Praise for S. M. Thayer

"When a novel starts the way this one does, you just know things are going to get worse. In this fast-paced, chilling novel, S. M. Thayer invokes F. Scott Fitzgerald's characters from *The Great Gatsby* as both a nod to the age-old compulsion to choose money over everything, and a cautionary tale to its ruinous powers. *I Will Never Leave You* is a dark and addictive read."

—Kaira Rouda, *USA Today* bestselling author

"This sly and sinister novel explores just how wrong a love triangle can go. Chilling."

—Peter Swanson, author of *Her Every Fear*

I WILL NEVER LEAVE YOU

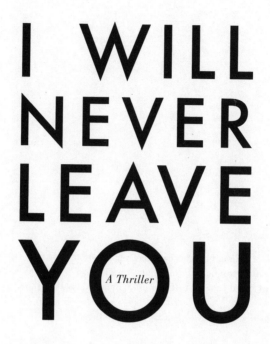

I WILL NEVER LEAVE YOU

A Thriller

S. M. THAYER

THOMAS & MERCER

Published by Thomas & Mercer, Seattle
www.apub.com

Amazon, the Amazon logo, and Thomas & Mercer are trademarks of Amazon.com, Inc., or its affiliates.

ISBN-13: 9781503951679 (hardcover)
ISBN-10: 1503951677 (hardcover)
ISBN-13: 9781503901186 (paperback)
ISBN-10: 1503901181 (paperback)

Cover design by Shasti O'Leary Soudant

Printed in the United States of America

First edition

To Alison, Stephen, Sebastian, and Ellie—
I'm so proud of each of you and so proud to have you in
my life.

PART ONE

Chapter One

TRISH

A newborn generates its own heat. Sleeping, wrapped in a pink candy-stripe receiving blanket and a matching knit hat, the baby's a hot coal threatening to burst into flames, and yet my husband, beaming, assures me—as nurses have assured him—that she's not feverish, that she's perfectly healthy, but the baby's heat worries me. It's impossible not to feel as if she's burning up, not to feel as if, holding her, I'm a twig, a tuft of dried grass, a crumpled sheet of newsprint, tinder that will be consumed by her fire. She's a forest fire, a conflagration waiting to happen, and there's nothing my money can do to tamp the destruction this baby's going to cause in my life.

"Relax, Trish," James says, easing his hand onto my shoulder. His voice is calm, soothing, and bursting with confidence, a loving voice tailor-made for uttering the "breathe in, breathe out" reassurances expectant fathers must coo to their partners during childbirth. Workmanlike and responsible, he has read the essential baby manuals, streamed the important YouTube videos, subscribed to the necessary magazines, and can mansplain away the natural anxieties of ushering a new life into this world. "Babies can sense tension, and it does them no good, psychologically and emotionally, if their first hours are filled with distress."

The baby makes the faintest snoozing sounds, and yet the sound seems impossibly loud coming from such a small body. I concentrate on the inhalations and the slight wheeze when she exhales, and though it takes time to feel comfortable holding her, the soothing sounds lull me into a hopeful reverie, and suddenly I'm filled with a generosity of spirit I haven't felt in ages. It's like what I'd hoped would come during all the years we tried to conceive.

It's true what they say: nothing is softer than a newborn baby. Ninety minutes earlier, just after the birth, nurses washed her, but there's a newborn scent attached to her, something amniotic and yet endearing. I've never held anything so soft and delicate, and I can see this baby is no ugly Cabbage Patch doll but already beautiful, with a strong chin and fine eyelashes. Her eyelids are pinched tight in sleep; I can't wait for her to awaken so I can look into her eyes and determine their color. Her face is still red, her head slightly conical from her passage through the birth canal, but these imperfections will pass with time, and I can see now why women joke of wanting to eat their newborns, envisioning the buttery chins, nougat-like chewiness of their fleshy thighs, the cheeks' velvety warmth.

Anne Elise weighed seven pounds, nine ounces at birth, already a notch above average.

Because of how she was positioned in the womb, sonogram technicians were unable to get an accurate glimpse as to her sex, and for months James allowed himself the assumption he'd fathered a boy. He'd wanted a boy, spoke often of it. I caught him peeking at sporting-goods catalogues and ducking into toy stores with visions of the Nerf balls, miniature plastic basketball hoops, and glistening yellow Tonka trucks he'd lavish on a son, and yet, looking at his considerate face, how filled with happiness he is, I know he'll be satisfied with a girl. He'll nurture her and nourish her self-esteem, tell her she's beautiful and smart, and give her the courage to fight for herself in whatever arena she chooses to enter in life. He'll cherish her, invite her to explore and discover lifelong passions. He'll keep up with her interests, send her links to interesting internet articles relating to them. He'll commit to being part of her life for the long haul. In short, I know he'll do with her everything he has failed to do with me.

We've been unable to conceive, James and I, during our twelve years of married life, and in recent years we've done outlandish things, things that go far beyond the pale of the exorbitantly expensive in vitro fertility treatments that have become standard fare for couples within our social circle. Despite our perseverance and the medical, spiritual, and hormonal specialists we consulted, "unexplained infertility" was the closest we came to an explanation of our difficulties. Like friends and acquaintances in similar circumstances, we wondered why people like us—well educated and drug-free, economically viable with good teeth and stylish wardrobes—had trouble doing what came naturally to everyone else: have children. We clung to each other in our silk pajamas, prey to every foul speculation as to the reason for our barrenness, blaming everything from climate change to the polyethylene in the bottles of our drinking water, the unseemly zeitgeist of our modern times, and the hollowness of our souls. We prodded ourselves on counselors' couches and on the examination tables of well-meaning doctors who spoke in terms of sperm counts and ovulation cycles. Some nights, we prayed as only a man and woman can pray, playing with positional experimentation that led to foot cramps and bruises but nary a disruption in my monthly cycle.

We started the process with so much hope, imagining our life filled with baby this and baby that, cradles and baby monitors and the beautiful mobile of dancing lambs we'd hang above the crib to lull our child to sleep each night. At our most vulnerable, succumbing to rumors of a Chinese practice with an astronomical success rate, we jetted off to Beijing, where, in a modern *siheyuan* constructed of concrete blocks and faux bricks, we nodded enthusiastically when a Buddhist monk told us that Western practitioners had only the barest glimmer of the spiritual aura surrounding fertility. We were so hopeful, so naive. Shorn of his hair and cloaked only in a thin saffron robe and a pair of bamboo sandals, our monk spoke in a dry, unaccented English that reminded me of how a Nebraskan might speak. We repeated his incantations in somber tones. So much did we believe him that we swallowed the acrid tea he poured from a terra-cotta pot and became violently ill, both of us falling to our knees and vomiting beneath a flowering jacaranda tree. If I hadn't been able to arrange for an emergency airlift through my father's embassy connections, we would've died under that same jacaranda, the purple blossoms settling down upon us in the *siheyuan* courtyard, victims of dehydration, intestinal duress, and our own naive desperation.

We cried. I took refuge in my inheritance, flexing my birthright privilege to buy designer evening gowns from the latest Dolce & Gabbana and Naeem Khan collections. At a certain point, James stopped crying. Unlike me, he had no wealth of his own to fall back on. One night, he groveled for the sleek silver Tesla Model S with ludicrous options that could be his for only $125,000. I congratulated him for his taste. No gaudy vroom-vroom Porsche or Ferrari, a Tesla was a machine of solid engineering with an environmental conscience. "You mean you'd buy me one?" James said.

I laughed. I wasn't going to do any such thing with my money. "But you've got your Volvo," I said of the midnight-blue station wagon we'd bought two years earlier in a fit of procreative optimism when we still imagined children would one day fill its back seats.

But now, bringing the sleeping baby to my shoulder and nuzzling my cheek against hers, it astounds me anew like a tidal wave: the innocence, the miraculous nature of life that eluded me for so long.

Tears stream down my cheeks. Anne Elise is the sweetest, most precious being on the planet. How could I have doubted this? So firm is this knowledge, this shock and awe, that I kiss her slender lips, and just like that, her eyes pop open. Her inquisitive eyes are exactly like mine, a rich cobalt blue with fine flecks of copper and gold. Am I staring at a miracle?

I'm crying great tears of joy, thinking of the wretched years James and I experienced, the love that had vanished from our lives and how we flailed our bodies into each other night after blessèd night, all the sex and raw exasperation. And fruitless. I shall never forget our fruitless years.

"Honey, are you okay?" James asks. He's still in the crinkly green birthing room hospital scrubs. Sentimentalist that he is, I wouldn't put it past him to sneak the scrubs home and whip them out as a conversation starter between courses at some future dinner party of ours.

The baby starts crying, which James warned me might happen when she awoke, and I'm helpless, for although I rub her swaddled back and rock her gently, Anne Elise wails. No one has told me how to soothe a crying child. Surely, there are techniques to learn, words or incantations that might do the trick, but I stand there, patting her, nuzzling her, praying calm upon poor Anne Elise, who balls her tiny fists up as though she's about to smack me. She kicks her legs, whipping her feet free of the pink blanket that had wrapped around them. Her toes are small, each no bigger than a fingernail. A strip of elasticized fabric bands her ankle like a bracelet. A white plastic disc about the width and thickness of a half dollar is affixed to the elasticized fabric. Upon entering the maternity ward, I saw the same medallions on other babies. A pair of red lips (not unlike the familiar Rolling Stones logo) appears on each medallion, and as I run my fingers over the disc, the image of Mick Jagger puckering his lips and kissing me pops to mind, filling me with revulsion.

The baby's cries awaken her mother, James's mistress, who's been curled up asleep in the hospital bed. Laurel Bloom. That's her name. Exhausted from an arduous ten-hour delivery, she fell asleep soon after nurses cut the baby's umbilical cord. This is the first time James has invited me to meet her face-to-face. She looks at me sharply, her face still splotchy from the strain of labor, her long blonde hair tied back in an unkempt ponytail that fans out on her bed pillow. I don't begrudge James the baby. But it goes without saying that I begrudge him the mistress.

Chapter Two

TRISH

A year ago, long before Laurel entered James's life, my father flew back to DC to greet James and me when we returned from our disastrous Chinese fertility treatments. Having recently retired to the Cayman Islands following a mostly distinguished banking career, my father was his usual effervescently cynical self. Although the color of his hair ebbed from jet black to what he preferred to call "the Paul Revere Pewter section of the palette," his wrinkle-free face up until recently gave the appearance of a man thirty years younger. His jowls had begun to sag in the year since we last saw each other. We were still close, but though we talked on the phone several times a week, I wasn't prepared to see the extent of his physical decline. His gout had flared up, impeding his mobility. Liver spots splotched the back of his hands, and the scaly skin brought on by geriatric xerosis covered his arms. He was seventy-five years old. He had called in a few favors to arrange our medical evacuation from Beijing. People who hadn't spoken to him in years had begrudgingly stepped to the plate to help us, and yet now that we were safe, those same people refused to take his calls thanking them for their assistance. Owing to the well-publicized scandals that beset his bank—a bank that bore our family name—official Washington had distanced itself from him. Though he rarely let on how much being persona non grata hurt him, the humiliation had contributed to his decision to leave the city for the balmy Caribbean.

"Grandchildren. It's the only thing that'll keep me coming back to this city much longer," my father said, limping across a crowded restaurant to a corner table where he invited us to dine with him. Though no longer a power player in town, he still preferred power restaurants—steak houses that boasted of grain-fed offerings and the K Street eateries where the food was bland and flagrantly overpriced. Had James or I chosen the place, we'd have picked Obelisk or Nora, a pair of Dupont Circle restaurants that had been around for decades but still offered surprisingly innovative cuisine. This particular restaurant, the Coterie, dated back to the years when three-martini lunches were the norm and Senate Majority Leader Lyndon Johnson would drag colleagues to his table and challenge them to eat Rocky Mountain oysters with him. Glossy signed photographs of the restaurant's illustrious patrons lined the oak-paneled walls. My father would be mortified if he knew that, this early into his retirement, the restaurant had already removed one of his three photographs.

"I love you two dearly, but I need to be a grandfather," my father said, laying his walking stick on the unused seat at our table.

"We're still trying," James said. He placed his hand on mine. "Lord knows, we try several times a week."

This talk, especially in public, where anyone might listen in on our intimate woes, irked me. I pretended to distract myself with the intricately folded swan-shaped cloth napkin atop my dinner plate. James, too, was uncomfortable discussing our sex life with my father. He tried to steer the discussion to the cache of Johnny Mercer 78s he had acquired a few months earlier. It was their shared passion—the music of the 1930s and '40s—but right after we placed our cocktail orders, my father was back on us about children.

"Listen, may I . . . ah-umm . . . throw out a radical solution?" my father asked.

James and I glanced at each other. My father, a straitlaced banker with conservative tendencies, was not a radical man.

"Sure. Let's hear it, sport," James said.

"Surrogacy," my father said.

We'd never discussed it before, James and I.

"It's the best idea for your particular plight," my father said. Over the years, I'd kept him abreast of the fertility doctors and outrageous therapies we had tried, but now my father told us in the same reasoned voice he used when delivering congressional testimony that he understood how painful our trials must be. My father isn't a touchy-feely man, but his eyes became glassy. "I want what's best for you. You both want a baby. You've seen . . . ah-umm . . . what? A dozen or so doctors over the last ten years? You're angry it's not happening for you. So I thought I'd throw surrogacy out there for you. As a suggestion. In case you haven't considered it yet."

The idea repulsed me. No one but me was going to carry and give birth to my child. I wanted to experience the morning sickness firsthand. I wanted the full breasts and the healthy glow of pregnancy, the minor irritations and weepiness, and the flights of fancy I heard were common in pregnant women. I wanted to wake James at three in the morning and sweetly ask him to drive to the market and buy me a jar of pickled herring to satisfy a sudden craving. More importantly, I wanted the intimate bond that would form in utero between mother and child. Adoption, which we'd discussed once, wasn't an option for this reason.

For years James had talked about the things he'd pack for me in the event I'd need to be rushed to a delivery room in the middle of the night. These endearments filled our pillow talk after we made love. He pledged to pack Gillian Flynn and Mary Kubica novels, flannel bathrobes, calfskin moccasins, and Debauve et Gallais chocolates for me. "Debauve et Gallais chocolates? You'd give me Debauve et Gallais?" I'd ask, genuinely touched. Produced by a Parisian chocolatier, Debauve et Gallais chocolates were the creamiest, most luxurious chocolates in the world. Just thinking about them made my toes curl. Every time he said the word, I pictured the blue ribbon tucked around the corner of their trademark blue, gold, and gray embossed boxes and the pure chocolate aroma that would escape from the box when I'd break its seal and eat the first piece.

"Sure, Trish. Nothing's too good for you," he'd answer, kissing my nose.

The waiter returned and set a manhattan on the table for my father. Condensation beaded on the bowl of the stemmed cocktail glass. My father speared the cherry that bobbed in the drink with a swizzle stick, and then, after my father voiced approval of his cocktail, the waiter deposited drinks on the table for James and me—Scotch for James, a brandy alexander for me. While my father sat across from us sipping his manhattan, James reached over and held my hand. He squeezed it. "So what do you think, Trish? About surrogacy?"

"I don't want to discuss this."

"These days, surrogacy's not outlandish anymore," my father said. "No one looks down at the practice anymore. Or the people who are doing it. These days, everyone's doing it."

"Dad. Please. I don't want to discuss this."

"Be reasonable," James said.

Sensing a disturbance, people at the surrounding tables peeked discreetly at us. I felt under attack. My father explained what surrogacy involved—as if I couldn't figure it out for myself. I got up from my seat, threw down the cloth napkin I'd been fingering, and walked away. James and my father called out to me, beckoning me back to the table, but after retrieving my sable coat from the coat check, I hailed a cab home, alone.

Just as the cab let me off at my house, I spotted my closest friend in the whole world, Allie Carlson, crossing the cobblestone street with her triple stroller. We'd known each other since we were eight years old, having met while taking horseback-riding lessons in Rock Creek Park. We'd gone through elementary and high school together at Georgetown Day School, one of Washington's exclusive private schools, all the while privately kibitzing about our aging instructors' stunningly poor fashion sense.

As soon as I saw Allie and her stroller full of children, I burst into tears. Unlike me, Allie was a baby machine. She'd only been married five years but already had so many children.

Allie put her hand on mine. "What's wrong, Trish? You can tell me."

"Nothing," I said, trying to hold back the tears. I'd burdened her so often with stories about my fertility problems that I couldn't possibly think of telling her how much it hurt deep inside, at this particular moment, to see her beautiful, healthy children. Allie often said she envied me, being married to a man as handsome as James. In her way, she loved her own husband, Clive, but he was balding and nearing sixty. He chaired Georgetown University's Art History Department and was always away on business for long stretches, traveling to one museum or another to lend his expertise on their holdings. Whereas I had James to comfort me, she had her children; decorum prevented me from admitting that, at times, I wished our positions were reversed—who wouldn't trade a husband for a baby?

Gradually, I pulled myself together. Her three children—Ellie, Sebastian, and Stephen—sat inside the stroller bundled in cutesy panda sweatshirts she'd bought at a National Zoo fundraiser. Ellie, the youngest at barely two, looked up at me from the stroller's front seat. In one hand was a lollipop and, in the other, a Raggedy Ann doll. How could one woman be blessed with three children and me, none?

"We're going to the playground. Got time to join us?" Allie said. Usually, I loved going with them to the playground three blocks away. Allie and I would take turns pushing her children on the kiddie swings and entertaining them with stories of fairy princesses and hoary goblins.

I begged off, saying I had housework to deal with. Allie squinted at me. We'd known each other so long that she knew when I was lying. Her eyes lit up. "Is it trouble? Trouble with James? Is that why you're so upset?"

The speed with which she formed these questions took me aback. Instinctively, I gathered what she was getting at. Most women would be supportive when they suspected a friend's marriage was collapsing, and yet with Allie, I sensed schadenfreude.

I tried to laugh away her suspicions. The last thing I needed was my best friend spreading rumors about the state of my marriage. "That's silly. What could possibly be wrong with James?"

Allie looked cross, as if disbelieving me, but then her expression brightened so quickly that I wondered if I had misinterpreted her earlier questions.

"That's good," Allie said, nodding. We made small talk for a moment longer, and then I watched as she pushed the triple stroller down the sidewalk toward the playground.

In the weeks and months that followed, however, I began to suspect Allie was right—trouble had entered my marriage. I had lost James at surrogacy. Wheels turned in his head in the months after my father brought up the subject. A woman knows these things. No longer did he tie his prospects for a child to the viability of my reproductive organs. I'd find him reading websites about choosing the right woman to carry your child and ensuring her adequate compensation. Once, while in line for complimentary steamed shrimp at a reception in honor of a newly opened exhibit of Mary Cassatt paintings, he leaned over my shoulder and asked, "What about her?" He pointed to a shapely young blonde attired in a full-length black dress and said, "Her. We could pay her to have our baby. Look at those childbearing hips!" I was shocked. I elbowed him in the gut and, drawing him aside next to one of Cassatt's mother-and-daughter portraits, explained to him in no uncertain terms that I wouldn't consent to surrogacy.

James started working later into the nights and taking long business-related dinners. He wouldn't come home until after midnight, complaining the clients he wined and dined spent too much time wining and not enough time dining. Despite his long hours, his spirits were high. The extra work, he said, energized him. Normally solicitous and free-flowing with the flattery, he became even more so, which I enjoyed. What woman does not relish hearing that her husband finds her to be the loveliest creature on earth? Yes, the over-the-top compliments reeked of insincerity, but I appreciated the effort he made to be nice to me. What was I supposed to do—ask that he quit being pleasant?

One idyllic Saturday afternoon, Allie dropped by to see if I wanted to go to the playground with her and her children. James surprised me by asking to tag along. James, too, liked Allie's children. He hoisted one child after another onto his shoulders and galloped around the playground giving them "horsey rides." The children laughed. They couldn't get enough of him. As soon as he let one child down to pick up another of Allie's brood, the child would immediately tug on his chinos, begging for another ride.

"Don't give up," Allie said when she caught me looking at her. Although we hadn't talked about my conception woes in months, I knew immediately what she meant. "He's going to be an excellent father someday."

James's cheeks were pink with exhaustion from all his galloping. Ellie, Allie's youngest, was on his shoulders, squealing at him to "go faster, horsey, faster!" One of James's phones rang. He pulled it out of his pocket. It was a new red phone I hadn't seen before, a cheap-looking flip phone unlike the two iPhones he carried with him at all times. Seeing some message flash across its screen, he seemed even happier. There was a delirious glaze to his eyes. He sucked in a breath, glided his tongue over his lips.

A wife knows what her spouse is thinking. I had seen that same lustful sparkle in his eyes many times over the years directed, thrillingly, at me. Seeing it directed at his phone, I panicked.

James stuffed his phone back into his pocket. "Something's come up at the office."

"On a Saturday?" I asked.

James planted a rueful kiss on my forehead. "Work happens, honey. Even on a weekend. It's the price of being employed—distractions like this. I'm sorry, but I've got to run to my office and . . . and put out some fires."

Never before had I suspected James of having an affair. For weeks, this suspicion ate at me. I told myself I was imagining things. We never quarreled, James and I, and he seemed happy with our homelife. He complimented me endlessly and never failed to notice when I wore a new dress, did something different to my hair, or set fresh irises on our dining room table. And yet I sensed again and again that, even while he sat next to me on our living room couch, his mind was elsewhere.

Should I have confronted him? In retrospect, I wish I had. He probably would have denied everything, and I probably would've believed him.

Instead, I contacted a private investigator. A few days after I emailed him about my predicament, he sent me two pictures. In one picture, James and this other woman—Laurel—walked hand in hand over the sweeping white marble floor of the Mayflower Hotel's lobby. I sucked in a breath and fumed. A half hour later, I summoned the courage to click open the second photo, which showed James and the same woman climbing the steps of the Lincoln Memorial in broad daylight. I studied this photo endlessly, trying to figure out what James saw in this woman. She was younger, yes, but plain looking and abundantly pregnant, dressed up in a pink novelty PSST! I'M NOT A VIRGIN ANYMORE! T-shirt that blatantly advertised her condition. She was what I'd always wanted to be: pregnant and happy.

∽

Today, an hour ago, James raced home, his cheeks flushed with excitement. Claiming he had "something of importance" to show me, he urged me to get into his Volvo. Instinctively, I guessed the reason for James's excitement—my private investigator had told me his mistress was a week overdue. When confronted with evidence of my father's affairs, my mother would lock herself in her room for weeks and sometimes months. I was determined to show the world I was made of sterner stuff. I grabbed my cashmere cape, slid on my ruched leather gloves. He drove us through the midday Georgetown traffic with an uncharacteristic abundance of caution, stopping at rather than running the red lights. Throughout our drive, he glanced at me with a nervous insistence. Poor, silly James hadn't realized I'd guessed what was happening. While waiting at a stoplight on Foxhall Road, I tapped his hand and asked, "So. Let me guess: your mistress just had her baby."

The light changed. The car behind us honked at him to get moving. James shifted the Volvo back into gear. We clanked through the slushy streets slower than before. He stared at the bare trees lining the road, no longer glancing at me. Signs along the road indicated we were traveling toward Sibley Hospital. When one of the signs indicated we should veer right to get to the hospital, James veered right—but despite the road signs, I couldn't believe he was actually taking me to see his mistress.

"You know about her?"

"Of course I do." Despite our twelve years of marriage, James has yet to learn that nothing gets past me. It didn't help that, in recent weeks, he'd been so careless with his secrets. I'd catch him reading baby manuals while watching televised golf tournaments. What grown man reads baby manuals? With or without a private investigator, the hackles on the most trusting wife would have been raised by that. And yet now that I was in his Volvo with him, I had no idea why he was taking me to her maternity suite.

Chapter Three

TRISH

Laurel points at me from her hospital bed and, in a slow, medicated voice, asks, "What's she doing here?"

"Relax, honey," James says. He takes the baby from me and, walking the five paces across the airy room, places the baby on Laurel's lap.

Because Laurel's been asleep, she's hardly held her baby yet, and I expect her to gaze upon Anne Elise with the same reverent joy as I'd done. Instead, she stares at me. No joy lights her rosy cheeks; no giddy happiness expresses itself in her eyes. There's something hard about her, as if she's had an uncomfortable upbringing. IV tubing snakes up from her tattooed arm; wires from an electronic heart monitor coil up from the folds of her gold terrycloth bathrobe. A plastic medallion like the one on Anne Elise's ankle is strapped to her wrist. She, too, has been kissed by Mick Jagger. The two plastic discs graze against each other, causing a simultaneous electronic smooching sound to squeak out from them.

"You let her hold the baby?" Laurel asks. Although she looks at me, the question is intended for James. I know so little about this woman James has been carrying on with. My private investigator has given me the basics on her, such as her name, age, and cell phone number, and clued me into her financial needs—her mountains of student loan debt, her penchant for Italian-crafted boots and fine leather goods. But he's been less successful in assembling her personality profile, her psychological profile, anything that might be useful in helping me *understand* her. "That witch? That bitch? After all the things she's done to you, you've let her hold our baby?"

Seeing the needy jealousy that overtakes her, I know precisely the kind of woman she is: lowlife. That's the vibe she gives off. I wouldn't be surprised if there's something criminal in her background. And as I'm realizing this, a plan hatches in my mind. A woman like her would have no shortage of nasty secrets. With my private investigator's help, I'm certain I can ruin Laurel. Or, at the bare minimum, convince James to dump her. She's carried on with my husband, seduced him, bedded him, and probably filled his head with fantasies of the bliss he can expect if he leaves me. None of this would have happened if I'd been able to conceive a child for James. Laurel's only means of ensnaring him was to offer him the one thing I couldn't: a baby. But now, I see her jealousy.

Every woman reacts differently when confronted with her spouse's infidelity. Initially, like my mother, I chose a predictable path: paralysis. Indecision plagued me for months, but at heart, I wasn't my mother's daughter so much as I was a child of my father. My father was a pragmatist who taught me that though the world was an ugly place, complaining served no purpose. After my private investigator informed me that James was having an affair, I had endeavored to figure out how to tilt things in my favor. Laurel's pregnancy was a complicating factor. She had no money, no sophistication. If something were to happen to the baby, James would undoubtedly tire of her in due time. That is what I chose to believe. Yes, I hoped there'd be a miscarriage, an abortion, some permanent rift that would develop between James and his mistress. More than anything, I hoped James didn't love her, and yet seeing the way he fawns over her and her baby, I see he loves them both. Which breaks my heart.

"Laurel. Honey. You were asleep. What harm could be done by having Tricia hold Anne Elise while you rested?" James's honeyed yet persuasive voice always strangely reminds me of roasted cashews. Any woman could fall for a confidence man with such a voice.

Laurel rubs her eyes. "What do you mean, 'Anne Elise'? We agreed on 'Zerena' if she was a girl. Zerena. With a Z like we talked about. Don't you remember? We *talked* about this."

James lays a hand on Laurel's shoulder, and with his other hand, he "coochy-coochy-coos" Anne Elise's chin.

"Don't you remember? Zerena. With a Z. That's what we agreed."

"Honey. Don't get angry. A baby can pick up on a mother's stress, so please act calmly. Zerena's a wonderful name. An awesome name! But I was projecting forward, thinking long haul for our daughter, envisioning the awkwardness she'd face in job interviews, constantly having to explain her name. I work in a conservative financial services firm. You know this. I work with troglodytes. I work with people so pigheaded that should they happen upon a résumé from someone named Zerena—*Zerena with a Z*—they'd start laughing. Or utter disparaging wisecracks. No way would they call her in for an interview. Even if she was the most eminently qualified candidate in their whole stack of résumés. I want our daughter to succeed. If that means giving her a, um, *less distinctive* name, so be it."

Laurel looks at James with wide, glaring eyes. I wouldn't have thought someone so ill-tempered and strongheaded would give in so easily, but she takes his hand, squeezes it, and thanks him for thinking "long haul" for their baby. James always knows the right tone to take, the right buttons to push. That is his power, his gift, his ability.

"Names are important," James says. "Hospital officials came by with the paperwork an hour ago. You were asleep. I didn't want to wake you, so I took it upon myself to fill out those forms, making it official. I hope you don't mind, honey."

Laurel nods. She's still smitten in the blush of love, totally taken in by her confident, sweet-talking philanderer. No doubt she looks upon James as the answer to all her financial worries. Twenty-four years old and saddled with $200,000 of student loan debt: she was foolish enough to leave her small but prestigious New England college with only a degree in liberal arts and a puny certificate in gender studies, dismal credentials that had so far landed her nothing more than waitressing opportunities.

Again, Laurel points at me. "So why is she here? I don't want her to have anything to do with our baby."

"Honey, I thought it would behoove us to introduce Tricia to Anne Elise as soon as possible."

I shudder. James must be crazy. There's no earthly reason he should've introduced me to his new baby unless he means to humiliate me. I'm hopping mad. Even now, I'm surprised I haven't given in to my better senses and walked out of this room.

"Why?" Laurel asks.

James's tone is measured, calm. He looks over to me, nods. "Earlier, while you were asleep, I saw how kindly Tricia responded to Anne Elise. She had goodness in her face, a gentleness that poured over her as she held Anne Elise." As he's saying this, I remember how dazzled I was to be holding the baby. I can't believe a word James says about me, but I'd never be hostile toward the baby. "For years, we tried to conceive a child ourselves because I knew Trish would be a perfect, loving mother. Just now, watching her kiss Anne Elise—"

"Wait. Are you telling me you let that witch kiss our daughter?"

James holds out his hand to calm her, but anger blooms in Laurel's face. I have no idea of the hormones rampaging through her, wreaking havoc with her emotions. I would have thought blissful happiness was the hormonal fate of every new mother, but as she grips the stainless steel bars at the sides of her hospital bed, Laurel's as unhappy as anyone I've ever met.

"Honey, hear me out," James says. "I'm on your side. Trust me. I want what's best for our little daughter. And I know you do too. When I saw Trish kissing Anne Elise, I realized we're in a win-win-win situation."

"Huh?"

James walks up to me, takes both of my hands. We stand inches apart, and he stares into my eyes, and my knees go squishy like the first time he introduced himself to me. His hands are warm, his smile tender.

"Trish, be honest with me. You want the best for my daughter, don't you? You wouldn't hurt Anne Elise, would you?"

I shake my head, for how could anyone wish to harm a baby?

"Then divorce me," James says.

Things crumble inside me. I can't believe what James just asked. I feel dizzy, nauseous. James stares at me compassionately as if about to butter me up with another damn dose of his flattery. He reaches over, touches my arm, and it takes every ounce of my self-control not to burst out in tears or push him away, and yet when I start to say something, he raises his hand to hush me.

"Hear me out," James says. "I wish it didn't have to be this way. Honest. I wish there was some other way. Divorce me so I can do the right thing and marry Laurel. Divorce me so I can make sure Anne Elise grows up in a strong, loving nuclear family. Divorce me so she will grow up with the confidence that she's loved by both her parents. You know the studies. You know the odds. A child growing up in a two-parent home is far more likely to succeed in life. This is especially true for girls. Trish, you're not an ogre. Divorce me so I can be a daddy."

Pleading to be a daddy, he trembles, bringing tears to my eyes. The pain of living with me, being married to me, is etched all over his face. I'm horrified. He doesn't want me. He doesn't want my love, my continued support. This much I already guessed by his willingness to leap into his affair with Laurel. But it's more than that: after twelve years of fruitless marriage, he's cutting his losses, casting me aside because of my barrenness. A woman in his eyes is only as valuable as the baby she's capable of gestating, and it pisses me off, this biological reductionism. Laurel, too, looks at me with glistening eyes, and now that I'm helpless with shame and tears, I remember that, by the terms of our prenuptials, James needs me to divorce him if he is to have any claim on my fortune. It is the most ironclad of prenuptial agreements: if he even threatens to bring divorce proceedings against me, he forsakes all of my money and four-fifths of whatever assets we've jointly acquired. Because he is reckless with his spending and reckless with his investments, I've always insisted that we keep our finances separate.

I let go of James's hands. I'm not going to divorce him. In fact, I've already planned how to force him to toss Laurel aside. I turn toward the window. My eyes settle upon the snow-covered gazebo across the hospital's grounds. Beyond the gazebo is a small pond. Though now skinned with ice, it is the type of pond where ducks flourish in idyllic summers, the type of place where Allie would take her toddlers to feed stale bread and broken crackers to the mallards.

"So what do you say, Trish? Will you let me do the right thing? Will you let me be a daddy?"

I turn around. The baby is asleep again on Laurel's lap. James and Laurel are holding hands. Both have hopeful expressions. If I were to say yes, they'd thank me and promise to invite me into their house whenever I wished, but my father—a contractually minded banker with no compunctions against foreclosing on businesses, farms, homes, and families—was always proudest when declaring he hadn't raised any suckers in the family.

"No, James. Why would I divorce you? I love you," I say, holding my hands to the chest of my ruby-colored Armani sweater, and as I'm saying this and seeing my grinning face in the mirror atop Laurel's bed table, I'm thrilled by the horror that comes over them. Laurel in

Chapter Four

LAUREL

I'm no special snowflake, no precious girl who demands to play by her own rules. Every dawn must have its day and every monkey its—what?—comeuppance. A woman in my position, having given birth to the daughter of another woman's husband, can expect no favors from that other woman, but I can't stand the dismissive, belittling way Tricia glares at me. She struts through my—*my!*—maternity suite with a sense of ownership as if it's one more room in her own private little snow globe. Possession is her game, so Jimmy has let on, but she can never have me or Zerena, and although Jimmy promised he was going to ask for a divorce as soon as our baby was born, I hadn't expected he'd call his wife to the hospital and do it right in front of me. I'm proud of Jimmy for allowing her the opportunity to do the decent thing and divorce him, but now that she's declined to board that train, it's time for us to move on.

Ten, maybe even five years ago, Mrs. Patricia Wainsborough (née Riggs) would've been beautiful. Jimmy showed me a picture of them at a ridiculously extravagant museum benefit, she in a strapless black Dior with a high-low hemline that showed off her long slender legs and impossibly thin waist, and you could see, both in the picture itself and how he fawned over the photo as he handed it to me, that he must have considered himself the luckiest duck in the pond to have had her as his arm candy. The dress must have been a size 4, something that even after I lose all the baby fat, I'd struggle shimmying into. She's in her forties, about as old as Jimmy. No longer does her skin naturally glow. Nor is the skin as supple. If you look closely, you see wrinkles have begun to pinch her eyes. Furrows crevice her pale forehead. A wiser woman of her means would avail herself of Botox or other procedures, but her eyes, the color so breathtakingly blue you'd swear they were costume jewelry baubles, still compel attention.

"Mrs. Wainsborough, please be reasonable," I say.

At the sound of my voice, Tricia curls her lip. "I am being reasonable. I'm simply not going to divorce James." She takes out a gold compact from her handbag, and her anger is evident in how she powders her cheeks, caking the cosmetics so thick she must be poisoning herself. To limit the risk of birth defects and miscarriages, at Jimmy's suggestion I refrained from cosmetics throughout my pregnancy, and now the smell of whatever she's dusting onto herself makes my skin crawl. "I've simply made up my mind, and I'm not going to discuss it any further."

"Mrs. Wainsborough. I'm asking you to leave. Get it? This is my private—*private!*—room. So why don't you vacate the premises, 'kay?"

She flinches, the first rise I've gotten from her since waking. Despite the color pasted onto her cheeks, her face is pale. She turns to Jimmy and is about to say something, but one of his cell phones goes off, emitting the pompous opening four notes to that famous Beethoven symphony—*bah bah bah bum.* Like a drug dealer, he carries three separate phones, and when he answers the call, a smile flashes across his lips, and he slips into portfolio-management mode, telling whoever's calling about the benefits of transitioning from front-loaded to rear-loaded mutual funds. It's how this vainglorious peacock displays his plumage, showing off to his wife and me his mastery of arcane investment wisdom and going off about yields, risk rates, and debt/equity ratios. Three minutes into the call, just as I think it's winding down, Jimmy raises a hand to signal he needs to continue his call away from our prying ears. There's a bounce to his step, a happiness that comes to him only when talking about money. He walks out of the maternity suite and into the hallway, and when I can no longer hear his voice, I turn again to his wife.

"Mrs. Wainsborough, I don't want to be difficult. I—"

"Tricia," she says, interrupting me. "Call me Tricia. Even people who don't like me call me Tricia."

"Okay. Whatever. Tricia. Please leave. I don't know how much clearer I can be without morphing all rude on you."

"It's going to have to wait."

"Why's that?"

"James drove me here. I have to wait until he finishes his call so he can drive me back."

"He *drove* you here?" It doesn't make sense. I assumed Tricia came here by herself. After Zerena's birth and as doctors stitched me up from the episiotomy, drowsiness from the anesthesia and the pain meds got the better of me. Although I longed to stay awake and hold Zerena and hear the sound of her breath, I drifted off to sleep. Jimmy squeezed my hand and said he'd stay with the baby until I awoke again. I trusted him. Instead, he abandoned Zerena and me so he could go back to his wife and bring her here.

"He's not a bad driver. Or at least no worse than every other idiot on the road."

Zerena wakes up again, crying. She looks at me with angry eyes and shakes her fists, and suddenly I feel so sorry, so selfish, so inadequate for having done whatever I've unknowingly done to make her so angry. How could I have let my baby down already?

I'm heartbroken Jimmy hadn't stayed true to his word and remained with us while I slept. He's the only man I could imagine spending my life with, but I've always questioned if I can really trust him. The baby's my lifeline to a better life, a means to escape my troubled past. Being the other woman is no easy task. Jimmy loves me. I know he does. And I love him. He has to love me. He just has to love me. Otherwise, how can I raise Zerena on my own?

What Jimmy said about a child—especially a daughter—needing the active love of a father in her life is true. Growing up, especially when I was really young, I always thought I was missing out not having the kind of father who'd read bedtime stories or take me to the park, help me onto one of the playground swings, and stand behind me, pushing me. My friends spoke glowingly of their own fathers. Me? I hardly knew where he was most of the time. What was so wrong with me that he couldn't stick around much or even every so often ask, "Hey, girl! How was your day at school? I'm real proud of you, sugar, for all those As on your report card."

Zerena needs Jimmy. I need Jimmy.

I first met Jimmy when he brought some clients to the restaurant where I waitressed. Looking at him from across the floor, I broke out in a cold sweat. I saw his gold wedding ring. Alarm bells zinged in my head, warning me to stay clear of him, but I couldn't resist. How often can the man of your dreams float into your life? Handsome, with dark-brown hair and eyes that set me on fire, he asked me what was good on the menu. I stuttered out a description of the *risotto del giorno* and told him the chef's signature braised lamb dish had recently been featured in the *Washington Post Magazine*. As I spoke, he slid his eyes up from the menu, taking me in, and smiled. I wrote down his table's orders. His manners were impeccable. Other men at his table looked up to him. He possessed a level of self-assurance that I'd never encountered before.

Until then, I'd defined myself solely by what I didn't possess—money, good clothes, and a respectable upbringing. I was the goose who could pass unnoticed in even the smallest of gaggles. I was no rich girl, no beauty queen, but he complimented me on the way I poured a glass of Barolo for him and thanked me for grinding just the right amount of pepper on his lamb. I basked in these compliments. I was a chasm, an abyss needing to be filled. I was a quantum, and he was the leap I needed to take.

I wanted Jimmy more than I'd ever wanted any man. He returned to my restaurant every night for a week. Sometimes, he'd stay just for a drink, but mostly he ate alone at a corner table. When the restaurant was slow, I hovered around him, inviting conversation. I didn't care that he was married. One night after closing, I let him walk me back to my apartment. He broke down and cried about the difficulties he and his wife had been having trying to conceive a child. They'd tried the whole hornet's nest of therapies and fertility treatments, nutritional supplements and fertility drugs, everything. He was at wit's end. Any man so distraught at the idea of never being a father deserved a child. I led him to my sofa bed, slid off the cushions, and opened the mattress before taking off my simple cream-colored cotton peasant blouse and drying his tears with it. He stood still and startled, and I snapped off my bra and watched as he instinctively pulled away as if having second thoughts about being in my apartment, alone, with me. So much can be said without saying a word. I wanted him so bad. I wanted to be the woman who'd bring purpose to his life. I caressed his shoulders, and after some moments he gave in to the temptation and caressed me back.

We'd been seeing each other for two months, him calling me whenever I had a night off from waitressing gigs. He'd book us into expensive hotel suites and take me to dive bars where he couldn't possibly run into anyone he knew. One night he took me to a brightly lit Nuevo Latino restaurant in Adams Morgan where pulsating Caribbean club music thundered over the sound system, making conversation impossible. The walls were loud and yellow and soft and pink, the murals a fauvist's Day-Glo reckoning of mauve palm trees, turquoise beaches, and lime-green oceans. A waiter approached our table. Because of the loud music, Jimmy raised his voice to be heard, something a classy guy like him doesn't do much. "Bring me a glass of your best sipping rum,"

Jimmy said, not bothering to open the leather-bound cocktail menu. Turning to me, he asked what I wanted to drink.

"Ginger ale," I responded.

Jimmy wriggled his eyebrows. It wasn't the answer he expected. In our previous outings, I'd made a point of ordering elaborate cocktails, gin fizzes I'd compel bartenders to whip up using fresh egg whites and Hendrick's gin or chocolate concoctions of my own fancy—jiggers of amaretto Disaronno liqueur mixed with Courvoisier, pale white rum, and maraschino cherries. Half the fun of dating me, I often joked in a flirty giggle, came from being able taste the outrageous cocktails I ordered, but no man acted so oddly in my presence as when I requested that simple ginger ale. Jimmy sidled his chair over to mine. Bougainvillea blossoms sprayed out of the bud vase atop the batik tablecloth. Already, this early in my pregnancy, my sense of smell was greater than it had ever been. The flowers were fragrant. Jimmy leaned into me, whispered into my ear, asked if I was all right.

"I've got a zygote problem," I said, aiming to be humorous, but the terminology tripped him up. The concern in his face deepened. He asked if my condition was contagious. I cast my glance into my lap and confessed to peeing onto the absorbent tip of a home pregnancy test that morning and watching its indicator change from a minus sign into a plus sign, simple arithmetic that informed me the sum total of my life was about to change. He scanned my face with deadly serious-ness to judge whether I was kidding. Never had I felt so vulnerable or so much at the mercy of another human being's compassion. I thought he'd be happy, overjoyed. He'd never explicitly said he wanted me to get pregnant, but I assumed that was his intention. Now, though, in his hesitation to embrace this news, I realized I'd let myself forget he was a married man and that, being married, he might not cotton to the news that his mistress was pregnant.

After some moments he squeezed my hand, his hand warm and pliable, like the modeling clay public school art teachers had doled out whenever my creative urge slouched toward sculpture. Jimmy said he'd take care of everything, that I'd have nothing to worry about, and in the weeks to come I thought he'd hand me a check or offer me transit to a clinic and sit with me in a sterile examination room as clinicians vacuumed out my womb. Driving me back to my apartment that night, he stopped off at an all-night drug store. I waited inside his Volvo—what kind of man *willingly* drives a Volvo station wagon?—while he ducked into the store, and when he emerged carrying a small paper bag and a bottle of water, I thought he was going to ply me with some caustic poison—something to rid my life of more than just the zygote. He opened the plastic water bottle, handed it to me, and tossed the bag onto my lap. Prenatal vitamins were inside the bag. I didn't normally cry, but jacked up as I was on mommy hormones, stupendous gratitude overtook me. Tears rushed from my eyes, and I knew at that moment he'd be one of the few decent people I'd ever meet. But I also understood I could never take the solidity of our relationship for granted.

Now, I'm holding our baby, who's crying. Jimmy is nowhere to be found. What am I supposed to do? Jimmy read the baby books. He was supposed to be here, coaching me, calming me and my child.

"Your baby," Tricia says, approaching my bed. "She's crying. Do something about it. Feed her, why don't you?"

I feel suddenly stupid. "How do I do that?"

Tricia throws up her arms, a sanctimonious fireball of rage. With not an iota of her husband's grace, she storms out of the room, leaving me to listen to the clack of her heels in the hospital corridor.

Wrapped in her pink receiving blanket, Zerena squirms in my lap like an angry burrito. I wonder how motherhood will change me. Will I be a good mother? Will I be able to love her, nurture her, or at least calm her? Nothing makes you feel as all alone and hopeless as being unable to calm your screaming baby. Zerena reaches toward my chest and puckers her lips. I loosen the sash of my terrycloth robe and raise her to my breast. She latches on instantly, making sweet glurpy sounds.

I expect breastfeeding to hurt, but the sensation of her mouth and tongue and the cute way she swallows between mouthfuls of nourishment make it all tickle.

I slip my finger into Zerena's little palm. Instinctually, her fingers clasp around mine, and like that, as if she flipped the switch to my heart, I'm flooded with this sense of devotion to her. I didn't expect this to happen so fast. My free hand rests on the back of her head, supporting her. Her skin is so soft, so warm. Only hours ago, she was a melon-sized question nestled in my uterus, someone I'd seen only through smudgy sonogram pictures. This is our first time alone together. Her fingers are so small, and yet her grip is firm, as if she never wants to let go of me. I don't want to let go of her either. I'll be a good mother. I'll teach her to be good, but not so good that she won't be able to stand up for herself.

Tricia trots back into the room with a middle-aged woman in tow. As soon as Tricia sees me nursing, she freezes. A polite woman, barging in on another woman with a newborn on her breast, would excuse herself and leave, but Tricia stands there, stricken, her fingers over her lips, a longing gaze in her eyes. The other woman, short and graying and wearing a white hospital uniform, comes at me with a smile on her face. She, too, ought to turn around, but she slips her hand over mine on the back of Zerena's head and gently adjusts the angle at which I hold her to my chest.

"Do it like that, so her mouth is straight over you," the other woman says, smiling with an air of talcum powder and happiness. "I'm Lois Belcher, by the way, the lactation consultant here at the hospital. Your mother had a nurse fetch me. She said you were having trouble getting a handle on breastfeeding, but frankly, it looks like you're doing everything right."

"My *mother?*" I stare at Tricia, aghast. She cringes like a chastised poodle.

The lactation consultant adjusts my fingers over Zerena's head and instructs me to shift her to my other breast—"To even things out," she says, offering the kind of practical breastfeeding advice most new moms probably receive from their own mothers. In a fit of panic and worried I'd need my mother's help, I called my parents a week ago for the first time in over eight years. They thought I was still in Vermont, didn't even realize I'd already graduated from college. When I mentioned I was pregnant and about to give birth, my father responded that there was no way—*no way!*—I could move back home again. As if. Last night, when my water broke, I called them again. They said they'd meet me at the hospital. I haven't heard from them since, which isn't surprising, since my parents happen to be about the sorriest critters imaginable.

The lactation consultant, seeing I've got the breastfeeding thing under control, leaves the room. I wish Tricia would leave too. She's still standing against the wall, utterly rapt and creeping me out. I'm topless, and she stares at me and Zerena, unable to take her eyes off us. She's jealous. She wishes she were me, young and blessed with a newborn girl. I've tried not to think of the pain I've caused her because there's nothing I can do about it now. I need to take care of Zerena. I don't want her to end up with the fuzzy end of the lollipop, which is what will happen if Jimmy ups and leaves us for Trish.

"So you were a liberal arts major, were you? At Ethan Allen College. Right?" Tricia asks, sitting down on the padded brown recliner next to my bed.

Warily, I nod. I'm not sure how she knows this. She peppers me with more questions about my college degree, engaging me in small talk, but it's unsettling how much she knows about my classes, my grades. It's like she's memorized my whole transcript.

"So along with your liberal arts diploma, you earned a certificate in gender studies. What's that for?" Tricia asks. A thin snide smile spreads over her lips. "Has that been *useful* in your career search?"

Unlike everything else she's mentioned, this statement about me having a gender studies certificate is flat-out wrong. "I don't have a gender studies certificate."

The look she gives me is of a cat that's just had a whisker yanked off. "You don't? Are you sure about that?"

"You don't know what you're talking about. I didn't go through five years of college just to amnesia out on everything. Women's studies. That's my certificate."

"Women's studies," Tricia says, as if committing it to memory, but even after she says this three times, her initial mistake still troubles her. I earned the women's studies certificate in part by counseling teenage girls on how to develop greater self-esteem so they won't be easily victimized or exploited.

Tricia bounds up from the recliner and puts her hand on the window. The sun's already beginning to set, but something catches her attention. "I'm going to have to call for a cab."

"Why's that?"

She points to something in the parking lot outside the window. "James must've forgot he promised to take me home. He just hopped into his car and is driving toward one of the exits."

"He is?" Jimmy had promised to sleep this evening on the recliner in my maternity suite. Zerena was going to be with us, sleeping in her stainless steel hospital bassinet. It was going to be the first time we would have spent an entire night all together—*baby's first night!* We had talked about this, chosen an extradeluxe maternity room just so we could be together for the occasion.

"What's the matter?" Tricia asks, fumbling through her handbag for her cell phone.

I tell Tricia about the plans we made. James knows how meaningful I wanted this to be for us. "We were going to spend the baby's first night all together. The three of us. That's what I told Jimmy I wanted us to do." Disappointment is making me tell her all this. I'm so distraught that I can't stop myself from talking. It's what I do sometimes: blab. Listening to me, Tricia softens her expression. A look of genuine sadness falls over her. She touches my hand, shakes her head in commiseration, but then, as though she apparently remembers she considers me dirt, her snide smile reappears, making me feel worse.

"Actually, I'm glad James isn't around right now," Tricia says. She picks up her pink cashmere cape from the back of a chair and drapes it over her shoulders. "This extra time's allowed you and me and Anne Elise to get to know each other. Hasn't it been fun?"

"Her name's not Anne Elise," I say, clearing my throat. "It's Zerena. Or, at least, it's going to be Zerena."

Tricia tilts her head, narrows her eyes. "But I thought James said—"

"I know what Jimmy said. And I know his reasons." The one thing life's taught me is that you can't let anyone push you around. Though he signed the birth certificate listing Anne Elise as the official name, I'm guessing ways exist to amend the filing. I've never had the chance to name anything in my life—not even a goldfish or a stray cat—and I'm sure not going to let anyone name my daughter for me. "Let me tell you: Jimmy and me are going to have more discussions about this."

Tricia eyes me for several moments, and I sense her begrudging respect for digging in my heels on this. She calls the taxi company, tells them to meet her at the hospital lobby in five minutes. When she's through with her call, she turns back toward me. "Can I give you one piece of advice? From my own experience?"

I nod.

"Next time, if you're going to make plans with James, prepare yourself to be disappointed," Tricia says, patting the top of my head with an unnerving condescension that makes me want to smack her down, but then the knowledge of how to truly hurt Tricia comes over me.

"It could be worse," I say.

"How?"

"Tonight, I'll be snug and comfy in this bed and breastfeeding my darling little girl. You? You'll still be old and alone. You tell me what's worse."

Tricia gasps, stung. I fear she's going to slap me—or worse—which would be great because I know I can take her in any brawl. Instead, though, she stalks toward the door, but before she leaves, she spins around, her cheeks red and angry. "You've made the worst mistake you could ever make."

"Why's that?"

"Why?" Tricia laughs a deranged laugh. "A woman with a vendetta and lots of money can cause great harm. That's why."

Chapter Five

JIM

Ten hours have passed since I left Trish and Laurel at the hospital. For much of that time, I'd been ensconced on a barstool tipping back tumblers of Scotch with a farm belt commodities insider who, upon hearing I'd just become a father, gifted me the investment tip of a lifetime. Fatherhood and a lucrative investment tip have fallen into my lap on the same day, but my life's a train wreck. I'm a congenial portfolio management specialist offering investment advice to the most risk-averse clientele you'd ever hope to ring up on speed dial. I'm not a genius, but I'm smart enough to know that one way or another, I'm going to pay for what I've done.

I'm standing on the front porch of Trish's house, Savory Mew, debating what to do. Located in the same Georgetown neighborhood as Dumbarton Oaks, the historic mansion where delegates from five nations hatched out plans to create the United Nations, the house has belonged to her family for four generations. And it's gorgeous, an ostentatious twelve-room Georgian brick manor house with a portico entrance, lead glass windows, molded ceilings, a tall slate roof, and the kind of storied past that lends itself to magazine feature stories. How can one walk away from such a home?

I fumble through my pockets for my house key, thankful Trish hasn't changed the locks on me yet. The house is dark. Trish must be asleep, meaning that for the moment I'll avoid the horrendous argument I know we're going to have in the not-too-distant future. I'm in it over my head with Trish and Laurel. There's a black stain on my conscience, a growing guilt that's getting harder to suppress, a sorrow that consumes me nightly before I drift off to sleep. I've got no good way of making right this situation. What does one do when one's screwed up as bad as I have? I let Trish down. I should never have stumbled into an affair, but in the months after Jack Riggs served up the idea of surrogacy, the idea that another woman might bear me a child gnawed on me. Having felt the sting of abandonment myself while growing up, I can't just walk out on Trish. Or Laurel. Or my newborn daughter.

At the hospital, I wanted Trish to yell at me, scream and shout, tell me how horrible I am. Last week, Laurel said she'd make sure I'd play no role in our baby's life if I didn't divorce Trish. A baby needs a daddy. I can't risk Laurel taking our baby away from me. I knew Trish would never divorce me because of the financial implications, but I needed to show Laurel I was doing what I could. Trish was going to find out about Laurel soon enough even if I didn't bring her to the hospital. Laurel's been tightening the screws on me to be done with Trish ASAP. Lately, she's been threatening to mail photographs of us together to Trish as a means of hastening our separation. Although I do wonder how Trish found out about Laurel, I was almost relieved when she told me on our drive to the hospital that she knew, because it meant I no longer had to live with that secret hanging over my head.

As strange as it sounds, I don't want Trish to eject me from her life. She's not the easiest person to be married to, but I love her. I really do. She's erratic, often acting on rash impulses or a logic that's near impossible to divine. At times, I've worried about her mental health, but I've not been able to convince her to see a psychologist. Like every other wealthy person I've met, she's uncommonly stubborn. Once she latches on to an idea, regardless how ridiculous or demonstrably false it may be, she'll never shake it out of her head. But I love her.

"James? Is that you?" Trish calls downstairs from the bedroom. "Are you home for the night?"

The question silences me.

Trish pads down the stairs, and in the dark, she sniffs the air, searching for me. Though I can't see her, I can tell she's cross at me by how she taps her foot on the marble floor.

"James. Have you been drinking?"

"Not drinking," I say, trying to put the best foot forward. "Contemplating."

Flipping on the light, I stumble forward and wrap my arms around Trish. She stands at the base of the grand staircase in her full-length cherry-blossom-print pink kimono. She used to cook incredible dinners: hollandaise sauce that was to die for, herbed lamb roasts, fresh-baked croissants. Every meal was spectacular. Years ago, upon arriving home, I'd grab her hand and twirl her around on the pink marble floors as if we were ballroom dancers. As newlyweds, I couldn't believe my good fortune. Through her, a brand-new world opened up for me, a moneyed extravaganza I never quite believed actually existed beyond the pages of *Vanity Fair* and the *Washingtonian*.

Coming from a long line of bankers, Trish's father served in Nixon's Treasury Department and, thereafter, in executive positions with the bank that bore his family name and controlled the commerce of this capital city for generations. Trish and her twin sister, Julie, seventeen years deceased due to a ruptured splenic artery aneurysm, were named after Nixon's daughters. An oil portrait of her father hangs above the fireplace in the living room. He was a dapper man who strolled the city with a silver-handled walking stick and top hat long after it had been fashionable to do so, and through these Gilded Age eccentricities and his financial muscle, he carved out a revered position for himself in Washington's social milieu. He possessed a patrician's jaunty chin, discerning eyes, and a smooth, chiseled, haughty nose. All children bear the scars and blessings of their parents. Sometimes, I doubt Trish realizes how much she resembles her father.

Growing up, I was never in Trish's league. Extravagance for me used to mean nothing grander than an extra scoop of ice cream or a new winter coat at Christmastime. But as a young man, in college, I fell under the thrall of F. Scott Fitzgerald's *The Great Gatsby*. Like all strivers, I took the novel to heart, appreciating it as a manual for how to get ahead in life rather than for its substantial literary merits. Having grown up in Buffalo (coincidentally, the city where Fitzgerald spent much of his early years), I snagged a half scholarship to a private DC university that billed itself as "the Harvard on the Potomac." I wanted to be rich. I was a Gatsby-in-training, an aspiring parvenu, a man on the make. Through Fitzgerald, I learned all men of consequence were either on the make, like Gatsby and myself, or, like Tom Buchanan, wealthy but careless people who relied on others to clean up their messes. A frequent though private game of mine was to walk into a party and assess everyone in the room—were they Gatsbys or Buchanans? Even before I met Jack Riggs, I pegged him, rightly, as a Buchanan. And he probably knew I was a Gatsby.

"I don't care if you were out 'contemplating.' Or whatever it was that you were doing. You shouldn't be driving after you've been drinking." Trish takes another exaggerated sniff of my alcohol-soused breath and flutters her hand, clearing the air of the odor. "Why don't you go to bed and sleep off whatever you've been 'contemplating'?"

"Did I ever tell you why I love you?"

Trish tilts her head, her eyes narrowing as if she's wary of being outsmarted. "Why?"

"Darling, I love the way you care for me. Even if I arrive at your staircase less than sober, you are compassionate and kind, gentle and sweet," I say, hoping against hope that a few generous compliments might temporarily erase the sins of my inebriation. "Beautiful. Silky. Sexy. You're everything a man could want in a wife."

Trish flicks the back of her hand at me, catching me on the shoulder. "You're impossible."

I kiss Trish's dry lips, trying to amuse her, but she leans away from my kisses, arching her back against the hand-carved wooden pineapple adorning the head of the staircase newel post.

"Hey? What gives?"

"Tomorrow. When you're sober. We're going to have a talk."

I turn away from Trish, glance once more at the portrait of her father above the mantel. It's strange how you can look at one thing and see another. Every time I look at that painting, I wonder what kind of home run he was trying to hit, naming his daughters after those of a disgraced president. Was he banking on Nixon returning to power? Was he trying to impress whatever Nixon admirers hadn't been booted out of office by the time Julie and Trish were born in 1975? Or was he naturally Nixonian, a cynical beast fully on board with Nixon's "screw my enemies" mentality?

Nixon once erroneously proclaimed, "I am not a crook." Technicalities and plausible deniability being the mother of all reckless assertions, I could say the same: I am not a crook, for my shenanigans are so far beneath the radar that no one but Trish cares about them. Although I've guided my financial clients into solid if conservative portfolios, I've been far more reckless with my own personal investments. And far less successful. I've lost staggering amounts of money. To impress Laurel, I booked us into $1,000-a-night hotel suites for our assignations. French doors opened out onto private balconies that overlooked the White House, the Potomac, the C&O Canal, and the national monuments scattered throughout town. I booked dozens of these hotel suites in the months we've been seeing each other. Now my credit cards are significantly overdrawn.

"Honey?" I say, leaning back against the wall until I feel the flocked wallpaper on the back of my neck. "Honey, if I told you how confused I am, you wouldn't believe me."

"I'd believe you," Trish says, slipping her hand into mine. "You're not the only one who's confused."

We stand like this for several minutes. Everything's quiet save for the occasional car on the cobblestone street in front of our house and the tick-tock of the grandfather clock in the next room. Moonlight shines in through the windows, its silvery light changing as clouds ebb and flow over the sky.

"Do you want to talk about this now?" Trish asks.

"No. Please. I'm in no shape to say anything sensible right now," I answer, slumping down against the wall.

$\sim$

Months after I met Trish, I received a phone call from her father, Jack Riggs, inviting me to lunch. I arrived at Savory Mew at the appointed hour expecting her to be present, but opening the door, Jack informed me she was away with friends. "Let's get to know each other," he said, decanting port wine for us into a pair of cut crystal glasses. I'd been to Savory Mew often enough that the house no longer intimidated me, yet on this occasion, alone with Jack Riggs, the blinds drawn, I realized an interrogation awaited me. Lunch was the stated purpose of my visit, but food was nowhere in sight. He offered me a cigar, which I declined.

"Sit down," Jack said.

I sat on the living room sofa, a priceless antique, and eyed the ancient windup Victrola in the corner of the room. During a previous visit, he'd commandeered my attention by bringing out rare Billie Holiday 78s on the Okeh label, but entertainment wasn't to be had on this particular afternoon.

"You're not a very smart man," Jack Riggs said.

I sucked in a breath.

Jack Riggs produced a folder containing my college transcript. I had majored in business but had been on academic probation for several semesters. Having just barely graduated six years earlier, I hoped my poor college performance could no longer be used against me. Previously, Jack Riggs had laughed amiably at my jokes, stroked his chin while considering my more thought-provoking comments. I thought he liked me. I thought he was glad I was dating his daughter.

"And your professional prospects are, shall we say, underwhelming."

"I'm circulating my résumé around town again, sir. Something will pop up. I'm sure of it."

Jack Riggs smirked. "Should I make a few calls? See what I can rustle up for you?"

My eyes widened. I hadn't considered asking Jack Riggs, as big a player in the Washington business scene as I was likely to meet, to help in my job search—an oversight that, I suppose, lent credence to his contention that I wasn't very smart. "I'd love to work at your bank, sir. I promise to work hard. Even if you started me off in an entry-level position, I promise you won't be disappointed."

"You? At *my* bank?" Jack Riggs glanced at my transcript and frowned. "I'm afraid that wouldn't be wise."

My shoulders sagged.

"But I'll do what I can. Trust me on this. And now I need to trust you on something." Jack Riggs pushed a photograph across the mahogany coffee table. The photo was of a beautiful woman with short blonde hair and ample cleavage barely contained by her red lace lingerie halter top. She looked to be about thirty, a tad older than Trish and me. "What do you think?"

Unsure how to respond, I sipped from my port glass.

"Tell me." Jack Riggs looked at the photo again and grinned. "You think she's attractive?"

Suddenly, I understood what he was getting at. Or so I thought. His wife, Trish's mother, had died five years earlier after a protracted bout of lymphatic cancer, and from the bashful way he grinned, I gathered he'd brought me here for a man-to-man conversation not about my professional problems but to seek advice on his own affairs of the heart. I took another sip of port. "You've got excellent taste, sir."

"Damn right I do. She cost me four million dollars too."

The figure flabbergasted me. I let go of the photo. It fell from my fingers and fluttered to the table.

"Four million. Easy. Between what I paid to keep this quiet from her husband, extract a pledge that she won't press charges against me, and the trust fund to take care of the baby's upbringing and eventual college costs. Hell, the agreement she signed requires that she says nice things about me if anyone asks. But take it from me: floozies are expensive." His term—"floozies"—was distasteful, harkening back to the Kennedy administration if not earlier, but though he expressed regret, his tone conveyed bad-boy bravado. He was an old goat, a grizzled player. His cheeks bloomed with pride. "Everything's got a cost. Especially if you make as many bad choices as I have."

In the years that followed, I've thought often of this conversation. He laid his cards on the table. We both understood each other's faults. My own father had abandoned my mother and me when I was thirteen. I'd already begun to look at Jack Riggs as a substitute father figure, but his crudeness appalled me. He talked of groping secretaries, grabbing women by their pussies, and planting kisses on the female associates who came to him for business or career advice. He told me about the harassment suits, the out-of-court settlements, and the cost of maintaining silence about his shenanigans through NDAs.

"Take my advice: don't follow my example." Jack Riggs lifted a cigar from the Spanish cedar humidor at the corner of the table. Tobacco products had never interested me, yet the process by which he went about lighting that cigar fascinated me. He struck a long wooden match against the striking strip of its matchbox, and then, after the sulfurous smell dissipated, he held the cut tip of the cigar at an angle to the match, rotating it in his hands so that the tip burned evenly. "You sure you don't want one of these? Arturo Fuente God of Fire. About the smoothest smoke you'll find anywhere in the world."

"No, sir," I said. "I'm good."

Jack Riggs put the cigar to his mouth and, still holding the match to its tip, drew in a few breaths. He released his breath. A small flame flared from the tip of the cigar. He took another puff until the flame extinguished itself. Setting the cigar down on a ceramic ashtray, he let out a puff of smoke. To this day, though it's been years since he last smoked a cigar at Savory Mew, I sometimes sit down on the same sofa and smell the nauseating aroma of that cigar and feel again the nervousness of that afternoon.

"Take my word: less expensive ways exist to get yourself in trouble. Stay clear of floozies, because you don't have the jack to deal with that."

"*Jack?*"

"Money. You don't have jack. At your level, one extra woman will exhaust your entire net worth."

"And you?"

"Let's just say all the extra women in the world haven't made a dent in my net worth." He produced a business card with the name of a private investigating firm printed upon it.

"Charles Simpkins?" I said, reading the name off the card.

Jack Riggs picked up his cigar and puffed on it. Its tip glowed. "That's him. The guy's a fixer. He fixes problems. He curtails the damages from my floozy problems. The girl wanted seven million," Jack Riggs said, gesturing to the photograph. "Simpkins talked her down to four. He also secured a copy of your transcript for me, by the way. If you have a problem, *any problem*, go to him."

I pictured Charles Simpkins as a shadowy silver-haired éminence grise, like Clark Clifford or Vernon Jordan, someone a guy like Ted

Kennedy or Bill Clinton would turn to, to solve an affair of the heart entanglement or a sticky business proposition. Jack Riggs was a wealthy man of the world. Was he warning me not to interfere with his affairs? A man who'd boast about the millions he tossed around to smooth over his indiscretions could surely ruin me if I ever upset him. In revealing his need for a professional fixer, he confessed to being a morally flawed man. I took the business card and buried it in my wallet, vowing to be better than him. Never would I put myself in a position where I needed a professional fixer.

Chapter Six

Jim

Seven hours after wobbling home drunk, I wake in bed, alone, and shut my eyes in reaction to the light filtering through the gauzy bedroom curtains. My tongue is a dehydrated strip of parched shoe leather, and there's an überache in my head. I remember being irrationally happy about Anne Elise's birth. I remember a conversation with a commodities insider about an investment opportunity, how for just the $250,000 buy-in on a livestock futures contract, I'd rake in millions of dollars almost overnight. But where am I to get a quarter million dollars? I remember Trish guiding me upstairs and the plop of my head as I passed out on the bed pillows.

Now, I hear Trish walk upstairs trilling a *la-da-da* breakfast melody. She opens the bedroom door and, with a smile on her face, says, "James, mornings like this just do not become you."

Trish's right: mornings aren't my strong suit, yet it's not in my nature to utter the stressed and hangover-blighted thoughts roiling through my head. As my mother, a single mom who put me through college on the strength of her alimony checks, used to say, "This world's got no stomach for whiners, hon."

"You're lucky you have such a caring wife," Trish says, setting down a Lucite tray containing my favorite hangover remedies: glasses of Gatorade and V8 juice, a mug of chamomile tea, a bottle of ibuprofen, Visine, aspirin, vitamin pills, a toasted poppy seed bagel slathered with cream cheese and lox, and two hard-boiled eggs that sit in antique soft-paste porcelain egg cups. "I bet Laurel wouldn't tolerate you on mornings like this."

I pour a glass of V8 juice down my throat. Hangover mornings are all about rehydration and replenishing the fluids and electrolytes alcohol has dried out of me. Medical experts should devise an easy-to-operate IV hookup to allow drinkers to plug into saline solutions overnight so they wake the following morning fully rehydrated, but for now, the next best thing is power chugging Gatorade and V8 juice. The more liquids I drink, the better I feel, and while this reemerging sense of well-being might only be psychosomatic, one must, in the immortal lyrics of Johnny Mercer, "Ac-cent-tchu-ate the positive."

"Thanks, darling. I feel better already," I say, almost believing it.

The only thing on the tray I don't drink is the cup of chamomile tea—a favorite of Trish's but something I can't stand.

"Come on, James. Chamomile is natural. It's an herb. It's totally safe and harmless."

I bring the teacup to my nose and sniff it.

"It's funny. Yesterday. Seeing her. I couldn't believe how much she looks like me," Trish says.

I do a double take. Trish is a petite yet imposing adult woman dressed in supertight designer jeans and a snug-fitting seamless camisole the color of crushed raspberries. With her black hair and wide forehead, she doesn't look anything like my blonde Laurel. Not even her manners or how she tilts her head when admonishing me are similar.

"Don't tell me you couldn't see the similarities," Trish says. "Just like me, she's got the bluest eyes."

"Far be it from me to be the contrarian, honey, but Laurel's eyes aren't blue. They're more like gray."

"Not Laurel. Anne Elise! That's who I'm talking about. Don't tell me you didn't see from our eyes how similar we must be."

"Oh."

"So. Tell me. When you first held Anne Elise and looked into her eyes, did you feel an instant special connection to her?" Trish's eyes mist up. She holds her hands together, starving for my response. "Let me live vicariously through your experiences. Did you love her immediately? How soon does love set in?"

Seismic sensations had poured through me at the moment of Anne Elise's birth. Time slowed down, becoming elastic. A nurse snipped Anne Elise's umbilical cord. Laurel was flat on her back, getting sutured. I held the baby to Laurel's face. We kissed her on either cheek. Our three noses touched together. In the expansiveness of the moment, my good cheer verging toward giddiness, Anne Elise's *presence* overwhelmed me.

I pop open the ibuprofen bottle, shake out a tablet. Guilt surges through me—not only because of my affair but from creating a baby who doesn't belong to the woman I've loved for the last fifteen years. Though my love for Anne Elise was instantaneous, saying so would only compound Trish's pain, hurting her more than I already have. She doesn't need me to tell her the joy she's missing out on by being childless. I run my hand through my unkempt hair, swallow the ibuprofen, and shrug. "I guess it was okay."

Trish's mouth drops open. "Only okay?"

Though I've said and done a lot of stupid things over the years, Trish has never been so surprised. She sits down at the corner of the bed, takes a small breath. For twelve years, for better or worse, we shared every experience of our lives, but I'm now experiencing things in which she can play no role. She crosses her legs. Her lips tighten as if she's bracing herself for a shock. "James? I need you to do something for me."

"What's that, honey?"

"You need to stop seeing *that woman*. She's a dalliance, James. That's all she is to you. You know this. Deep down, I know you know this. Get her out of your life. Do you understand? Get rid of her."

The way she says it—*get rid* of her—I think she expects me to kill Laurel, which I'd almost understand if she ever finds out how much money I've blown on Laurel. Three weeks ago, I received my annual six-figure performance bonus. Rather than paying off my credit cards, I used the money to move Laurel into a stunning three-bedroom riverfront apartment. On the night I told Trish I was at work preparing a client presentation, I painted the walls of one room goldenrod yellow. The room was going to be our child's nursery. I had discussed so little with Laurel about how we were to proceed once the baby was born. Perhaps Laurel assumes I, too, will move into the apartment. Perhaps she envisions nights on the balcony sipping wine together while the baby sleeps. Nor, beyond pleading for a divorce yesterday, have I talked with Trish about my living arrangements. Everyone in our presumptuous little triangle is just assuming things will work out to their liking.

I rise out of bed. Still hungover, I'm prepared to feel the room spin beneath my feet, but after I take a wobbly first step, the urge to vomit subsides. I walk to my closet and pull a winter-weight blue pinstriped suit off a heavy wood hanger.

Trish crosses her arms, taps the toe of her open-toed flats against the floor. The color of her shoes matches her crushed-raspberry camisole. "You married me, James. You vowed to love, honor, and cherish me. Don't you remember? Don't you remember the sacred vows you made to me?"

I kiss her on the forehead and touch her chin. "I'll always love, honor, and cherish you, darling. Why do you think I come home to you each night? Even if, you know, you no longer want me living here with you, I'll always cherish you. Why do you think I wrap my arms around you and kiss you as often as I can?"

Trish's cheeks redden until they match the color of her camisole and flats. She starts to cry. I haven't seen her cry since the time two years ago when an eminent doctor sat us down in an office decorated with potted ferns and advised us that, after two unsuccessful rounds of in vitro procedures, "you ought to embrace your childless future."

"I love you," Trish says.

"I love you too. You're right, honey. Maybe I ought to stop seeing Laurel," I say, testing the idea out aloud. Sooner or later, I'm going to have to do something. Not that I'm in a position to do something immediately.

Trish looks up at me, startled.

"I need to be smart about this. As you might imagine, I'm in an exposed position. Give me time. I need to figure how to get myself out of this."

Trish takes in this information, a needy sponge gladly absorbing a raindrop of hope. She brightens, and for a moment, I fear she'll press me for details, commitments, a precise schedule for when I intend to tell Laurel I'm dropping her. Behind every plan A is a top-notch plan B, but for now my plan B is to wrangle more time for myself so I can devise an even better plan C. Thankfully, one of my cell phones goes off. It's almost eight o'clock, the hour at which clients seek out my insights about European and Asian overnight trading activity, a topic that today, I'm ill prepared to answer. But when I grab my phone, I discover it's not one of my clients calling. Instead, it's my credit card company asking for payment for the amount I've overdrawn my account. It's the third such call this month. All my available cash went into the rent for Laurel's apartment.

"What's wrong?" Trish asks after I put down my phone.

"Wrong? Nothing's wrong. What could possibly be wrong when I'm at home with such a beautiful, lovely wife?"

No smile materializes on Trish's lips; no joy lights her face. It's as if, because of the heartbreak I've put her through over the past day, my compliments no longer have an effect on her. She looks glum faced and tired. "James? Why don't you call in sick today? We could go back to bed for a little bit, and then, after you're feeling better, we could bundle up and drive out to Rock Creek Park for a walk."

Rock Creek Park. This is her improbable peace offering to me. It's our favorite place in the city, a forested two-thousand-acre park in Northwest DC where people flock in the summertime for Shakespeare performances and tennis tournaments. We walked there often, roaming the grounds under cotton-clouded skies, the forest's layer of dried leaves crunching beneath our feet, our lungs filled with the woodsy air. In the dead of winter, meandering off and beyond the hiking trails, one feels totally alone on the isolated leaf-strewn woody slopes. In this city of marble monuments, obstructionism, and brutal egos, it's the one place you can feel kidlike, alone with nature. In 2002, the park came to national attention when the skeletal remains of a young woman thought to have been the mistress of an influential congressman were found on a remote bluff under heavy foliage. The body had gone undiscovered for more than a year, which didn't surprise me, since there are so many desolate and isolated pockets within the park.

"So what do you say? Do we have a date for Rock Creek Park?"

"Er . . . emmm," I say, sneaking a peek at my watch. Although I'm open to the temptation to shirk business and work responsibilities, running off with Trish on a nature hike doesn't feel right. The smile that had been on Trish's face wanes as I hesitate. I shake my head, tell her I shouldn't traipse off and have fun when I have obligations at my office—"Responsibilities are responsibilities, you know"—but we both know the real reason I can't go with her.

To my surprise though, Trish reaches over and kisses me again, her lips lingering on mine for precious moments. Although I'd never admit it to Laurel, Trish is a far better kisser. She takes my hand, cups it in both of her hands, and looks up at me. "James. I'm not prepared to give up on you."

And this is when I know I've got her right where I want her. She's not prepared to give up on me, which gives me time to figure out what to do about Laurel.

Chapter Seven

TRISH

James's touch is like no other. Because he's conflicted and confused, I must push harder on him to stay with me. If I were pregnant, none of this would've happened. We may have our differences, but the bond between us is unbreakable. Drunk as he was, he returned home last night rather than going to the hospital for the special celebration Laurel planned with him. If his desire was to straight-out abandon me, he would've done so already. Instead, he needs time and my encouragement to end his fling with Laurel.

We first met on the scariest day in history. People were frantic, pouring out of their DC office buildings at ten o'clock in the morning. Hijacked airliners had slammed into New York's World Trade Center towers, while here in DC, across the river, the Pentagon was in flames. Buildings throughout the city were evacuated, the federal government on emergency shutdown. With traffic at a standstill and the streets congested, hailing a cab to get home to Savory Mew was out of the question. Never had I felt so unsafe. I stared into the brilliant blue sky expecting it to be filled with hijacked aircraft. Sirens blared from every conceivable direction. My father was attending a shareholders' meeting in New York, and as I crossed an intersection on K Street, panic seized me. My father, I realized, might be dead. My mother had been dead for five years, and my sister had died earlier in the year. People teemed around me, everyone fleeing their office buildings, but I feared I was all alone, an orphan with no one left in my life to care for. Cell phone networks were down. None of my calls went through. People crowded shoulder to shoulder on the sidewalks. No one felt safe going down into the metro. Rumors that would later prove false peppered the conversations around me. Someone said a truck bomb had exploded outside the State Department. The breeze was heavy with the charred smell from the Pentagon fire a mile or two away. I started to cry, thinking about my father.

A man next to me in the crowd reached into the breast pocket of his navy-blue suit jacket and handed me a soft white handkerchief to dry my tears. He had light-brown hair and dark, comforting eyes that brought out my immediate trust. Until that moment, lost in my thoughts, I hadn't realized we'd been walking apace for several blocks. In tears, distraught, I told him I feared my father was dead. He drew a breath, put his hand on my shoulder, and, touching my chin, implored me to think positive thoughts. The man said I owed it to my father to visualize him happy and healthy, that if by chance my father was struggling to free himself from under tons of rubble, my "positive psychic projections" would energize him. I'll never forget it. Under James's persuasive gaze, I willed myself to believe my father was still alive.

"In order to *be* lucky, you've got to *think* lucky. Subconsciously, we feed off the energy others give off to us. Karma," James said, tapping his heart. "It's what we live by."

I stared into James's eyes, and he did not flinch from my gaze. We were in the nation's capital, in the middle of a national emergency, people running every which way, sirens wailing, and yet I had his entire attention. As if by magic, my phone beeped. My father's number lit up on the screen. Somehow, he had gotten through to me; somehow, he was alive. My father, never one to text before, sent the briefest of messages: Im OK U?

Hurriedly, I texted back a simple Yes.

So overjoyed was I that I wrapped my arms around James and kissed him, hungrily, digging my fingers into the lush fabric of his suit jacket and feeling the muscular flesh of his shoulders beneath the fabric. His mouth tasted of chewing gum, and his cheeks smelled of Acqua di Giò cologne, a combination of innocence and sophistication that drove me wild with desire. My need for him was animal-like and desperate. People in our midst were looking at us, pointing at us, and I had it in my mind we were reliving some kind of celebrated scene and that, like the famous Times Square photograph of an uninhibited sailor kissing a nurse on V-J Day, our kiss would take on talismanic proportions in the popular imagination.

James straightened his jacket, straightened his tie. He could've been forgiven for thinking me unhinged or, at the least, a bit too *forward*, and yet, as he turned to face me, I sensed again his unflappable calm, his supreme confidence. He held out his hand and introduced himself, prim and proper. He told me his name. Wainsborough. It sounded English. The name of a duke or a lord, someone of consequence I'd feel confident introducing to those in my social circle. He kissed my hand, an over-the-top gesture that, compared to my passionate embrace, seemed positively restrained. My heart raced. I stuttered.

"The pleasure of meeting you is entirely mine," James said, letting go of my hand. "It's a pity it takes a national disaster for me to meet someone as charming as you."

~

Now, showered, dressed, and having spooned down a bowl of blueberries and instant oatmeal, James plants a kiss on my cheek. Back when we first dated, we talked without words, letting our eyes do the talking as we stared at each other across restaurant tables. Though he won't call in sick to spend the day rekindling our love with a winter's stroll through Rock Creek Park, I'm determined to hang on to him. He is my husband. I bat my eyelashes, and he raises an eyebrow.

"Do you want to know what I dreamed last night? I dreamed I was pregnant," I say, and as I tell James about the dream, he slips his hand over mine. Though he asked me to divorce him yesterday, I look into his eyes, yearning to see that divorce isn't what he really wants. I tell him about the bloating I felt in the dream, how I thought I'd burst out of my skin. "It was simply the most exciting dream I ever had. Would you like it if I were pregnant?"

James glances at the kitchen clock. The clock is plastic and black and shaped like an elegant cat, and with each passing second, the cat's tail swishes from one side to the other.

"Would you like it?" I ask again, but I already know from his reluctance to answer that he thinks it impossible I'll ever get pregnant. He doesn't want me to get my hopes up. Plus there's Laurel, his fertile young mistress who apparently doesn't share my difficulties with conception.

"Hey, I forgot to compliment you on how well your shoes match your camisole. It looks lovely. What do you call the color?"

Both items are new, bought the previous week while boutique hopping, but rattled with the feeling he's slipping out of my life, I can't remember the details. Reds, greens, and blues no longer exist in couture. Instead, we have shades like bruised plum, rosemary sorbet, and smudged banana, monikers deriving from produce aisles and fanciful imaginations. My friends are always amazed at how attentive James is of me, how he notices the little things—the accessories, the color coordination—that their own lackadaisical husbands overlook.

"Hey, why so glum?" James asks.

I shrug. In my heart, I know unless I do something, James will eventually leave me. None of this would have happened if I'd been able to become pregnant. Fundamentally, he's a good man. I doubt he's ever dallied with another woman before Laurel dug her claws into him. Now that he's a father, he will endeavor to be a good father. For the sake of his baby, he will eventually commit himself to Laurel, tossing me aside. How is it supposed to feel when a marriage dissolves? I'm overwhelmed by the mawkish sentimentality for this shared life that's rushing away from me. Back when we dated, I deduced that his love for my money helped cement his love for me, which was why I consented to his marriage proposal only on the condition he sign the prenup. As long as it was clear he'd never get a penny if he divorced me, I figured he'd be mine for life. Sooner or later, his love for Anne Elise will outweigh his love for my money. Eventually, he will leave me for Laurel. But I won't make it easy for him.

"Are you coming home tonight?"

"Why wouldn't I?" James says, opening the front door. Over his shoulder, beyond the circular driveway and the snowed-over front lawn, I make out the cobblestone street in front of the house. "Why wouldn't I want to come home to the most wonderful wife in the city? Please don't think a little tiff or two will make me run away."

A *little tiff*? He's trying to downplay his affair and all that's come between us, but I'm not going to let him distract me. "So what time are you coming home?"

James squints at me. It's not like me to pester him about his comings and goings, for I'm not one of those henpecking wives who feels incomplete if she doesn't know where her husband is every time the cat's tail on her kitchen clock swishes another second or two. "I'll be home. Just like I always am."

"At what time? I need to plan something. How about seven o'clock? Is that good enough? Do you think you can be home by seven?"

James shrugs. "Sure."

A moment later, James snaps his fingers. "Crushed raspberry."

"Huh?"

"Crushed raspberry. That's what they should name the color of your shoes and top. It's the perfect name for a color. Don't you think, darling?"

~

My father had multiple affairs during the course of his marriage. A woman internalizes these things. A father's infidelity teaches a girl that, ultimately, as a woman, she's disposable. A mother's silence about her husband's infidelities teaches acceptance. Yes, I was affected by it. My mother, who traced her ancestry to the *Mayflower*, was the most generous person I'd ever known. Each night, instead of reading bedtime stories to my sister, Julie, and me, she recited poems by the American fireside poets of the nineteenth century. Henry Wadsworth Longfellow, John Greenleaf Whittier, James Russell Lowell. Her delicate voice lilted with the rhythms of each verse. She was a porcelain flower, fine and fragile and utterly unable to withstand the fissures my father's affairs introduced into her marriage. She took to bed for months on end. In the mornings, Julie and I dove through the heavy curtains that surrounded her four-poster canopy bed, trying to cheer her up. We'd brush her brittle hair, pretend she was our fairy queen and we her fair handmaidens. We'd lay out the elegant pleated skirts and silk blouses we'd hope she'd wear, but rarely could we coax her downstairs for breakfast or outside for a rambunctious hide-and-go-seek game like we once enjoyed.

"What do you do all day?" my sister and I asked her one morning four months after she first retreated into her bedroom. We were trying to figure out why she no longer played with us or even asked after our school activities. During the months she'd become bedbound, winter had turned into an unseasonably warm spring, and now it was nearly summer, the twittering of songbirds in the air whenever we galloped outside. Julie and I had somehow discovered a passion for badminton. We wanted her to come outside and watch us volley birdies over a net we'd strung up between two maple trees.

Our mother stared at us, her face gaunt and her eyes ravaged with worry.

Until that moment, I assumed that, in bed, she slept throughout the day, but seeing the pallor in her sun-starved face and the purple shadows under her eyes, I suddenly realized that, quite to the contrary, she hardly slept at all. This knowledge frightened me. I wanted to flee the room, afraid that if I stayed another minute, I, too, would never be able to sleep again. Her skin was as white as the powder she used to dust onto herself.

"I pray," our mother whispered. "That's all I do anymore."

Always much braver than I, Julie sat down beside her. "What do you pray for, Mommy?"

"I pray that I can die soon."

Years later, I'd understand our mother had fallen into an irrevocable depression, but back then, still in my girlhood, I couldn't fathom why she never left her sour-smelling room. I hated her for being so weak. I am not proud of this.

My mother once had long, luxurious hair. She once had a pretty smile, a dainty figure, and calm, compassionate eyes. I pleaded with her to open the windows and let the sun flow into her room. I pleaded with her to be happy. I pleaded with her to fight for her life even though, at that young age, I wasn't sure what that meant. As I grew into my teens, I gradually understood why young women sometimes called our house for my father at odd hours. Or dropped by in person, only to be ushered upstairs into one of the guest bedrooms by him. He was wrong for doing what he did, but I hated my mother for not being strong.

Staying in bed, she was giving up on life. This, in my mind, meant she was giving up on being my mother.

So, yes, my father's affairs affected me, and yet I was never mad at him; I was mad at my mother. All my resentment and bitterness, even that which I was too angry to verbally express, was directed at her.

Now, even after what James has done with Laurel, I'm determined not to suffer the same fate as my mother.

Chapter Eight

TRISH

This morning, I gulped down two Valiums as I whipped up the breakfast tray of James's hangover remedies. Yesterday, after returning from Laurel's maternity suite, I met with my internist. I didn't want to be like my mother and fall into depression in the face of James's affair. Hopping onto the doctor's examination table, I unveiled my troubles to him, letting him know depression ran in my family along my mother's line. He put a stethoscope to my chest, the cool metal bell of that instrument causing me to shiver, and slipped a rubberized belt around my arm, pumping it up to gauge my blood pressure. Physically, nothing was wrong with me, and yet, as a precaution, he scribbled a Valium prescription for me. I was skeptical. What were the possible side effects? He told me about the sleepiness it induces, the difficulty in coordination some people experience. "Is that all?" I asked.

He glanced at his tablet, scrolled through the drug's complete profile. He told me about the suicidal ideation, aggression, agitation, confusion, unusual thoughts and behavior, memory loss, and depression that can occur.

"Unusual thoughts?" I asked. My doctor put down his tablet. "Some people react strangely to Valium in rare cases. Since you're without preexisting psychiatric concerns or mental health issues, I doubt you need to worry." In the seventeen hours since I filled my prescription, I've taken several Valiums, but I've yet to experience the calm moods promised by my doctor. Now, watching James step into his Volvo, I take another tablet. And then another.

Throughout his life, my father raved about a particular private investigation agency. They were the crème de la crème in his book, the ne plus ultra. So far, except for the gender studies snafu, they've provided me with excellent information on Laurel. In recent years, I remember my father saying that some unpleasantness had developed between him and the agency, sullying their relationship. They had charged him exorbitantly for their services or double billed him or some such nonsense. Because I don't want whatever happened with that to impact the quality of services they offer me, I've only given them my married name—which was easy enough to do since all our previous communications were conducted through email. They don't know I'm Jack Riggs's daughter. Now, though, because I need them to dig up more information—*uglier* information—if I'm to convince James to stop seeing her, I jump into my car and drive to their offices.

DC's Chinatown, where Simpkins & Simpkins is based, is a section of town that, today, scarcely exists. Once or twice a year, before my father's affairs ruined their marriage, my parents took my sister and me there for dinner at one of the small restaurants, where the dining rooms smelled of sizzling peanut oil, cardamom, and ginger. Authentic Chinese waiters appeared at our tables bearing pots of green tea and little ceramic teacups that looked unlike any of the fine porcelain cups I used at home. Roasted whole ducks, their heads still attached, their skin glistening with an orange glaze of Elmer's-like viscosity, hung in the windows of these restaurants, ostensibly to attract customers, but I couldn't imagine anyone wanting to be served one of those ducks. What do you do with the head? The neck? The beak? Often, we'd be the only Caucasians in these restaurants, everyone else being as authentically

Chinese as our waiters, and I'd close my eyes, fling back my head on the metal-framed chairs, and listen to the yammering Mandarin of the conversations around me as my father pointed to items on the menu, calling them out by their numbers: "We'll have numbers twenty-three, sixteen, and forty-nine. And bring us some egg rolls too."

But, today, for all intents, Chinatown is no longer Chinatown. Developers have rushed in, razing whole blocks of longstanding Chinese stores and replacing them with gaudy brewpubs, Fuddruckers, Hooters, and the brightly lit homogenized chain stores found in every shopping mall across the nation. Tenement buildings that had housed generations of Chinese immigrants were leveled to make room for luxury condominiums. Most of the authentic Chinese restaurants are gone. Nary is there a roasted duck in any of the storefront windows or a bowl of soy sauce–drenched bean curd noodles on any of the tables. Time and circumstance change neighborhoods and relationships. What is a Chinatown without any Chinese businesses or residents? What is a wife without a husband?

When I arrive at the address listed on the firm's website, something's amiss. Consigned to the subbasement of a spanking-new office building, Simpkins & Simpkins's quarters are barely bigger than my walk-in wardrobe closet. The office is windowless, airless, a claustrophobe's nightmare. A man looks up at me from behind a dented metal desk, where he's playing computer solitaire on his cell phone. He's about twenty-five years old, maybe younger. With no sign of a wedding band on his ring finger, my guess is that he's unattached, the kind of aimless young man who spends his nights on a secondhand couch watching college basketball games in a studio apartment. I've never been in a private investigator's office before, but it is exactly as I imagined it—low-key and unkempt. Electronic gadgets—laptops, tablets, scanners, handheld radar guns, and parabolic eavesdropping microphones—surround his desk. A DC private investigator's license hangs on the wall beside posters of athletes from Washington's underperforming basketball and hockey teams.

"Is Charles Simpkins going to be in anytime soon?"

The man blinks. "Charles Simpkins is dead. He was my grandfather."

There's a catch in my throat. "I'm sorry for your loss. Was it recent?"

The man looks at his wristwatch. "It's been a few years." He rises from his chair. Sporting wire-rimmed glasses and a short-sleeve button-down plaid shirt, he holds out his hand. His face is long and freshly shaved, red with razor burn and the discomfort of having been reminded about the loss of a loved one. "I'm Larry Simpkins. I've inherited what's left of my grandfather's practice. Can I help you?"

"You told me it was gender studies, when all along it was women's studies," I say, sliding a printout of the report he emailed me onto his desk. Simpkins puts down his cell phone. Another phone rings atop a sheet-metal filing cabinet. He turns to answer it but, taking note of my displeasure, lets the call go into voice mail. "So what do you have to say for yourself? I'm paying good money, don't you forget, and I want accurate information. How can I trust you if you can't get a simple thing like women's studies right?"

Simpkins stares at me for what seems like an obscenely long time. Though we've never met, I get the impression he's searching his memory and trying to place me. He grabs the report I've flung onto his desk, his bushy eyebrows rising and falling as he reads it. It's a mere seven pages, but he stops on page three where I highlighted "gender studies," circling it twice with a fluorescent blue felt-tip and amending the page's margin with a big "NO!"

"How do you think I felt confronting her yesterday? I wanted to rattle her cage. I wanted to convey the impression of menacing omnipotence. Instead, I came off looking like a fool, insisting she had a certificate in gender studies when she had none. She told me I didn't know what I was talking about."

Simpkins gives a little laugh that lasts only as long as it takes me to glare at him, compelling him to wipe the smirk from his face.

"I want reliable information. Good information. Troubling information. That's what I want." Meeting Laurel yesterday, I sensed immediately an unseemly past lay in her background. James is malleable, easily subject to suggestion. I must convince him that Laurel is unfit to take an active role in Anne Elise's upbringing. Better yet, if I can demonstrate a history of criminality, drug use, or lewd or otherwise morally objectionable behavior, I can persuade social service agencies to take the child from her, which would save our marriage. If you pay a good lawyer enough money, you can accomplish anything you want. We could raise Anne Elise ourselves, James and I, and legally adopt her.

"I'm sorry," Simpkins says. "What can I say? I never knew there was a difference between gender studies and women's studies. I thought they were synonymous. Were there other things wrong with my findings?"

I think long and hard about everything he's sent so far. "As far as I know, there were no other inaccuracies. But listen: I need you to dig deeper. I need to ruin this woman's life, Mr. Simpkins. I need the skeletons in her closet, her juiciest secrets, information so toxic it'll curl the toes of the bleeding hearts I'm likely to encounter in family court and the city's social services offices when it comes time to petition someone to declare her an unfit mother."

Simpkins raises an eyebrow. "Did she already have her child?"

"She gave birth yesterday. At Sibley Hospital."

Simpkins's face is blank.

"You didn't know, did you?"

"You never requested day-to-day surveillance from me. And besides, hacking into medical records is illegal."

Two photographs on Simpkins's filing cabinet catch my attention. In both, Simpkins stands shoulder to shoulder with Mark Zuckerberg, the freckled boy billionaire Facebook founder. Both grin at the camera, as if sharing a joke. Simpkins follows my gaze to the pictures and blushes. Instantly, I sense he's that rare Washingtonian who doesn't like the attention earned by his accomplishments.

"How do you know Mark Zuckerberg?" I ask.

"I did an internship at Facebook's Menlo Park headquarters last year. I worked with him one on one, putting together a special project for him."

My initial impulse is to chalk this up as a tall tale, for I can't imagine someone of Zuckerberg's stature relying on someone as young as Simpkins, but then I remind myself that, supposedly, in the technology fields, young slackers like Simpkins find great success.

"What's he like?"

"Mark? He's cool." Simpkins clicks his fingers together and, flashing a bashful smile, comes alive for the first time since I entered the office. "Mark gave me the best advice anyone's ever given me."

"What's that?"

"He urged me to drop out of Harvard just like he did and follow my bliss."

I let this sink in. Though I'm less than twenty years older than him, I'm constantly astounded by how people of his generation have such different life priorities than my own. In the proper hands, a Harvard degree is the ticket to a good life and abundant social connections, something no right-minded person ought to reject.

"So what's your bliss?"

"This," Simpkins says, gesturing with his hands to his beat-up desk, dented filing cabinet, his paltry laptop, and the entire office around him. "I wanted to follow in my grandfather's footsteps. Congressmen, senators, and even a president relied on his services. It's been hard for me, though. The cost of doing business in this town is sky-high." He sucks in a breath, looks at me in dramatic fashion, his eyes stretching out big and needy like those of a puppy begging for a scrap of food. "I'm not going to lie to you. Right now, I'm two months' in arrears on rent."

Is Simpkins looking for sympathy? Or more money? As far as he knows, I'm the cash-strapped middle-aged woman I professed to be when I first inquired via email about his services. So far, though, he's provided good information at a good value. If I'm to succeed in getting James to dump Laurel, I need to keep Simpkins happy. I reach into my brown leather Prada tote for the packet of cash I withdrew earlier from the bank. Seeing the crisp hundred-dollar bills, Simpkins sucks in a breath. Everyone dreams the devil will come round tempting him or her with a million dollars to commit one minor indiscretion, but my father taught me most people will gladly sell their souls for significantly less. "Never be afraid to lowball," my father used to say, puffing on one of his robust full-flavored Arturo Fuente cigars. "The devil's no sucker. Why blow a million dollars on some poor sap when a few hundred dollars will do the trick?"

Like the devil, I'm no sucker. A good private investigator would charge ten thousand dollars to get the information I need, but Simpkins locks his eyes on the money. He's already told me he's behind in his rent. I peel out twenty of the hundred-dollar bills and lay them on his desk. His hands tremble.

"It's a take-it-or-leave-it offer, Mr. Simpkins," I say, confident that a man with so much need in his gaze will do just about anything I ask of him. "I need whatever dirt you can dish out on Laurel Bloom, but I can't afford to give you any more money."

Simpkins reaches across the desk and holds one of the bills to the overhead light, inspecting it. "It's genuine."

"Of course it's genuine."

Simpkins's tongue glides across his chapped lips, moistening them until they glisten in the overhead fluorescent light. He looks at me and then eyes the cash again.

"I'm going to need you to work fast," I say.

"How fast?"

"Do you have serious hacking skills?"

"This is America. You can believe what you want to believe, but I do seriously good work," Simpkins says, and in the pride that glows on his cheeks, I sense my trust in him isn't misplaced. He isn't a stupid man. He's worked for Mark Zuckerberg, a certified tech genius, so technical skills must be in his arsenal.

"Everyone's got secrets," I say. "Find hers however you can. I don't care how you find them, but I need them. The more debauched and scandalous, the better."

Chapter Nine

TRISH

After my father retired, but before he relocated offshore to the Caymans, he moved into an eight-room postwar brick colonial not far from Sibley Memorial Hospital so James and I could have Savory Mew to ourselves. The colonial was a step down for him, both in the status of its neighborhood and its lack of palatial splendor, but he claimed to love it. A previous owner, a highly placed congressional aide who landed big in the lobbying business, had whitewashed the exterior brick walls twenty years before my father had bought the property. The vestige of white remaining on the brown clay bricks was like the mold that fuzzed over fine cheese: something to distinguish it from the newfangled homes, condos, and cookie-cutter townhouses that flooded the market.

It was my father's wedding gift to me, deeding me Savory Mew, and in the years that followed, we brunched, James and I, at my father's new house on Sunday afternoons. We were very close, my father and I. All our finances—our banking accounts and investment portfolios—are tied together under both our names, but as much as I valued my father's sound investment advice, I valued him more for the effect he had on James and me. My father was always his usual effervescently cynical self on these occasions, and although we teased him about his inability to toast a bagel with any real authority, my father's camaraderie helped James and me soldier on as man and wife despite our inability to conceive. For these brunches, he eschewed the neckties, gold cuff-links, and customary silk pocket squares that would accessorize his sports jackets and suit coats on any normal business day, instead attiring himself in what he characterized as "Sunday casual" code—khaki slacks, brown penny loafers, and a blue Brooks Brothers blazer over a blue oxford shirt. The brunches were high-spirited affairs, and James usually restrained himself from drinking too many mimosas. Every fifteen minutes or so, conversation would halt while ambulances raced past the house, their sirens wailing on their way to Sibley. It baffled me how my father could live amid such constant noise. Wouldn't he be happier in the peaceful horsey surroundings of Middleburg? Or how about Great Falls? Or McLean? I pictured my father living in genteel comfort, and yet he pooh-poohed my concerns, laughing, telling me, "Honey, I didn't thrive in Washington for as long as I have just to be driven off by sirens and ambulances."

Now, driving to Sibley, I pass by my father's whitewashed house and am surprised by the **For Sale** sign staked in its front lawn. Though he hasn't stepped foot in this country for a year, he said he'd keep the house so he can visit us often once his first grandchild was born. I thought we were close. Following my mother's death, I forgave him for his egregious philandering, which compounded the misery of my mother's last years. I'd have thought he'd mention this to me, email me some notice or explanation. What drove him to put the house on the market? Seeing the sign staked in his yard, I half expect we'll never see each other again. Has he finally given up on me ever bearing him a grandchild?

∽

My father used to say, "Keep your friends close but your enemies closer." With this in mind, I head back to Sibley Hospital after meeting

Simpkins. Awkward as it might be, I need to learn more about Laurel in order to know what I'm up against. As I step off the elevator onto the maternity ward, the cries of a baby from a nearby room make my knees go weak. The crying fills me with longing and anxiety, reactions I would've thought mutually exclusive of each other. I imagine holding the baby, trying to soothe it. I imagine the moment Laurel realized she became pregnant. How soon after bedding my husband did she realize she'd conceived? Was it minutes? Did her breasts ache as he pulled out of her? Did her heart suddenly lurch, delirious with joy? Or was it morning sickness that gave away her condition?

Lois Belcher, the lactation consultant, approaches me in the hallway. Being around babies must give her special powers, for she looks like someone's idea of a fairy godmother, a kindly woman possessing a glittery magic wand capable of transforming pumpkins into stagecoaches. Cheerfulness abounds from her. Although every job has its stresses, it must be refreshing to work in a profession where positive outcomes overwhelmingly outnumber the bad, where the people she serves are so abundantly accepting of her assistance. Seeing me, she waves.

"She's still recovering. Her episiotomy wound's giving her some trouble, but I think she's doing well," Ms. Belcher says.

"Who?"

Ms. Belcher laughs. "Your daughter, of course!"

Despite this prompt, it takes a moment to realize she's still under the assumption that Laurel is my daughter, which stings me because my hunch is that she also assumes James is Laurel's husband, not mine. And yet my ears perk up. I hadn't realized Laurel had an episiotomy—something that, frankly, I wouldn't wish on anyone.

"Is she awake?"

"You bet! So is your granddaughter! They'll be glad you're visiting them again!"

"Thanks," I say. There's not a chance Laurel will be glad to see me. The maternity ward smells of antiseptic iodine and the fresh-cut flowers friends and relatives deliver to the new moms. Should I have disguised my intentions by bringing her a big bouquet of zinnias, irises, maybe even roses?

Two babies from rooms directly across from us start crying at once. Another baby, swaddled in blue blankets on the lap of a convalescing mother being wheeled down the hallway, starts wailing. The babies in the ward are like a flock of crows: as soon as one squawks, the others join in.

"Is it always this loud in here?"

Ms. Belcher grins. "Isn't it wonderful?"

A girl with long caramel-red hair, the kind I'd wished I had when I was eight or nine, walks past us carrying what must be her baby brother. She looks at the baby in her arms with rapturous care, and it's as if I can read her thoughts: she's pledging to be the most wonderful, tender, loving big sister the world has ever known. She wanders through the hallway so focused on the baby that our presence doesn't register upon her. As she reaches the end of the hallway, Lois Belcher calls out to her, telling her to stop.

The girl looks up at Lois as if awoken from a daze.

"You can't go past that door," Lois says, pointing to the glass door the girl was just about to open.

The girl apologizes and then walks back down the hallway, again staring at her baby brother.

"Why couldn't she go past that door?" I ask.

"Security. Babies can only leave the maternity ward with someone whose KISS bracelet code matches the baby's KISS bracelet," Lois Belcher says, explaining that the plastic medallions with Mick Jagger lips I've seen on babies and new mothers are electronic security devices. "That little girl doesn't have a bracelet. If she went past that security door, or if she tried to go onto the elevator with the baby, alarm buzzers would go off immediately."

"So if she'd have taken the baby through the door, you would've issued an Amber Alert or something?"

Lois laughs. "It wouldn't have come to that. Believe it or not, the bar is set pretty high when it comes to issuing Amber Alerts. Authorities want to avoid overwhelming the system with false alarms, so they need to be a hundred percent certain an actual abduction has taken place before they issue a full Amber Alert."

We walk toward Laurel's room.

"I'm going to register you for your KISS bracelet. That way, you can stroll with Anne Elise while Laurel's napping and not have to worry about setting off alarms."

"You can do that?" I ask, incredulous. The purpose of security devices is to protect the baby. Handing them out willy-nilly to everyone defeats their purpose, but then I remember she thinks I'm Laurel's mother. A woman as kindhearted and helpful as Lois Belcher must do this for every grandmother she meets.

We stop at a computer at the nurse's station. Lois Belcher asks for my personal information—legal name, address, birth date, social security number. She swipes my driver's license into a yellow digital scanner the size of a baseball and then directs my attention to a computer monitor, where all this information appears. I press "Enter," verifying the accuracy of everything. She pulls out a KISS bracelet from the pocket of her hospital smock, scans it into the machine. A minute later, Lois Belcher wraps the bracelet around my wrist.

"To activate it, press it against Anne Elise's bracelet within the next sixty minutes," Lois Belcher says.

"How will I know if I do it right?"

"Don't worry. You'll know!" Lois Belcher says and then excuses herself so she can go on her rounds and help the ward's other new moms cope with the demands of breastfeeding.

Peering into Laurel's room, I spy Anne Elise nestled on Laurel's lap atop the bed. Out of all the babies in this ward, she alone remains quiet, calm. Unaware she's being watched, Laurel coos to Anne Elise, her high-pitched squeals cute and goofy, and I'm filled with the desire to do the same: rush in and snatch Anne Elise from Laurel so that I too could bring delight to Anne Elise. A coo, a funny face, kind words, and maybe a kiss. I could do it, too: I could be Anne Elise's mother.

Laurel's hair is undone and unwashed. I doubt she's showered since stepping foot in the hospital. Without makeup, her face is the plain-Jane visage of the gal-pal character in a television sitcom, someone integral enough to the show's plot to be granted a few compassionate lines of dialogue in each episode but anonymous enough that the show's producers would never think of building romantic scenes around her. Her eyes, though large, are set slightly too wide apart, her flat nose a tad broad. Not for the first time do I wonder what James thought when they first met. Had he been drinking? Did he look across a smoky bar with beer-goggle eyes?

Laurel's focus is totally on Anne Elise. She doesn't notice me until I'm standing next to her bed, my shadow looming over her. She shields Anne Elise from me with her arm, her hand covering the baby's eyes as if I'm something she never wants Anne Elise to see, and the IV tubing connected to her arm pulls tight, causing the stainless steel IV stand that holds her IV bag to roll a few inches on its caster wheels.

"What are you doing here?" Laurel asks, instinctually distrusting me. She pulls Anne Elise closer, sits up a few inches higher on the bed. "Who let you in here? Did Jimmy send you?"

"Your baby's so adorable," I say, unable to take my eyes off Anne Elise. Like a magnet, I feel instinctively drawn to her. "Can I hold her?"

"No. Of course not."

"I'll be gentle. I'll hold her tight and secure."

"He sent you, didn't he? Why did he send you?"

James, I surmise, hasn't called Laurel since walking out of this room yesterday, and for a moment, I sympathize with her. She isn't the beatific young mother of a Renaissance painting but a confused young woman with bloodshot eyes wrapped up in the most emotionally charged situation of her life. In her own way, she's like me: trapped in a predicament not entirely within her command to change. James, her lover, the man who only yesterday asked to divorce me so he could devote his life to her and the baby, hasn't so much as called her. She's probably only now realizing what a cad he is and what a mess she's in.

"He was with me last night," I say, settling into the recliner beside her bed that is neither comfortable nor uncomfortable. Technically, what I say is true: soon after I led him upstairs, James flung off his clothes and passed out on our bed beside me. Laurel's expression deflates from defiant combativeness into outrage. "He was with me last night, enjoying my comforts. You may think, Laurel, that I'm nothing but—what? A dried-up bitch?—but I can assure you there's nothing dried up about me. Ask James, if you like."

Laurel's mouth opens a notch. She gulps.

"So how's your episiotomy healing?"

Laurel looks up at me with horror and embarrassment. I can only imagine how painful the wound, the incisions, must be and how discomforting it must be for her to talk to a near stranger about something so intimate and private. "You know about my episiotomy? How'd you know about my episiotomy?"

"Laurel. Laurel. Laurel." Clearly, I've struck a nerve with her; right now, I'm so thankful Lois Belcher gave me the ammunition to get under her skin. "There's one thing you should know about me: nothing gets past me."

Laurel removes her protective hand from Anne Elise and wipes the tears forming in her eyes. Anne Elise, flashing a dimpled smile, must think it's a game of peek-a-boo, her mother's hand blinding her eyes one moment, and then, when the hand lifts, she sees the brightness of the room—and me. Her eyes so radiantly blue, her abundantly blonde hair softer than corn silk, she bedazzles.

"Your daughter. Anne Elise. She's smiling at me."

"Newborns don't smile. If she looks like she's smiling, it's because she's passing gas. That's what doctors told me. So how does that feel? Knowing the merest glimpse of you makes an innocent baby fart? I pity you."

I laugh. "*You?* You pity *me?*"

Laurel wraps her free hand around the railing of her hospital bed. She's bigger than I am, a woman who probably had her share of girl fights over the years. Color rises in her pale face, an unsightly vein throbbing at her temples, but she's a cooler cucumber than I thought, for she doesn't launch into the kind of visceral verbal attack I expect. She pulls Anne Elise to her chest, turns her around so she no longer faces me. "I pity you because you wanted a baby but can have none. I pity you because you wanted a husband and are realizing you can't have the husband you wanted. I pity you because, very soon, you're only going to have your money to keep you company at night. And money, let me tell you, is no substitute for a loving man. Or a baby."

I sink into the recliner. It's the same recliner James was supposed to sleep in last night. The room becomes silent, leaving me to contemplate Laurel's icy assessment. She has identified my weakness: my futile desire to be like she is—a mother. She looks toward the window and the snowy grounds outside the hospital and then undoes the sash to her robe. As if she were a magnet drawn to metal, Anne Elise attaches herself to Laurel's breast, and the sound Anne Elise makes, a gentle *slup slup slup* as she's gulping down the milk, is both just about the cutest sound I've ever heard and the most painful.

"I'm going to be the world's greatest mother," Laurel says, and then I see the glow on her cheeks and the caring way she glances down at her daughter. She's a woman like I would have been if I, too, had a baby at my breast. Every woman must go into motherhood with the same intention: to nurture her child with love and adoration. That's what I wanted to do. I, too, wanted to feel what it was like to be generous.

"I'm going to be a way better mother than my mother was to me."

Birds chirp outside the suite's window, a rare sound during the winter months.

"Were your parents pretty bad?" I ask, amazed that she's revealed this much to me.

Laurel glances toward the window, where a red-breasted robin perches on the brick windowsill just outside her window, and in the way she purses her lips, I sense regret. "You have no idea how bad they were."

The regret in her face deepens into resentment. My initial impression of her background is probably correct: her parents must be criminals or drug users or alcoholics, rude, abusive jerks who made her childhood truly miserable. I should be gleeful, and yet I feel sorry for her. I, too, had a miserable childhood.

"My father had anger issues. Bad anger issues," Laurel says. "Whenever I'd hear him coming home, his car grinding to a halt on the gravel outside our trailer, I'd duck under my bedcovers and pretend to be asleep. Day or night, it didn't matter. The slightest thing would send him screaming, throwing things, and punching holes in the trailer walls. My mother, she had her problems too, but at least she wasn't a yeller."

I pat her hand, shake my head, expressing more sympathy than is probably prudent, but I can't help myself. I don't know how it happens, but we start talking, and ten minutes later I realize I'm actually enjoying the conversation. She's a mere child with few people in her life she can talk to, and once she starts talking, she can't stop. Once I scrape beyond her hard-edged veneer, I find she's shy and smart but full of self-doubt, which likely owes to her troubled upbringing. She tells me more of her plans to be a counselor for at-risk girls, but she worries about the difficulty of the grad courses she'll need to take to make this happen.

"I'm not a do-gooder. But I want to be a do-gooder. Does that make sense?" Laurel says. "I want to be a great mom. All my rich classmates at Ethan Allen always talked about the altruistic need to 'give back.' That's what I want to do too."

"So why don't you?"

She turns silent, avoids my eyes, her lips sad little things conveying introspection and the fear of failure. "I haven't yet told Jimmy about my plan. It'll take years of study—grad school, training courses, professional certification requirements—and it hurts knowing how far away I am from getting where I need to be."

"Bah! Don't let your fears dissuade you from enrolling in these courses. You got a 3.85 GPA at a very good private liberal arts college. How hard could grad school be for someone as smart as you?"

"Thank you," Laurel says. A moment later, she looks at me with cheerful eyes. "Thank you for saying that."

For several seconds, neither of us says a word, and again I sense she's feeling awkward and angry at my presence.

"You asked how my episiotomy was healing."

"Huh?"

"It's not healing well," Laurel says.

I'm astounded by Laurel's candor, but I also realize I helped draw her out with my sympathetic touch and the commiseration I demonstrated when listening to her talk about her parents. James firmly adheres to the old proverb that you catch more flies with honey, but until this particular fly flew into my web, I hadn't put much faith in that way of thinking.

"Last night, doctors came by to examine me. I could barely lift my legs for them, and when I did, their reactions told me something wasn't right. It hurt just trying to do what they said. 'What is it?' I kept asking, but they wouldn't answer me. It's not like I could see what they were doing. They talked among themselves, all of them. And it's like, let's not tell the sick girl anything. More doctors were paged. They wheeled me into an examination room where the lights were hot and bright, and I felt queasy inside because of how they were moving me around. Prodding me. Pushing me down there as if I were Play-Doh. Nurses promised they'd look after Zerena—'In the event something happens,' they said, which made me think I was at risk of *dying*. I panicked. I felt scatterbrained, dead-dog stupid. My temperature spiked at one hundred and five. An infection, they finally said, had set in. Which explains why I woke up still connected to this IV unit."

Doctors had performed the episiotomy on Laurel because, due to a miscalculation, they believed Anne Elise would be so abnormally large as to cause extensive vaginal tearing if delivered normally. I cringe as Laurel describes the procedure performed upon her. In the doctors' rush to perform the episiotomy, the mediolateral incision from the vaginal opening through to the perineum was deeper than it ought to have been and not cut at the right angle, and hence, the doctors had difficulty suturing it properly after delivering Anne Elise. That an infection set in this quickly isn't good.

"I wish the doctors could make me better, like, *right away*," Laurel says. "I've hardly been able to stay awake for an hour straight since yesterday."

Sympathy, like hatred, is another of the weaknesses my father disdained. Laurel was needlessly and clumsily cut open. Anne Elise isn't abnormally large, meaning there was no justification to perform the procedure. More care should have been given to making the incision and more thought given to prevent its infection. Had this happened to me, I'd phone my lawyers to initiate malpractice suits, but Laurel, in debt up to her bloodshot eyeballs, has no lawyers to plead for redress. All she has is the pain of the episiotomy. And pus.

"Laurel, forgive me for asking, but are you able to pay all the hospital bills?"

"Jimmy will take care of everything."

"He will?" I can't imagine James, perpetually strapped for cash because of his harebrained investment schemes and ballooning credit card debt, has the wherewithal to foot what could grow into a mid-five-figure hospital bill by the time Laurel's discharged. "Don't you have health insurance of your own?"

"Nope. I used to have Obamacare, but I missed the open-enrollment period this year. Then I quit my job—"

"When did you quit your job?" As far as I knew, Laurel worked as a waitress at a moderately well reviewed Italian restaurant off Dupont Circle.

"I quit my job months ago."

While we talk, Anne Elise nurses on her mother's milk. Laurel lifts her to her shoulder and pats Anne Elise's back. The baby's sweet-smelling milk breath washes all over me. When Anne Elise burps, Laurel sighs with satisfaction. She shifts Anne Elise from one shoulder to the other, elicits a second burp, and then lowers her back to her other breast.

"She can drink so much," Laurel says, flicking back her head and displaying an amount of pride that's good to see. "All I have to do is sit back and heal and take care of Zerena. I can do this."

"But the hospital, the medical costs," I say, my mind racing back to the practicalities. Rather than opting for a more economical room or sharing a room with other new moms, Laurel's installed in a private room furnished with leather-upholstered sitting chairs and a state-of-the-art 4K widescreen television. "Aren't you worried about where the money will come from? Doesn't that concern you?"

"Jimmy will take care of everything."

"Have you asked him?"

"Why would I need to do that?"

Laurel must think James is made of money, a knight who'll rescue her from her money woes. He's a smooth-talking master of outward appearances and genteel manners who, in the fine tailored dark suits I buy him, dresses the part of a well-to-do financial strategist. He hasn't even brought her flowers. Laurel hasn't caught on to James's bifurcations: to the risk-averse clients with whom he has a fiduciary responsibility, he's an astute and upstanding advisor who never fails to paddle toward the cautious side of the financial rivers. And yet James is nothing if not reckless when managing his own affairs.

Soon after we started dating, James and my father bonded over the ancient Victrola that to this day still occupies a spot in our living room. Glenn Miller. Frank Sinatra. Billie Holiday. James enjoyed these artists as much as my father, and for years, every time they met, my father would pull out his stack of fragile shellac 78s. To my father's surprise, James had his own modest collection of 78s. Rather than collect recording artists, James's 78s were all of songs written by Harold Arlen, Johnny Mercer, and the Gershwin Brothers. Whenever my father and James met over a glass of port, a tumbler of Scotch, or a fine red wine, the conversation would turn to the Great American Songbook, a term I scarcely knew existed until hearing the two of them sing its praises.

One day, James hit up my father for $100,000 to back him in one of his investment follies. Because of their shared interests, James considered my father a friend, but even then, my father recognized James for what he was: an amiable huckster. "Don't let that man flimflam you," my father said, taking me aside into the wood-paneled hideaway nook behind the retractable facade of an elaborate, custom-carved walnut bookcase on Savory Mew's second floor. The wood-paneled nook was his private lair, a secret room in this ancient house where he beckoned me whenever we were to have a serious conversation and the room that he'd flee to whenever my mother sulked after finding out about another of his affairs.

"You don't like him, do you?" I asked. My father chuckled to himself. "Ah-umm. On the contrary, I like him the way I like every raconteur who crosses my path. But be aware he's a weak man. As long as you insulate yourself, and your money, from his weakness, he might be good for you—he's tall, handsome, and, ah-umm, eminently presentable." Rather than plowing money into James's investment schemes, my father made a few calls and found James the job he still holds to this day.

I close my eyes and listen to Anne Elise nursing. It sounds so pure, so wholesome, the little movements of her lips, her sighs, her short breaths.

"Listen, Laurel. We may have started on the wrong track yesterday. I said a lot of mean things, but in all honesty, you can't trust James. Some people are born with a sense of responsibility, and then there's James. He is not a responsible person. Don't rely on him to help you or support you or even to be there when you need him," I say, purposely painting James in the worst possible light to get Laurel more inclined to leave him. "He's not the man you think he is. He's debonair and handsome, but he has no real money and no real follow-through on the promises and commitments he makes."

Laurel stares at me, struggling with two different emotions: embarrassment and contempt. The contempt is for me, the embarrassment reserved for herself and the mistakes she might've made in overestimating James's good qualities.

"You're wrong," Laurel says, raising Anne Elise to her shoulder with such innocent and gentle care that I feel ungenerous for bringing up James's faults. The baby's about to fall asleep. Laurel looks at me with big, droopy eyes. "You're jealous. That's why you're making up these lies about Jimmy. I know he drinks, but I can deal with that. I can get him to change. Love can do that, you know, make someone go against their instincts to become a better person."

Romantic notions cloud Laurel's mind. It's almost endearing how protective she becomes of James. Surely, in her way, she loves him; she hasn't yet learned, as I have, that love has its limits.

"I hope you're right," I say.

"I am."

And then Laurel does something that surprises me: she hands Anne Elise to me.

"Can you lay her down in her bassinet? Doctors don't want me to get up from bed if I absolutely don't have to."

Anne Elise's eyes flick open. Her eyelashes are long and beautiful. There's something sublime about holding a baby who looks straight into your eyes. She smiles. I walk her to her bassinet, lay her down on the spongy sleeping pad. She stretches her short arms and yawns. By the time I stop gazing at Anne Elise, Laurel, too, is asleep. When she said she was unable to stay awake for a full hour since giving birth, I thought it was one of the hyperbolic complaints a new mother might make, but something is clearly wrong with her. Her breathing is loud and labored, not the near-silent snooze of her baby but the wretched snore you might expect from a geriatric asthmatic.

It seems unfair to banish Anne Elise to a stainless steel bassinet just because her mother's too tired and infected to care for her. Listening to Laurel wheeze and snore, I realize that this is my opportunity to have Anne Elise to myself. Was not Lois Belcher virtually begging me to take Anne Elise out for a walk whenever Laurel conked out?

Chapter Ten

LAUREL

It's a dim, dim world when I wake up, and my mind is a feather in the breeze, the thoughts drifting in and out. My face bumps against the stainless steel bed railings, and it's like I'm behind bars again, but then the realization of my current circumstances pounces on me. The room is dark, the blinds closed. Beyond the room's closed door comes the muffled sound of babies crying. My thoughts leap to Zerena. I'm uncannily aware she's not in her bassinet. Someone has taken her, and then I remember how Tricia crazily pleaded with me not to trust Jimmy.

I press buttons on the control panel at the side of the bed to summon a nurse, but the buttons I press must be the wrong ones, for they do nothing but activate the bed, pushing my legs up and then my head up, wedging me V-shaped between the mattress. Another button tilts me sideways. I bump again into the bed railings. The slim plastic IV tubing tangles around my neck. Somewhere in this room, buttons exist to reset the bed, turn on the lights, summon assistance, and bring Zerena back to me, but it's like any button I press, any choice I make, will be the wrong one. The door opens. A shaft of light from the hallway enters into the room. From the doorway, a woman gasps. She flicks on the light and stares at me, speechless, her hands on her hips, and only after some moments do I recognize her as the hospital's lactation consultant.

"Where's Zerena?" I ask, wedged against the bed rails. I'll be damned if I've given birth to Zerena and suffered the consequences of this botched episiotomy just to have her be snatched away from me. "Someone stole Zerena. We've got to find her!"

"Are you all right?" the lactation consultant asks.

Which is, like, the stupidest question in the world, because any idiot should be able to see I'm not even close to being all right. A grown woman should not be held hostage by her bed. Emotionally exhausted, I can't even answer her. The lactation consultant strides across the room and presses a button on the control panel. The bed frame rumbles beneath me. Gears crank mechanically, loudly. The mattress begins to lower itself, first at my legs and then at my head. No longer is the mattress V-shaped. No longer am I splayed into an awkward position, but lying flat and seeing the button to correct my wrongs had been within my grasp all along, I feel doubly incompetent.

"Who are you?" I ask. "Tell me again. I forgot your name."

"Lois Belcher," the lactation consultant says, extending her hand toward me. She's uncontrollably happy. "I'm so glad I came here when I did. Please tell me you weren't tied up like that for a long time."

"We've got to find Zerena. Someone stole my daughter!"

Lois puts a consoling hand on my shoulder and grins.

"It's not funny," I say, unable to comprehend this woman's inability to take me seriously. A baby girl has been stolen. We should call police officers, summon hospital administrators, but this woman fluffs a bed pillow as if comfort is my overriding concern. "We have to do something about it. My baby's gone."

"Your daughter is with your mother."

"My *mother*?"

"They've been walking up and down the hall for the last half hour. Your mother wanted to go outside and show your daughter the snow, but I convinced her that wasn't a good idea. Your daughter isn't wearing a jacket!"

"Huh?" I don't understand how my mother could possibly be walking around with my baby, but as I'm trying to process this information, Tricia comes into the room tra-la-la-ing a lullaby to Zerena, whom she cradles in her arms. Tricia's no nightingale—her voice screeches off-key. Zerena is wide awake, unsoothed by Tricia's jackdaw warble, but Zerena's mouth is open in amusement, igniting my jealousy. Love is a slippery slope. Already I fear Zerena prefers Tricia's companionship to mine, but just seeing Zerena safe and happy turns me into a puddle of joy. Tricia picks up a soft pink washcloth from Zerena's bassinet and wipes clean the drool that gathers on Zerena's chin. At the touch of that cloth on her skin, Zerena coos.

Tricia dresses so ridiculously young, like a teenager, in her tight designer jeans and snug pinkish-purple—or is it purplish-pink?—camisole. The outfit screams of someone desperate for attention. In high school, she was probably the girl who stole everyone's boyfriends, but then, thinking about this, I feel a stab in my heart because, damn, I must be the kind of woman who steals husbands. Tricia canters over to the lactation consultant, a ditzball smile pasted on her face, and gushes about the "invigorating constitutional" she and Zerena enjoyed.

"I really think she would have adored the snow! How she would have flipped out over the sensation of snowflakes falling on her face. But look at her!" Tricia says, holding Zerena up. "She looks just like me! Isn't that amazing?"

Lois, the lactation consultant, giggles. Of course she'd hit it off with Tricia, both of them from the same generational tribe, but as much as she yaps with Lois about eye color and chin similarities, Tricia's looking squarely at me every time she brings up another way that Zerena is just like her. "She's a carbon copy of me! I mean, look at her lush eyelashes. They're a perfect match for mine. She could've been *my* daughter!"

It's demeaning how Trish carries on as if the baby were hers. She talks with Lois Belcher as if I weren't here. Finally, when I can take it no more, I clear my throat. "There's one other way she looks like you."

Tricia tilts her head. "How's that?"

"The way she drools. That's got you written all over it."

My remark knocks the stuffing out of the rapport Tricia's been feigning. She stares at me, slack-jawed in shock, but she pulls herself together quickly. Her smile reappears. People like her with moneyed backgrounds and society-page upbringings aren't like real people; she's that rare kind of circus performer who's astutely aware of and eager to control the reactions she provokes. She glances at Lois Belcher, rolls her eyes, and laughs, putting Lois Belcher back at ease. "Gosh, Laurel. You're always so amusing."

"Gee. Thanks."

Tricia peeks at her platinum wristwatch. James has bought me remarkably little bling, but someday he'll buy me a watch as extravagant as the one Tricia wears. What must it feel like to wear a watch that's worth a year's rent? Seeing the time, Tricia gasps.

"What is it?" Lois asks.

"Reality's calling. It's four o'clock. I've got to rush home and cook dinner for my husband."

I don't have to look at Tricia to understand she's looking straight at me, deliberate and wicked. She's not averse to playing the "wife" card to get a rise out of me. Had Lois not been in the room with us, my reaction would be different, but for now I accept Zerena when Tricia places her in my arms. A baby should be more than a consolation prize, a booby prize, but the stony face Tricia employs as she adjusts Zerena's knit hat makes me think that's all she thinks Zerena is to me: a booby prize.

"I almost forgot to tell you something important," Tricia says.

"What's that?"

"It's not gas. That's not what doctors believe. Isn't that wonderful?"

I'm totally at a loss for what Tricia's talking about.

"Anne Elise's smile. Doctors used to believe newborn babies couldn't smile. That what we interpreted, facially, as a smile was in fact just the strain on the baby's face from passing gas. That's what they used to believe. But they're wrong. Lois was telling me this while you napped. Isn't that right?"

Lois nods. I couldn't have been asleep for more than an hour. What else have they talked about? They're so chummy, as if in cahoots with one another.

"So why, then, do babies smile?"

"Well-being, mostly. Not happiness per se, and not because they find something amusing or cute or funny. Isn't that simply amazing?"

"Why's that so amazing?"

"You make her smile! Don't you see it? Already, this early in her life, you've endowed her with a sense of well-being!" Tricia says. She, too, is smiling, confident in her own privileged sense of well-being. "Doesn't that make you feel wonderful?"

It *does* make me feel wonderful, but I don't get Tricia. She's a witch in sheep's clothing. One moment, she says the meanest, nastiest things, and the next, she says something so totally gorgeous that it makes me want to cry. She's a disorienting yo-yo, not even conscious of how she makes my emotions boomerang inside me. She's about to lose her husband to me, but I wish—one way or another, sweet or bitchy—she'd settle upon consistency.

Tricia pats my hand. "And speaking of wonderful, I need to go and cook dinner. I think I'll make lamb tonight. My husband loves lamb."

Lois and I watch Tricia head out of the room so she can run home and make supper for Jimmy.

"You've got the sweetest mother. You know that, don't you?" Lois says.

Chapter Eleven

Laurel

I'm no pincushion, no dartboard, no jailhouse snitch about to be shiv-ved, but an hour after Tricia departs, a half dozen nurses bring out the needles and stick me with medicines, drugs, antibiotics, things one of the sloe-eyed nurses declares "will juice your system up something good," and when they're not injecting me with one wonder cure or another, they draw blood samples. I'm feeling better, I tell them, asking if they might discharge me later today, and still they produce the hypodermics. Needles and me never mix well. When I was young, I passed out three times from the sight of blood being drawn from my arm.

Zerena awakens from a nap and immediately fusses for a feeding. One of the nurses hands her to me without speaking, treating Zerena as if she's but an obstacle to her attempt to draw another vial of my blood. I wish they'd let me be alone with Zerena. It must not do her any good, seeing her mother prodded and probed like this. I long to hold her, comfort her.

"You're my little sponge," I say, bringing Zerena to my breast. No matter how much I feed her, she always wants more. Each time she clamps down and nurses, a jolt of electricity charges through me, connecting us. Zerena gazes up at me, her blue eyes shining, and I think she feels it too, that jolt of electricity that passes between us. Before she was born, I looked at her as being my key to hanging on to Jimmy. But she's a key unto herself. Rather than being just a means to an end, she's her own little lovable self. Already she owns my heart.

Two doctors—different from yesterday—enter my room without knocking. They're a pair of smug monkey thirtysomethings, one male and one female, both holding translucent blue acrylic clipboards to their chests. A nurse asks me to make a fist so she can draw more blood, and it's an unnatural feeling, making a fist with one hand while holding my nursing newborn with the other hand. One of the doctors lowers her clipboard. Her name—Dr. Helen Magee—is stitched onto her white hospital lab coat.

"So how are you feeling?"

"Truthfully? Needles freak me out," I say, lifting Zerena to my shoulder. My blood streams from the nurse's hypodermic through a thin stretch of transparent plastic tubing and into a glass test tube. I glance at it and immediately turn away, so queasy does the sight of my blood make me feel. When the first test tube fills, the nurse exchanges it for another one because multiple blood tests are needed. Either that or she gets her jollies by watching me squirm.

"Gotcha," Dr. Magee says, writing something onto the papers on her clipboard. "Otherwise, though, you're doing a remarkable job taking care of your little one amid this chaos."

"I guess it's true what they say: motherhood is all about multitasking."

"So how are you healing?"

I tell the doctors about the fatigue and my inability to stay awake for more than an hour, how it hurts to shift my legs on the bed. Half the time, I feel feverish, and the other half I'm so cold my teeth chatter. Pus weeps from my wound, causing the bandages to become too slick to stay put, their adhesive backing no longer sticky enough to hold to my skin.

"Could you spread your legs and let us look?" Dr. Magee asks.

I stiffen. Along with multitasking, motherhood is all about indignities. It feels *wrong* to spread my legs and let someone, even a doctor, look at me down there while Zerena is at my breast. Dr. Magee asks a second time, stressing she wants to help me. I oblige. An ammonia-like odor wafts out as I spread my legs apart. Zerena's nostrils flare at the smell.

Two other figures appear at the door. Neither wears a white hospital lab coat. The woman, dressed in a shapeless blue-and-white polka-dot shift, sticks her head into the room as if unsure what she's looking for. She's followed by a man in dungarees and a gray sweatshirt stained with mechanic's grease. Seeing me, the woman gasps. Her front top tooth is discolored and noticeably cracked.

The man she's with waves at me, a sheepish grin on his face. He's no doctor. Neither is she. These people are my parents, Tully and Belinda Bloom. I haven't seen them since police locked me up in juvenile detention as a tenth grader for helping myself to a pair of iPhones at the local Best Buy. I did it at their urging, palming items that could be pawned off to pay for their financial shortfalls. On parole themselves for a variety of offenses and fearful of what a "corrupting the morals of a minor" conviction might mean to their personal liberties, they swore to the court they had no prior knowledge of what I was doing, and I, too naive for my own good, said nothing to contradict their lies. It was my third offense in six months, a tipping point that landed me a three-month juvenile detention stint. Although I didn't know it at the time, my parents' own legal issues would make it unfeasible for me to be released back into their custody when I completed my initial sentence. So three months became six months. Which became a year. Which was extended until I reached my eighteenth birthday.

"Look at you!" my mother, Belinda, says, rushing into the room. Instinctively, I tense up. Though I called my parents the other night, I never believed they'd actually come here—and now I'm not so sure I want them to be here. I've lived for years under the assumption my parents were a pair of mean dogs I'd best steer clear of, but they look older, wiser, and less needy.

Doctors and nurses, unfazed by the disturbance, attend to me. The nurse eases her hypodermic from my arm and presses a cooling alcohol swab against the spot where the needle had been.

"My gosh, are you all right?" my mother asks, her chest heaving with concern. I can only imagine how sick I appear. Two sets of earrings are in each of my mother's earlobes: silver hearts and a pretty pair of blue diamond studs set in white gold. Back when I was growing up, there was never enough money for her to afford jewelry. She presses a hand to my forehead, like a real mother might do if her child was feverish. "You're sick, aren't you? Tell me how sick you are. You didn't have to go through with the pregnancy. If you'd called us months ago, maybe we could've helped pay for an abortion."

Dr. Magee looks up at my mother sharply.

"What your mother means is that you should have come to us sooner," Tully says. For as long as I could remember, he insisted I call him by his name. Never "Dad." Never "Father." Always "Tully," which he fancied sounded more authoritative. "It broke our hearts when you wrote that letter saying you no longer wanted us to be in your life, but we forgive you. Honest. We do."

"Wait. *You* forgive *me?*" The letter my father mentions was written while I was in juvenile detention months before my release. I had literally aced my GED while behind bars and was eager to get a fresh start to my life. "I was locked up for three years because I didn't want you to get in trouble for sending me into stores and shoplifting things for you. Don't you know how bad that is? To have your own daughter locked up because you can't take responsibility for your own mistakes?"

"We all make mistakes," Belinda says.

"Okay. Okay. So we weren't the best parents back then. Who is? That's why you stopped talking with us," Tully says, slicking back his graying hair from his eyes. Age—or maybe it's the whisky—has gotten the better of him: his face creased with worry and neglect, he's wiry, antsy, nervous. "Everyone's parents screw up once or twice. But we were good, mostly."

"Once or twice?" I say, almost speechless at how hindsight conveniently allows him to forget how miserable my childhood was. My parents would go missing for days. There'd be nothing in the refrigerator. I stole apples or oranges from the school cafeteria at lunchtime, begged gumballs from friends, knowing I'd need them for dinner. "A screwup is, like, forgetting a birthday or something. Because of you, I was locked up for three years. *Three freaking years!*"

"What your father's trying to say is we're sorry." Like my father, worry lines etch my mother's face. She takes a deep breath, sighs, closes her eyes, and bites her lips. Her fragile tooth looks as if it'll fall out should she chew into a Jolly Rancher or a cube of caramel candy. "Honest, we are real sorry. Both of us. We should've been better for you."

"If we goofed in the past, we goofed. Don't go digging up old bones," Tully says. Unlike my mother, his teeth are pearly white. Somewhere along the way, he must have paid a cosmetic dentist good money to bleach his teeth. "Family's family, right?"

While we're staring at each other, Zerena burps a wet burp, meaning that along with her burp, she regurgitates a teaspoon or two of something onto my shoulder. Lois Belcher led me to expect this might happen, but this being the first time, it startles me. The milky-white regurgitated mucus seeps into the cloth of my hospital gown.

"Listen, your father's right," Belinda says, sitting on the recliner. She takes off one of her sandals, a plastic pink flower half-de-petaled over the toe strap, and, sighing, knuckle massages the sole of her foot. "Family's family. We would've helped you if you'd given us a chance. You called way too late for us to help with your pregnancy. Do you think it's too late to put the baby up for adoption? Or maybe it's too early? Don't give up hope! There's got to be an orphanage in this city we can call."

Dr. Magee lowers the skirt of my hospital gown back over my knees. I've caught her glancing angrily at my parents. Whatever she's seen down there, assessing my episiotomy, has knocked the smugness right out of her monkey. She looks at me with utmost seriousness. Watching her, my parents—normally no quieter than a pair of yipping schnauzers—become silent.

"God bless you," Dr. Magee says. Her hands smell like hand lotion and latex from the powder-free exam gloves she wore while examining me. Some people, like her, naturally ooze sympathy. She takes my rough hands into hers.

"How bad is it?" I ask, gritting my teeth, knowing she must've found something really bad down there. Although I'm better than yesterday, antibiotic-resistant infections are a leading cause of death in hospitals. Everyone knows this. People walk into emergency rooms all the time with minor mishaps—sprained ankles or a bad cold—and hobble out with untreatable staph infections or communicable hepatitis. "I must be in pretty bad shape if you're already invoking God to protect me."

"You're going to be fine. We'll still need to keep you here a few more days, but you're healing, and the infection shows signs of improvement."

I should be elated, but Dr. Magee glances to my parents, a glance only I can see, and frowns. She pities me, and it's humiliating, once again being an object of pity. It was the same when I was a kid—everyone in Oyster's Edge, our small town on Maryland's Eastern Shore, would look at me with pity when they saw me with my parents. Ever since meeting Jimmy, I've felt special, like a someone. It's impossible not to be messed up big time after being locked up in juvenile detention, but Jimmy helped me push aside my hopelessness. Meeting him, I made the decision to be normal again. To be trusting. To be pure. People would see me with him, and I'd watch their esteem for me rise. I wasn't just another young twentysomething wallowing in downward expectations and a going-nowhere waitressing gig but an intelligent young woman worthy of a middle-class life. Slowly, I became someone I wanted to be. Someone capable of applying to grad programs—psychology or social work—that would lead to a career of helping girls like me.

"It's . . . how to say this?" Dr. Magee says. She's maybe a decade older than me, but as she strokes her chin Einstein-like, it's like she's the personification of Wisdom. "We have counselors on staff, people who can connect you with social services and WIC benefits. Do you understand?"

My cheeks burn with shame. I'm not in anywhere near as bad a predicament as Dr. Magee assumes, and it feels unfair—no, *horrible*—to be characterized like this. I'm no charity basket case aspiring for food stamps or a sometimes placement in a homeless shelter. I have a college degree. I have hope for a decent future. I have a man who loves me. But it stings, being mistaken for someone too stupid and irresponsible to take care of herself.

My father glares at me after the doctors and nurses vamoose. He taps his fingers against the veneer table on the opposite side of my bed, a rat-a-tat-tat rendition of "Taps" to ratchet up my indignation. "You heard that: you're in a tough position. Let's be smart about this. You aren't in any shape to raise a kid by yourself. You know that. Adoption or orphanages aren't bad things. Plenty of kids go that route, and some of them end up okay."

"Dad. Shut up, will you?" I say, shocked. All my life, my father's always assumed the worst things possible about me. We haven't seen each other in years; he doesn't know anything about me. "I'm not giving up Zerena. I love her more than anyone I've loved in my life."

Tully slaps his forehead, shakes his head as if I'm either too flighty or just plain stupid. "Honey, don't you know love's expensive? How are you going to afford a rug rat?"

My mother weeps in the recliner. Her sandal in her hand, she fingers the remaining petals on the pink plastic flower. My parents don't know about Jimmy and the happiness he brings to my life. They don't know about this incredible bond I feel with Zerena. They don't know about the riverside apartment Jimmy bought for me or the nursery in that apartment Jimmy hand painted and furnished with a crib, stuffed animals aplenty, a changing table, and an old-fashioned cane rocking chair on which I'll spend warm, harmonious hours rocking Zerena to sleep each night.

"I hear you, Laurel," my mother says in a voice so quiet my slightly deaf father cannot possibly hear. She tears off a plastic flower petal from her sandal and pinches it between her fingers. Sometime in the past, perhaps with me or perhaps at the announcement of an unwanted pregnancy she never told me about, my mother might have heard the same lecture from my father. "Where there's a will, there's a way. We'll think of something to do with your baby. Don't worry."

Jimmy knocks on the door, catching my eye, a generous smile on his face. He's a tall, cheerful, broad-shouldered man, a proud new father eager to see his family, a prosperous man in a magnificent blue pinstripe suit and polished black wingtips. Though glitches remain in our relationship, he'll love me, cherish me, be an awesome father to Zerena. He strides past my father, kisses me on the lips, and sweeps Zerena up into his arms, hugging her. The excitement is too much for Zerena. There's a smile on her lips, zazz in her cobalt-blue eyes. Hard as it is to believe, I sense Jimmy loves Zerena even more than I do. I can't imagine my father ever whirling me about with the same glee when I was a baby. And yet, watching Jimmy, I'm reminded about Tricia's warning—that Jimmy's not the responsible person I think he is. Can that be true? Will he one day punch a hole in the wall of some trailer if he ever finds out Zerena spilled a glass of milk? Can any man be as good as you think he is?

But one thing's for sure: we're not going to give Zerena up. We're not going to put her up for adoption or abandon her in a wicker basket on the steps of an orphanage. She's ours.

Jimmy sways around the room with her, kissing her again and again, and my parents are flabbergasted. In Jimmy's hands, Zerena looks as if she is the craziest, coolest toy ever to come into his possession. She giggles. Delight in a baby is an amazing thing to behold. But then Zerena wet burps on him, a dollop of regurgitated mother's milk spitting from her lips onto the lapel of Jimmy's gorgeous blue suit. Jimmy's eyes widen. He sniffs the dollop. His nostrils flare at its scent, and I can't help but think he's going to show me an angry side of him I've never seen before, but then he shrugs and looks at me with no hint of reproach. He doesn't let little things derail his emotions. Fingering the white goo, he laughs. "Isn't this the damnedest thing?"

"Believe it or not, the lactation consultant told me that's perfectly normal," I say. "It's called 'reflux.' As long as it doesn't happen all the time and as long as she's not burping up, like, *gallons* of it, we shouldn't be concerned."

My parents, speechless, stare at Jimmy. He's suspicious too, wondering who they might be, but gentleman that he is, he broadens his smile. With each sweep around the room, he glances at them as if trying to place them, but finally, handing Zerena back to me, he bends down and whispers, "Hey, who are these people? They give me the creeps."

I've not mentioned my parents to Jimmy. Ever. Partly because I wanted to forget them but also because I feared they'd be a deal breaker in our relationship, a pair of baggage-laden straws objectionable enough to break any camel's back. Jimmy is all about class, and though they might be clean and sober now, there's nothing classy about my parents. Taking a deep breath, I cringe. "Jimmy. That's my father, Tully. And my mother. Her name's Belinda. They came down to see Zerena."

Jimmy scrunches his brows. "Zerena?"

"Anne Elise," I say, correcting myself, for this is still another conversation we need to have, for she's way more Zerena-ish than Anne Elise-ish. Zerena's the name of an adventurer, a superhero, a warrior princess—*not* an old-fashioned stay-at-home do-nothing name like Anne Elise.

"Your parents, you say? These are your parents?"

Biting my tongue, I nod.

Jimmy's eyes narrow upon my uncouth parents. There's skepticism in his stare, caution in the way he brings his hand to his chin. He's calibrating how far an apple falls from the tree, glancing back between my parents and me, and my stomach turns, knowing my future may still be tied to them. Jimmy could walk away from me and Zerena—discard us like a couple of empty beer cans—should he judge we're destined to be as sketchy as my parents. He stretches his arms, and my stomach knots up when I see indecision on his face, but then his generous smile reappears as if he's actually happy to make my parents' acquaintance.

Jimmy saunters toward my mother.

"Ahh . . . Belinda. Laurel's told me so much about you." Jimmy takes my mother's hands, one in each of his. My mother, rarely the center of anyone's attention, becomes uncomfortable, but then Jimmy says, "My, my. I totally see it."

My mother flinches. "Huh?"

"You're where Laurel gets her beauty. You really are. Please don't be offended, but for as long as I've known Laurel, she's told me she gets *all* her beauty from you, and now I can see she's right."

My mother blushes enthusiastically. It still amazes me how Jimmy sets people at ease and earns their confidence. Never is there an unkind word from his lips. Part of me feels angry at him for being so nice, but it's his good manners, his propensity to be generous, that first attracted my eye. I've never met a man like him, and neither has my mother. It's like he's too good to be true. She flutters her eyelashes, stutters a bashful thank-you.

My father, not to be outdone, sticks out his hand. "What has she told you about me?"

Jimmy, swimming in his rarefied financial circles, never met a man like my father before. Jimmy takes a good look at him. An expectant expression comes over my father. He rolls up his sweatshirt sleeves, revealing the tattooed cobra on his arm he acquired during a two-week stretch in prison after pleading guilty to an aggressive panhandling charge.

"Ahh. Tully. Tully. Shall I be frank?"

My father's eyes widen with the realization he may not like what he's about to hear. Giving a barely perceptible nod, he braces himself.

"Tully, you were a strict father."

My father takes a breath. He expected high praise, but now he's about to be cut down to size.

"But never too strict," Jimmy says.

"What else does she say about me?"

"You were wise, but like most children, Laurel didn't learn to appreciate your wisdom until after she left home. Isn't that true?"

"Damn right," Tully says, looking at me from the corner of his eye. "You got that right. Even now, she doesn't give me the credit I deserve."

"Don't be harsh. Everything comes in good time. A daughter like Laurel is like a fine instrument: treat her with respect, and she'll pay you back in spades. You're an intelligent man, right? The past is past. No sense crying over what happened back then. Look forward. That's the way to go."

"Who is this wonderful friend of yours, Laurel?" my mother asks.

Jimmy's eyes rove toward mine, eager to see how I'll introduce him. So much in our relationship remains unsettled, but he's been an absolute gentleman so far, showing more mercy to me and my parents than we deserve, so I decide to take a calculated gamble and make the announcement I've longed to make.

"Mom. Dad. This is my fiancé, Jimmy Wainsborough. He's Anne Elise's father. I'm sorry if this seems sudden, but we've been seeing each other for a while now, and we're getting married soon."

Jimmy arches his eyebrows, and then, just as quickly, his expression returns to normal. I know we're going to have to talk about this more, but this is the first time I've ever told anyone about our relationship, and it feels like some magnificent threshold has been crossed. My parents are speechless. Moments ago, they looked at me as if I were a pitiful coyote who's come roaming back to the burrow with her tail hanging low between her legs. Now, my father slaps Jimmy on the back, offers his congratulations, while my mother asks Jimmy if she can hold our baby. This is her first actual contact with Zerena, and emotional as I am, I reach for my cell phone and snap a picture. My mother and Zerena are in the foreground, right in front of Jimmy and my father.

"So what kind of business are you in?" Tully asks Jimmy. "You've got a job, don't you?"

"I'm a financial advisor."

"So you peddle stocks, do you?"

Jimmy laughs, but he's wary of telling too much about what he does because he doesn't like being tapped for free investment advice. Nor does he relish being hit up for loans, as happens sometimes when strangers discover he's wealthy.

"So what firm do you work for? Are you a salary man, or do you work on commission?"

As my father deluges Jimmy with questions, it dawns on me that he's elated but also that he feels obligated to do the prudent father thing, making sure my suitor is a good prospect or, at least, financially solvent. As if he couldn't otherwise figure as much from the quality of Jimmy's elegant suit.

"I work for O'Neill, Joseph, and Fitzgerald."

My father, who likes to believe he's an investor because he once opened an IRA account when he held a Midas garage job for two whole years, scratches his head. "Never heard of them."

"It's the kind of wealth-management firm that flies under the radar unless, well, you need a wealth-management firm," Jimmy says, and then, when my father starts to say something more, Jimmy puts his finger against his lips. Zerena is asleep on my mother's shoulder, and he takes her and lays her in her bassinet and sweeps the little pink baby blanket over her.

"Maybe we should turn off the lights?" Jimmy asks.

My father, uncharacteristically obedient, walks across the room and flips the light switch off. I, too, am feeling tired. Motherhood is all about multitasking, but it's also about getting enough rest so you can do the things you need to do. As much as I'd like to prolong the good feelings and chat, soon Zerena will awake again, crying to be nursed.

"Hey, maybe we should give the new mom a little naptime?" Jimmy says, attentive to my need for rest.

Before she leaves, my mother circles back to me and whispers, "Hey, congratulations. I'm so happy for you."

"Thanks, Mom. It's good to see you again," I say. Before today, I hadn't realized how much I missed seeing my mother. "Those blue earrings you have are real pretty on you."

My mother blushes. She tilts her head and takes the earrings off, being careful to stick their backs onto their pins, and lays them in my palm. Her hands clasp around mine, and it's almost painful, seeing how happy she is to be giving me these earrings. "Be sure to soak them for a bit in rubbing alcohol before you wear them. If they looked good on me, lord knows how beautiful they'll look on you."

Chapter Twelve

JIM

Two days ago, Anne Elise didn't exist. A day ago, I didn't realize she'd have this euphoric effect on me, but as I sweep her into my arms and sway around Laurel's hospital room with her, happiness explodes inside me. Laurel's still asleep, and her parents have gone for the night. Moonlight peeks through the blinds. Everything feels charmed with magic. I close my eyes and wonder if the rest of my life can be as perfect as this moment. There must be a way to bottle this feeling, prolong it, keep everything else at bay. My conundrum about what to do with Trish and Laurel seems insignificant compared to this monumental sense of joy. I cup the back of Anne Elise's head in my palm, supporting her, and when she opens her eyes, she stares straight into mine. Mirth lights her eyes.

"You like her, don't you?" Laurel says, awakening. With only her hospital bed's stainless steel railing between us, she looks at me, her face pale and radiant. Although hormonal acne blemishes erupted over her cheeks since giving birth, she truly never looked more beautiful. "Isn't our baby the fanciest fly? The cutest Chihuahua?"

I laugh, amused by Laurel's phrases. Her quirky expressions can be strange to my ears—things that may be the slang of her generation or stuff she totally makes up on her own—but it's one of the endearing things about her that first caught my attention.

"Do you ever wish a moment can last forever?" I'm rarely tongue-tied but, attempting to express exactly how taken I am with Anne Elise, I struggle to leap past the hackneyed superlatives: *She's wonderful! I love her so much!* "It's strange. From the moment I first saw her, I felt this instant, irrevocable love for her. Powerful. Emotional. Affirming. But it's more than that. It's like—god, this is going to sound silly."

Laurel reaches through the steel bed-railing bars and pats my hand. "Go ahead. You can tell me."

"When I was a boy, before my father left us, my parents sent me to a Catholic elementary school. A parochial school. We weren't Catholic, but my mother thought the Catholic school was better than the public schools where she taught, so they sent me there. Every Friday, nuns from the convent gave us religious instruction. There's this prayer Catholics say when confessing their sins. We had to memorize it. In this prayer, there's a line about God being 'all good and deserving of all our love.'"

"The Act of Contrition," Laurel says.

I look at Laurel. So much of what we know about each other—our favorite cocktails, basketball teams, classic rock bands, and superhero movies—amounts to trivial stuff. I hadn't realized she, too, went to a Catholic school. Or perhaps she is Catholic. But she's right about the name of the prayer. The Act of Contrition.

"That's how Anne Elise is—all good and deserving of all my love. She makes me want to be someone better than me."

Laurel gasps. "Oh my god! That's *exactly* like I felt too."

I sink back into the recliner and listen to Anne Elise's short snoozy breath. It's remarkable how much better you hear when the lights are off, how depriving yourself of one of your senses kick-starts the others to greater perceptivity. I can see how wonderful Anne Elise is, not only how wonderful she is *now* but the supersmart girl she'll be in the future, the valedictorian accolades that will follow her through school, and the accomplished businesswoman she'll grow into. At some point, Anne Elise is destined to look at me with that same embarrassment that seized Laurel when she introduced her parents to me. I'm nothing but a get-rich-quick man who fails to get rich. Without Trish, I'd be broke, a flat-out loser who'd otherwise be sleeping on sidewalks.

"Do you think it's possible for people to change?" I ask.

"I don't want you to change. I love you the way you are."

Laurel. Poor Laurel. She doesn't know who I really am. All she sees is who she wants to see—a tall, debonair man with good manners and a natural gift for flattery, which, let's face it, is all most people want, but she doesn't know my humiliation every time Trish bails me out of another financial mess. I'm not all good, nor do I deserve anyone's love. I should be bankrupt and destitute. Even now, in debt up to my eyeballs, I have no available funds to invest in what might be my best ever chance to make an investment killing. Where am I going to get a quarter million dollars? Laurel doesn't know any of this. Instead, she sees a wildly successful financial genius, and it feels good, knowing someone—*anyone*—believes in me, even if her trust in me is misplaced.

"Seriously, do you think people can change? For the better?" I ask.

Laurel looks down at her hands and stretches her fingers. Pregnancy hasn't done her fingernails any favors. Unlike most women, whose fingernails get stronger, her nails became weak and brittle, cracking and splitting more frequently since we learned she was with child. Torn and ragged, they look as if she's been biting them. "I've been wondering the same thing." Her head bobs up. She looks me in the eye. "Hey, where'd my parents go?"

Laurel's parents slunk out of the hospital an hour earlier, claiming a long drive lay ahead of them. Before leaving, her father pulled me aside in the hospital waiting room. He looked me over, drumming his meaty fingers against a blue-graveled aquarium where goldfish stared out at us. It felt weird, him coming up to me and thinking I was his daughter's fiancé. I feared he was going to hit me up for money. That or threaten bodily dismemberment if I ever, so help me god, lift a hand in anger against his daughter.

"What can I do for you, Tully?"

"Tull," he said.

"Huh?"

"Call me Tull. All my friends do. Besides, family's family. Now that you're about to be family, I'd be proud to get to know you better."

"Okay, uh, Tull." It made my skin crawl, thinking that if I were to marry Laurel, I'd have him as a father-in-law. If I were to set him straight right there in the waiting room, I was pretty sure he was the kind of man who'd make a scene. Or resort to violence if he knew I was unprepared to make an honest woman of his daughter.

"You weren't bullshitting me, were you? Laurel's really coming round to respecting me again?"

Two bug-eyed goldfish swam around the fish tank. It was the kind of brightly lit splashy aquarium designed to hold a child's attention. Seashells and fluorescent-blue gravel lay on the tank's bottom. In one corner, a plastic deep-sea diver figure stood next to a treasure chest. Every few moments, the lid to the treasure chest swung open to reveal pearls and gold coins.

"Admittedly, I don't know everything that happened when Laurel was younger, but I can tell you this in all truthfulness: she's never said a bad word about you to me."

Tully glowed. He was like me: a man who screwed up big time during the course of his life, but, hope being the eternal cog that keeps us all going, he wished to be redeemed through the love of his daughter. He fished a rubber band out of his pocket, pulled back his long gray hair, and slipped the rubber band over it, bundling his hair into a ponytail. I couldn't get a handle on him. Neither Gatsby nor Buchanan, he's a hardworking man reeking of the Big Mac and french fries he wolfed down prior to arriving at the hospital. That's who Tully is, a character so earthy and real that Fitzgerald never deigned to write him into his fictions.

"Hey, can you do me a solid?" Tully asked.

"What's that?"

"Tell Laurel I love her. Tell Laurel I'm happy for her. And happy that she reached out to Belinda and me again after all these years."

"Sure. I'll do that."

Tully reached around and slapped my back, a loose affectionate gesture he probably shared with the grease monkeys at the garage where he worked. He smelled of chewing tobacco and the type of heavy-duty hand cleaner designed to cut through the automotive lubricants, manly scents that took me back to the days of my youth before my father abandoned my mother to run off with another woman. On weekend mornings or at nights after he came home from his grocery store job, my father would pop open the hood of the family Chevy, put a socket wrench in my hands, and point to the bolts that needed to be unfastened. Tune-ups. Oil changes. Resealing head gaskets. My father did all his own automobile repairs. The smell of Tully's hand cleaner brought it all back to me, the early mornings with my father and the thermos of coffee that would keep us awake. Nowadays, I can't change a sparkplug, so rusty have my mechanical skills become.

"Hey, it's going to be good having a tycoon like you in the family," Tully said.

I laughed the kind of self-effacing laugh that was expected of me. "Tycoon? Me? Ha! Unfortunately, I'm not Warren Buffett."

Tully slapped my back again. "You're still young. Give it time."

I looked into Tully's eyes. He believed I had the capability to be everything I pretended to be.

Telling all this to Laurel is strangely heartening. She's amused I could actually converse with her father, but then she flicks on the switch that controls the fluorescent wall lamp above her bed. Her expression hardens. "Jimmy. You should know something about my father. He's a viper. He honestly is. Beware of him. I'm not joking."

I get that there's bad blood between the two, but I try to make light of it. "Bah! How bad could Tully be if he helped create a wonderful woman like you?"

Laurel takes a deep breath and closes her eyes, and I feel more than foolish, for it's not often my effort to put people in better spirits fails so miserably. "Jimmy. You don't understand. He's not a man to be messed with."

"Fine. Okay."

"I don't want anything bad happening to you, okay?"

"Sure. I get it." I have no idea why she's making such a big deal over this. "Listen, I don't know why we're arguing, but let's brighten things up. This tension's not good for either of us."

It takes a moment, but Laurel eases up. I imagined the days she'd spend in the hospital after the birth to be a form of quarantine, severe and cut off from all the normal comforts of home. I'd stuffed her suitcase with things designed to make her stay more endurable: extra pairs of slippers and nightgowns, toiletries, and spare pillows. To this, I added a box of Debauve et Gallais chocolates. I wanted her to enjoy something sweet, a reward for bearing our child, especially since she'd otherwise eat nothing but hospital food.

Laurel reaches over and touches the spot on my suit jacket where Anne Elise did her reflux spit-up thing. A crust has formed over the dollop, which smells rank, like spoiled milk. Next time I pick Anne Elise up, I ought to drape a towel or something similar over myself as a precaution. "I'm surprised you didn't go apeshit mad when she did that," Laurel says.

"What's a dry-cleaning bill compared to the love of a baby?"

Laurel laughs. She thinks I'm sweet and gentle, and for the most part, I am. "Actually, I'm glad my parents are gone because there are a couple of things we should discuss. How did you feel when I introduced you as my fiancé?"

A woman who introduces me to her family as her fiancé is not someone who's going to jettison me out of her life (and my baby's life) anytime soon—so I was actually glad to hear it. And yet her pronouncement raises inevitable complications. The screws are tightening on me. One way or another, Laurel and Trish are both trying to corner me into making a decision I ultimately would rather not make. "Laurel—I understand why you did it. You needed to say something to your parents to explain who I was. But please, don't go around telling other people we're engaged, okay?"

"Why?"

I shake my head in disbelief. Discretion, apparently, is not part of Laurel's vocabulary. I can't believe she doesn't understand why a married man might object to having someone going around saying he's about to marry someone else. "Laurel, please. What do you think will happen if, god forbid, my wife's friends hear that we're engaged? How will that look? That'll only make Trish dig her heels in deeper when it comes time for the alimony negotiations. Think about my wife."

"Your wife? Why are you still worried about her?" Laurel says, her face pale, her emotions cold. I think of Tully's crude cobra tattoo, the snake's forked tongue darting out of its mouth, its fangs exposed, ready to attack. It chills me, thinking this part of his personality might have rubbed off on Laurel. "You told me you were going to get Tricia out of your life. Out of our lives. The sooner it happens, the better."

"These things take time," I say. I used to believe my best thinking was done while standing up—under the pulsing warm water of my morning shower or while working at my standing desk—but now I plop down on the recliner. As young as Laurel is, she has no idea how hard it is to break away from a long-term relationship. "Are you aware of what one wrong mistake could mean? These things take time."

"You've had, like, *nine months* to figure out how to disentangle yourself from Tricia. How much more time do you need? No more chillaxing. It's time you bailed on her."

My life's as complicated as it's ever been. I owe Trish *millions* of dollars. Literally, millions. Each time Trish covers my investment losses, she summons me upstairs to the same secret second-floor study her father used as his little hideaway nook. Inside, ornately carved wooden filing cabinets contain old communiqués from the decades when the world's financial elites communicated with each other via transatlantic cables and wireless telegraphy. Dusty bank ledgers dating back to the nineteenth century line the shelves. The first time I saw them, I mistook the bank ledgers for the kind of thick leather-bound Bibles that are passed down through the generations, the kind that if you open the front flap, you'll find handwritten genealogical notes detailing the begots and begats of an entire clan. I've tried to get Trish to tell me how she activates the hallway bookshelf that swings back and retracts into the wall to reveal this nook, but she's never divulged the secret. Instead, she sits me down at her father's old desk and makes me sign papers her lawyers draw up in which I pledge repayment of the money should, as the documents spell out, anything ever happen to our union. The legalese in Trish's documents is impeccable, yet over the years, it never occurred to me that someday, the union of our marriage would falter and that I'd be accountable for the money.

"Honey. Dear. Do you know the adage about a woman scorned? Do you know why men lose entire fortunes during divorce proceedings? Anne Elise needs us to be on a solid financial footing. Precautions are needed. I can't have Tricia fleece me for every penny I'm worth in divorce court. Do you understand that, honey? I'm trying to do what's best for us. What's best for Anne Elise. Give me time—that's all I'm asking. You've got to trust me."

Laurel crosses her arms. "Do you remember me saying I'll make sure you'll never see our baby if you don't divorce Tricia? So help me god, I'm serious about that."

Our argument is interrupted when someone steps into our room with a huge bouquet of pink roses in a cobalt-blue vase. The flowers are stupendously fragrant; seated in the recliner, I smell them. Laurel brightens immediately upon seeing them. The delivery person looks at the card that's attached to the vase and then looks at Laurel and asks, "Are you Laurel Bloom?"

"Yes!" Laurel says. And then she turns to me and says, "Thank you, Jimmy. Thank you! I was hoping someone would send me flowers."

I tip the delivery person a couple of dollars and walk the flowers to Laurel, who brings them to her face and inhales lustily. The flowers are beautiful, the pink tips of their petals dark and vivid, but something's wrong: it's not me who bought the flowers for Laurel. My thoughts turn to her parents, but Tully doesn't strike me as someone who'd splurge for what must be a seventy-five-dollar bouquet. As far as I know, Laurel doesn't have another close friend in the city. I'm the center of her world. Or so I thought. Certainly, she must have other people who'd send a congratulatory bouquet. But who?

"Open the card," I say.

Laurel, all smiles, does exactly that. I can tell she expects the card to contain some bold declaration of love from me, but because she's sitting with her back to the wall, I can't peer over her shoulder at what she's reading. At a certain point while she reads, her eyes narrow. She looks up from the card, confused.

"Well? Who sent it?"

Laurel hands the card to me. Immediately, I recognize the handwriting.

You're going to be a wonderful mother, way better a parent than either your mother or father were to you!

—Tricia

Trish?

A bell clangs in my head, telling me something must be wrong. My heart whooshes, flooding me with guilt. How could I think of abandoning Trish when she's capable of such generosity?

"She's killing me with kindness," Laurel says. "Is it possible I've misjudged her?"

"See? Trish is great! That's what I've been trying to tell you. How bad can Trish be if she sends you flowers?" I say, but random acts of generosity are not in Trish's retinue of tricks. Why would Trish try to get on Laurel's good side? And then a sudden chill stirs through me—is it possible she's trying to get on Laurel's better side so she can turn Laurel against me?

"Just because she sends flowers doesn't mean I want you to stay married to her."

"We've got the best thing imaginable, you and I: love," I say. "The love we share for each other. The love we have for our baby. I need time to make sure we don't get dinged too badly, financially, when I divorce Tricia."

Laurel snorts. "Jimmy, this is going to shock you, but I'm not a nice person."

"Sure you are."

"With parents like mine, I've got trust issues, okay? I've been burned too many times trying to make my parents happy to ever trust anyone blindly again. And right now, you're stretching my trust just as far as it can go. Certainly you can understand that, can't you?"

～

Leaving Laurel's room after saying good night, I spot a pay phone in the maternity ward hallway. I hadn't realized pay phones still existed, and from the dust that's settled onto its crevices, I doubt anyone's used it in years. Deep in my wallet is the business card Jack Riggs gave me long ago. Never before have I needed a professional fixer, but there's no one I can turn to for advice. Laurel's trust in me is wearing thin. I can't divorce Trish because of money issues. Plus, as I stretch further from Trish because of Laurel and the baby, I'm filled with regret. Just the possibility of divorce is making me realize how much I still love Trish. How much I rely upon her. But unless I divorce Tricia, I won't be allowed to have a relationship with my baby daughter. I don't dare use any of my own cell phones for fear that, if things go wrong, someone (Laurel? Trish?) will be able to trace my actions. I plug quarters into the pay phone, dial the number. Someone answers.

"Is this Simpkins and Simpkins?"

"It could be," a man says. "Can I help you?"

Chapter Thirteen

TRISH

Driving home from the hospital, I stop at Dean & DeLuca, Georgetown's M Street gourmet market, and purchase a rack of pasture-raised New Zealand lamb and bundles of asparagus so fragrant you'd swear they were picked this morning. I cooked for James every night when we were first married and living in a Capitol Hill apartment. He used to love it when I cooked for him. Inwardly I quivered with delight at the way his face lit up when I set evening dinners down on the table, but then my father vacated Savory Mew for us. Along with the house, we inherited the services of a professionally trained chef, meaning I cooked rarely thereafter.

Now, though, I reach into the pantry bookshelf and grab a Julia Child cookbook. There are many ways to secure a man's heart. I pop another Valium. My hands are calm, steady, but my mind is all jittery. James told me he'd be home by seven o'clock; I've just enough time to create a meal he won't soon forget.

Even childless, I thought we'd survive. So many of our friends were on second or third marriages, yet we were still a team. We took walks in Rock Creek Park, my hand in his as we stepped along stone trails that led to remote thickets where, undisturbed, we kissed and hugged. How did we get from the happiness of our Rock Creek strolls to this moment when the continuation of our marriage is in doubt?

I think of my mother barricading herself in the bedroom for weeks at a time. The way my father stood idly watching her decline was criminal but not prosecutable. But what my mother did to herself was indefensible. She sank into depression. She quit trying to live. My father never would've done that if their positions were reversed. Thirteen years after my mother first prayed to die, cancer called for her. Doctors, and my father, will say it was the cancer that killed her, but they're wrong: her refusal to fight for her place in my father's life was what killed her. I'm not going to succumb to the same fate. If the choice is fighting or dying, I choose fighting. And are there not many ways to fight for a man?

Once I arrive home, I coat the lamb with sea salt, rosemary, crushed garlic, and cracked black peppercorns, letting the garlic's natural oils carry the other seasonings with it as it's absorbed into the meat. I look at the black plastic cat clock, shocked to see it's already past six o'clock. James will be home in less than an hour. I pop another Valium, tell myself to remain calm, and listen to the swish-swash of the cat clock's tail as it marks the passing seconds.

Remembering that a moist lamb is a happy lamb, I sear the garlicked lamb in a cast iron skillet. When the fatty side of the lamb sizzles, I turn it over to brown its bottom and sides. Once, when we were in Florence, James ordered Bistecca alla Fiorentina, the classic Tuscan grilled steak dish. Neither of us spoke Italian. Our *ristorante* waiter, unable to otherwise converse with us, flipped over his hand and pointed to a vein in his wrist. "*Al sangue?*" he asked to discern if James wanted his steak rare, or bloody, as Florentines are fond of their meat. To this day, James still raves about that meal, and ever since, I've cooked his meats rare. A moist lamb is a happy lamb, just as I hope my well-fed husband will be a happy husband.

Juices run from the meat when I lift it out of the skillet. James will admire its rosy pinkness and the way the garlic has caramelized on its surface, forming a crust. I've enough time to prepare the side dishes: port-wine-glazed carrots and a hollandaise sauce to be served over the asparagus. There are many ways to a man's heart. Water boils in the asparagus steamer. It's all coming back to me: the pleasure of making a meal for James's enjoyment. The swish-swash, swish-swash of the cat clock's tail seems to be getting louder. In ten minutes, the asparagus will be steamed to perfection. I dip a finger into the hollandaise sauce that I've made. The sauce is flawless. I've got just enough time, just enough swishes of the kitchen clock's kitty-cat tail, to rush everything to the dining room table.

Chapter Fourteen

Jim

Simpkins suggested meeting at eight o'clock, meaning I've got a half hour to kill. The venue he chose is new to me, Taylor's, a Tenleytown sports bar catering to the American University college crowd.

"Get you a refill on that drink?" the barkeep asks, motioning to the empty tumbler of twelve-year-old Scotch I just finished. With a head full of curly blond hair reminding me of Harpo Marx, he's barely older than the frat boys getting hammered playing quarters at a table in the back. In keeping with the bar's football theme, the barkeep's dressed in the black-and-white zebra stripes of a referee, a silver whistle hanging from an orange lanyard around his neck, but judging by the way he pours pitchers for the frat boys, I'm guessing he's not about to flag anyone for overconsumption.

"Food," I say, reminding myself that it's better to drink with a full belly. "A plate of chicken wings. Can you do that? Something hot. Unsportsmanlike spiciness. That's what I'm after."

Two millennial slackers nurse MGDs at one end of the bar, oblivious to my presence as they compare notes about the computer networks they've compromised. One of them got paid today and brags about how he can finally make rent on his office space. He's wearing a sheepskin jacket, the kind of rough-stitched thing that looks like something the Marlboro Man would wear when rustling cattle. He orders another round of MGDs for himself and his pal. DC is full of computer geeks, NSA and CIA types tasked with hacking into Chinese intelligence agencies and terrorist cells, but I fear for our nation's security if these two cyberwarriors are the best we have. You'd think our spies would know to keep quiet, but the one who just got paid gabs about the juvenile court databases and medical records he's scoured.

"Sealed juvenile court records? How'd you do that?" his pal asks.

"This is America. You can do anything you want. I programmed a new app for that. That's how I did it," the man says, pulling out his iPhone and unlocking the screen. "Through reflexive locator algorithms, I mimic the request as if it's coming from inside the network, and then, through rapid response generation, I attack the database root password, temporarily changing it so no one else can enter the DB while I'm inside. Everything's conducted through a network of rotating VPNs so if the hack's detected, it can't be traced back to me."

"Wow."

The two of them geek out, speaking a dialect of computerese unintelligible to me. They talk of back doors, bots, MySQL infiltrations, and brute-force attacks, lamenting how much harder hacking's become over the last five years since governments and commercial entities started clamping down on digital security.

"She paid me two thousand dollars. I feel skeezy taking her money after what her father did to my grandfather. But not bad for an hour's work, huh? In cash too." The guy dips his hand into the front pocket of his jeans and pulls out a wad of crumpled cash. "She paid everything up front with hundred-dollar bills."

It's only these two guys and me sitting at the bar. I'm eavesdropping so blatantly it's impossible they'd be unaware of my presence. Neither, I realize, are spies, but only gradually do I understand one of them must be my private investigator—a euphemism, I assume, for "professional fixer." I can't imagine Jack Riggs entrusting someone so young to handle his problems—but, then again, anyone who charges $2,000 an hour must be talented. Still, it's hard to believe this is the guy who'll tell me how to keep both Trish and Laurel happy. Once his drinking partner leaves, I'll slide over to the stool next to him, introduce myself, and see how he can fix my dilemma.

The private detective talks about the specifics of his current case. "The woman gave birth yesterday at Sibley Hospital. A baby girl. She got knocked up by the woman's husband, and now the woman's all sore about it."

My head jerks up. He's talking about Laurel. Trish must be his client.

The detective's pal shakes his head.

"So the wife charges into my office saying I need to dig up any dirt I can find so she can get city social services to take the baby away from the mistress. How's that for vengeance? Vicious, huh? Rich women play for keeps, don't they?"

Playing hardball is part of the Riggs family ethic, but I'm still staggered. Scotch scorches the wrong way down my throat. I had come prepared to lay down my situation and seek this fixer's assistance, but Trish has somehow beaten me to him.

The private detective's attention veers toward one of the television screens above the bar. Two hockey players are squaring off at center ice ready to fight each other. They throw off their gloves, grab hold of each other's jerseys, and slam fists into each other's jaws. Within moments, blood flows. If I don't do something, Trish is going to get the city to take away my baby. My head spins and spins. Instead of booze, it's life that's gotten the better of me.

"Holy shit," the detective says, transfixed by the hockey fight. "I think he just popped the other guy's teeth out."

I'm eager to learn more about the detective's findings, but three drinks into the evening, the need to relieve myself comes over me. I head to the men's room, do my business, and think about what I can possibly do to interfere with Trish's plans. When I return, the private detective sits alone scrolling through messages on his iPhone. He's taken off his sheepskin jacket, folded it over the stool where his friend had been sitting. Knowing that Trish is taking action against Laurel forces my hand. If I'm to prevent Trish from getting the city to take away Laurel's baby, I need to intervene. Maybe he's already emailed this information to Trish. Maybe social services has already initiated actions to take Anne Elise away from Laurel. If they can strip Laurel of her rights to keep her child, they'll surely do the same with me, meaning I'll likely never see Anne Elise again.

"Spot me a round," I say, sliding onto the stool next to the private detective. His eyebrows twitch. Up close, he's even younger than I pegged him, maybe in his early twenties. About the only thing he has going for him is his intelligence because, in a plaid shirt and outdated wire-rimmed glasses, there's nothing about him that would make you think he's anything special. "Make it something good too."

"Why me?"

"Because you're the one who bagged two thousand dollars today. That's why. When the gods of good fortune shine upon you, never be afraid to share your winnings with others. The world is a giant roulette wheel. Karma's real. Let your luck rub off on total strangers. That's what I always say."

The detective's bushy brown eyebrows twitch again. He peers down to the other end of the bar, where my plate, now piled with the chicken wing bones I've thoroughly picked clean, still sits. "You were sitting down there?"

"Two double Scotches on the rocks," I say, catching the barkeep's attention. "Put them on my friend's tab."

Surprisingly, my new friend doesn't flinch. He looks me over, says nothing. Despite how gabby he'd been with his friend, he suddenly becomes taciturn. His mouth is a tight smile, his eyes small slits through which he peers at me. He doesn't ask my name or what I do for a living, but maybe for professional reasons, it's better he doesn't know too much about his clients. Should I request he perform some act that stretches the limits of legal permissibility, it's to his advantage to maintain as much plausible deniability as possible. When the drinks arrive, his nostrils flare at the peaty aroma. I thought private detectives were still the hard-drinking lot portrayed by Humphrey Bogart and Raymond Chandler, but he recoils from the smell.

"How long were you listening in on my conversation?"

"I take it you're a private detective?"

"Are you the guy who called earlier?"

"I might be."

He peers back at his drink, listens to the clink of the ice cubes as he swirls the tumbler around in his hands.

"You're all right, sport." At this pleasant mellow stage of inebriation, my thoughts are crystal clear, the alcohol enhancing my thinking abilities, my logic not yet the incoherent rage it sometimes becomes when I've been drinking. I slap the private detective's back, just as Tully slapped mine. A certain kind of man, usually the young and eager to please, will respond to that kind of gesture, but the rest of us will bristle at the touch of a stranger and the implicit desperate tug for trust. "Plus, you're smart, demanding payment in cash. That way, you won't have to pay taxes on it."

The Scotch is, shall we say, filthy atrocious with an aftertaste not unlike kerosene, and within a couple of minutes, his tongue loosened, the detective tells me all the great things about being a private detective, how he's developed fail-proof ways to break into databases and decrypt password-protected documents. On a hunch, I reach into my coat pocket and activate the record button on my cell phone, which I've used often to tape business lunches, conferences, and face-to-face client meetings.

"So tell me the work you do. What kind of cases do you take on?"

"Domestic stuff. Husbands or wives contract me to track down a spouse suspected of being unfaithful. Every time that happens, I'm, like, 'Hey, you really don't want me to do that,' but they're all, like, 'I *really, really* need to know.' Smartphones are, like, the greatest gift to a private detective—anything you want to find out about someone is linked to their cell phone. So I trace cell phone records, track down cell phone locations, hack into text messages. Then I surveil that person with a telephoto lens, snap a few photos of them entering or exiting hotels, motels, sometimes even the back seat of a car in an empty parking lot." He shoots his hands through his shaggy hair, quaffs down the rest of his Scotch, and exhales a satisfied sigh. "It's amazing how careless people are."

"So how much do you charge to ruin someone's life?" I ask, imagining the reactions of his clients when he unveils the photographs, romantic texts, and intimate emails proving their spouses have been unfaithful. As soon as they see this shit, his clients must break down, sobbing.

"I'm not ruining anyone's life."

I raise my eyebrow. "You aren't?"

"I'm giving people what they want."

All along, I've wondered how a private eye could be as unaware of the consequences of his investigations, but then I get it: if he were any more in touch with what he's doing, he wouldn't be able to live with the devastation he brings to people's lives. As cynical as I am, I've never drawn pleasure at provoking misery in others. Pale and withdrawn, he must've been a troubled youth who got his ya-yas out by kicking kittens or poisoning the neighborhood stray.

The detective reaches for one of the empty MGD bottles he drank with his pal and peels off the label. In the back of the bar, one of the frat boys sinks a quarter in a glass he hadn't been aiming for, and the whole lot of them erupt in the kind of enthusiastic high-fives men my age can't pull off anymore with authenticity. Twenty years ago, I would have walked up to their table and asked to join their drinking game. Now, though, I've got responsibilities.

"You find out anything good about the woman you were looking into? The one who had, um, a girl over at Sibley?"

"You bet. I'm good at what I do. I found plenty."

"And the woman who hired you. What did she say when you told her all this?"

"She doesn't know yet. I'm not supposed to get back to her until tomorrow."

I have no idea what deeds Laurel may have committed, what dirt this lowlife detective might've unearthed. If Trish convinces authorities that Laurel's not a fitting mother, who knows what might become of Anne Elise? Social services would take one look at me, or at least my bar tabs, and declare me equally unfit for parenthood. Foster homes, orphanages, adoption agencies. That's what might become of Anne Elise. I might never see her again. Hours ago, swaying her around Laurel's hospital room, I silently pledged to be her father and protector, and that's what I intend to be. Trish's plotting to rid Laurel of Anne Elise, and I'm not going to let it happen.

"So tell me what I can do for you?" the detective asks. "Why'd you call me?"

"If you haven't told the wife yet, don't do it."

The private detective jerks his head up. "Why shouldn't I?"

"I'll make it worth your while if you *don't* hand over the information to the jealous wife. How's that for a business proposition?"

The detective lifts his wire-rimmed glasses off his nose, grabs a napkin off the bar, and rubs a speck off one of the lenses. I sense some consideration, some mental calculations, going on in his mind. What I'm suggesting is a ballsy double-cross of my own wife. He tilts his head, examines me, puts his glasses back on. "Why would you do that?"

"Because I'm a good Samaritan. That's why. What difference does it make? Don't question the motives of your business associates. All that should matter is that my money's green. That's what I'm saying. A smart businessman like you ought to know not to look a gift horse in the eye."

"What do you know about the wife? I hear she's bad news."

I'm shocked anyone could think of Trish as "bad news," but I try not to let the shock seep into my expression. "Buddy, I don't know anything about the wife."

The private detective peers down at the torn strips of the beer label. We listen to the frat boys' drinking game behind us. Quarters bounce on the table. One of the frat boys lets go of his quarter, which rolls onto the floor. The detective lays the beer-label strips onto the glazed oak bar, jigsaw puzzling the label's image back together again.

"Impressive," I say.

The detective nods. The reassembled beer bottle label is laid out on the bar. He reaches into his wallet, plucks out a business card, and places it atop the label's American eagle logo. The business card is different than that which Jack Riggs handed me years ago. Charles Simpkins is not listed. Nor is the firm still located on Pennsylvania Avenue across from the White House.

"Larry Simpkins," I say, reading the name off the business card.

"That's me. Who are you?"

"Me? I'm the guy who'll be calling you again real soon. That's who I am. That's all you need to know. Got it?"

Chapter Fifteen

Jim

Savory Mew's lead glass windows blaze like full moons; every light in the house appears to be on as I drive up the cobblestone street leading to our house. It's eleven o'clock. Or maybe eleven thirty. I might think there's a party going on, but Trish isn't someone who endorses spur-of-the-moment revelry—which is too bad, because I could use a party right now. Or at least more alcohol. Having left Taylor's with enough room in my belly for a few more drinks, I'm all revved up with no place to lush out.

"Hello? Honey pie? I'm home," I say, stepping through Savory Mew's front door. An eerie emptiness touches me to the bone: this is a house that love has abandoned. Though lit up to the nines, the house is its normal, desolate self with no alcohol, drunken revelry, or partiers in sight. I dim the foyer sconces, step into the living room, and, seeing the room empty, extinguish the stained glass Tiffany mushroom lamps next to the armchair Trish usually uses when watching the police procedurals she loves on television. "Trish? I'm home. Where are you, sweetie?"

From somewhere deep in the house, I hear Trish mumble. I walk through several more rooms, flipping off the light switches as I go, until I eventually find her in the dining room. Although she's dressed in a strapless black dress as if to go out for the evening, a white fur wedding shawl covering her shoulders, she looks like she's been sitting here for hours, frowning. Mascara and traces of glimmering blue eye shadow streak down her cheeks from tears that have not quite dried. Nothing in her sad countenance squares with the confident woman I imagine must've charged into Simpkins earlier in the day and demanded dirt on Laurel.

Two place settings of our blue-rimmed Noritake wedding china sit on the table. Silver serving pieces reflect the light of the candles that flicker romantically on the pair of enormous nineteenth-century gilt bronze candelabra we bought years ago at an Old Town Alexandria antique shop. Crystal wine glasses are filled with red wine. The elaborate details take me aback. Our linen napkins are folded into origami swans that face each other, beak to beak, nuzzling. Dinner lately for us hasn't consisted of much beyond store-bought microwave entrees scarfed down together or individually at the rough-hewn table in our kitchen breakfast nook. A few years ago, Trish informed our cook her services were no longer needed, letting her go with an uncharacteristically lavish severance package. We had stopped inviting people over for dinner parties or cocktails because the questions our ever-fertile friends (all blessed with one or two or even three children) would ask about our own efforts to conceive would send Trish sobbing to the bedroom. By firing our cook, she was throwing in the towel on home entertaining.

"Honey. Dearest. Are you all right?"

"You told me you'd be home by seven o'clock. You promised."

Trish's insistence this morning that I come home at a decent hour comes back to me. I'd forgotten all about it. Not only am I unfaithful, but I've become a man who can no longer be troubled to keep track of his commitments. Trish has cooked this lavish meal for me, and now it's cold and inedible because I've forgotten to come home. "I'm sorry, honey. I screwed up. Can you forgive me? Please?"

Curdled fat globules float over the asparagus spears. Only after some moments do I realize this had once been a hollandaise sauce. She made it for me, put herself out in its intricate preparation because she knew I loved it. A man with two women in his life is a fool. It's hard enough to keep one woman happy, but it amazes me how Trish still wanted to keep me happy. I picture her as she must've been for the last few hours, running the sauce and the asparagus back and forth from the stove to keep them warm. The heat of the stove would have caused her to sweat, increasing her anxiety. I picture her beating the sauce, whipping it. Is that how you keep a good thing from going bad? I picture her doing everything she could, praying that it would keep until I came home, and I picture her despair when it finally separated.

Trish lifts the silver dome off a silver serving tray to reveal a garlic-and herb-crusted rack of lamb. Her hand trembles. The meat is cold, the pink juices gathered at the bottom of the tray congealed into a leathery-skinned Jell-O. Hours ago, it would have been perfect.

"You were supposed to be home at seven o'clock," Trish says, letting go of the dome so that it crashes onto the table. She had set our dinner plates side by side as if she anticipated us leaning into each other, close and comfortable, the wine an aphrodisiac to rekindle playful touches and intimacies. We used to eat like this years ago, back when we talked of having a baby of our own. She'd make the meals herself, taking pride in the smiles she put on my face.

Pulling out the chair next to her, I sit exactly as she anticipated had I arrived earlier. "Darling, to tell you the truth, I wasn't sure you wanted me to come home tonight. Everything looks delicious. But I thought you didn't want me anymore."

Trish's eyes widen, becoming brilliant blue marbles. When we were first dating, I loved looking into her eyes, and now, seeing the candle-light in them, I'm reminded of the hours we spent holding hands and staring into each other's faces. "Why would you think that?"

"Why? Because of Anne Elise. Because of Laurel. It's a terrible situation I've dug myself into, and I thought you'd reject me. That's why." I rest my chin in my outstretched hands. "Trish. What am I supposed to do? I barely know Laurel. I barely know what I've stepped into. Tonight, I met her parents."

"Let me guess: they're drug users. Or criminals."

Trish's assessment is an exact match for what I'd been thinking. "How'd you know?"

"I know people. Anyone who ends up like Laurel must have started in a bad place. Can I tell you a secret?"

"Tell me anything you like."

"I simply think Anne Elise is beautiful. I so much wanted to hate her too. I so much wanted to pick her up and see that she was nothing but a grubby little piece of junk."

"She's not junk, dear."

"I know she's not." Trish brushes back a fresh tear, the glimmering traces of her eye shadow smudging onto the back of her hand. "That's what's so unsettling. From the moment you slipped her into my arms at the hospital, I could tell she was wonderful, perfect, an absolute angel. It was like I had a baby-sized hole in my heart she snuggled into perfectly. Don't you see? She's all I ever wanted: a baby of my own. She should have been the baby we were meant to have. You and me."

"You're right," I say, brushing the side of her face with my fingertips. I felt the exact same way staring into Anne Elise's eyes. Even when she spit up her regurgitated milk onto me. A baby who will spit up on you will never leave your side. That is what I think.

"James. We need to talk."

"Why talk? Let's enjoy this moment together. Let's savor the calm before the storm."

"There doesn't have to be a storm. We could still have a child. We can try again. We can create a sister for Anne Elise. Or a brother." Trish tells me again how electrifying it was to hold Anne Elise. "It was like she was mine. If it wasn't for that mistress of yours, she would have been mine," Trish says. "Get rid of her."

"I could never get rid of Anne Elise."

"Not Anne Elise. That's not what I meant. I meant Laurel. Get rid of her for us."

I wince, shocked. This is the second time Trish has asked me to get rid of Laurel. She's tightening the screws on me. And this time, the way she says it all jittery and trembling, I'm convinced she expects me to kill Laurel. Her eyes are agitated and bloodshot. She grabs hold of my shoulders and digs her fingernails into my shoulder with an urgency I hadn't suspected. Her nails are piercingly sharp and painful.

"Get rid of her for us. We can raise the baby ourselves. Don't you see it? If you get rid of Laurel, we can have the baby to ourselves."

"Honey . . . honey . . ." I say, not wanting to enrage her any further. "You're not thinking clearly."

Trish lets go of my shoulders. I glance at the hole she jabbed into the right shoulder of my suit jacket. I wouldn't be surprised if, underneath my shirt, I'm bleeding. My shoulders are sore, aching. She pushes back hair that has fallen in her eyes. "Yes, I am! You owe me this. You *owe* me. Anne Elise was supposed to be our baby. We've been talking about having her ever since we met."

The timbre of Trish's voice is so unlike its normal crisp tone. She's never suggested something so irrational, but I know where she's coming from. I take her hand and warm it between my own hands. Her hair falls over her eyes. Something curdles in my throat, for while I'm responsible for her anger, I never wanted to bring her sorrow, and yet I'm fearful of what else she might do to me . . . or make me do for her.

"Are you going to do it? For me?"

"Honey, I can't toss Laurel aside and stand by while you snatch away her baby. Ethically, I can't do that." It pains me to say that word—"ethically"—for it makes me feel like such a hypocrite to brandish this word after stupidly doing something as unethical and immoral as having an affair. Yet I'm responsible for Anne Elise. Which means I'm responsible for Laurel. Trish slumps her head down, her dainty chin resting on the white fur shawl she's wrapped around her shoulders. I feel her sorrow. I wouldn't be surprised if she orders me to vacate the premises, and yet I wonder if I'd be truly better off if she tosses me out.

"Honey, I'll do the right thing. Trust me. Trust me. But I need time. You've got to trust me on this. You've known me for fifteen, sixteen years. Have I ever let you down?"

I expect my words will reassure Trish, but something has dulled her emotions. She stares off into the distance. She reaches into her Prada handbag for an amber plastic prescription bottle, pops open its childproof safety lid, and flings a pill into her mouth. Even deep into a Scotch buzz, I understand there's a connection between the amber pill bottle, Trish's doped-up sounding voice, and her wild suggestions. Following my gaze to the pill bottle, she blushes and then hurriedly tucks the bottle back into her handbag.

I take a sip of wine. A wise drinker knows never to mix Scotch and red wine, but I've screwed up so much recently that wisdom surely has no finger on me. "What's that, honey? In the bottle? In your purse?"

"Nothing."

"How many have you taken?"

"It's just Valium. To keep me calm while I sit waiting for you to do the right thing, like you just said you would."

"How many did you take?"

"My doctor said to take them as needed. Tonight, I've needed them a lot."

"Trish. Honey."

"Don't worry. I'm not going to take too many. It's not like I'm going to overdose or anything."

"You can overdose on them?" I say, alarmed. "How many would you need to take?"

"Beats me. But don't worry. It's not like I'm going to kill myself or anything. I've just been worrying a lot. It's not just you and Laurel and Anne Elise. I'm also worried about my father."

"Jack?" I haven't seen Trish's father, Jack Riggs, since he broached the subject of surrogacy on us. I presumed he was living in comfort and good health. I envied his Cayman Island paradise, where he sits under the shade of palm trees, listens to the ocean surf, and dines on a heart-healthy diet of broiled lobsters, sea bass, and tropical fruits.

"I can't reach him. Today, I found out he put his house off MacArthur Boulevard up for sale. He said he'd never sell it so he'd have a place to stay when he visited us once we have grandchildren for him. Don't you think it's strange he'd put it on the market without telling us?"

In the 1990s, Jack Riggs sold his shares in the family bank but insisted on maintaining a seat on the corporate board so he'd continue to exert real control over the institution. At its peak, it was, by far, the largest bank in town. Presidents deposited their federal paychecks with Riggs Bank. It was a bank unlike any other in the nation, its finances intricately entwined with the federal government. Jack initiated a campaign to make the bank become the financial institution of choice among the foreign embassies and diplomats stationed in town. The bank sought to maximize profits. Foreign embassies sought to minimize oversight on their accounts. Jack's a smart man. He put two and two together. Repeatedly, he turned a blind eye to foreign money laundering. Money used to finance the 9/11 terror attacks was funneled through the bank, leading one influential senator to suggest 9/11 never would have happened had it not been so ridiculously easy for foreigners to launder money through the bank. Jack, beleaguered and aging, was ousted from the board, disgraced by the scandal. The bank that had borne the Riggs family name since 1840 sold its assets to a rival banking firm in 2005. Its former branches now fly under the PNC Financial banner. His house off MacArthur Boulevard might fetch a couple of million dollars in today's market, chicken scratch compared to the wealth he presumably still has tied up in various offshore accounts.

"He's not returning my phone calls or my emails."

"He isn't?" Jack has never been anything but punctual and responsive. We still talk from time to time about the joint investments we might one day make. Whenever I've tried to reach him, he never fails to return my calls. I can't see him dodging Trish's calls, but strung out on Valium like she is, she doesn't need me to alarm her any further. "Don't worry. He's probably out enjoying himself. He'll get back to you soon enough."

"Argh." Despair falls upon Trish. She reaches across the table for a rosewood-handled steak knife, hacks off a diamond-shaped chunk of lamb from the cold roast, and stuffs it in her mouth. She chews the meat, and in her breath I smell the garlic from its crust and the perky red wine that she washes the lamb down with. When she catches me watching her, she sets down her cloth napkin and says, "I've been wanting to do that for hours."

"Are you sure you should be doing that? Drinking wine while taking Valium?"

"Pah! You're one to talk about drinking!"

She's right. I have no moral authority to stand on when it comes to the subject of alcoholic abstinence, and for a moment I feel I've let her down. And then I feel doubly bad, remembering that it's not my alcoholism that's let her down but my infidelity.

Trish offers me her steak knife so I, too, can hack off some lamb, but the sight of the cold lamb repulses me. Meat that's been cooked so rare shouldn't be left out in the open for too long. I tell her about food-borne contamination, how consuming bloodred rare meat that has sat on a table for four or five hours will make her sick, but she doesn't listen. She slices off a couple of lamb chops and piles them onto a plate. Even mellowed out on Valium, she must have been in a private hell, staring for hours at this elegant meal but not wanting to lay a fork into it so that I would appreciate the trouble she'd gone through preparing it for my sake.

~

An hour later, we're in the kitchen together cleaning up. We had cleared off the table and transferred the leftovers into Tupperware containers. My alcoholic buzz has dissipated, much to my chagrin. Washing dishes used to be one of my favorite parts of the evening, both of us standing shoulder to shoulder amid Palmolive and running tap water, one of us running a soapy sponge over the dishes while the other dries them off with a dish towel. Hard to believe we were once a functional couple. Washing dishes will be one of the things I'll miss should the time come for me to move out of Savory Mew.

Upstairs, as I change into my flannel pajamas, Trish saunters up beside me in an alabaster silk chemise, engulfing me in her tender smile. Her lustrous black hair swept to one side, she's as fetching on the eyes as ever. Shalimar, the perfume she dabs behind her ears for special occasions, scents the air around her. "Do you want to see what else the doctor prescribed me?"

"Sure. What?"

Trish opens her hand and offers me a trapezoidal blue Viagra tablet.

"Your doctor prescribed this? For you?"

"I don't want you to be confused about us. Let's work out our problems," Trish says. She wraps her arms around me, displaying more physical affection than at any time since I started seeing Laurel. Something about her is wrong. An hour ago, she'd dug her sharp fingernails into my shoulders. Now, she's outright seductive. She purrs into my ear. "James, we can still try to make a baby of our own. Just because we've failed before doesn't mean we'll fail again."

Chapter Sixteen

Trish

James opens his arms and holds me. His hands are warm and strong, and I savor the embrace. If he's to leave me, I want to remember this moment and the sensation of being in love with him. He's awkward and uncharacteristically clumsy, unsure whether to respond to my advances. I pull his hand, tugging him toward the bed while simultaneously undressing him button by button of his flannel pajama top. I slip a Viagra tablet into his hand, and he looks at it dubiously. He's never outright needed these types of pills, but I've sensed his frustration at himself for not being as young and virile anymore. Pushed by the excitement of experiencing the pill's vaunted effects, he will want to make love to me. I brush one of my chemise's spaghetti straps off my shoulder and then the other, and as the chemise shimmies onto the floor, he inhales a breath and places the pill on his tongue. Elation surges through me. I am giving myself to him. I guide his hand to my chest. He squeezes my breast. "Harder," I say. There's only so much one person can do to keep hold of another person, and I'm doing everything I can.

～

I wake shivering with intestinal cramps, my whole body on fire, slivers of morning light shining upon me through the windows. It's late, maybe nine or ten o'clock. James is long gone for his office, his musky scent lingering behind on the pillows, and I remember dreaming how comforting it was to walk Anne Elise around the maternity ward yesterday. Because of my KISS bracelet, I strolled through the whole hospital with her, unimpeded. Now, when I step out of bed, nausea wrenches up from my intestines, roiling over me. I crawl to the bathroom feeling light-headed, and after I throw up, I stay on the floor, the cool ceramic bathroom tiles hard on my knees, and listen to the whoosh of the toilet's automatic flush. Water is what I need, something to wash the acrid taste out of my mouth. I can hear everything going on within me: the thump-thump of my heart, the grumble in my stomach, the crinkle of my skin as I scratch a dry patch on my wrist. Glimpsing myself crouched at the toilet in the bathroom mirror, I see a desperate, pathetic woman . . . a woman much like my mother had been. I don't want to become my mother. I don't want to be pathetic. I vow to fight for James so that I don't end up like her. And then, pulling myself to an upright position, I'm startled: just like that, I feel better, clearheaded and optimistic about my place in the world. No longer do I feel sick. How can this change have happened so quickly? My breasts feel tender. Looking at the mirror, I'm displeased at the bloating in my face, my arms, but ecstatic at how my face glows with unnatural warmth.

And then I get it.

I must be pregnant.

How else can I account for the nausea—morning sickness—and the peachy glow that lights my face?

Just as Laurel must have known the moment of her conception, now I do too. We made love last night, James and I, clutching and grasping each other like raccoons and howling sweet nothings, a near-bestial experience unlike the whispers and normal soothing motions of all our previous lovemaking. I was aflame with jealousy, wondering if James's newfound animal-like rambunctiousness owed to Laurel's coaching, but as we progressed, I gave in to the same spirit, responding in kind, biting, scratching, flipping him onto his back, crawling on top of him. James laughed, riotously. We hadn't laughed in bed since shortly after we married—on a spring afternoon I remember well for how we opened the apartment windows and let raindrops blow upon us during the act. I found myself thinking of Debauve et Gallais chocolates— James had always talked about bringing them to my maternity suite when I became pregnant. Even then, lying in his arms, I felt warm and achy, a postcoital drowsiness coming upon me. Never having been pregnant before, I didn't identify these symptoms as the signs of conception, but now, after experiencing my first bout of morning sickness, I know.

Downstairs, the robust aroma of a fresh pot of coffee fills the kitchen. James, ever considerate, cleaned up after himself before going to work, his coffee mug and oatmeal bowl both washed and rinsed and drying in the bamboo dish rack. A note lies on the breakfast table.

Didn't want to wake you this morning, but thank you for last night. Again you amaze me. I am so lucky to have a wife who accentuates the positive so well!

A little red heart lies below where James signed his name. He's never embellished his notes this way before. I feel special, knowing that he enjoyed himself. I wonder if he feels it too: our conception. Might he have awoken to an intuitive ping? A moment of startling clarity when, while snapping on his gold cuff links, he bolted upright with the glorious suspicion that we finally conceived?

I dress quickly. Much of the morning is already lost to me. Although I'm riding a mellow high, I pop a Valium and walk out of the house in a full-length down-filled black bubble jacket. The day is bright and bracingly cold, the February sidewalks sheeted with ice. I'm walking for two right now, taking small, slow steps and being careful not to slip, especially because my knee-high black leather boots are more suited for a fashion show runway than a treacherous sidewalk. Turning onto Wisconsin Avenue, I find a shoe store and buy a pair of fleece-lined snow boots with thick rubber treads on their soles that are guaranteed not to slip even on the iciest of surfaces. The salesgirl boasts that her boutique is the sole distributor of these boots in the metropolitan region. "Are they really good?" I ask. She flips the boots over and shows me the high-tech-looking hexagonal treads on the boots' soles. Paying for them at the register, I lean in and tell her I'm pregnant. She's the first person I've told, and since I've hoarded this secret to myself for the last hour, it's an exciting relief to share my good news.

"I want to be a good mom. I don't want to risk harming my child should I slip."

This salesgirl, a smart-looking college student with a fresh face and beads in her hair, wishes me well. She hands me my receipt. "I never would have guessed you're expecting. You're not showing or anything."

I assume she means this as a compliment. "Thanks."

Ever since ingesting my first Valium tablet, I've been jittery and prone to wild bouts of fancy—exactly the conditions I thought the pill would prevent. Everything feels different, charged with excitement—but then I wonder if it's the Valium or the pregnancy that's doing this to me. Do all mothers-to-be experience rickety thoughts, ecstatic emotions, and clammy palms?

With the new boots on my feet, I walk across Wisconsin Avenue to a drug store whose seasonal aisles are optimistically stocked with gardening supplies and suntan lotions, even though last week the groundhog predicted six more weeks of winter. The pharmacist is a large African American woman who has the calm, happy disposition I've always associated with midwifery and a wholesome diet of organic foods. I ask her about home pregnancy tests, if they're reliable and which brand she'd recommend as having the best early-detection ranking. She tells me all the kits are about the same despite the wide price differences.

"Save a few dollars and go with the cheapest one. How many days late are you?"

"None yet." Thinking backward, I count the days since my last period. I'm one of the few women who are 100 percent regular. "My next period won't be for another week."

The pharmacist scrunches her eyebrows. She weaves her fingers together, places her hands on the faux-wood counter that separates us. "Ma'am. You wouldn't be able to get positive confirmation with the over-the-counter tests we carry. Even a doctor wouldn't be able to tell you yet with any accuracy. Why do you think you might be pregnant?"

"I just sense it," I say, remembering the great sex James and I had last night. Within my womb, cells are dividing, triggering hormonal changes, preparing my body for the changes to come. Maybe that's why I feel so jittery now. I've never wanted anything so bad in my life. In nine months, James will pack Debauve et Gallais chocolates into a suitcase and rush me to the hospital. By that time, he'll have left Laurel and recommitted himself to me. I almost feel sorry for Laurel—she's about to lose James. Our babies, Laurel's and mine, will cancel each other out. The other positives I bring to our relationship—the home, the money, the comfort, the stability, and the respectability—will weigh in my favor. There'd be no reason for James to stay with Laurel. "Look at my skin! It glows. Everything feels different within me. I threw up this morning."

The pharmacist separates her hands from each other, reweaves her fingers.

"Morning sickness! Don't you understand? I've already got morning sickness!"

"Are you sure it's not something you ate?"

The store is brighter than I've seen it before, the vinyl counter on which I tap my fingers more solid, more trustworthy. "It's like the air smells different. Not its aroma but its whole texture. Does that make sense?"

She lifts her hands off the counter, places them on mine. Her touch is solicitous, calming, a pat on the back of my hand delivered for no other purpose than to bring comfort and joy. She regards me with sad, judgmental eyes. "I'm speaking from what I know, which is that it's clinically impossible to test for pregnancies so soon after the *potential* moment of conception."

"Point me the way to the prenatal vitamins," I say.

My cell phone vibrates. I pick it up, expecting it to be my private investigator, but I'm greeted by the welcoming voice of my father. He says he is well, but he sounds haggard, as if he's been under some stress on his Caribbean beachside paradise. Cayman phone lines are notoriously dodgy, and in the background I hear the faint, ghostlike sounds of other conversations, echoes, and a strange pinging sound that tick-tocks the seconds of our conversation. I ask why he didn't return my calls and emails, to which he confesses he hasn't been able to check his messages lately.

"Dad! Guess what? I'm pregnant!"

As I say this, I sense the shock both in my father's voice and in the way the pharmacist's eyes widen. You'd think she'd feel privileged, sharing in this enthusiastic moment, but she takes a breath, stares at me, and shakes her head. My father, at least, is happy for me. He asks what we plan to name the child, if it's a boy or a girl, but before I can say it's too early to tell, the pinging tick-tock that had been in the background becomes louder. My father starts to apologize.

"Dad. Is everything okay? You can come and visit me again. I'll be able to present you with a grandchild!"

My father's voice becomes fainter, the pinging louder. "Ah-umm . . . I'm running out of time."

"Dad!"

He starts to say something more, but the line goes dead. I stare at the phone, expecting him to call right back. The pharmacist looks at me with concern, as if something unfortunate or maybe tragic has just happened to my father. I try to return the call, but a message appears on the screen alerting me that the number he called on does not accept incoming calls. I send him a text: Im OK U? A moment later, my phone pings. There's an alert on its screen telling me the text was undeliverable.

"Is he all right?" the pharmacist asks.

"Probably a bad cell," I say, shaking my head. Rich or poor, telecommunications are the great leveler: as wealthy as anyone might be, reliable cell phone service remains out of all our reaches. Of course I'm concerned, never having a chance to ask about his house, but my father will call me back soon; he always does.

"That's good," the pharmacist says. "But listen to me: it's impossible to tell, mere hours after engaging in a sexual encounter, whether you're pregnant. There's no physical, psychological, or emotional sign this early that will reliably indicate conception."

"But I can tell."

I start to reexplain myself, tell the pharmacist she's wrong—has she never been pregnant herself?—but the possibility she might be right suddenly rocks me. There were times in the past when I imagined myself pregnant—but I was sure this time was different. My heart plummets. Is it possible I'm imagining this pregnancy? Can the symptoms of pregnancy be induced by stress or by the overeager desire to be pregnant? Or maybe the Valium is messing with my perceptions. I feel dazed, unsure of myself. I grab the pharmacy counter railing to steady myself.

"Ma'am. Ma'am? Are you all right?" the pharmacist asks.

Tears come over me. My inability to bear a child has cost me dearly. If only I were pregnant. The pharmacist pats my shoulder, but I'm still blubbering about my infertility. "Ask your doctor about fertility treatments, in vitro, things like that," she says, but she doesn't know about the procedures we've already tried. She doesn't know about the diminishing chances that I'll ever conceive or the doctors who've instructed me to embrace a childless future. Pretty soon, it'll be a husbandless future as well. Doctors have been unable to pinpoint the cause of our problems—was it James? Was it me? Fifteen years of sleeping together yielded no children. Laurel's pregnancy puts to bed the notion that James might've been the sterile one. Anne Elise's birth is proof that his sperm is fine. It's my ovaries, my eggs, my fallopian tubes, my womb, or some other facet of my reproductive organs that's at fault.

The pharmacist hands me a tissue. People have lined up behind me, waiting to have their prescriptions filled. I wish they'd all disappear.

Chapter Seventeen

TRISH

Laurel's hospital room is fragrant with the scent of the pink roses I bought. Pink roses. Is that not the flower Emily Post would send to an adversary? With every breath, Laurel will smell their scent and be reminded of me. The scent will get under her skin. That is what I hope. The wild emotions I felt at the pharmacy have subsided, but I'm still devastated not to be pregnant. It's the ache of barrenness that I feel, a longing that at this point in my life I doubt will ever be fulfilled. God chose Laurel to be pregnant instead of me, and it hurts like hell.

Laurel and Anne Elise are asleep and, in Laurel's case, snoring. It amazes me how, in a maternity ward, you can enter any room regardless of whether the patient is awake or asleep or even wants to see you. None of the doors are locked. I prowl through the room, opening drawers and closets and medical cabinets. I look at the wet boot prints I've tracked into the room. The floor is covered with hexagonal tread marks. Just like the salesgirl promised when I bought my new boots, I haven't slipped all day. Laurel stirs in her bed, murmuring in her sleep. At times, it's as if she's about to awaken, but then she rolls to her side and starts snoring again. I could totally mess with her—ransack her room and its belongings or maybe write foul messages onto the room's television screen with lipstick—but I can't let my worst instincts take hold of me. I am better than that, and I need to remember this.

Anne Elise stirs in her bassinet, reaching out and begging me to lift her into my arms. I smell the reason for her liveliness: she needs a diaper change. I watched nurses perform this duty yesterday when her diaper wasn't quite so fragrant. Disposable diapers, wipes, and a jar of petroleum jelly are stored in a drawer in the bassinet, and as I unwrap Anne Elise's swaddling clothes, the liberating act of freeing her from her blanket and diaper brings delight upon her face. She makes a sound—not quite a giggle but more like a squeak. At her age, unable to talk or express herself through more than a couple of facial expressions, much of what she thinks and feels is open to interpretation, but she clearly likes the cooling sensation of the room's mild air against her warm flesh. Perhaps it's because I was one of the first people to ever hold her, but she's disturbingly trusting of me. I lift her legs and slide a fresh diaper beneath her. After wiping Anne Elise clean, I spread petroleum jelly on her warm bottom to prevent diaper rash, and she falls almost immediately back to sleep in her bassinet.

Two days after she's given birth, Laurel's IV bag still hangs from a stainless steel IV stand. Tubing from the bag extends to where it connects to a catheter in her arm. In her sleep, Laurel crosses her arms, jostling her IV tubing. The line from the IV bag is long, bordering on unmanageable. You would think the tubing would be shorter to decrease the possibility of entanglements.

As I look over the cheerless room, something on the nightstand catches my attention. I don't know how I could've missed seeing it. Right next to the flowers is a gift box of Debauve et Gallais chocolates. Those should've been my chocolates. We talked for years, James and I, about sending me to the hospital with a box of Debauve et Gallais. When we talked about having a baby, the taste of Debauve et Gallais chocolates would fill my mind. I'd think about it while making love, think about it whenever I imagined myself cuddling my newborn baby.

Now, my insides turn to acid, a boiling, bubbling mess of dreams gone bad. My knees knock together. I feel sick, unable to breathe, and barely able to think properly. More than his affair and the sex and the sneaking around behind my back, this box on Laurel's nightstand smacks of betrayal.

Those should have been my chocolates.

I feel like waking Laurel and yelling at her, but then a better idea comes to me. Laurel's asleep. I watch her eyes wriggle under her lids. She looks incapable of doing anyone harm, but I know better. I'm trembling with anger, everything haywire and jittery inside me. Without the antibiotics, she might die from her episiotomy infection. I run my fingers over her IV tubing. I could tie it in knots, cutting off her flow of antibiotics. Evil isn't beyond me. Anne Elise stirs in her bassinet. It's like she can sense her mother is in danger.

I tug on the IV line, pinching off the flow of antibiotics. Still asleep, Laurel squirms in her bed. I see the rise and fall of her chest beneath the blankets as she takes in a long, whistling breath. I wrap the IV line around the open rail of her bed railing. Laurel's not going to get a drop more of antibiotics as long as I'm in the room. With luck, it'll be hours before nurses notice what's happened. And by that time, her infection could be past the point where it can be easily remedied.

I open my Prada handbag, pull out my KISS medallion bracelet. Lois Belcher told me I'd know when the bracelet was successfully activated. I step over to the bassinet, where Anne Elise still sleeps, and press my medallion over hers. Both discs glow pink, and then, from nano-sized speakers embedded in the medallions, I hear the faint smooching sound of a kiss. Hearing the sound, Anne Elise opens her eyes. I pick her up and peek outside the door. Anne Elise is snug against my shoulder, and when I zipper up my black bubble jacket, only the top of her pink knit newborn's cap peeks out. No one is at the nursing station. I walk out into the hallway with Anne Elise. Every crime has its penalty, every bad bargain its purchase price. James shouldn't have given that Debauve et Gallais box to Laurel, nor should Laurel have seduced him. The hallway's totally empty. Just before the elevator opens for us, I look down the hall to make sure no one's spying on us. There's not a single person anywhere around. The elevator door opens. We step inside. When the elevator door closes behind us, I unzip my jacket a few inches to give Anne Elise more air. She's pleasantly warm against me, a snoozing bundle whose only crime is having been born to the wrong woman. A moment later, the elevator door dings open, letting us off. We walk through the sunshine-filled lobby, my new boots making a squishy sound with each step. Laurel's had her opportunities with my husband, and now I've got an opportunity with her baby.

PART TWO

Chapter Eighteen

JIM

I'm the celebration at the end of Laurel's day, the friendly face who'll stride into her room and make her forget the dreariness of being confined to bed. Tonight, I will tell her how beautiful she is, how darling and dear. This is what I tell myself as I hop out of my Volvo in the hospital parking lot. Today's my lucky day: an uptick in the precious metals market netted hundreds of thousands of dollars for even my risk-averse clients, and although, overdrawn on my credit cards, I was not positioned to take advantage of the market myself, it feels good knowing I had a hand in someone else's gravy train. Karma is a comes-around, goes-around thing: sooner or later, the luck I bestow on others will flow my way too.

Inside the hospital lobby, I'm greeted by a sign in the gift shop window proclaiming a two-for-one candy sale. "Make mine a Hershey's Bar and an Almond Joy," I say, whipping out my credit card. The young woman manning the cash register—probably a high school student working nights to earn a little weekend spending cash—tells me her other customers are not so enthusiastic as I am, prompting me to tell her of the miraculous birth of Anne Elise, "a girl who, if we're lucky, will one day grow to be as beautiful as you."

The girl blushes at the compliment, weaves her hand through her caramel-brown hair.

"I have a baby girl! And soon I will have two delicious chocolate bars: one for me and one for the new mother!"

The salesgirl swipes my credit card through her machine, but the message that displays on its screen is not to her liking. She frowns, scans the card a second time. "You say this is your first child?"

"My very first!"

She frowns again at her machine. This isn't the first time my card has been declined, but she's too young and polite to burst the bubble of my good fortune. She hands me back my credit card, hands me my chocolate bars, and cannot look me in the eye. Rather than making excuses for my overextended credit line, I feign oblivion at her generosity: she's taken it upon herself to commit a minor act of theft on my behalf, and what could be luckier than that?

I take the elevator up to the maternity ward, where weakened but elated new mothers, their faces rosy with exhaustion, stroll the hallways with their babies. Visiting hours in baby land is the most joyful time on the planet, people's spirits still soaring from witnessing the miracle of childbirth, and though babies cry, the sound that catches my ear is the cutesy baby talk new mothers, fathers, grandpapas, and friends coo to soothe the newborns.

Laurel's room, alone among all the rooms lining the corridor, is dark. A used Pampers lies on top of Anne Elise's bassinet—someone changed her diaper but forgot to throw out the old one—but Anne Elise herself isn't in the room, and Laurel is asleep, her sleep interrupted by her fitful moans and groans that make me believe her dreams are the stuff of struggles and foes. Though the room's lights are off, light pours in from the hallway. I sit on the leather recliner, fold my hands behind my head, and listen to the periodic laughter floating in from the hallways. Someone should bottle the good cheer and sense of well-being that seem to coat the entire maternity ward.

Laurel's not well when she awakens. Her eyes are hollow pits, little sinkholes that flutter open at intervals, flashing glimpses of panicked confusion. Her hand is a burning coal, hot, feverish. For the last half hour, I wondered where Anne Elise might be. More than likely, nurses carried her to the nursery so Laurel could sleep, but now Laurel croaks out Anne Elise's name. She pulls herself to a sitting position in her bed. She might be delusional, caught in a fever dream, so frantically do her eyes dash around the room.

"Laurel," I say, grabbing her hands. I'm not sure my presence even registers on her. "Are you all right?"

Laurel jerks her hand, but she can't move it far because her IV cord is wrapped around her bed railing, restraining her. She groans, the sound of her groan like two sticks clacking together. "I hate this thing," she says, freeing up the IV tubing with her free hand. "It's always getting snagged on something."

"Should I get a doctor? I can do that, my dear."

"Where's our baby?"

"She's okay. She's in the nursery."

"I'm c-c-cold," Laurel says, stuttering.

An extra blanket sits in the drawer of the nightstand. I toss it over Laurel, tucking its flimsy corners tight around her. She's burning up but refuses to let me call in a doctor because she says every time they treat her, she ends up feeling worse for their efforts. Sooner or later, the nurses or doctors are going to drop in on their rounds and check up on her anyways, so I stay close, holding her hand. Laurel's always struck me as a lost soul, a feral but fragile child who never learned how to develop friendships and stable relationships; admittedly, this was one of the things that drew me to her. She needed a friend, and I was patient and kind. She ate up my flattery and readily believed I was as wealthy as I represented myself to be.

"What's that smell?"

"Chocolate," I say, plucking the gift shop candy bars from my jacket pocket. "Today's your lucky day: Do you want Almond Joy or Hershey's?"

"That's not what I meant." Laurel breathes in deeply, the air passing through her nose in thistly scratches. "Something smells like shit."

It's the diaper she smells. I should have thrown it out when I saw it. "It's one of Anne Elise's dirty diapers. Someone left it out. I'll take care of it."

"She was here again."

"Who?"

Laurel points to the boot prints on the floor. "Tricia. That's who. She must have dropped by when I was napping. Thank god I was asleep so she couldn't harangue me again. She creeps me out."

"She wants to be friendly," I say, though I can't rightly think of an innocent reason Trish would choose to pal around with Laurel.

"Why are you always sticking up for her?"

"You catch more flies with sugar, honey. That's why," I say, not telling Laurel about Trish's private investigator or my surreptitious work to neutralize her efforts. Instead, not wanting to ramp up Laurel's alarm, I paint Trish as a harmless spurned lover working her way through the stages of her grief so that one hopefully soon day she'll give in to my request and divorce me. "Tricia's clinically depressed. She's popping Valiums as if they were candy. Last night, she made an elaborate meal and set the table with our good china and our silver setting pieces. She lit candles around the dinner table and then stared at the food for hours, too distraught to even eat. When I came home, the candles were little shrunken stubs, their dripping wax pooling beneath the candelabras, puddling onto the table. She's not well enough to think things through rationally. We've got our whole lives ahead of us. We can wait a few weeks. Trust me, honey. I'm not going anywhere."

"I don't care. You need to divorce her."

"I'm working on that."

"Not fast enough."

"Honey, let's not argue. You need your strength. Right now, you don't need tension. You've had medicines and antibiotics; what you need are happy thoughts. Toss aside your anger, your anxiety and jealousy. Project the thoughts you want to have. The future is built upon our expectations. Visualize yourself serene and happy if you want to actually be serene and happy. That's your prescription for happiness."

Laurel looks at me skeptically.

"I was thinking about you all day, honey. Can I tell you what I was thinking when I walked into the hospital to see you just now?"

Laurel never tires of hearing what I have to say about her. I give her a long look. Her unkempt hair hasn't been washed for days. Three days in the hospital have undone her exuberance and the healthy glow that pregnancy had bestowed upon her, replacing them with acne blemishes, an oily sheen, and an exhaustion that is almost palpable. Shadows hang beneath her eyes.

"As soon as I stepped onto the elevator, I looked forward to telling you how beautiful you are. It is something I like saying and something you deserve to hear as often as possible."

Laurel blushes, the color rising in her chalky cheeks. She looks at her feet, which stick out from the flimsy blanket I wrapped around her. "Thank you."

I raise my hand, gesturing for her silence. "But now I look at you, and what I see is tension and worry and fatigue. Don't do that to yourself. Don't worry about Tricia; worry about yourself. The Tricia thing will sort itself out."

"But how?"

I kiss Laurel. Her breath is sour, and she looks sick, but I've put her at ease, buying more time for me to figure out what to do about her, the baby, and Trish. For now, at least tonight, she won't tighten the screws and press me further to ditch anyone. It may not quite be happiness that spreads across her face but something more long-lasting: acceptance.

She wraps an arm around my shoulder and sighs. Someone else enters the room. My back is to the door. Laurel, seeing whoever comes into the room, becomes excited.

"Mom!"

"How sweet! You two were hugging!"

I turn around. Laurel's mother, Belinda, stands in the doorway, her face more made up than yesterday, her eyes ringed with kohl eyeliner. Polka-dot shifts must be her thing, for today she's wearing a green-and-red polka-dot shift, the kind of dress one might wear to make an impression at a holiday party.

"Ahh! Belinda! So good of you to visit Laurel again," I say.

Belinda sways over to Laurel's bed. She takes Laurel's hands and smiles. "Tully's out parking the car, but I wanted to run up and see you as soon as I could. I was thinking about you all night last night. I'm so glad you're keeping your baby."

Laurel starts shivering again, whether from emotion or infection, I can't tell. "Thank you, Mama."

"Oh, look! You're wearing the earrings I gave you," Belinda says, noticing one of the blue diamond studs on Laurel's earlobe. "They look good on you too."

"Oh, Mom. They're awesome. Thank you."

"Say, where's your baby?"

"She's in the nursery. The nurses took her there so Laurel could catch up on her rest."

"But I can still see her today, can't I?"

"Of course you can," I say, though I'm unsure exactly how to reclaim our daughter. Is it like a coat-check system? Do nurses give claim tickets every time they take your baby to the nursery? Or is retrieval conducted on the honor system, whereby you ask a nurse for your baby, and it's magically delivered to you?

Tully steps into the room carrying a grease-stained paper lunch sack I assume holds a sandwich, condiments, maybe a bag of corn chips he may or may not share with Belinda. Something's different about him, a businesslike courteousness that's inconsistent with the image I formed of him yesterday. The clothes he wears today—a button-down white shirt and gray slacks—seem plucked from a different closet than the one that supplied yesterday's dungarees and sweatshirt. He slaps me on the back and, straightening his gray-and-green-striped necktie, asks, "Hey, can I talk to you about something in the hallway?"

"You bet."

There's a bounce to Tully's step as I follow him to the hallway. Rather than steering us to the comfy couches in the waiting area, he stops at a trash can across the nurses' station. Mothers with their babies stroll around us. Tully drums his fingers against the glossy white wall. Though I have no doubt he could tell an entertaining story or two, he gazes at me as if he's got weightier matters in mind.

"So what do you want to talk to me about?"

"I didn't want to talk in front of the womenfolk. You know how they get." No one is anywhere near us, but Tully looks over his shoulder as if to make sure we're alone. "Now that we're family, I need your help."

Laurel's warning about Tully being dangerous comes back to me. Something about his slippery grin, his cosmetically too-bright smile makes me think he's about to ask something horrible of me. "Uh. Sure, Tully. What's up?"

"Tull. With you and me, the name's Tull. With everyone else, Tully." He crosses his fingers together the way people do when hoping for luck, yet with him, it's like he's signifying the formation of a pact between us. "I respect you. You know what I mean? So I want you to call me Tull. Okay?"

"Sure, Tull. That's mighty fine of you. Thanks."

He nods, slaps my back, gauges my reaction. "Say, can I trust you? I can trust you, right?"

"Trust me: I've got nothing but Laurel and Anne Elise's interests in my heart."

"That's not what I'm talking about. I'm not talking about them. I'm talking about me. What I'm asking is"—again he crosses his fingers—"now that we're family, you're going to be upfront, totally honest with me. I mean, you're not some jack-off who's going to piss me off something stupid, are you?"

"Tull. With you—*especially* with you—I'll be upfront. Count on that. Seriously. You can trust me. Lots of people do. I make my living helping rich people park their money into solid wealth generators. If I ever screwed any of them, I'd be in jail by now. So you can trust me."

Tully sucks down a breath of air. "Here's the thing: I do all right making money—at least lately—but I've got zero investment smarts. So here's where you come in: since you help rich people with their investments, help me with mine too. Okay?"

I feared this was going to happen—being hit up for free investment advice—but, frankly, I'm afraid of what he might do if I decline to help him. "Tull, what kind of investments do you want to make?"

Tully looks me in the eye. "The kind of investments that make money. Got it?"

"Tull. Please. You need to be more specific. Stocks, bonds, mutual funds, equity agreements, commodities, real estate—what are you comfortable with?" I ask.

Tully blinks, taps his fingers to the wall. A baby wails not far from where we stand, and Tully asks me to repeat myself. He's what people in my profession would call a rube, but I'm not going to take advantage of him.

"Tull. You're a smart man. Investments aren't like horse races. You don't just waltz up to the pari-mutuel window, slap down your money, and five minutes later when the race is over, collect your winnings. Even with a solid short-term investment, your money won't be accessible for six to twelve months."

"That long? Months?" Tully grimaces. "Can I just give you the money and let you take care of everything?"

"How much money are we talking about?"

Tully hands me his oil-stained paper lunch sack with a solemnity that makes me suspect there's more than a ham sandwich inside. Holding the bag, my hands shake. He locks his eyes on me, and instantly I know a terrible secret of some kind lies within the bag.

"Go ahead. Open it."

I peek inside. The bag is stuffed with hundred-dollar bills. Thousands of dollars' worth of honest-to-goodness Benjamins. "Holy shit."

Tully beams with pride. "Now you see why I wanted to talk to you in private?" The money smells like motor oil and battery acid, smells I've never associated before with currency. Every single note is covered with grease or discolored with caustic chemical substances. "I've been keeping it in my toolbox at the garage, earning zero interest on it, so I know you can do better than that."

I've never seen so much cash stuffed into a bag before. "Are you a drug dealer or something?"

Tully's eyes flare open. "It's not nice to question a man's livelihood. If we're going to be doing business, I don't need you asking questions. Got it?"

It takes me a moment to gather my wits and utter an apology. "Tull, I swear, I've never seen so much cash before in one spot. I've handled checks for millions of dollars, but it doesn't have the same effect, you know? I mean, man, what I'm saying is that you've done real well for yourself."

Again, Tully beams. "I have, haven't I? You going to tell Laurel how well I'm doing?"

"Totally your call," I respond, thinking this might be a trick question designed to test my loyalties. "I understand if you wish to keep this to yourself, but I'm sure Laurel would appreciate knowing how successful you've become."

"Sure. What the hell. Let her know her old man is doing good. She'll treat me with more respect this way."

"That's the ticket."

"So you're going to help me," Tully says, tossing me the bag. "I want you to take this money and make me more money. Invest it like you think it needs to be invested. There's something like ten thousand dollars in there, and I can probably get you some more fairly soon. Okay?"

What Tully's asking—to parlay this bundle of undocumented under-the-table cash into bona fide fungible assets—is the textbook definition of money laundering, a violation of countless federal SEC statutes that could land my butt in jail, but it's my suspicion that federal watchdogs are more adept at flagging multimillion-dollar laundering schemes than the small-potatoes ten- or fifteen-thousand-dollar stuff.

We head back into Laurel's room, where Laurel and Belinda still chat about earrings, but though Laurel's been awake for only an hour, she can barely stay awake. I'm about to disobey Laurel and fetch a doctor but am beaten to the punch when Lois Belcher, the lactation consultant, arrives. Immediately, she asks if Laurel's all right. Has she been breathing well? Is she feverish? Does it still hurt around her episiotomy? To each question, Laurel shrugs, deepening Lois Belcher's concern. She asks me how long Laurel's been like this, and I tell her the truth: "Ever since giving birth, frankly."

"You should've told someone she's been like this," Lois Belcher says. Until this moment, I haven't seen her so cross. The astonishment I'd been feeling over Tully's bag of dirty money dissipates. I tell Lois Belcher I suggested as much to Laurel, but Laurel told me not to bother anyone, which doesn't impress the lactation consultant. She bends over and presses a button on the panel at the side of Laurel's bed, summoning doctors.

"Do you think she'll be all right?" Belinda says. "I was telling her about this other set of earrings I wanted to give her. Real pretty ones, with little bitty freshwater pearls."

"Hey, can you get someone to fetch our baby from the nursery for us?" I ask Lois Belcher, eager to see my baby again. For all the thrill of seeing Tully's money, I'd rather lay my eyes on Anne Elise. "Please bring us our baby. Someone took her to the nursery. Can you get her for us?"

Lois Belcher shoots me a quizzical look. "She's in the nursery? I thought—"

"Yes, bring my baby to me," Laurel says. She closes her eyes, takes a deep breath. "I bet she'll be hungry again."

Something's not quite right in Lois Belcher's expression. She tilts her head as if momentarily lost in thought. "Okeydokey. Let me go get her for you," she says, going toward the door. "I'll bring her back in a jiffy."

I watch her as she leaves the room. As soon as she's in the hallway, the speed of her footsteps quickens. Laurel, too, senses something's amiss. Tully drums his fingers against a nightstand and then a table and then Laurel's bed railing. A thin, jittery man pokes his head into the room. He's no doctor, just someone from the hospital's housekeeping staff. He rolls a bucket into the room and mops away the dirty boot prints from the floor. We watch him dip the mop into his bucket and wring it dry, the dirty water sloshing around in his bucket as he rolls it from one end of the room to the other.

"Damn. Someone sure had messy feet," Tully says.

"You're telling me," the housekeeper says, leaning on his mop. He looks to be about seventeen, maybe the same age as the gift shop cashier downstairs. He pulls a bandana from his back pocket and wipes his forehead. "I cleaned tracks all up and down the hallway. They went all the way to the elevator."

"Thank you. Thank you for cleaning," I say.

"Anytime," the housekeeper says.

We watch the housekeeper roll the bucket out of the room. And then we look at each other, each of us wondering why no one has returned with Anne Elise. Laurel moans. Minutes pass. A tedium that's not to my liking enters into our unspoken conversation. I stretch out my arms, look at my wristwatch, and feign surprise at how late it's become.

"Oh my gosh! I just remembered I'm supposed to call one of my clients and update him on the precious metals market."

"You and your calls," Laurel says, shaking her head.

"Hey, a man's gotta work, right?"

To this, Tully says, "Right on, man."

And with that, I'm out in the hallway and at the pay phone in the waiting area again, dialing the number that's on the business card Larry Simpkins gave me yesterday.

"Hey. Remember me?" I say when Larry Simpkins answers. "I'm the guy from last night who said he was going to call you."

Simpkins remembers all right. "I've been waiting by my phone. I thought you were never going to call."

"Well, I'm calling right now. Let's talk."

"No can do," Simpkins said. "Another client just stepped into my office. Let's make it in an hour. Is that okay? And let's do it face-to-face. Come down to my office. You have the address, right?"

I look at the business card. "Sure do."

As we hang up, I feel sorry for whoever has parked himself or herself on a chair in Simpkins's office. In a few minutes, after Simpkins unveils the bundle of black-and-white photos documenting the spouse's infidelity, the customer's life will be torn asunder. Sacred "for better or worse till death do us part" vows render a cruel mockery. Simpkins is a merchant of despair, a ruiner of lives. But as I dwell on Simpkins's perniciousness, I'm hit cold with the realization that it was probably through Simpkins that Trish first learned of my affair. What must she have thought when Simpkins opened up his dossier file and handed her a picture of me and Laurel? She must have been gutted. Just thinking about it makes me regret everything. She must have stumbled out of his office and felt like killing Laurel. Or killing me. Or killing herself.

What's strange is that so far Simpkins has given no indication he recognizes me from his earlier investigations. Is he that unobservant? Or were his pictures of Laurel and me so blurry that he couldn't get a good read on me?

Downstairs, I stop off at the gift shop again, but though the two-for-one candy sale sign remains in the window, the salesgirl's less enthusiastic to see me this second time. She bites her lip, apologizes, and tells me she can't sell me any more candy bars.

"That's okay," I say. "Today's your lucky day."

"Huh?"

I reach into Tully's lunch sack and place a hundred-dollar bill into her startled hands. She probably doesn't earn so much money in a week. "When the gods of good fortune smile upon you, never be afraid to let a little of your luck rub off on total strangers. Spread the karma far and wide. What comes around, goes around. That's what I always say."

Chapter Nineteen

TRISH

My whole body is electrified as I walk through the sunlit hospital lobby with Anne Elise under my coat. Everything is jittery and wonderful. No one gives me a second look. I know the difference between right and wrong, but I'm stunned how easy it is to steal a newborn. Everything is pleasantly warm, the sunlight pouring into the lobby through the huge windows and skylight, dappling the terra-cotta tile floor. Nothing seems amiss. Nurses rush across the lobby, responding to an emergency on one of the upper floors, and an elderly lady sits alone on a bench by the coffee kiosk saying a rosary to herself. I'm a pampered-looking woman of a certain age whom no one would suspect of felonious intent. There's a burbling fountain half-surrounded by potted palms and enough greenery to make anyone forget it's the dead of winter. People walk with trepidation to the information desk, bracing themselves for the in-patient procedures that will be performed upon them. Others inquire on the status of convalescing relatives. In the atrium, a glass door opens to let me outside, and when I step through it, I'm amazed no alarms go off, no flashing lights or klaxons alerting the world to my theft.

Halfway to the car, I look over my shoulder, expecting security officers to burst out of the hospital and chase after me. Wind whips icy snowflakes against my cheeks. The siren of an approaching ambulance catches my attention. No plausible reason exists for how or why someone might innocently abscond with another woman's baby, and yet it's already too late to turn back. I fumble for my car keys, open the door to my Mercedes.

I've taken six or eight Valiums, and thoughts zip through my head with a jangled alacrity that, in and of itself, takes my breath away. Motherhood, I tell myself, is a great adventure: where you get on is not as important as where you get off. Taking Anne Elise was a crime of opportunity, but by the time I stick the key in the ignition, plans have solidified in my head. Already my thoughts plow forward to the future. I'll be a better mother than Laurel could ever be. Anne Elise's girlhood will be a magical adventure of foreign-language-immersion classes and petits fours, horses and purebred puppies. I will be the mother every child dreams for. Together, we'll stroll into the Ritz-Carlton for mother/daughter tea dates, we'll shop till we drop, dress in matching skirts, subscribe to Kennedy Center ballet performances, and drink chocolate milkshakes whenever we damn well please.

But now, not having a proper baby seat, I conceal Anne Elise under my bubble jacket while we drive into Chinatown. Emerging clouds cast gloominess onto what had been a bright afternoon, the streets slick with February frost and slush, prompting extra caution and a light foot on the gas pedal. Anne Elise's soft downy head wobbles against my chest. Such a bright, inquisitive baby; she's probably trying to peek out from my bubble jacket, the curiosity in her surroundings almost palpable in how she opens her eyes to take in not only my Mercedes' nut-brown napa leather interior but also the bustling city blocks around us, the honking traffic, and the flashing lights and bright signs of the storefronts around us. Her first taste of DC is of bumper-to-bumper traffic and street-side vendors standing behind tables piled high with T-shirts, baseball hats, and shot glass kitsch geared toward the tourist trade. Pedestrians crowd the sidewalk.

All my life, I've maintained control of situations and emotions, but twenty minutes with Anne Elise have transformed me into a reckless felon. At the next stoplight, I pop a Valium and another, and then guilt overtakes me, for the prescription bottle warns against operating automobiles while under Valium's influence. I don't want to endanger Anne Elise. Already, I'm discombobulated by the fear of being apprehended. I haven't thought this through. How could I not think this through?

I can't remember where I'm going, but then I remember the appointment with my private investigator. He's due to present evidence that Laurel's not fit for motherhood—which, now that I've stolen her baby, is information I no longer need. However, if I fail to keep the appointment, Simpkins will become suspicious. I can't just barge into his office one day and demand he dig up the nastiest secrets and foulest deeds someone committed and the next day lose all enthusiasm in the subject. And yet he'll be more suspicious if, on the same day Laurel's baby disappears, I show up in his office with a newborn child I can't account for. He's a smart man. He'll find out Laurel's baby is missing. He'll connect the dots, and when he does, I wouldn't put it past him to call the police.

I breathe deeply, count to ten, gather my wits, and channel my father's wisdom and the inner Riggs ruthlessness of my bloodlines. My father once told me I can handle any situation thrown in my path. That's what makes me different from my mother—I'm not taking James's affair lying down, sulking, in bed. On the most stressful day of his life, my father called me into Savory Mew's hideaway office. Leaked documents had just revealed that money laundered through his bank financed the al-Qaeda 9/11 terrorist attacks. Journalists were harassing him. Senators and congressmen called the house trying to make sense of what happened. "Dogs may bark," my father said, looking up at me from the pile of papers scattered around his desk, "but the caravan needs to move on. We've got the diligence, you and me, to keep the caravan moving. That's what Riggses do: we shove past the barking dogs."

I grab my phone at the next stoplight, call Simpkins's office. When he picks up, I ask, "What did you find out about Laurel Bloom?"

Simpkins hems for a moment as if trying to place who I am. "Weren't you supposed to come by my office? In a half hour?"

"I can't meet with you today, actually. But what did you find out?"

"There's nothing to tell. I searched. I searched big time. There's no dirt out there on Laurel Bloom."

"How can that be?"

"Because she's clean. That's why. She's a decent person who happened to get knocked up by your husband. It happens. In all my time investigating people, I've never seen anything like this before: a person with no skeletons in her closet. Besides hooking up with your husband, that is."

I think back to Laurel's awkwardness, her brusqueness, her downright rudeness and disdain toward me. These are not the traits of a young lady with a proper upbringing or someone with no skeletons in her closet or the traits one expects of a law-abiding citizen, but rather they're harbingers of criminal activity, drug and alcohol use, licentious behavior, disciplinary actions, academic expulsions, a string of mental health issues, and perhaps a spate of homelessness, moral failings that will induce queasiness in anyone. Though I no longer need to petition the city to take away her child, Simpkins's refusal to dig in to Laurel's past angers me. Why can't he do his job right? If something goes wrong with my plan to keep her baby, I'm going to need all the dirt I can get on her to blackmail her into not pressing charges against me. Why can't Simpkins give me the satisfaction of finding out the details?

"Do you want to know what I think?" I say, just as Anne Elise erupts with a loud cry.

"What's that?"

I rub Anne Elise's back, worried that Simpkins might have heard Anne Elise's cry. It's been hours since Laurel last nursed her, but miraculously, I succeed in soothing her within moments, making me think I really *am* cut out for motherhood. She looks at me with her big baby-blue eyes, and my attention on her is total. I adjust her newborn's cap, tickle her chin, which, surprisingly, produces no reaction from her, and yet I sense the affection in her eyes, the latent mirth about to explode from her pink lips.

"Ma'am. You were saying?"

"Huh?"

"I don't have all day. You were going to tell me what you think about my findings?"

"Mr. Simpkins, how do I know you even bothered to investigate Laurel Bloom? How do I know you're not a scam artist? For two thousand dollars, a client deserves evidence that you've at least tried to do a proper investigation."

If I wanted to be nasty, I could phone my lawyer and petition the appropriate city regulators to revoke Simpkins's license. That much I'm sure of. But the process would take months, depriving me of the immediate satisfaction I crave. "Mr. Simpkins. Do you want to make a deal? I'm not going to file a complaint about you. I don't want the city to strip you of your license, which I'm sure they'd do in light of all the money you've so far defrauded me of."

"Why not?"

"Because I want you finish the job. Destroy that woman. Do you understand? Tell me everything about her. Tell me significant dirt, even if it means, well, *accidentally* accessing confidential legally protected databases. Am I making myself clear?"

The temperature around me seems to increase by ten degrees. The light changes. I step on the gas. Simpkins clears his throat. "Mrs. Wainsborough. You do understand the risks you're asking me to undertake will come at an extra fee, don't you?"

"I'll give you, say, fourteen hundred more dollars if you finish your investigation to my satisfaction," I say, making up the number on the fly. "One thousand, four hundred dollars. But only if you dig up something really incriminating on that woman."

"You said yesterday you didn't have any more money."

"I miscalculated. So do we have a deal?"

"I think there's a fair chance I can find something of interest for you," Simpkins says. "Give me another day, and I promise I'll move things forward on this investigation to your satisfaction. Shall we meet tomorrow? In my office? Say, about noon?"

Chapter Twenty

LAUREL

I'm no forget-me-not, no drip-dry girl to be left hanging from the shower-curtain rail, but this is how I feel, waiting for the doctors to examine me. Time is flippy-floppy. I'm feverish, and every time I open my eyes, it's like ages have passed since I last stared out at the water-stained acoustic-tile ceiling above my hospital bed. My parents sit beside me making stilted conversation, none of us knowing what to make of each other after this long absence in each other's lives. Every inch of my body is sore, inflamed, perspiring. Milk leaks out of my engorged breasts and slicks warm and oozy over my chest. Even my earlobes hurt.

"What's keeping them so long from bringing Zerena here?" Belinda asks. She stares into a compact mirror and touches up the kohl around her eyes. She never used to wear much makeup, and it's good to see she's making an effort to look good. "You'd think they'd be quicker getting your baby for us."

"Relax. They've got gazillions of babies in the nursery, and they're making sure they bring the right one." Tully gets up from the recliner. Like a caged wolf trying to outpace the confinement of a zoo cage, he paces the length of the room, back and forth and back again, grinding his teeth.

"Can you sit down?" Belinda asks. "You're making me nervous."

"I've got things on my mind, okay?"

"You did it, didn't you?"

"Did what?"

"You know. You gave our money away."

Tully tilts his head to one side, gathers his graying hair in one hand, and with a rubber band, bunches it into the kind of high stylish ponytail you see on badass thugs in music videos and old *Miami Vice* episodes. "I didn't give it away. I invested it."

"It's his new look," Belinda says of my father's ponytail. Ten years ago, he would've questioned the manhood of any guy who wore a ponytail. "It's still hard for me to get used to him looking this way. What do you think?"

Although I can barely keep my eyes open, I raise my head off the pillow to give Tully a better look. He holds his head high, beaming with a boyish pride. I, too, can't get over his new look. Unable to muster the energy to shampoo my hair these last few days, I wish I had half his vigor for hair care.

"So what do you think, Laurel?" Tully asks.

"You look nice. So what is it you're investing in, Daddy?"

"Do you think I can trust that man of yours?"

"Jimmy? Sure, you can trust him. He's as solid as they come."

"How'd you meet him?"

"One night, he brought in a couple of his clients for dinner at the Italian restaurant where I was waitressing, and straightaway, we hit it right off," I say, telling my parents an edited version of our courtship. Jimmy had been upfront with me, telling me he was married. At first, all he wanted to do was talk and take long walks. He was slow to ask to hold my hand, but as soon as I met him, I knew I had spotted the man I was destined to spend the rest of my life with. While I'd been in juvenile detention, I'd been made to feel that, even after I was released, I'd always be viewed as an inmate, a reprobate, a criminal, in most people's eyes. Embarking on a new life with him would mean I could forever close that previous incarcerated chapter of my life. "The night after that and every night for the next week, Jimmy showed up at the restaurant alone, grabbed a seat at a corner table, ordered a plate of calamari *fritti*, and nursed glasses of grappa. One night, after I got off for the evening, he sauntered up to me and said—and this, I'll never forget—'Let me be your Mr. Wonderful.'"

"Yeah? So what happened?" Tully asks.

"So I let him, silly."

I think back to those first encounters with Jimmy. Washington is best experienced on mild spring evenings when the temperature is neither cold nor warm. Most nights, we hailed evening cabs to the Jefferson Memorial and strolled around the Tidal Basin, hand in hand, the glow of the city lights on the water, the lingering scent of the cherry blossoms in the air, the sound of the breeze rippling the water, and the excitations of love filling me with longing. I leaned my head on his shoulder when we sat on park benches, called his name just to hear the sound of it coming from my lips. Nothing I did or said irked Jimmy. He had dark-chestnut hair and crushed-velvet-brown eyes, and he was the handsomest man I'd ever met. He said things he knew would make me laugh. He complimented me for my quirky sense of humor, whispered how beautiful I was.

I knew it was wrong to be spending time with a married man, but I needed to take the one chance I'd so far been offered to snatch a semblance of a respectable life for myself. I invited him into my apartment. Having spent my teenage years in juvenile detention, I missed out on the normal first crushes and nervous pecks on the cheek a regular high school boyfriend might have provided. Before I met Jimmy, I feared that having lost out on that necessary introduction to healthy romantic relationships, I would forever be unsuitable for an adult relationship. Jimmy put me at ease, made me feel like a decent person. Taking him back to my apartment hastened the connection between us. I began to see him as more than a man who needed a child and more than just a means for me to break out of my slumdum waitressing life. I began to see him as a humorous, caring man. A nice man. A man who needed me in his life.

"Jimmy serenaded with me old songs when we walked, dropping down to his knees and making me feel as if I were in a movie. Sinatra songs. Big band songs. Songs that were popular before any of us were born. That's how far back Jimmy's mind works."

"So that's why I should trust him? Because he sings Sinatra?" Tully says, saying "Sinatra" in a snooty voice. Music, for him, scarcely exists beyond the bourbon-voiced confines of what used to be called "southern-fried rock." Lynyrd Skynyrd. ZZ Top. That kind of lazy-boy unimaginative junk. He crosses his arms and drums the fingers of one hand over his elbow. I hadn't remembered him being so antsy, but he paces the room as if looking for something to wallop.

"Dad. You can trust him. One night, we were walking in Georgetown. You know that old bank at the corner of Wisconsin and M Street? The one with the gold dome that was built centuries ago?"

"The old Riggs Bank building?"

"That's the one. One night we passed a homeless bum sitting cross-legged against the marble columns with his palm out, begging for cash. Jimmy pulled out his wallet and gave the bum a crisp fifty-dollar bill. Fifty dollars! I asked Jimmy if he worried the bum would waste the money on booze, and do you know what Jimmy said? Jimmy said, 'What makes you think *I* won't waste the money on booze if I kept the money for myself?'"

"That's why I'm supposed to trust him? Because he wastes money on bums?"

"Dad. Jimmy didn't care about the money because, to him, it was nothing. He told me his family used to *own* that bank. They used to own the whole Riggs banking chain!"

"Holy shit! You've hooked yourself a Riggs man?"

"Uh-huh!"

Tully whistles. "See, Belinda? I knew I could trust him. I was right giving him your tooth money."

My mother turns to me, her expression that of resignation. "I need root canals and serious work on my molars. Tully's been making some money on the side so I can get dental surgery to repair my teeth."

"That's great, Mom!"

"Maybe. We'll see. Your father gave all that money to Jimmy tonight to invest for us."

Tully throws up his arms. "It's going to be all right. Jimmy's A-okay. You heard our little girl tell you that. A guy like that—a *Riggs* guy—ain't ever going to screw you out of your teeth. Isn't that right, Laurel?"

Someone knocks on the door, and when I look up, I see Lois Belcher with two men dressed in gray suits. Thirty minutes have passed since she left to fetch Zerena, and the uneasy concern on her face raises my anxiety. None of the bunch has my baby. It strikes me that this is the first time anyone—nurses, doctors, orderlies, or even the boy who sweeps the floor each morning—has seen fit to knock before entering my room.

"Miss Bloom?" Lois Belcher says, stepping forward. "We've been looking for Anne Elise in the nursery. Do you recall when she was taken there? Or who carried her there?"

"I was napping when that happened. Jimmy was here. Jimmy told me someone came and took Zerena to the nursery so I could sleep better."

The two men behind Lois Belcher exchange glances. One turns his attention to the beat-up clipboard he's carrying while the other asks, in a low voice, "Zerena? Who's Zerena?" Both men are linebacker big and meaty, tall, muscular men with electric gizmos in their ears and walkie-talkies holstered to their belts, but it takes me an extra moment to realize neither are doctors: they're hospital security staffers.

"Ma'am . . . please think carefully," the man with the clipboard says. Despite his huge size, he's got normal-sized hands and the kind of chubby face that under any other circumstances would give him a friendly appearance. Now, though, he speaks with a slow, deliberate voice. "Was there anything suspicious earlier today before you fell asleep? Where did Jimmy go? Is it possible to talk to him right now? It's real urgent we get to the bottom of this as soon as possible."

"Where's Zerena?" I ask, though I'm already afraid what the answer might be. "Why haven't you brought her to me like you said you were going to do?"

"Your daughter's missing," Lois Belcher says.

The news knocks me senseless, overwhelms me, muscles into the very core of my being. I feel things draining inside me, my hopes and dreams washing away. I stutter, "Miss-ss-ing?"

"Ma'am. We're doing our best to locate her."

"Where is she?"

"We don't know, ma'am. She's missing."

Everyone—the security officers, Lois Belcher, even my mother— seems to be saying that word at once: "missing." I lower the bed railing so I can hop to the floor. I'm not about to take any of this lying down, but as I lower my feet to the floor, dizziness comes over me. In my clumsiness, my IV cord snags on something. It's been days since I last stood up on my own power, and it's like I'm a baby wobbling on my feet, and the next thing I know is that the IV stand smashes against the wall.

"Ma'am. Stay calm. We're doing everything we can."

"Oh my god. Before I fell asleep, Tricia was here," I say, catching my breath. I remember dreaming about her in the room, but as I think about it, it seems like it was more than a dream. A fuzzy memory, maybe. A sickly green feeling rushes over me. I remember her lifting up the box of chocolates Jimmy bought her, how she cursed my name. Strange, hexagonal boot tracks covered the floor. Surely, those were her boots that made those marks. I can't believe Tricia would run off with my baby—but then, thinking it over, I can totally believe it. Everything clicks in place in my mind. However many times that snake sheds her skin, she'll always be a snake. Tricia was with me before I fell asleep—I'm convinced of this. She was the one who changed Zerena's diaper. When I woke up, my IV cord was wrapped around the bed railing, cutting off the antibiotic's flow into my arm. At the time, I thought somehow I snagged it myself, but now there's no doubt in my mind she was responsible. "Tricia. She must have done it."

My mother, alarmed, reaches over and places a hand on my shoulder. "Honey? Who's Tricia?"

Chapter Twenty-One

Jim

Simpkins's entire office is about 150 square feet, not much bigger than the interior of the cargo vans parked in the parking garage just beyond the room's hollow-core metal door. The decor is minimal—a coat rack, upon which hangs his sheepskin jacket; metal chairs; metal desk; metal filing cabinets; and a credenza—all the furniture painted battleship gray to match the concrete floor and the shadows that hang below Simpkins's eyes. Maybe camouflage is what he's after, but some office-supply store must've had a serious gray sale around the time Simpkins started up his little operation. Even the coffee mugs and the computers and inkjet printers are gray.

Simpkins rises from his chair and extends his hand in greeting. "I didn't know if you'd show up."

"A successful man abides by his schedule," I say. The lone plant in the office, a hanging philodendron, looks like it died six months ago, so shriveled are its vines. With no windows or appreciable air circulation, spending eight or more hours a day in this cramped space must be seriously soul sucking, the kind of fate you wouldn't wish on anyone but your boss. Something hisses on the other side of the shared concrete block wall where, likely, the building's boiler room is located. "Dude, you've got a sweet little detective cave going on in here!"

Simpkins lifts his wire-rimmed glasses and rubs his eyes. "To be frank, I'm trying to save on office expenses. It's all part of my master business plan. For now, I'm working in this pit. That's why I don't like to meet new clients here. In a couple weeks, though, if I play my cards right, I should be able to afford better office space."

I swivel my chair around to take in the sports posters on the walls. "Simpkins, trust me. You're making a smart move, eschewing pricier office space so you can pocket more money for yourself. Who wants to pay more rent than they have to? Who needs flash? Who needs a penthouse suite or an office window when you have money in your pocket?"

Everything about Simpkins looks turgid and bloodshot. A newbie to the world of boozy bonding, he's still hungover from our encounter last night, but I've got just what he needs. Having stopped off at Potomac Wines & Spirits, an M Street purveyor famous throughout the city for its selection of Scotland's finest exports, I lay on his desk a bottle of twenty-one-year-old Macallan single-malt Scotch I purchased with three of Tully's Benjamins. I pull open the bottle's cork top and inhale the peaty vapors.

"This'll go down way smoother than the rotgut we drank last night," I say, tilting the Macallan toward Simpkins. "Drink up, sport!"

Simpkins, green at the gills, takes a pusillanimous swig, barely enough to wet the whistle. His bloodshot eyes widen as the Scotch scorches his throat. He winces.

"Pretty smooth, eh?"

Simpkins nods, his lips braced tight as if in pain.

"So suppose we get started. Did you pass on any information about that Laurel Bloom to the spurned wife?"

Simpkins lifts up his wire-rimmed glasses and, tilting his head, squints at me. Without his glasses, he looks older, wiser, and prone to bouts of alertness. "How did you know the woman's name?"

"Huh?"

"Laurel Bloom. You said her name. How'd you know her name?"

I'm not sure what he's getting at—but then it hits me: he'd been operating under the assumption I had no personal knowledge about the case, which is good because that means he truly has no clue who I am. Nothing is to be gained if he knows of my involvement with Laurel. Or with Trish. "You must have mentioned it last night. At the bar."

"No, I didn't," Simpkins says, his voice firm, insistent. "I never publicly acknowledge the name of someone I've been investigating."

"Sure you did. Maybe after your second or third drink." I weave my hands together, plant them on my knee. "Liquor loosens lips. Everyone knows that. Otherwise, how else would I have known?"

Simpkins puts his glasses back on but continues to stare at me.

"So tell me: Did you pass on any information about the girl in the hospital to the wife?"

"You told me you'd make it worth my while if I don't. I held on to my end of the bargain. This is America. Now make it worth my while."

Money. It always comes down to money. I grab $2,000 out of Tully's paper lunch sack, matching the amount Simpkins said Trish gave him yesterday. Simpkins reaches for the moola. Many of the bills are crumpled, mangled, or otherwise greased and torn at their edges. But money is money: it's all good. Simpkins, however, wrinkles his nose at it.

"Don't you like money?"

"This money's dirty."

"It's not polite to question a man and his money." Saying this, I'm reminded of Tully and the affront he took at the accusation of it being drug money. Maybe the money's dirty, but it's the only money I have. Simpkins picks up another hundred-dollar bill and scrunches his eyes at it, a grimace on his face. Perhaps it's the hangover or the sip of top-notch hooch, but it's almost as if he decides he doesn't need my money. He grins contemptuously. I surreptitiously switch back on my phone's recording function, so suspicious am I of his change in behavior. "Hey, who's to say which money is cleaner than others? All money is dirty when you come down to it."

Simpkins paws one of the bills, rubbing it between his fingers. When he opens his hand, releasing the bill back onto his desk, his fingertips are black with grease. "That's what I meant."

"What's a little dirt between friends, right? If God didn't want money to be dirty, he wouldn't have invented hand soap. Or regulatory agencies."

The quip gets a little rise out of Simpkins. He grins, but just as I think I've got him coming around to being friendly again, he opens his desk drawer, pulls out a bottle of hand sanitizer, and squirts a dab into his hands. Years ago, I met Al Gore at a meet-and-greet for would-be venture capitalists looking to fund a renewable energy start-up he was fronting. This would have been two or three years after he lost the 2000 presidential election, and Gore was already viewed as a political has-been, yet I found him charming and in firm control of the facts and figures of his presentation. Afterward, Gore pulled me aside for a glass of port. We shared a dry sense of humor and swapped anecdotes about my father-in-law, whom I gathered had a hand in Gore's 2000 presidential fundraising operation. Later, as we shook hands and bid each other heartfelt *Hey, it's been great meeting you!* adieus, an aide appeared at Gore's side with a bottle of lemon-scented hand-sanitizing gel, making me feel as if Gore and/or his aide suspected me of being contaminated with germs—which is how I feel watching Simpkins sanitize his hands: icky.

"So, Mister—hey, what did you say your name was?" Simpkins asks.

"I didn't. Remember?"

Simpkins takes another underwhelming swig of the Macallan. I'm honestly surprised he hasn't figured out who I am or why I've such a vested interest in the affairs of a spurned wife and the young woman who gave birth at Sibley.

"I've got bad news," Simpkins says, setting down the bottle.

My head jerks up.

"Inflation. It creeps up on you. You know what I mean?"

"What are you talking about?"

"That woman yesterday, the one who thought she was getting a good deal at two thousand dollars for all the dirt I could dig up on that chick in the hospital?"

"Yeah? What about her?"

Simpkins eyes me for what seems like an exceptionally long time, unnerving me. "She ponied up another fourteen hundred dollars today."

I grab the bottle and take a healthy, man-sized swig of the Macallan. Closing my eyes, I hold the Scotch in my mouth for a good five seconds, reveling in its taste. "So what's this mean?"

"You're in a bidding war. That's what this means. I can't say for certain, but I'm pretty sure I could squeeze a couple hundred dollars more out of her, too."

"A couple hundred?"

"Yep." Simpkins folds his hands together again. His smile is the greasy smile of a used-car salesman fleecing an aging pensioner out of his last $1,000 for an ancient Ford Festiva that'll break down as soon as it's driven off the lot. As much as I want to hate him, I'm astounded at his stupidity: Trish could afford to fork over way more than a few hundred dollars. Surely, he knows this. But he doesn't. He has no idea who Trish is. Simpkins takes the Macallan bottle from my hand and raises it to his lips, but rather than taking another slight sip, he gulps down the kind of huge desperate swig a man takes when throwing himself at the mercies of stupid fate or searching for courage. He wipes his mouth against the arm of his Adidas track jacket. "So how much more do you think I might be able to squeeze out of you?"

It's me against Trish in a bidding war I can't afford to lose, which is unfortunate: me, with no real money of my own, pitted against my wealthy wife. If bidding is to go on piecemeal, each day Simpkins hitting us up to raise the ante, I'm bound to lose. My only hope is to blow Trish out of the water with an insanely high opening bid.

"I can guarantee you one thing: I've got way more money than your other client."

"Prove it."

Loath as I am to part with Tully's cash, I toss the entire bag onto Simpkins's desk. Even after what I've already given to him, plus the gift shop candy bars and Macallan, about $8,000 remains in the oil-stained lunch sack, enough dirty cash that Simpkins will need two bottles of hand sanitizer by the time he's through counting it.

"How much is in here?"

"A shitload. That's how much. Do I win the bidding war? Or should I take my money and walk away?"

Simpkins glances into Tully's money bag.

"You've got ten seconds to make up your mind, Simpkins. What are you going to do?"

Simpkins, like me, has likely not seen so much cash in one place before, but, greed being the world's greatest motivator, he rubs his thumb through the stubble on his chin and angles his head at me as if to figure a way to outsmart me out of more cash.

"By your silence, I'm assuming you'd rather I take my money back," I say, eager not to appear too anxious.

"I'll take your money. I won't tell the wife anything I found out."

"Ahh! You're as smart as I thought you were, taking the bird in the hand rather than gambling on what the wife might be willing to throw into the bush."

Simpkins should be ecstatic, but instead he's underwhelmed. That or he's an incredibly calm poker-faced man too wary and wily to let anyone guess his emotions. Tonight, he'll stroll into Taylor's and tell his pal how he gamed me out of a whole shitload of money, but tomorrow, after he fills out a deposit slip and drops off the money at his bank, he'll rack his brain for ways he could've extracted more money out me. I, too, should be elated, but I'm no closer to amassing the boatload of money I need to make good on my investment tip, and now I'm ten grand in the hole to Tully.

"Tell me what you found out about this woman who had the baby. At Sibley, you said, didn't you?"

"That was never part of the deal." Simpkins's voice hardens. Perhaps he believes I was bidding against Trish out of purely altruistic notions. "You never told me you wanted the information yourself."

"It's the winners who make the rules. That's the first rule you should know about operating in this town. Whoever pays the most gets to write the rules of the game. How could a man as smart as you not know this? Tell me about Laurel Bloom."

Simpkins reaches behind him to open a drawer of his metal filing cabinet. The manila folder he grabs out of the drawer is slim, perhaps containing ten sheets of paper, but the first thing I notice is one of Laurel's sonogram pictures. I have no idea how he hacked into the hospital records to get that sonogram picture, but my esteem for his sleuthing abilities skyrockets, and yet, watching the way he studies that sonogram picture, I get nervous. A grin appears on Simpkins's face. He picks up a pencil and writes something in the folder, takes another drink from the Scotch bottle, and then fishes out a nude photo of Laurel and some young blond-haired, blue-eyed guy who must be as young as her. They're lying on sumptuous red silk sheets atop a four-poster queen-sized canopy bed, sated smiles on both their faces.

"Who's that?" I ask, steadying my voice to mask the jealousy rocking through me. In the photo, Laurel's gorgeous, more gorgeous than I've ever seen her in real life, but there's that other guy nuzzled up against her, his possessive arm around her naked waist.

"That's the girl—Laurel Bloom—with the guy who fathered the child. Her phone's got intimate selfies the two of them took together back last May and June. If you do the math, going back nine months from when she had her baby, this is the guy who would have been with her back when they, um, you know."

I take the photo in my hands. Though I maintain my calm, inside, I'm sobbing. The evidence is unmistakable. Looking at the man in the photo, I think of Anne Elise. The resemblance, especially in their sleek noses, is uncanny. For years, I tried to have a baby with Trish. When that failed, I did stupid things, such was my desire to have a child of my own. I wanted so bad to have a child. Is that a crime?

"Are there other photographs?"

"You bet. This one's the most salacious, though. I mean, get a load of her!"

Involuntarily, my glance wanders to the breasts that Simpkins points at. He's right: Laurel's magnificent. I want to punch Simpkins, shove the dirty money down his throat, do him bodily harm. Up until now, I looked at Laurel as being naive and innocent. I will never be able to look at her the same way again; I will never be able to love her again.

"Are there photos of her with other guys?" I ask, clinging to the hope that Laurel valued me enough to store photos of me, too, on her phone.

"Nope. There's only a few photos of her and this guy. And nothing whatsoever from the end of June onward. She must have deleted everything else. If I had the actual cell phone, I might be able to recover some of those, but hacking into it from a remote location, there's only so much I can do."

"What else did you find?"

"Plenty." Simpkins flips through pages and printouts, but I haven't the heart to look at any of it. "She was arrested on thievery charge as a teen and spent her high school years at a juvenile detention center, where she was disciplined for a plethora of misconduct charges—namely, insubordination and fighting with the other inmates."

Laurel hasn't told me any of this. From what she mentioned of her past, I assumed she spent an idyllic girlhood playing in the sand dunes on Maryland's Eastern Shore. Meeting Belinda and Tully should have clued me in that this was unlikely, but I wanted to believe in her girlish goodness.

"And her parents!" Simpkins says. "They're both messed up."

"Wait. You investigated her parents?"

Simpkins grins. "You were right about me yesterday. Can't you tell? I get off on this!" The dirt he gathered on Laurel's parents is significant. Belinda's been in and out of drug treatment centers for years for meth and opioid abuse. Assuming she hasn't used since her most recent rehab stint, she might've been clean for all of three months. "So her mother's been in and out of rehab, and her father, Tully, has been in and out of jail. Quite a pair, huh?"

My head whirls.

"Weird, huh?" Simpkins says. "I never heard of anyone named Tully before. Right now, there's a string of outstanding warrants on him."

"What for?"

"Skipping bail in Ohio. Petty thefts. Larceny. Grand theft auto. Possession with intent to distribute. Stuff like that. But in Delaware, he bashed in some guy's face with a crowbar. Or maybe it was a tire iron."

"Holy shit."

"Yeah. I sure wouldn't want to cross that guy's path."

My stomach is all tied in knots. I've fucked myself over, giving all of Tully's cash to Simpkins. Once Tully finds out I've squandered his money, it's my face he'll reconfigure with a tire iron. Or a crowbar. I'm angry at Laurel for deceiving me about Anne Elise's paternity, angry at Trish for forcing me into this rabbit's hole of an investigation, angry at myself for wasting Tully's money, and angry at Simpkins for divulging the sordid details about Laurel. An hour ago, I was happily, blissfully ignorant. I thought Laurel was wonderful. I loved her.

"Pretty cool stuff, huh? I gotta say, this has been one of my more interesting cases." Suffused with professional pride, Simpkins beams. He really does get off on the lurid stuff. He grabs Tully's lunch sack and dumps out the money, the crumpled-up hundred-dollar bills spilling out into a pile that takes up half his desk. He paws the bills, rubs them between his palms. Money spills onto the floor and into his coffee mugs. For me, life couldn't be much worse, and I've had a major hand in creating Simpkins's gravy train. No good karma will rub off on me tonight. Simpkins smooths out one of the wrinkled bills and holds it to the overhead fluorescent light. His expression changes. Scowling, he picks up another hundred-dollar bill and holds it up to the light too.

"Hey, wait a sec," Simpkins says, eyeing me. "All this money's counterfeit."

Chapter Twenty-Two

TRISH

Dusk falls. Ever since I finished my call with Simpkins an hour ago, I've been driving in circles with Anne Elise concealed beneath my jacket. The traffic light changes from green to a cautionary yellow, and after I coast to a stop at an intersection, people pour out onto the crosswalk to traipse to the other side of the street. Most stare at their cell phones as they walk, but a lone woman in a fake mink coat turns and smiles unexpectedly at me as she crosses in front of my car. My pulse quickens, for she's spotted Anne Elise, and while she might think this is cute—a mother harboring her baby under her winter coat—later tonight, when news bulletins and missing-baby Amber Alerts appear on television, she'll likely remember this moment. Would she be able to identify me? She's looking at me, expecting me to return her smile, and then, because she sees my anxiety, she frowns. The traffic lights change. I stomp on the gas pedal, screeching the car to a roaring start.

Anne Elise starts crying. Nothing seems to soothe her. I sing lullabies about the twinkling stars, hug her, kiss her, rub her back, and yet no amount of twinkling stars can put her back to sleep. Brushing my hand over her cheeks, I feel the moistness of her tears. Finally, just like that, she closes her eyes, all tuckered out. It's not good for a baby to go hungry, and yet I hadn't the foresight to grab formula or bottles or other baby necessities before walking out of the hospital with her. I must get this caravan moving, and yet at every red light, stop sign, intersection, I worry about the pedestrians who turn and look at me as they cross the street. I'm bound to be caught. I drive back toward Sibley, and yet too much time has passed for me to return to the hospital grounds and pretend I was just promenading in the snow with Anne Elise. Nearing the hospital, I veer the car away onto a different street. Loughboro Road becomes Nebraska Avenue. Driving past American University and through Tenleytown and Connecticut Avenue, I find myself going toward Rock Creek Park. In the dead of winter, the park is underused, the perfect desolate place to disappear and never be found.

I park near the planetarium. Judging by the lack of tire tracks in the snowy lot, no one's been here for days. Icy rain begins to fall. I walk down a path and then another path. Left outside in these elements, even the healthiest and hardiest would catch cold or pneumonia. No joggers, dog walkers, or bicyclists are in sight, no summertime ice cream vendors beckoning children with Nutty Buddy cones and Fudgsicles, and it's hard to believe that in a city as populous and wild and self-important as Washington, you can ever be truly all alone. But I am not alone: Anne Elise, asleep, snuggles beneath my coat.

Moonlit and snow glazed, the park seems magical, a fog-shrouded fairyland where anything can happen. I walk down a trail and am reminded of strolls with James. In the distance, a stream burbles. I used to fetch stones in that stream. When it was hot, we took our sandals off and let the water run over our toes, telling ourselves our lives would be perpetually sunny, perpetually filled with happiness.

"This is where your father and I sliced open a watermelon once. Right at this picnic table. And there—over there where the two maple trees are—is where we tossed Frisbees," I say, remembering the feel of the sun on my shoulders. Though Anne Elise is asleep, it's important she learns of the love her father and I share. "We laid out picnic blankets and unpacked salami and Havarti sandwiches from a picnic basket. I freckled easily, and your father would rub Coppertone on my shoulders, my arms, my face to prevent sunburn."

Anne Elise looks so intelligent, so wanting of information, a sponge for any dollop of insight about her father and me, but as I tell her of the past, my mind swims toward the future. I'm seeing the springtime grass on which she'll crawl, the oak trees she'll climb when she's older, the red bicycle with squeaky training wheels. Kindergarten soccer games, Saturday afternoons at the National Gallery of Art's Impressionism exhibits, and the Christmastime performances of *The Nutcracker* at the Warner Theatre, James and I on either side of her in the plush velvet orchestra seats, all of us rapt in "Dance of the Sugar Plum Fairy."

But then, as snowflakes dust my hair, I know it can't be. Sooner or later, I'm bound to be apprehended. By tomorrow, there's a fair chance I'll be behind bars, the subject of a messy scandal splashed out all over the front pages and the lips of the snootiest socialites of my acquaintance. And what kind of future would there be for either of us if that happens? What would my friend Allie have to say, and what will a prison sentence do to my chances of ever being named an honorary chairwoman for any of the charity cotillions I attend?

I cannot return Anne Elise to the hospital. There is so little I can do with her, but as I mull my options, a new path emerges in my mind. Should Anne Elise disappear, James will eventually return to me. Even solid marriages and long-standing relationships would crumble from the emotional turmoil of losing a newborn. James and Laurel, scarcely having known each other for more than nine or ten months, do not have the kind of stable, loving relationship to withstand such a test. Of this, I am positive. And while they may band tighter immediately following the disappearance, the bond would be ephemeral. Sooner or later, they wouldn't be able to look in each other's eyes without being reminded of tragedy and heartbreak. They might still fuck each other, but they'll never be able to love each other again.

In a clearing beyond a stand of river birches, not far from where Rock Creek's burbling icy waters bisect the park, lies the perfect spot. I stop and watch my breath in the cold air. There's a baby-sized indentation in the snowy ground, enough fallen leaves, branches, and bigger rocks to hide her from anyone who should happen to jog past. I unzip my jacket and feel the rush of cold air come over me. Anne Elise, in her sleep, has already mastered the art of sucking her thumb. She looks so cute in her sheer baby clothes as I lay her on the ground.

Chapter Twenty-Three

LAUREL

I'm in my bed, still stunned the hospital let Zerena disappear. "Where is she?" I keep asking. No one has any answers. Lois Belcher comes to my side while the two men in suits speak into their walkie-talkies about a possible abduction. Zerena isn't in the nursery, nor has she been there for the last eight hours. One of the men in suits puts his hand over his walkie-talkie's mouthpiece and tells me, "Hell or high water, we're on this thing," confiding this as if it's supposed to bring me comfort. My parents stand in bewildered alarm, Tully's arm on my mother's shoulder. It's the closest they've come to an affectionate gesture in my presence, but Tully, tugging on the collar of his white button-down shirt and glancing at his watch every other minute, eyes the security guys.

"Who's Tricia?" Tully asks. "Some friend of yours?"

"Tricia is Laurel's mother," Lois Belcher answers matter-of-factly.

"No, she's not," Tully says. He pushes Belinda a few steps forward. "This here's Laurel's mom. And her name's not Tricia."

"It's Belinda," Belinda says, flashing an uncomfortable smile. She's never liked being thrust into others' attention. "My name's Belinda, not Tricia, but I've been Laurel's mother ever since she was born. Honest, I am."

"See? This woman's Laurel's mother. Just like I told you."

"Oh, dear," Lois Belcher says. She puts her hand to her chin and turns two shades paler. "Is this true?"

I take a breath, close my eyes, and nod. Though I'm lying in bed, I feel as if I might fall. More people rush into the room, which seems to spin around me. Someone says something about a system-wide failure plaguing the hospital's video surveillance cameras. The hospital security officers lower their walkie-talkies. One of them shakes his head. The other says, moaning, "Just our luck, man."

When I was locked up in juvenile detention, I hated how security alarms blared whenever an inmate committed an infraction, but now I'd fork over my left hand or maybe a kidney to hear a klaxon, a wailing siren, some signal of hospital-wide alarm to jolt everyone into action finding my baby. Instead, the security officers look at each other with regret. One of their walkie-talkies crackles with static, reminding me of the secondhand pair of beige walkie-talkies I got for Christmas when I was eight or nine. Unwrapping them, I thought they were the coolest gift ever, and for days thereafter, Tully or Belinda would humor me with silly messages walkie-talkied to me from the other end of our trailer, but as their Christmastime cheer whittled down to the humdrum of another workaday new year, their willingness to engage in such shenanigans faded. Being an only child to frequently absent parents is lonesome. Alone most nights, I walkie-talkied myself, holding the walkie-talkies in either hand and making up pretend conversations to amuse myself in the hours I was left alone.

"So who's Tricia then?" Lois Belcher asks.

Everyone turns to me. My throat gets dry. If I'm ever to see Zerena again, I need to be upfront about this, but embarrassment gets the better of me. Everyone's opinion of me is about to drop ten notches as soon as I tell them I've been sleeping with Trish's husband, a married man. I bite my lips. No matter what happens, I have to admit the truth. For Zerena's sake.

"Tricia is Jimmy's wife," I say. "I never should have done with him what I did."

The people around me exchange glances, slow to make sense of what I've said. There's no Act of Contrition big enough to forgive the sins I've committed. A voice cackles out of one of the walkie-talkies so loud and electronically distorted that I momentarily mistake it for the voice of God casting judgment on me. I bring my hands to my face, shielding myself from everyone's judgmental stares.

The news that I'm an adulterer hits Lois Belcher hard. I catch her biting her tongue. She leans against the wall, turns her gaze away from me. I wouldn't have pegged her for the moralistic type, but birds of a generational feather flock together. Because she's friendly with Tricia, she must look at me as some kind of whore. Though I've played no part in Zerena's disappearance, this wouldn't have happened if I hadn't messed around with a married man.

"Oooh," Belinda says, the first to understand the implications. She sits down beside me, runs her hand through my unwashed hair. There's compassion in her face, compassion she never expressed while I was growing up. In this moment, when I'm more desperate for compassion than ever before, it's exactly what I need. "I'm so sorry. I feel so bad for what you must be going through." Belinda puts her arm around my shoulder, drawing me into a sideways hug. "It'll be all right. You've got the hospital doing everything they can to find your baby girl."

Tully drums his stubby fingers on the side of the nightstand. "Wait. Wait. Hold everything. Are you telling me Jimmy's not even your man?" Tully's face reddens. He paces the room, walks back, drums his fingers on the wall next to the IV stand. He's a caged animal, Tully is, indignant and trembling with anger. He points his finger at me. "Don't you know you shouldn't be having babies with other women's husbands?"

"Quit picking on your little girl," Belinda says. "Don't you think she knows this? Don't you think she's been trying to figure out what to do without you shouting at her?"

"I'm not shouting. That man took our money."

Tully makes a fist, and at the sound of that fist smacking his other hand, Belinda panics. Tully looks as if he's about to explode. Belinda lets go of me and, getting up from beside me on the bed, edges up to him. She slips her hand consolingly onto his bicep to calm him, her voice the soothing voice of an elementary school teacher trying to pacify an angry child. I've seen her try to calm him down before, but rarely did it work. "Don't worry, honey. It'll work out. Everything will be okay."

"How do you know?" Tully asks. Suddenly, he starts yelling. "He's not the family man we all thought he was, is he? Don't you get it? He's not family. He's not *our* family, anyways."

One of the security men lays a hand on Tully's shoulder and, with the patience of a man trained at managing stressful situations, says, "Sir. Sir. Please don't shout. This is a hospital."

Tully thrusts out his chest. No one's quicker to take anger, or quicker to amp that anger into violence, than Tully. That's one thing I remember as a child: the bar fights he got into, the parking lot melees that began with someone stealing a parking space he wanted. Belinda urges him to stay calm, but he shoos her away. Turning toward the security man, he stares him in the eye. The security officer is huge, beefy. Standing up to him, Tully's a comparative pipsqueak. "Get your hands off me, buddy, and don't fuck with me. I'm not shouting. I'm upset is all."

"Sir. Sir. Do you wish us to call the police on you?"

Tully's going to pounce on the security man, or—worse—the security men will pounce on him. Any moment, something bad's going to happen. My mother hides her face beneath her hands. Tully grabs the clock radio from the nightstand, rips its cord from the wall, and makes as if to throw it. The security men, sensing danger, stand tall and unflinching, broadening their shoulders and puffing out their chests.

"What are you going to do with that clock?" one of the security officers asks.

"Sir. Sir. Do you wish us to get the police involved here to calm you down?" the other asks.

"The police?" Tully repeats.

"Yes. The police."

The recognition that he's about to have the cops called on him comes slowly to Tully. He raises his hands up in a classic "Don't shoot me!" posture and steps back half a step, which amazes me. Never before has he flinched at the prospect of a police confrontation. Maybe he really has changed. Or at least become smarter about when to pick a fight. "Don't you go calling the police. I haven't done anything, and you know that. It's you two who's done something—losing my daughter's baby."

"Sir. We're working on that."

The clock's still in Tully's hand, its four-foot cord dangling against his knee. He lowers it gently, the other hand still in the air in a non-threatening position. "Well, don't go bothering me then just because a baby's gone missing. I had nothing to do with that. And I wasn't shouting."

I expect Tully and the officers to apologize to each other, but instead, the officers turn their attention back to me.

"Can we ask you more questions?" one of the security officers says. He says again, "on behalf of the entire hospital," how sorry they are for what happened to Zerena and pledges to help get her back. And then he asks questions that all concern Tricia. Unfortunately, I barely know her. Pressed to recall her, my mind goes blank.

"She's really slender, right?" I say. I'm woozy and feverish, panicked and in despair, but one thing pops to mind: her eyes. "She's got these eyes . . . eyes like . . . like, *blue*."

"Her eyes?" one of the security men asks, looking up from his clipboard.

"Yes. Her eyes. She kept saying her eyes were the same deep-blue color as Zerena's." I expect the security officers to jump all over this description—it's the only real identifying feature I've yet offered—and yet they shake their heads, unimpressed, because, without Zerena, they're unable to color match her eyes. I dig deeper into my memory. I tell them how she seemed to think she knew all about my college years, which was off-putting. And then I remember something else that might do the security men some good.

"Jimmy says Tricia's been depressed lately. She's been self-medicating on Valium," I say, recalling Jimmy's worries about the pills she's popping. "He says she's taking so many that she's becoming illogical, loopy." In my mind, she must have worked her way into an irrational froth that culminated with her stealing my baby. "That's probably why she kidnapped my baby."

"So what about the man? Jimmy. Your, uh, boyfriend. What can you tell us about him?"

"Jimmy?" I'm jarred they don't see the relevance of my suspicions about Trish. They can't be totally stupid, and yet when I ask them—implore them—to look into Trish, they shake their heads dismissively. Clearly, they've got their own suspicions about what happened to Zerena.

Lois Belcher clears her throat purposely to catch everyone's attention. There's a perturbed look on her face, a scowl. "If you don't mind me saying so, I don't think I've seen Trish all day. I'm usually on top of things like this too."

The security officers nod at this assertion. No doubt they've worked with Lois Belcher before and view her as a trustworthy person. One of the security officers puts his hands on his hips. "And even if this Trish person were here today, she couldn't just walk away from the hospital because of all the security systems we have in place."

I glance back at Lois Belcher. Instead of gloating, she looks down at the floor, wide-eyed, her mouth ajar as if in shock.

"Usually it's the man in the relationship who takes the child or the baby," one of the security officers says.

"Jimmy wouldn't steal a baby. He's way too classy to do something like that."

But the security officers are insistent that I provide them a description of Jimmy, so I tell them how warm and caring he is, how kind he's always been—but they direct me to the immediately necessary facts concerning his identifying features—height, age, race, hair color, birthmarks, and visible tattoos, which, in his case, means none. I tell them about Jimmy's midnight-blue Volvo station wagon, how, while driving me home from my first sonogram appointment, he said it was the perfect car for a man setting out to start a family. At the time, I wept, thinking he was committed to me and the family we would have together.

"So where does he live?"

"I don't know."

The security men look at each other. "Are you serious?"

Although Jimmy bought the riverfront apartment for me, he doesn't live there. At least not yet. The security officers ask other questions. I know so little about Jimmy. Place of birth? Social security number? Place of employment? Nope, nope, and nope.

"How about his birth date? Do you at least know that?"

"He's a Leo," I say, remembering that, since I'm a Sagittarius, the astrology charts in one of the magazines I bought predicted he'd be my perfect love partner. But maybe because of all the medications I've been dosed with, I can't remember when in August his birthday falls. The second week, maybe. The astrology magazine predicted fireworks for us, romantically, a hot, sizzling romance that would consume our passions, but this additional detail fails to impress the security officers.

"Wait, wait, and double wait," I say, grabbing my phone. "I'll prove to you that Jimmy didn't steal my baby."

"What are you doing?"

"I'm calling him."

The two security officers look at each other, probably thinking they should've asked me to call Jimmy before making wild, horrible accusations about him. I punch Jimmy's number into my phone, already feeling the satisfaction of being able to hand my phone over to one of these guys so they'll hear for themselves that Jimmy didn't do anything. A couple of moments later, I hear a muffled ringing in the background somewhere. Jimmy's not picking up, but the security officers' expressions change. Eagerness lights their eyes. They peer at the recliner. One of them steps toward it. I'm still hearing the ringing in the background, and then, when the security officer lifts the recliner's cushions, the ringing becomes louder, and then I see what the security officer has found: a red flip phone had been buried into the cushions. The security officer flips open the phone, presses a button, and a moment later I hear his voice answering my call.

"Is this your, um, boyfriend's phone?"

Humiliation roils over me. I press end to cancel my call, and then I examine the phone in the security officer's hands. It's a cheap-looking old thing. I knew Jimmy carried three phones with him, but I never was in the same room with him to see which of those phones he used when answering my calls.

"It's just a basic little pay-as-you-go model," the security officer says, handing over Jimmy's phone to the other security officer. "He probably bought it at Walmart or 7-Eleven."

Somehow, I always imagined Jimmy using some lavish iPhone, something spectacular, whenever we talked. I feel so stupid. It probably slipped out of his pocket the last time he sat on this recliner. The phone must mean so little to him that he hasn't even realized it's gone missing.

"Ma'am. You have to know more about how we can contact this Jimmy guy. Where does he live?"

"He lives in Georgetown, I think. He and Tricia have a house in Georgetown."

Belinda perks up suddenly. "Tell them about that bank he owns. That should help them find him."

The security officer lowers his pen. He cocks his head, raises an eyebrow. "He *owns* a bank?"

"His family *used* to own banks. A whole slew of them. But Jimmy said they divested themselves of their bank holdings years ago so they could put their money into more lucrative, higher-yielding investments." Jimmy had used the exact phrase—"lucrative, higher-yielding investments"—on the night he handed the fifty-dollar bill to the bum. It sounded thrilling and vaguely illicit, the phrase rolling off his tongue with a bravado that made me love him even more. He's the smoothest, handsomest, kindest man I ever met. Who doesn't want to believe her lover is outrageously successful?

"So what bank was it?"

"Riggs Bank. His family owns Riggs Bank."

"So you're telling me that your boyfriend, Jimmy *Wainsborough*— that his family, the *Wainsborough* family—owned *Riggs* Bank?" Even I realize how absurd this sounds. The security man looks upon me with pitiful concern. In a delicate voice, he asks, "You don't know him too well, do you?"

A plunging feeling comes over me. Until now, I bought everything Jimmy told me about himself, asking nothing in the way of corroborating evidence beyond the love he expressed for me. Jimmy might still be the bright, generous, gifted financial consultant he represents himself to be, but if he had told me he was the King of America, I wouldn't have asked to see his crown, his scepter, or his royal throne before believing him.

"But he's rich," Tully says. "He's grade-A bona fide rich. Tell him, Laurel. Tell him how rich Jimmy is. Tell him."

I fold my hands in my lap, and when my mother runs her soothing hand again through my hair, I lean into her, nesting my head against her shoulder. I always envied the little girls I saw on the benches in playgrounds and shopping malls, how they'd curl up against their mothers, calm and safe. I hope Zerena will do that to me someday—lean into me for warmth, protection, and a hug.

"Tell him, Laurel."

"Sir. Jimmy never outright told me he was rich. He implied it though at every chance he could and never did anything to dissuade me of that notion."

I think the security man knows what I mean. Or at least, tucking his ballpoint back into the breast pocket of his suit jacket, he doesn't ask more questions. The other security man passes me his business card and instructs me to call him should I think of anything relevant. He tells me police officers will visit me soon with their own questions.

"How soon?" Tully asks.

"Actually, I'm surprised they're not here yet."

Tully looks down at his scuffed black dress-up shoes. Tomorrow, freed of the need to impress Jimmy, he'll return to Wrangler jeans and sneakers, which honestly suit him better. "Hey, Laurel? Your mother and me need to get driving home now."

"Already?" Belinda asks.

"Yes. Already."

Belinda hops off my bed and squeezes my hand. Tully's standing in front of her, his arms at his hips. With a disheartened sigh, Belinda says, "Hey, it's a long drive back home. You understand, don't you?"

"Sure, Mom. Hey, let me give you something." I reach around my head and unclip one of the blue diamond studs from my earlobe. Belinda asks me what I'm doing. I turn my head and unclip the other. They're the nicest things Belinda ever gave me, much nicer than any used set of walkie-talkies. I drop them into her hand. The blue diamond studs sparkle in her palm, each of the diamonds two carats huge, the blueness adding to their rarity and beauty. I've been dreaming of diamonds since I found out I was pregnant, envisioning the ring that Jimmy would one day present to me on bended knee.

"Don't you like them?" Belinda asks, and it's only then that I see the hurt in her eyes. She wanted me to have the earrings and sees my return of them as a sign that I'm rejecting her.

"Mom. I'm not worthy of them. Take them. Maybe you can sell them and pay for your teeth. Wouldn't that be nice?"

Belinda blushes. "Oh, honey. They're not real. They're like everything else I ever had: pretty but worthless."

~

Tully, Belinda, and the two detectives leave at the same moment. Lois Belcher leans against the window, her hand on the glass. Beyond her, outside the window, dusk squeezes what's left of the cold winter light out of the sky. I consider asking her to leave me alone, but I fear that, upset by how I'd been sleeping with Tricia's husband, she may go on a tirade about my loose morals. I close my eyes. Although I try to sleep, thoughts ping around my head, keeping me awake. A while later, unable to sleep, I open my eyes to see Lois Belcher sitting on the recliner next to me. She stares at the ceiling, not aware I'm awake. Her face is wrinkled at the eyes and upper lip in a way I'd imagine must cause her anguish when she longs to look in the mirror and see her younger self stare out at her. She looks wise and sorrowful, a straw woman, sallow and gray.

"You can go, you know," I say, catching her attention.

"I know I can. My shift ended an hour ago. I'm waiting for the police to come. And anyways, I can't stand the thought of you being alone at a time like this." Lois Belcher stands up, stretches her arms. "You must be exhausted."

"I can't go to sleep. I've tried."

A man knocks on the door and identifies himself as a Detective Lionel Adderly, a plainclothes DC police investigator dressed in the summer outfit of a rich boater—khaki slacks, lime-green polo shirt, and perturbed ennui. Although he asks the same questions as the hospital security officers, he pays more attention to my responses. He asks each question slowly, tilts his head when I respond. At times, he asks me to repeat myself. He's thorough. He asks follow-up questions.

"So, to your knowledge, who was the last person with the baby before she disappeared?" Adderly asks.

"Tricia Wainsborough. She's married to the baby's father. There's bad blood running there because of it."

"So you know *for a fact* that Tricia was the last person in the hospital to be with the baby?"

I tell Adderly about the dreams I had of Tricia in the room, how she was holding my baby with rage in her face. I tell him that the dreams were so real, more like a hazy form of consciousness than the fantastical and make-believe things I usually dream. I tell him about the soiled diaper on the bassinet and the crazy boot tracks that were all over the floor when I woke up. "Only a woman as batty as Tricia would ever wear boots like that, right?"

Adderly looks at me with sad concern, and I can see what he's thinking: I must be crazy. Anyone could've come in wearing those boots, and a person's dreams would never be considered evidence in any real criminal investigation. For all I know, a nurse might have peeked into my room and, noticing I was asleep, carried Zerena back to the nursery.

Adderly lowers his pen from his notepad.

And yet, I know in my heart and in every inch of my soul that Tricia's responsible for my missing baby.

"Right after Tricia found out about Jimmy and me, she made all kinds of threats that she's going to ruin our lives. Or ruin our baby's life. She's the Grinch who stole Christmas, that woman is, a woman with no generosity whatsoever in her heart. Jimmy tried to talk sense into her, actually brought her into this room to show her Zerena, hoping that if she saw Zerena, she'd be apt to be nice. But that didn't work."

Adderly walks around the room taking notes. At first, I think he's merely humoring me, not openly saying that he thinks I'm crazy. He opens the closet, the bathroom door, the drawers in my nightstand. He's not being nosy; he's just looking for clues. He opens the Debauve et Gallais chocolate box. For a moment, he looks like he might help himself to one of the truffles, which would be okay with me because, frankly, chocolates aren't my thing. He looks at the pink roses Tricia sent and asks, "Who sent these to you?"

"Tricia."

He opens the card that's next to the flowers, reads aloud Tricia's note of confidence telling me I'll be a great mother. "She send this to you too?"

I nod.

Adderly tucks the card back in its envelope. "You think someone who sends you a card like that is fixing to steal your baby?"

"But she did it. I know she did it." Up until now, I've been at a slow boil since Zerena disappeared, but I can't control myself anymore. I need to stand up for myself. Just because I'm a woman of low economic standing doesn't mean I shouldn't be taken seriously. I raise my voice and, trembling, go full-blown banshee. I'm scared. I want my baby back. I want to hold her tight to my chest, feel her warm breath against me. I need her like I've never needed anyone before. Inside, I'm all ache and crinkle, sad and lonely. I scream so loud that nurses stare at me from the hallway, afraid to step into this room. If the security officers were here, they'd tell me to stop shouting, but nothing can keep me from getting this off my chest. Zerena might be in danger. "How the hell do I know why she'd send that card? She's gone psycho or something, playing mind games with me, trying to get me to trust her, but there's no trusting that witch as far as I'm concerned. I know she's guilty. Flip her burger! You've got to arrest her. She stole my baby."

I lean back on my pillow. My voice is sore and scratchy, but my outburst makes an impression on the otherwise unflappable Adderly. If

I hadn't spoken up, he probably wouldn't even try to interview Tricia, but now he pledges to see her tonight. "Do you know where this Tricia Wainsborough lives?"

"Sir. I don't."

Silence greets my response. Adderly closes his notepad.

Lois Belcher gets up from the recliner, where she's been sitting throughout my interview. Catching my glance, she lowers her head. "I know where Tricia lives."

"You do?" I gathered the two of them—Lois and Tricia—were friendly, but I didn't realize they knew each other well.

"Yes. I logged her information in when I gave her a KISS bracelet. I was the one who gave her a KISS bracelet," Lois Belcher says. Her voice is weak. She speaks reluctantly, as if weighing what to reveal. As she speaks, I burn up inside. I trusted her, regarded her as my protector. Her face is expressionless. She knows she's done wrong. "I'm sorry. I thought she was your mother. Honestly, I did. I'm going to lose my job for this. That's why I haven't said anything until now. I'm sorry. I was the one who gave Tricia the security bracelet that might have enabled her to steal your baby."

Chapter Twenty-Four

Trish

James has his uses. He's a whiz at lighting a crackling fire in the fireplace. He can strike a match and set fire to the dampest kindling, run a lighted cone of newsprint up the flue to warm up a damper and draw the smoke up the chimney once the main fire is lit. Over the years, he's mastered the art of filling a silver tea ball with just the right amount of loose-leaf chamomile tea and letting it steep in a thermal-lined ceramic carafe for just the right length of time. I'm reminded of this when I sit in Savory Mew's living room. He's not home yet tonight. I'm cold, and I'd very much like there to be a fire in the fireplace and a spot of tea in my cup. How very much I'd like to feel the glow of the cordwood flames throughout the room, warming the Lalique lamps on the piecrust tables, the Grecian vases, ebony curio cabinets, sumptuous Simon Willard grandfather clock, and the curvilinear cream-colored Hepplewhite sofa upon which I sit. For centuries, a fire in the family hearth symbolized well-being, security, and an egalitarian happiness that even simple folk could enjoy, and yet lighting a fire is a skill I've not mastered. Whenever I try, the logs smolder for hours without bursting into flame, the smoke filling the room and sending its occupants elsewhere to catch a breath of fresh air.

Crown princes, sitting presidents, and titans of commerce have sat in this august room, placed their porcelain teacups on the mahogany drop leaf coffee table, and conversed about bond prices and the international financial agreements too complex for people not privy to their drafting to fully understand. For decades—up until the early 1990s, when it was quietly repatriated to the survivors' family from which Nazis had looted it—an enormous Monet haystack hung on the wall above the sofa. The painting was the pride of the room, more impressive than even the mantelpiece oil portrait of my father. Depending on the light of the day, the golds and blues became effervescent as sunlight poured into the room through lead glass windows. My father showed the painting to guests with pride. "Try finding a needle in that haystack," he'd tell them, slipping a glass of port into their hands. Once, in a moment of merriment, my twin sister, Julie, and I scotch-taped a darning needle swiped from our mother's sewing kit onto the canvas. If we perpetrated this stunt in a museum, we'd have been arrested, but my father laughed and laughed, and for years thereafter, until my sister succumbed to her aneurysm, whenever my father came into a room and found us standing together, he'd announce with mock surprise, "Ahh, my little needle girls." We were the apples of his eye, Julie and I.

∼

As I look at the cold andirons in the fireplace, blue and red flashing lights shine through the windows and interrupt my memories. Two squad cars are parked outside, and the amplified sound of someone speaking over a police radio jars me to attention. Valium softens the commotion and panic that would otherwise come over me in this situation. I think of James and his propensity to drive after drinking. I live in fear that one day I'll answer the door and be told my husband is dead. Or seriously injured. Or in jail. I imagine his Volvo screeching into a tree, a parked cargo van, a grandmother crossing the street in a wheelchair. I imagine the sound of impact, James's head smashing into his windshield, shattering it. I imagine him handcuffed and blowing into a roadside breathalyzer test. Despite his drinking, he's never had even a speeding ticket, but no run of luck can last forever. Some nights, upon arriving home drunk, he can barely wobble upstairs.

The doorbell rings, and I collect myself before answering. No hurry to be the recipient of bad news or a police investigation, I let the bell ring a second time before getting up from the Hepplewhite and walking across the house to open the door. Though I've rehearsed in my mind what to say, a somber nervousness churns in my stomach. A medium-built man in khaki slacks and a polo shirt stands in the portico, one hand pressed up against the marble column that partially supports the porch roof. Behind him, two uniformed police officers stand at attention by their squad cars. The man holds out his silver Metropolitan police badge, and after I glance at it, he asks, "Are you Mrs. Patricia Wainsborough?"

"Is this about my husband?"

The man blinks. "Why would you ask that?"

"He's late. I worry about him. He should be home by now."

"Interesting," the man says. Because he doesn't say more than that—just "Interesting"—I wonder if I've already spoken too much. He looks over my shoulder into the darkened foyer and the grand staircase beyond it. He's not here about James. His clothes are inadequate given that nighttime temperatures hover around the freezing point, and yet, because the case that calls him to my doorstep is urgent, he doesn't shiver.

"A wife worries about her husband. Is he the reason you're interrupting my evening?"

"No, ma'am. Are you Patricia Wainsborough?"

"Yes."

"I'm Detective Lionel Adderly," he says. Adderly shakes my hand and then motions to his colleagues standing by their squad cars. "Do you mind if we come inside?"

"If that's what you'd prefer."

Inside, I lead Detective Adderly into the living room, invite him to sit on the Hepplewhite, and apologize for being unable to offer him tea. The two uniformed officers stand in the corner by my father's old Victrola. Though they introduce themselves, Adderly does most of the talking. He's not a rocket scientist, just one of DC's finest, I remind myself. His eyes wander the room, taking in my antiques and paintings, the museum-quality furniture, the antique writing desk upon which a portion of James's 78s are stacked, and the seashells and millefiori glass paperweights in the curio cabinet. The brass andirons, with their vaguely Chinese-looking dragon motif, draw his attention. Peacock feathers bloom from a Ming vase set upon a lacquered pedestal. The detective takes this all in, seeing in each object a clue about my life; if he is like most people, he will assume that I, too, am as cloistered and fragile as the objects in this curated living room.

"I was thinking how nice it would be if my husband were home. He could light a fire, brew me a carafe of chamomile tea, and we could sit on the sofa and just . . ." Adjusting my legs, crossing and recrossing them, I don't complete my sentence. "Why are you here?"

"Is there a reason he's not home? Have you two—and I'm sorry if I'm blunt—not been getting along lately?"

Talking to the police is not the wisest thing, and yet suspicions would rise if I request my lawyer be present for this interview. My father insisted we be responsible for our own narratives, that we never cede control of our story lines. Adderly looks at me, eager for my reaction. At heart, everyone is an actor performing the story of his or her life.

"Do you feel uncomfortable talking about this, Mrs. Wainsborough?"

"Yes. My husband is, shall we say, drawn to women younger than I. His mistress had a baby the other day, so James has been coming home later than usual," I say, speaking softly, my evasive eyes darting to the fireplace and my father's portrait.

Adderly leans in closer so he can hear me. On his clean-shaven face, I smell his musky aftershave. He's a young man, still in his early thirties, and his face is young enough that it doesn't express concern as ably as an older man's might, but as I let down my guard and reveal to him my plight as the aggrieved wife, his face softens. He sees in me a preconceived notion: the stereotypical middle-aged woman about to be tossed aside for a younger woman, and because he is fundamentally decent, sympathy lights his coffee-brown eyes.

"I suspect James stopped off again at the hospital where his mistress and her baby are convalescing after the delivery. This has become, as you might well imagine, a matter of no small discomfort for me. Right now, he's probably rocking the baby in his arms, cooing at her. In another hour, he'll come home and ask why I don't have dinner waiting for him."

"He's not at the hospital. And he's not with the baby," Adderly says.

"He's not?" My eyes gape, as if taking in this information. "But you said he's okay. Is he okay? He's not hurt, is he?"

"The baby's missing."

"The baby? Are you sure?"

Adderly tilts his head, assessing my reaction. Some men speak first and save their thinking for later, but Detective Adderly is not of that persuasion. There's an intensity in his eyes I've rarely encountered. He's judging me, making up his mind on whether I'm responsible for Anne Elise's disappearance. Each moment under his gaze feels prolonged, uneasy. He raises his hand to his chin.

"Are you sure the baby's missing?"

Adderly lowers his hand. Although his clothes are clean, his fingernails are dirty, and yet a small satisfied smile appears on his lips.

He leans in close and, dropping his voice, says, "Between you and me, Sibley's record on baby security leaves a lot to be desired."

"This is horrible." I let my mouth fall open, expressing shock. Inwardly, however, I'm elated, for a man who confides in me his professional opinion about another organization's security record is a man who trusts me.

"Were you at the hospital, Mrs. Wainsborough? To see Laurel?"

"Yesterday and the day before, I was there. I might have been, like, the first person to actually hold the baby. James brought me there as soon as the baby was born." I glance at Adderly and see the shock in his eyes. Clearly, he can't conceive of a marriage where the husband so willingly invites his wife into his mistress's maternity suite. I shake my head, bat my hand through the air, as if I, too, can't fully comprehend this. "It's a messed-up situation. It truly is. But it's life, unfortunately. The baby, Anne Elise, is beautiful. Although I can't stand the idea of my husband messing around with another woman, I've never seen so beautiful a baby."

"I noticed the flowers you sent. That was a very nice note you wrote."

I smile, glad that Adderly noticed my capacity to be generous. Already, he seems inclined to view me kindly. "Thank you. Laurel was telling me she was worried she couldn't be a good mother. To be honest, I was prepared not to like her. But she's a young mother now, and I imagine a young mother's life must be fraught with horrible stresses, so I was simply trying to be supportive. For the baby's sake."

"Do you mind if my colleagues take a look around the house while we talk?" Adderly asks.

The two officers glance at me and then glance away in apparent disinterest to how I might respond. Consenting to a police search is unwise, and yet again I recognize that a refusal would increase suspicion. Adderly strikes me as competent. I've seen enough police procedurals on television. Should I decline a voluntary search, it wouldn't be long before Adderly reappears at the door with a search warrant.

"Your officers will be careful, right?" I ask.

Adderly tilts his head, unsure what I mean.

"The house is full of antiques, fragile things that, in some cases, can't be replaced if damaged." As I give this explanation, Adderly's expression softens. In his eyes, I'm an eccentric but harmless fuddy-duddy—the exact impression that I'd hoped to convey. I point to the three-foot-high blue ceramic vase stuffed with peacock feathers. Intricately carved red flowers are etched into its sides, making it a rare example of early Chinese porcelain. My parents acquired it as a wedding gift back during the Kennedy administration. "Believe it or not, that vase has been appraised at upward of a half million dollars."

Adderly's eyes flare open in shock.

"It's absurd, isn't it? It's so valuable I dare not even dust it anymore for fear of damaging it."

Adderly laughs. He assures me his officers will be "extremely gentle" with my belongings, and as they climb the stairs and open doors into closets and bedrooms, I tell him the approximate time of my visit with Laurel the previous two days.

"Do you know, I think that woman hasn't changed a single diaper yet. Not a single one. She sits around in bed all day expecting the nurses and me—*me!*—to do everything for her baby."

I expect Adderly to bring up the KISS bracelet, which is buried in my handbag, but he doesn't so much as open his notebook. Perhaps he will use questions about the security bracelet as a pretext for subsequent interviews. True to their word, the other officers return downstairs and declare they haven't so much as scratched a single antique, for which I thank them profusely.

"Laurel told everyone at the hospital that she looks at me as some kind of mother figure. Can you get over that? Apparently, she appreciates my companionship, which, let me tell you, is incomprehensible to me. Do you know what she said, though? She said she'd love it if I came again today but that I really shouldn't because someone was coming today who she really had to talk with."

Adderly's eyes widen. He picks up his notebook and jots something in it. Obfuscation is my game. I need to cast suspicion in as many quarters as possible if I'm to have a long-term hope of deflecting suspicion from myself.

"Who was this other person?" Adderly asks.

I shrug my shoulder. "Beats me. All day, I've been wondering the same thing. I mean, please don't think this presumptuous, but James told me Laurel doesn't have a single good friend in the whole world."

Adderly picks up his pencil again, starts scrawling more things in his notepad.

"Hey, you don't think James is responsible for Anne Elise going missing, do you?"

Detective Adderly narrows his eyes. In my purposefully silly, ping-ponging way, I'm throwing a whole lot of different possibilities at him. Until this moment, he hadn't considered that James might be behind Anne Elise's disappearance. "Why would I think that?"

"Nothing. Nothing at all," I say so hurriedly the words collide together.

"Has he been acting oddly?"

I gaze at the fireplace, stretch out my arms. "I love James. You understand that, don't you? James still loves me. I know he does. He still comes home to me each night. We have dinner together, tell each other about our days. It's almost like our lives were before he met that woman. I wish he would come home and light a fire in the fireplace for us. You understand that, don't you?"

"A baby's life is at stake. That is what I understand."

"We're all under a lot of stress. You can appreciate that. Sometimes, under stress, people do things you don't expect of them. In James's case, he's been drinking heavily. I worry about him. Do you know what I thought when, opening the door, I saw you—an officer of the law—on my doorstep?"

"What?"

"I thought you were going to tell me there'd been an accident. That, driving home drunk, James crashed his car. I thought you'd tell me I'd never see James again."

Adderly looks at me as if expecting me to say more, and in my reticence he sees a loyal wife, a wife who, however wronged, is constitutionally unable to cast aspersion upon her husband. I have said enough, however, to change Detective Adderly's focus on the case away from me. He may investigate James. He may investigate Laurel. But he won't be investigating me. There are many ways to a man's heart. Should James or Laurel discover Adderly's investigating one of them, they'd become distrustful of each other, grow apart, fall out of love.

Adderly points to the portrait hanging above the unlit fireplace. "Who's that?"

"That's a portrait of the finest man who ever walked the planet: my father, Jack Riggs. Of Riggs Bank fame."

"Riggs Bank?" Detective Adderly scratches his head. "Sorry. I never heard of them."

Ten years ago, in the aftermath of the regrettable scandals that consumed my father's last years before retirement, the bank's directors were forced to sell off its holdings. All branches were renamed during the PNC Financial takeover, so toxic had the name of Riggs become, and yet it hurts, learning how the name is now meaningless to a man like Adderly. Ten years should barely be a drop in the collective memory of this city. The name should still inspire awe and respect, not blank stares.

"Detective Adderly. I'm not in the habit of spouting off with unfounded allegations, but do you want to know my gut feelings about Anne Elise being missing?"

"Sure," Adderly says, whether out of real curiosity or to humor me, I cannot tell. He cracks his knuckles. "Go ahead."

"Look into Laurel. She's postpartum depressed and is frightened that James is going to dump her. James met her parents yesterday, and they struck him as shady people, both of them with criminal backgrounds or something terrible like that in their pasts. Erratic, slimy people. That's what they are. Drug abusers—that kind of people. James hardly has a bad word to say about anyone—'ac-cent-tchu-ate the positive' is his favorite expression—and yet he kept ranting to me about how horrible Laurel's parents are. Her father kept saying how Laurel should give up the baby, get rid of it. Put her up for adoption. Or leave her in an orphanage. What kind of man tells his daughter to get rid of her baby?"

～

Five minutes after Detective Adderly and his two officers leave, I decide to have some fun. Simpkins had given me Laurel's cell phone number, but so far, I haven't had use for it. Now, though, I ring her up. By the time I'm through with her, I'll rattle her so bad she'll have no choice but to leave James. The phone rings and rings. Laurel must be one of those graceless slackers who deigns not to answer her phone. So I leave a message. A long message.

Later, I'm sitting again on the Hepplewhite sofa, looking at the empty fireplace, and thinking how nice it would be if James were to come home and light a fire for me. The squad cars have driven away. No longer is the room lit by the unnerving glow of their red and blue flashing lights. Before he left, Adderly clasped my hands and promised to do "everything I know how" in order to find Laurel's baby. I thanked him for his efforts and invited him to phone me should he have additional questions.

Not having eaten all day, I think about gathering some leftovers from the refrigerator. Even cold, last night's lamb will be delicious. I contemplate whether to give James a call. If I catch him in a good mood, I'll invite him to come home and light a blazing fire for us and heat up a carafe of chamomile tea. There is so much I need to tell him. And I should probably call my father for advice. He'll know the strings to pull, the people to pay off, should Adderly and his men come to investigate again.

Chapter Twenty-Five

LAUREL

I'm a narcoleptic cat unable to stay awake for any decent stretch of time, and though I fall asleep wham-bam easy, I awake in fits of panic, the sweat pouring over my forehead soaking into my pillows and blankets. Doctors at either side of my bed ask, "Hey? Laurel? How do you feel?" Dry at my mouth and dry at my throat, I'm groggy beyond belief. My fingers feel crinkled, gnarled, dispossessed of their natural suppleness. They're not the fingers of a young mother but of a corpse, a cadaver, a grim reaper clutching a rusting scythe. I long for someone to slip Zerena into my arms, long to feel the comfort of her little body, the murmur of her gurgle, the lap of her mouth against my breasts.

"You're dehydrated, maybe even delirious," a nurse, or maybe it's a doctor, says.

Someone on the other side of me reaches over and touches my lips, and before I know it, she's forcing something hard and bitingly cold into my mouth—an ice cube—and instructing me to let it melt on my tongue, and while this is happening, someone else switches out my IV bag. Another person flicks on the room's overhead light. Perhaps it's the dehydration affecting my eyesight, but I jerk my hand up to shield my eyes from the too-bright light, and when I do so, the IV tubing snags again on the bed railing. A full two units of saline solution have been pumped into me over the past hour, not that anyone spells out for me how much fluid—a cup? a pint?—this represents.

"You're lucky," someone says.

I gasp, inflated with hope. "You've found Zerena! Have you found her?"

The person who stuck the ice cube in my mouth glances at the nurse or maybe doctor. Someone else, a man hidden behind what appears to be multiple layers of hospital scrubs and latex gloves, produces a hypodermic needle and a glass vial. Needles are my enemy. I've always been afraid of them, and I'm trying not to think of the needle. I wish Jimmy was holding my hand, his confident voice prodding me to be brave. The man jabs the needle into the vial, pulls back the hypodermic's plunger to draw the vial's medicine into the barrel. My stomach cramps up in anticipation of being injected, and then, as I think of Zerena, my heart sinks: no one has acknowledged my question about her, meaning she's still missing.

"This is vancomycin, which is a powerful antibiotic," the man says.

Looking at the needle, I think I'm going to faint. "Why do I need that?"

"It'll knock out your infection. That's why."

Someone else swabs down my arm. At the smell of the alcohol, my nostrils flare.

"Other doctors told me yesterday I was going to be all right. They told me that yesterday, and they told me that the day before, and now you're saying I'm not all right."

"We're doing everything we can. Vancomycin is extremely powerful on bacteria that's otherwise antibiotic resistant. The side effects are mild—mostly limited to the pain you'll feel at the site of the injection. It's safe for lactating women. We're running tests to see what's causing the infection, but there's a good chance this dose will knock out the bacteria even before the lab results come back. Plus, as soon as you're rehydrated, we won't need to keep you tied up to the IV anymore."

"You won't?"

"No, ma'am."

"That's the best news I've had all day. That means I can go home then, right?"

Though his eyes are focused on the hypodermic in his hands, I feel a sudden sympathy from him. "I'm sorry your day hasn't been better," he says.

"So am I. Do you ever have the feeling you were going to die?"

"Don't be silly," he says, patting my hand.

But it's a feeling I can't escape, this premonition of imminent death. All throughout the ward, babies cry, and I can't stop myself from thinking of the babies who are behind the crying. Somewhere, Zerena is still alive and crying, and I hope I can live long enough to hold her again and dry away her tears. Without her, I'm a duck with no pond, a flimsy pink airplane with no sky.

"Hey, where's Jimmy?" I ask. I wish I could phone him, talk to him, share all my worries with him, but he isn't here. He isn't here. I can't trust him to be here when I need him.

The man sticks the needle in my arm. I know I should turn away, close my eyes, pretend this isn't happening, but when he presses down on the hypodermic's plunger, injecting me with the vancomycin, it's like a cool wind breezes through me.

From somewhere across the room, my phone rings. It rings and rings, and I hope it's Jimmy calling me. Or someone else—anyone— who might bring me good news about Zerena's whereabouts, but my mind is a puddle of fear. Someone's holding me down and jabbing a needle into me, preventing me from jumping across the room and fetching my phone. The needle stays in my arm long after its contents appear to be emptied, and the man counts out the seconds—"Oh twelve, oh thirteen, oh fourteen"—and at the magical number of "oh fifteen," he raises his eyes from the needle. I feel myself fainting again, the borders of my vision becoming dark and cottony. His eyes widen, alarmed. He starts to say something. I catch his first two words—"Oh, shit!"—before things turn foggy.

Chapter Twenty-Six

JIM

There are no positives to ac-cent-tchu-ate, no ring-a-ding-ding cherishable moments to latch on to from this meeting with Simpkins. All of Tully's money is counterfeit. Simpkins runs his fingertips over another hundred-dollar bill, brings it to his eyes, raises it to the overhead light, and shakes his head. "Nope. Not this one either. It's all fake."

"How can you tell?" Everything around me feels as if it's falling apart. It's not only Trish and Laurel tightening the screws. Now Simpkins is doing it too. My hopes, my dreams, sink in this gray tugboat of an office. "How can I be certain what you're telling me is correct?"

Simpkins squints at me. "Because I know what I'm doing. That's why." He expounds with authority the errors of the currency—color-shifting ink that doesn't shift to the right color when he tilts the bill, the watermarks that don't appear when he holds it to the light, the blurry microprinting so sloppily rendered it couldn't have met the exacting standards of a federal printing press. "So now that you've tried to pass off a fortune in counterfeit money on me, how do you propose we proceed?"

It never occurred to me that money, of all things, might not be what it seems. The amount is so trivial—a mere $10,000—that most of my clients wouldn't think it worthy of a petty cash slush fund, but nothing, apparently, raises the hackles of the meek so much as the sense of being wronged, and so Simpkins launches into a rant. He can't believe I'm so reckless as to sully our good relationship with counterfeit money. "You're lucky I'm so ethical," he says, shaking his head disapprovingly. "I'll give you forty-eight hours to bring me some honest money to replace this junk."

What happens if I fail to replace the bogus currency with legal tender? One way or another, Simpkins vows he'll get his money. "If I have to, I'll sell the information to that Wainsborough lady. And as for you, I'll let the police figure out what to do."

"Ha! How are you going to do that?" I fortify myself with another swig of the Macallan, congratulate myself for being such a smart boy. Anonymity is my trump card, a cloak of invisibility allowing me to evaporate mistlike from Simpkins's grasp. But then I remember the sonogram picture in his file. My throat tightens up, goes dry. He's crafty and devious enough to break into hospital databases. Even if he doesn't know who I am, he surely has ways of finding this out. "Do you even know who I am?"

"Buddy, I know plenty about you," Simpkins says, grinning. He tells me my social security number, date of birth, current address, and license plate number, rattling them off by memory. "What's more— you're a deadbeat alcoholic loser driving a midnight-blue Volvo station wagon, but you'd much rather be driving a Tesla, a Maserati, something with the glitzy class to match your sense of entitlement."

I stare at him.

"I'm a private investigator. *A private investigator.* Secrets are my business. I don't have all the pieces on you yet, but so help me god, give me fifteen minutes, and I'll figure out your credit card numbers and their security codes, your bank accounts, and the PIN number for your ATM card."

"What good will that do? I'm broke. I have no money. All my credit cards are overdrawn," I say. Never before had I considered insolvency to have its benefits. "You won't be able to get any money off me even if you try."

Simpkins shakes his head. "Buddy, listen to me. One way or another, you're going to give me the ten grand you owe me. Passing off counterfeit currency is a federal offense. If you fuck me over on this ten grand, I'll pinpoint you so deftly that prosecutors will have no choice but to prosecute you to the fullest extent of the law. Got it?"

~

Driving away from Simpkins's office through the downtown streets, I don't know where to go. I'm a slacker in search of a stupor, a wallet in search of some cash. I don't want to see Trish. I don't want to see Laurel. Nor do I wish the embarrassment of having my credit card declined at the watering holes that are my usual refuge. Years ago, as I drove these exact streets home from a rollicking Fourth of July barbecue at some senator-in-law's Chevy Chase manse with Jack Riggs, he waxed poetic about this being the land of opportunity, the wide DC boulevards paved with kickbacks, government-funded bailouts, and under-the-table agreements. Like any Gatsby, I wanted to believe America was America, a land of hopeless opportunity where, if you scratched the dirt deep enough, you'd find streets paved with gold. A land where, on a clear day, you could see Prosperity in the distance.

Freezing rain plinks against my windshield. Regrettably, I left the Macallan behind at Simpkins's office, having imbibed just enough to strand me in that melancholy middle state of being: neither drunk nor entirely sober, nothing seems bleary or cold, just unbearably sad. I reach into my back pocket for the phone I bought just to call Laurel, but it's not there. I must have dropped it in Simpkins's office, but there's no way I'm going back there just to reclaim it.

Only after Simpkins told me of Laurel's betrayal did I realize how much I loved her. I am not a dog. I did not flee into Laurel's arms at the first sniff of pheromonal attraction. Trish had been arguing with me about surrogacy. In the weeks immediately after Jack Riggs mentioned it, the idea of surrogacy ricocheted and triangulated through my thoughts. My mind wandered to the idea that another woman's womb might carry the child I long hoped Trish would carry. From there, I let my mind wander to how my child might get into this other woman's womb. The thoughts were insidious, overtaking me for hours at a time. I couldn't tell any of them to Trish, so ashamed was I for thinking these things.

When I met Laurel, thoughts of surrogacy again popped into my mind. I looked at her and felt bouncy. Mired by our infertility problems, Trish succumbed to despair. She moped around the house, rarely letting us accept the cocktail party and dinner invitations friends extended to us. I'd long since ceased to be a source of constant happiness for Trish, but Laurel ate up my flattery, and it felt good being able to make someone happy again. When I set eyes on her at her restaurant, she laughed and bantered with diners, totally comfortable with her role and surroundings. With her, there were no connivances, no drama, no despair. Instinctually, I knew she'd be the mother of my child. I hadn't approached another woman since first laying eyes on Trish, but with Laurel I felt this compulsive need to introduce myself and seduce her over with geniality and intimations of wealth. I wanted her to love me. I wanted her to bear my child.

Weeks prior to Anne Elise's birth, I moved Laurel out of her dank Woodley Park basement efficiency and into a gorgeous five-room riverside apartment in a historic complex not far from the Kennedy Center. Seeing it the first time, Laurel brought her hands to her face and erupted with astonishment when I opened the gilt-green living room curtains to reveal the spectacular view of the placid sun-drenched Potomac that would be hers for the six-month duration of the lease I signed on the apartment. Sliding floor-to-ceiling windows led out from what would become her bedroom onto a balcony where, on her first night in the apartment, we held hands and kissed, our lips warmed by thoughts of a shared future and mugs of brandy-laced hot chocolate. Two rowboats were on the water, beating back against the current. We stood together, watching them, listening to the splash of their oars. Since the lease was renewable, and since I preferred not to think of myself as perpetually strapped, I let her believe the apartment was hers for keeps.

With nowhere else to go and wanting to be alone, I head to this apartment. Three days' worth of newspapers are piled up against her front door. No one has been inside since I rushed Laurel to Sibley on the morning she gave birth, and when I key open the door, I see the signs of an interrupted life: the can of chicken noodle soup sitting on the blue granite kitchen countertops that she opened just before her water broke; the nappy amber towels I threw down to absorb the amniotic fluid that gushed out of her onto the tile floor; the living room television on mute but still stuck to the Weather Channel, informing us that for the third straight day the DC area will be overcast with intermittent wintry tempests.

The apartment's furniture is blond and retro mod, the kidney-shaped living room tables, low-slung chaise longue, and bucket chairs all items that wouldn't look out of place in a *Jetsons* episode. Laurel wanted furniture with a sense of whimsy, something that would point to the excitement of the future but also hearken to the comfy well-defined past of Saturday-morning cartoons and a tight-knit nuclear family. I tidy up the apartment, putting a few things back in place, and then wander into the nursery, the one room where the furniture is all new and bought, rather than rented, and because the walls still smell of fresh paint, I open the windows to air out the room. Sitting on the cane rocking chair, I plug in the coolest device I bought for Anne Elise—an orb-shaped nightlight that projects pink stars and a crescent moon onto the ceiling. Gazing into the illuminated firmament of twinkling stars, I think about how much I looked forward to showing her these exact stars. "Grab them!" I'd tell her as she lay on her back and stretched out her arms to the astral illuminations on her ceiling. "Reach as high as you can!" I can't believe Laurel tricked me, used me, took advantage of my desire to be her George Jetson.

One of my other cell phones rings. It's Trish asking where I might be and when I might come home. She's tired and hungry but not upset. "I'm sitting by the fireplace. I'd like you to come home and build me a fire. Brew me a carafe of chamomile tea, and we could snuggle."

"I want to be alone tonight."

"Where are you? Maybe I could come over and keep you company."

"No."

"Tell me where you are. You're not with *her*, are you?"

"No." Although Trish would appreciate the irony of me renting Laurel an apartment in the same complex where, forty-plus years ago, a spectacular break-in led to the national crisis that indirectly cost Jack Riggs his Treasury Department job when his chief benefactor was removed from office, Trish doesn't know about this apartment.

"I should tell you a police detective visited me tonight."

A cold gust blows river mist toward the open window. As I think about the counterfeit cash, my pulse quickens. Simpkins was supposed to give me forty-eight hours before calling the police. I hadn't thought he'd double-cross me like this, giving me barely—what?—forty-eight *minutes* before unleashing the law on me. DC cops aren't supposed to be this tenacious pursuing what only amounts to white-collar crime.

"A detective came to Savory Mew. He just left. It was you he wanted to speak with."

"Why? Why did he come?"

A moment elapses. "You honestly don't know?"

"Of course I don't know!"

"I'm so glad to hear this," Trish says, letting out a huge sigh. "You know nothing about it, do you? Anne Elise is missing from the hospital."

The news takes my breath away. "Oh my god." I can't think of anything else to say, any other way to express my dismay. "Oh my god." As angry as I feel toward Laurel, I'd never want anything bad to happen to Anne Elise. "Are you sure?"

"Uh-huh." Trish, too, seems upset by what happened. Until this moment, listening to her shock and anger at Anne Elise's disappearance, I hadn't realized just how much she must love the baby. "It's horrible. She's been missing for hours. They can't find her anywhere. You didn't know?"

"Why do you think I'd know?"

"I hesitate to tell you this, but the police think you've run off with her. Or worse. I tried to tell them you'd never do anything like that, that you're calm and gentle. I think Laurel's been talking to them."

"Laurel?" I can't make sense of this. Why would Laurel say anything against me when she's the one trying to bamboozle me into thinking Anne Elise is mine so that I'd support the both of them all their lives?

"Think about it. She's not a stable person. You told me yourself her parents are sketchy. So she thinks you're going to dump her—"

"How did she get that idea in her head?" I ask, interrupting Trish. Although I intimated to Trish that I was contemplating dumping Laurel—mostly to keep Trish from dumping me—I never suggested such a thing to Laurel.

"James. Hear me out. What matters is what *she* thinks. As she's lying in her hospital bed, depressed and infected, what she thinks is, 'Hey, James is still going home to his wife each night, making love with her, eating fantastic lamb dinners with her. I bet he's going to dump me.' That's what she's thinking."

Lamb dinners? How would Laurel know about the lamb dinner Trish cooked last night? Yesterday, when Trish visited Laurel ostensibly to spend time with Anne Elise, what she must've really been doing was spreading lies about the affection I still harbor for her. Trish's got Laurel believing I remain happily though perhaps unconventionally married. Which is ironic, because that's exactly what I wanted Trish to think, and yet she's preying on Laurel's insecurities and inclinations toward jealousy, cranking up her fears or encouraging her to take preemptive actions against me out of spite. As I listen to Trish, my whole body tenses up. I grab the sides of the rocking chair I'm sitting on. Everyone's tightening the screws on me.

"Do you know what I mean?" Trish asks. "She's so sure you're abandoning her that she turns passive aggressive and bad-mouths you to the police. It would be funny except that the police believe her lies. This could wind you up in jail."

"Jail?" I lower the phone from my ear and moan. Everyone is determined to put the squeeze on me. Simpkins. Tully. Laurel. Trish. In no mood whatsoever to ac-cent-tchu-ate anything but anger, I let out a howl. Darker numbers from the Johnny Mercer songbook play through my mind—"Blues in the Night" and "One for My Baby (and One More for the Road)"—songs of languor and alcoholically anesthetized heartbreak, a clickety-clack leading to the realization that "a woman's a two-face, a worrisome thing." Did Johnny Mercer ever write a song about a revenge killing? Because that's the kind of song I need to sing— something cold and vicious. Laurel's been lying to police about me. I'm liable to go to jail. I'm distraught, trying to figure out how I got myself into this position. If I had Trish's Valiums, I'd give them all to Laurel so she'd overdose and die. One thing's for certain: I'm never going to love Laurel again.

"Hey? Are you all right?" Trish asks.

"Sure, babe. What could be wrong? I'm a lucky man, having someone like you in my corner to alert me to what's going on. Thanks."

Chapter Twenty-Seven

LAUREL

An hour or more later, I awake so clearheaded that I'm zapped with the impression I must be dead. No nurses crowd around my bed, no needles prick my arms. Nor do smug monkey doctors tell me to spread my legs or take a peek down there. I'm alone, thankfully alone, but though I'm buried beneath what feels like six feet of blankets, I'm no sack o' bones waiting for the mortician's slab. The antibiotics have done their trick. I'm alert and more energetic than I've been in days. True to their word, the doctors have disconnected me from my IV: no tubing coils from my wrist, connecting me to an IV bag, a stainless steel IV stand, or anything else that threatens to topple down on me should I move my arm too suddenly.

Feeling like a rooster at the break of the day, I shrug off the blankets. In these early-morning hours, the maternity ward is quiet and dark. Though I may no longer be infected, the episiotomy itself still hasn't healed. I wince at the pain between my legs. A lesser rooster would be dissuaded by the pain, but I shimmy out of bed, step to the closet, slide into the cranberry peacoat I last wore when checking into the hospital, and grab my purse. The lights in the hallway are dimmed for the evening. No nurses, doctors, or janitors patrol the hallways. It's up to me to find Zerena.

An exit door leads to a brightly lit stairwell. Hospitals are no place for a healthy person. Yesterday, doctors said my infection had gone away, yet it came back. Now that they've cured me again, every minute I remain here increases the chances I'll catch another infection, and so I scooch down the stairs, neither nimble nor quick, a slow-and-steady tortoise intent on winning the race. Downstairs, I realize I left my phone in my room, but it's way too late to go back. I hobble across the lobby and pass through the revolving door. Outside, everything is calm, immaculate, the sounds of the city absorbed by the snow that falls in abundance. I pause, catch my breath, brace myself against a **No Parking** sign in the pick-up/drop-off zone. Cold will dull the pain that pierces me between my legs. This is what I tell myself. Snow is falling in thick, juicy flakes. Someday, perhaps in a couple of years, I will build a snowman with Zerena on a night like this. For now though, I need to find her.

"Hey, you need a ride?" someone asks.

I turn around. A taxicab has pulled up right behind me, its engine running. Perhaps the cab has been standing there all along, or perhaps it just arrived, dropping off its passengers while I stared out into the snowy surroundings. The cab driver, a Middle Eastern–looking man in a blue-and-gray hoodie, sticks his head out through the driver's side window and asks again, as if I hadn't heard his first question. And then he adds, "Hey? Are you all right? Do you need me to walk you back into the emergency room?"

"Huh?" Beneath my peacoat, I'm still wearing my maternity ward–issued pink hospital gown and the pair of fuzz-ball slippers I've had since college.

"You've been standing there for five minutes, leaning against the parking sign."

I let go of the sign, flex my cold-stiffened fingers, and notice it stopped snowing. Despite my earlier gusto, I feel weak. "I have?"

"Do you need a ride?"

"I need to go home." I tell him the name of my apartment complex. I've lived there only a couple of weeks, and the place still strikes me as some dream reality where everything is beautiful and well maintained. So new is the apartment to me that I mistakenly gave my old apartment's address when checking into the hospital, which will make it next to impossible for them to find me if I'm needed. Tomorrow, I'll track down Tricia's address and hunt for Zerena, but tonight I want to cocoon myself in a bed that doesn't have stainless steel safety railings at its sides.

The cab driver screws his eyes. "You live there?"

"It's nice," I say, wobbling over to the cab and opening the door to let myself into the back seat.

∼

Five buildings comprise the Watergate complex, three devoted to co-op apartments and the other two containing a hotel and office space. The complex's name, now synonymous with arrogance and corruption, derives from a large wooden gate in the water at the spot where the now-defunct Chesapeake and Ohio Canal entered into the Potomac River. History has a way of rearing its head, repeating and transforming itself. Someday when it's warmer, I intend to rustle through the brush at the river's edge and find what remains of that gate, but when the cab driver lets me off at the front of my building, snow starts falling again. With only slippers on my feet, I must be the worst-shoed person ever to shamble into the building. Jimmy is probably out, maybe even spending the night with Tricia, but my anticipation builds throughout the elevator ride upstairs. When the elevator door dings open, it's like I can smell the briny, woodsy wake of Jimmy's Acqua di Giò as if he, too, has stepped off the elevator moments earlier.

Inside the apartment, things are tidier than I remember. Before my water broke, I watched the Weather Channel for three days straight, fearful some freak storm was about to descend upon the city, stranding me snowbound when the time came for me to go to Sibley. A window, somewhere, is open, letting a winter draft into the apartment. Lights flicker in the nursery. Approaching that room, I'm astounded to see the nursery's ceiling aglow with stars and a crescent moon, the stars twinkling softly, poetically, as if in a lullaby. I tiptoe closer, peer inside. Jimmy's on the rocking chair. The nightlight star projector that he bought last week sits on the floor by his feet, beaming its stars upward. He hasn't seen or heard me. It's sweet, watching him in this quiet starlit room. He has no idea that our baby's gone missing, but I know that after I tell him what's happened, we'll be able to handle this situation together. He strokes his chin; as strange as it sounds, I've never felt closer to him than I do now.

I step inside the nursery and try to close the window, but the window hardly budges. The sound the window makes startles Jimmy. He glances up at me, alarmed.

"Jimmy, I'm so glad to see you." Perhaps because I've startled him, he looks angry, scowling mad, so I rest my hand on his shoulder to calm him, thinking that, together, we'll support each other. We'll be the shoulder the other can lean on, the solace we each seek. "Zerena's missing. They can't find her anywhere at the hospital."

"Shut up," Jimmy says, knocking my hand away. "I've about had enough of you."

PART THREE

Chapter Twenty-Eight

JIM

Anger is the least effective emotion when it comes to getting what you want in this get-along/go-along world, but unable to control myself, I hurl a plastic baby rattle so hard it shatters against the wall above Laurel's head. Grains of brown rice burst from the rattle like shrapnel, settling onto her hair, the shoulders of her peacoat, and the carpet at her feet. She looks at me wide-eyed, astonished, fearful for her life.

I've spent the last hour contemplating what I want in life. A week ago, I dipped a brush into a can of glossy yellow paint that smelled of linseed oil and painted the walls. The impression I hoped to create was of sunshine, happiness, and limitless opportunities. I wielded a Phillips-head screwdriver, a new Craftsman socket wrench, needle-nose pliers, and a ball-peen hammer to assemble the crib, the changing table, and this rocking chair upon which I sit. I made preparations, bought cases of Huggies disposable diapers, a Playtex Diaper Genie II Elite diaper-disposal system that billed itself as "your companion in your journey through early parenthood," a half dozen refills for said Diaper Genie, snap-on onesies of every color imaginable, Vaseline, baby oil, baby wipes, and an industrial-sized hamper to accommodate the baby's dirty clothes. I foresaw every contingency save the possibility that the baby wasn't mine. Nor had I figured her mother would finger me to the police as suspect *numero uno* in the event of her disappearance.

"You're evil. That's what you are," I say, clapping my hands together loud enough to make Laurel jump. "After all I've done for you. After all I've done for Anne Elise. What the fuck were you thinking? Dragging me into your white-trash life? You hoodwinked me, lied to me, fucked me silly until I was good and under your spell so you could convince me I was the father of another man's child."

Laurel cringes. She's no lily-white flower, no angel with feathery wings and ethereal longings. The love child of a lowlife criminal and a druggie, she spent years locked up behind bars, but she wants me to believe she's so innocent as to be offended by my accusations.

"But, Jimmy—"

"Don't 'but, Jimmy' me!"

I lift up my phone, play for Laurel's benefit my recorded conversation with Simpkins. Listening to the money negotiations between Simpkins and me, she's confused, but during the meat of the conversation, Laurel stiffens. She listens to Simpkins talk about the photos in her phone and how he's sure the blond-haired, blue-eyed man sharing a bed with her in one of the photos is the father of her baby. I'm watching Laurel as she listens. An icy breeze ruffles the open window's lace curtains. Her cheeks are red from tears, red from the cold. She brings her arms together and shivers.

I click off the phone, tap my foot to the floor. "So?"

"I should've been honest. There was another guy I was seeing back when we met." Laurel wipes back her tears with the back of her hand. "When I realized I was pregnant, I didn't know what to do. I didn't know if you'd understand. I wasn't sure whose it might be, but I was sure hoping it was yours. I should've been more honest."

"No shit. You were fucking another guy at the same time you were fucking me. At least with you, I was honest. I told you I was married, so I was honest about my infidelity. But you?" As angry I feel about Laurel

sleeping with another guy, it pales to my anger knowing I'm not Anne
Elise's biological father. I sneer, get up from the rocking chair. "Trish
wants me to kill you."

"Kill me?" Laurel gulps. Her forehead glistens with perspiration.
A disarming clarity comes over her eyes. She sits on the floor, crosses
her legs, and lays her palms upon her knees as if to summon strength
through meditation. She breathes in deeply, holds the breath, and
chokes back her tears. "I was lonely and had no real friends in the world.
The guy meant nothing to me beyond a warm cuddle and a chance
not to be alone for a night. I was so glad when I met you. You looked
at me as if I was more than just a piece of ass. You asked my feelings
about things and cared about what I thought. That was new to me. You
cared about me. The other guy never did. I fell in love with you. I'm no
dumb-dumb, no fly-by-night skank. You are the man I want to spend
the rest of my life with. I love you. You love me. I didn't want to risk
you turning your back on me if I told you about the other guy. Can you
blame me? It's you I want to be with, not any other guy."

"You do meditation?" I ask. We know so little about each other,
relying on gut instinct to fill in the particulars of each other's interests
and delights. I wouldn't have thought Laurel was into meditation or
yoga or any of those mindfulness exercises that are becoming popular,
but now that she's in the lotus position, I can see how she'd be drawn
to vaguely Eastern, vaguely spiritual practices. Things that are vaguely
pure or at least less susceptible to corruption. What kind of fool am I?
How could I have gotten so involved with someone I barely know? And
how can I get myself out of this situation?

Laurel brushes her hand against her sweat-drenched forehead. "I
don't meditate as often as I should."

"Why'd you tell the cops that you thought I'd—what?—kidnapped
Anne Elise?"

Laurel looks up, bewildered. In a previous life, she would have
been a free-love spirit decked out in hippy-dippy tie-dye hemp sandals

and love beads, seeking the good vibrations of an ashram or the rainy, muddy chaos of Woodstock. She lifts her palms from her knees, buttons the top button of her peacoat. "What are you talking about?"

"The police. Trish called and said detectives were swarming around the house, trying to find me. Apparently, they're looking for me."

"Why would they be looking for you?"

"Don't bullshit me."

Laurel stands up, lays an arm against the bright-yellow wall to steady herself. She closes her eyes and winces as if in pain and the mere act of pulling herself to a standing position winded her. "I'm not bullshitting you."

"Trish said you told them I took Anne Elise. Until she called me, I didn't know Anne Elise was missing."

"I'm not bullshitting you. I never said anything like that."

"But Trish said—"

"How do you know Tricia's telling the truth?"

I tell Laurel that Trish's my wife, that we've been married a dozen years and at the very least she's never misled or deceived me as badly as Laurel has. And now I see it in my mind: tomorrow morning, I'll go back to Trish, sit her down on the Hepplewhite, and tell her how sorry and foolish I've been. I'll light a fire in the fireplace, brew her a carafe of chamomile tea, and pledge never to stray again. I'll throw myself at her mercy. Trish will know what to do. We've traveled the far ends of this earth together. We've chartered private jets to see wonders few other Americans are lucky enough to experience: the white sands of Fiji, Easter Island's megalithic moai statues, genuine Inuit igloos on Baffin Island. I've not known Trish to lie. She can be exacting, demanding, merciless even when guarding her personal finances, but she doesn't stoop to dishonesty. But as I'm thinking this, Laurel's looking straight at me, the earnestness of her gaze piercing straight through me, and then, as if I'm walloped by an uncomfortable awareness, it hits me that

Laurel is right—not one but *two* women have been playing me, lying to me, using me.

"You've got to trust me," Laurel says. "Within weeks of meeting you, I stopped seeing that other guy. I don't know whose baby it is. It could be yours; it could be his, but even before I knew I was pregnant, I stopped seeing the other guy. Honest."

What Laurel says shocks me. Ever since Simpkins revealed those pictures of Laurel in another guy's arms, I assumed there was no way I could be Anne Elise's father. But a single picture proves nothing. Though Simpkins couldn't retrieve them, Laurel's taken dozens of pictures of me with her phone. She's stopped people on the boulevards we've walked and in the parks we've strolled and handed them her phone so they could snap photos of us. But can Laurel actually have stronger feelings for that other guy? Is that why she kept his pictures but deleted those that she took of me? But more importantly, can I really be Anne Elise's father?

"I'm scared," Laurel says. "What's going to happen to Zerena?"

"Zerena?"

"Anne Elise," Laurel says, correcting herself. In the minutes since stepping into this frigid room, her rosy cheeks have turned porcelain pale again. She shivers and, in a weaker voice, asks, "Can you shut the window? I'm catching cold or something."

"Sure." I get up from the rocking chair. The window slides shut easily.

When I turn around, Laurel's taken my seat on the rocking chair. She's still shivering, still cold. She stretches out her hand, looks around the room, and her face gets sad. "How did we get like this?"

Instinctively, I know what she means. No baby rests in the crib, no permanence affixes itself to our lives. We're living in-between lives, dodgy, precarious moments that threaten to evaporate as soon as one of us decides to walk away from the other. We're two smart people who've dillydallied ourselves into this situation where neither of us is sure what's going on. All along, I've been trying *not* to make a choice between Laurel and Trish, reasoning that as long as I didn't back myself into choosing one or the other, I could have both. Several times I've stopped myself and tried to imagine who I'd be with in another few months. Sometimes, I see myself back in Savory Mew, content with the fine clothes and fine wines Trish plies me with; on other days, I see myself in this apartment or some eventual homeless shelter living off nothing but Laurel's and Anne Elise's abundant love.

Ideally, you should accept happiness as it comes, but happiness is the most relative of all emotions: no matter how happy you might be, the mind always swerves to other situations that could make you even happier; no matter if I see myself with Laurel or Trish, I always imagine myself being happier if the other were true. F. Scott Fitzgerald wrote that "the test of a first-rate intelligence is the ability to hold two opposed ideas in the mind at the same time, and still retain the ability to function." That's what we were doing, "functioning." You can learn everything about America through Fitzgerald, but nothing in his stories and novels could've prepared me for this.

"Do you really think the baby might be mine?"

"Yes. I asked my doctors. We've gone over ovulation charts, figured out when my last period was. It's a fifty-fifty thing. As near as I can tell, our baby was conceived either the first time I made love with you or the last time I was with that other guy. We can get a paternity test if you want," Laurel says, nervously. "And then, if you're not the father, I'd understand if—"

"No!" I know what she's going to say—that if the baby isn't mine, she'd understand if we parted, but that's not what I want. For the first time since I slinked into Simpkins's office with my bottle of Macallan, I feel good, hopeful, desirous to stay alive. What's to be gained by a paternity test? Nothing. Having gone so long without a child, I don't want to risk throwing away my chance to be a father if the test proves negative. Ignorance has its virtues. I've wandered through half my life not really knowing everything that goes on around me. Why should I change now?

Laurel's teeth chatter. She rubs her hands together, crosses her arms. "I'm cold."

"Hey, shouldn't you still be in the hospital?"

Laurel winces. "The doctors said I'd be all right. That's what they said."

"They did?"

"Trust me. It's better I'm not there. They can't even sew up an episiotomy right. Can you bring me a blanket?"

I bend to my knees, and placing one arm around her shoulders and the other behind her knees, I lift her from the rocking chair. She's lighter than she ought to be, and though she claims to be cold, a feverish heat rises off her. She's a frail little bird, a plush toy of a new mother, someone who, in her inimitable unspoken way, is frantic and scared. With her in my arms, I walk toward the bedroom. I'm not muscular like that blond-haired guy in the photo Simpkins showed me, but aided by adrenaline and the wish to bring peace to this roller-coaster night, I carry her effortlessly. During our honeymoon, Trish refused to allow me to lift her into my arms and carry her across the threshold of our hotel suite, and although I tried not to let her denial bother me, I think of that moment as the first indication Trish was never prepared to fully give herself to me. Crossing from the hallway into the bedroom, I slide Laurel into bed, roll the quilted comforter over her. By the time I fluff up her pillow, she's fast asleep but sweating profusely.

Chapter Twenty-Nine

LAUREL

Shivering and wet, I'm melting away into nothingness. I must have fallen asleep hours earlier. Jimmy must have carried me into bed. There's a damp washcloth on my forehead dripping water onto my face, and though three blankets wrap around me, I'm trembling when I awaken on the bed in my apartment. Knowing Zerena's missing, I feel empty. Moonlight dapples the river outside the bedroom window, the light glistening on the water, but I'm woozy and achy. What presses upon me is darkness and peril. It's five a.m., an hour when no one should be awake. I'm scared and desperate, childless and alone in this apartment that still feels new to me, and because it is new to me, it feels like I'm a snowflake who doesn't belong here, an interloper, a temporary lodger who'll soon be told to pack her bags and take a hike. Hearing footsteps approach the bedroom, I duck under the covers. A hand plops on my shoulder, tugging me.

"Laurel. Please."

Peering out from underneath the blankets, I see Jimmy's insistent face. He sets a glass of water on the nightstand and shakes out a couple of capsules from a bottle onto his palm. Because he was not in bed when I awoke, I assumed he had gone away again, like he always does.

"Have you been here all night?" I ask.

"There's no place I'd rather be than here, sweetie, taking care of you," Jimmy says. Though his feet are bare, he's dressed in the same suit he's worn since yesterday. Shadows hang beneath his eyes. If I were to bet, I'd guess he had no sleep whatsoever. I'm oddly emotional, knowing he's been here all night. We've never shared a full evening together. When he checked us into fancy hotels, he'd duck away before midnight each night to return home to Tricia. I told him I understood—he didn't want to unnecessarily anger his wife—but I felt second-class, cheap, and slutty, knowing he didn't want to wake up and find me sleeping beside him. After making love, I'd rest my head on his shoulder and inhale his Acqua di Giò, his deodorant, and the musty tang of his perspiration. He'd hold me for joyous, satisfying moments and say he wished he could spend the whole night with me, and I never knew if he was telling the truth about this or not. Was our love situational? Was that all it was? I'd watch him gather his trousers, his jockey shorts, his black dress socks from wherever he'd thrown them before getting into bed with me.

"Jimmy? Can I ask you a question?"

"Sure."

"Where do you live? With Tricia?" This had bothered me ever since the hospital security officer made me feel like a fool for not knowing it.

To my surprise, James tells me the address—somewhere in Georgetown—and because he willingly tells me this address, I realize he trusts me. Or at least figures I can't possibly inflict any more harm on his marriage than I already have. When I repeat the address, committing it to memory, he nods. Sometime soon, whenever I'm with my cell phone again, I vow to look up that address to get a greater glimpse into his life.

Now, Jimmy hands me the glass of water. "Take these, okay?" he says of the two capsules in his palm.

"What are they?"

"Ibuprofen. To bring your fever down. Are you sure doctors didn't give you any other medicine when they discharged you?"

Perhaps it's out of concern for Zerena or perhaps because he's worried about my health that he chose to spend the whole night with me, but I'd like to think he's turning over a new leaf, finally ditching Tricia so we can live together. My throat is so dry I can barely swallow the ibuprofen capsules, but I swell with emotion. Through the fog of my happiness, I hear something thump against the front door, the sound distant and cloudy like a handclap heard when swimming underwater.

Jimmy cocks his head. "Newspaper," he announces. "They just delivered it. That's what the sound is."

"Do you think they published a story about Zerena's disappearance?"

Jimmy's head pops up. The possibility hadn't occurred to him before I mentioned it, but now that I have, he bounds out of the room to fetch the paper. I hear him open the front door and then close it. Moments later, he returns with the newspaper tucked under his arm and slides into bed beside me. His cold feet brush against my calves, sending icy shivers all over me, but for a moment it's easy to imagine we're an old married couple lazing away the early hours of a Saturday morning reading the newspaper in bed. Jimmy holds the paper so we can both read it, but no article about Zerena appears on the front page. Washington being a national and international city, stories of local interest go underreported in the *Post,* but it's impossible they'd overlook a sensational nugget about a newborn's disappearance from a local hospital. Jimmy sighs. Against my hot face, his breath is cold, icy like his toes are against my feet. We search the entire front section. Jimmy picks up another section and rifles through the pages. "There's got to be an article about her somewhere."

But there isn't.

"Nothing," Jimmy says. "How can that be? You'd figure there'd be an Amber Alert on her by now. Don't newspapers mention Amber Alerts anymore?"

"Maybe we should put out a reward to find her? Let's call the police and tell everyone we're offering—I don't know—ten thousand dollars for Zerena's return. We'll offer enough money so people take notice."

"*We* should offer money?"

We've rarely talked about money, and I'm acutely aware of the financial imbalance I bring into this relationship. I'm the penniless damsel, and he's my knight in shining currency who'll open up his checkbook to rescue our little princess. "I meant, maybe you can offer a reward. Even if she's not really your daughter—"

Jimmy presses his fingers over my lips. "She's my daughter. I love her too."

I squint at him. How could he now be so sure he's Zerena's biological father?

"Laurel. In order to be lucky, you've got to think lucky. Right now—and I swear, for the rest of our lives—I'm thinking lucky."

His words send a shiver of warmth all over me. I am so lucky. That's what I'm thinking. The sun is beginning to rise over the Potomac. Daybreak had been one of the things I'd been looking forward to enjoying in this apartment.

Jimmy's voice becomes quieter. "Honey? Can I tell you a secret?"

Something in the way Jimmy says this puts me on edge. No one but no one asks permission to reveal a secret unless it's something bad. The first thing that pops into my mind is that even after all he's said, he's doing a boomerang and leaving me for Tricia, but then my stomach clenches. Warning bells go off in my head. I remember what one of the security guards said yesterday. Everyone knows the narratives of domestic crimes are all the same—when a woman dies under suspicious circumstances or a child goes missing, it's usually the victim's husband/boyfriend/father who's guilty.

"Honey. I'm broke. I don't have the money to offer a reward."

I stare at him unblinkingly.

"I'm not the millionaire you think I am. I've misled you. I'm sorry. I'm not rich. I'm so in debt it would make your head spin."

"But your bank. Your family owns a bank. Or owned a bank."

Jimmy lets go of my hands. His mouth turns clumsy, and his eyes gape, giving the impression he's only now coming to terms with what he's saying. "I'm not rich. I've never been rich." Jimmy stares at the glorious sunrise outside our window. I can see that he'd rather not be telling me what he's telling me and also that he's telling me this with a deep sense of shame. I've never seen such anguish in his face before. Only in America do people feel ashamed for not being wealthy. "Tricia's family. She's Riggs through and through. She's the wealthy one. My own father was a deadbeat alcoholic loser who abandoned us when I was in my teens. My mother's a schoolteacher—nice work if you can get it, but it doesn't provide an heiress-level income stream. If it weren't for Tricia, I'd be a deadbeat alcoholic loser too. She's the one who keeps me afloat, bailing me out time and again whenever I teeter toward a bankruptcy filing."

"But this apartment you bought." I glance around the spacious bedroom. Despite what he said, I can't reconcile how someone as classy as Jimmy can be broke. Not every apartment has such picturesque windows, humongous chandeliers, and top-notch American walnut flooring. Though my knowledge of the DC real estate market is near zilch, my guess is the apartment is worth millions. Surely, Tricia wouldn't have paid to put me in an apartment this nice. "We can take a loan out on the apartment. What do you call it? A home equity line?"

"No, we can't."

"Why not? We'll use the money to set up a reward for Zerena. Maybe hire our own private investigator to locate her."

Jimmy snorts.

"What?"

"Laurel, honey. Private investigators aren't worth squat. Trust me. Only suckers hire private investigators."

"Okay. But we can still post a reward for Zerena."

"With what money?"

"With the money we'll borrow against this apartment."

"Honey. Laurel. Dear. It's impossible to get a second mortgage on a property we don't own."

"Huh?"

Jimmy's cheeks redden. "We're only renting the apartment."

"Renting?"

"The rent is twenty thousand dollars a month. It took everything I had to put down the money for a six-month lease."

"Six months?" Jimmy had told me he bought apartment for me. I'm positive that's what he said before I moved in. "But . . . but . . ."

"I'm sorry. I wanted you and the baby to have the best possible start in life. If I'm lucky, I might be able to squeeze out another month or two for you to stay here. Otherwise . . . well, otherwise, we'll figure something out."

I feel so stupid. It's not the money that leaves me dumbfounded. Belinda, my mother, struggled with addictions all her life. As a teenager, even locked up in juvie, I thought myself superior to her because I was drug-free, but I've succumbed to the cruelest drug of all: love. Love blinded me. Love caused me to rush into this relationship without fully investigating what I was stepping into. Under the euphoria of love, I trusted Jimmy unquestioningly. I didn't ask to see bank statements or mortgage papers. I didn't ask for a diamond ring, a kiss on the cheek, or a bouquet of flowers. I didn't ask for anything; instead, I gave him the only valuable thing I had to give: my love.

"Wait. What about my student loans?"

"What are you talking about?"

Although we never talked about it, I assumed Jimmy was going to pay off my loans. How am I ever going to get a couple hundred thousand dollars to pay off all the money I owe from going to college?

"Jimmy, you're not the only one in this relationship who's hugely in debt. I owe, like, a quarter of a million dollars. Can you help me?"

Jimmy closes his eyes, sighs. "I wish I could, honey."

It hits me like a pair of handcuffs being slapped around my wrists. I'm going to end up with nothing from this relationship. Maybe even worse than nothing. And it hurts, knowing that Tricia was right about Jimmy all along. He's not responsible. He's not trustworthy. "You lied to me. You let me think you were rich just so I'd sleep with you."

"I'm sorry." Jimmy hangs his head, scooches out of bed. Sunbeams angle over his shoulder from the floor-to-ceiling windows, but tired and dejected, he pays no attention to the beauty outside. Maybe he, too, succumbed to love. Maybe he thought love would make everything work out, that through love he might finagle a way for us to keep this glorious apartment forever. He picks one of his black socks off the floor. I'm not innocent. I lied to him, let him believe I hadn't been sleeping with another man, let him believe Anne Elise was his child. But I really hadn't been sure. Jimmy had been so joyful at the news of my pregnancy that I never told him it might not be his child. Now, he picks up his other sock and fishes his polished wingtips out from under the bed, and as he puts his left shoe on, I realize he's fixing to leave. If I don't get over my resentments quick about his money situation, he's going to walk out of the bedroom, perhaps forever.

Tired and feverish, I struggle to concentrate on what's going on. Being second-class poor myself, I should have more sympathy for Jimmy being poor, but anger rises in my throat. No one relishes being misled and outsmarted by a lover, and yet, if Zerena and I are to survive, if I am to find Zerena and make a better childhood for her than I had, it's up to me to find a solution to our problem. Already tying his black shoelaces, Jimmy is about to walk out of my life.

"Wait," I say.

He turns around.

"Maybe we could . . . maybe we could . . ."

"What?"

I toss my head back on the silky bed pillow. Jimmy's looking at me, expecting me to say something amazing, but problem-solving has never been my greatest skill, and his anticipation gives way to embarrassment as he shies his eyes from me. But then the answer comes to me all at once. I know what we have to do, and for the first time in days, I'm happy. I smile, lift my head up from the pillow.

Jimmy steps closer, bends down to hold my hand. "Honey? What is it?"

"The money Tully gave you. We can use that for the reward." It's my brightest idea ever, something so stupendously brilliant I'm surprised I hadn't thought of it earlier. Later, after Zerena's found, we can do a GoFundMe campaign or something to repay Tully—but later is later: we could put Tully off for a couple of months, which will buy us time to figure out what to do.

Jimmy closes his eyes, lets go of my hand.

"What's wrong?"

"We can't do that either. That money's counterfeit."

"What?" My father's no stranger to criminality—petty thefts, breaking and entering, small-time drug dealing, assault and battery— but counterfeiting, which requires some level of technical competence, seems too sophisticated for him. "Are you sure?"

"Positive."

"Well. Give it back to him. Tell him to give you more money. Real money."

"I can't do that. The money's with someone else who's not too happy it's counterfeit."

Jimmy starts to say more but his cell phone rings with those pompous *bah bah bah bum* Beethoven notes. It's the phone he uses for business, the one he tells me never to touch. He picks it up and starts talking about money, but while he's talking, I get the sick feeling that Tully's going to demand his money back, counterfeit or not, way quicker than either of us anticipates. As I'm mulling over what might happen when Tully finds out about this fake cash, Jimmy's call becomes contentious. He tells whomever he's talking to that "you gave me forty-eight hours to come up with the money. Forty-eight hours!" but the man's already switching boats on Jimmy. Whatever the money's about—financing or something—the guy tells Jimmy he needs to come up with the financing right away. That, at least, is what I think the guy says. Jimmy screams. And then he asks, "Say, how'd you get my phone number?" to which I hear derisive laughter coming from the other end of the line.

The call ends, none to Jimmy's satisfaction. He stands up and leans against the sliding glass windows, fuming.

"Who was that?" I ask, expecting to be told about some demanding client whose investment expectations are way too high.

"That was a private investigator, the guy who I gave Tully's money to."

I screw up my eyes at him. "You told me only suckers hire private investigators."

"So sue me. I'm a sucker, okay?" Jimmy hunches his shoulders. "That's who I am: a sucker."

Chapter Thirty

JIM

Laurel's hand is rough, her skin dried with fever, dehydration, and the demands of motherhood. As she drifts off to sleep again, I sing the pinnacle of Arlen and Mercer's songs to her—"It's Only a Paper Moon," "Over the Rainbow," "Jeepers Creepers," and "Ac-cent-tchu-ate the Positive"—all of them born out of the Depression-era ethos of raise-your-chin-up, can-do optimism. If we're to proceed happily through life, we need to embrace the lies that hover around us, collecting in every nook and cranny of our zeitgeist and our very being. From her slumbers, Laurel murmurs with what I choose to believe is delight over my performances, but I know my vocal limits—I'm no Sinatra, Bing Crosby, or even a serviceable Ray Eberle tenor. A casual listener might be forgiven for thinking the songs of the era died long ago, that people of Laurel's generation wouldn't recognize them, but how could any song that asks, "Where'd you get those peepers?" ever be outdated?

"Stay with me," Laurel says, rubbing her eyes in a half-somnolent state, her voice yawny with sleep.

"I will, honey. Of course I will."

"Stay with me. Stay with me until I wake up again."

"Of course I will." I pat her hand. "Of course I will."

My inclination is to lie beside her, but as I pull the stem to the alarm clock so I can wake up in a few hours, my mind races. I'm also concerned for Anne Elise. She's missing. I've been worrying about her ever since Trish phoned me with news of her kidnapping. I've vowed to myself to forevermore treat her as my own child. I've hardly been able to sleep, so worried have I been. My worrying isn't made any easier by Laurel. She, too, needs my help. She breathes unevenly, the rhythm of her raspy *whew-fruf-fruf* breaths like water splattering from a rusty pump. No hospital in the world had any right to release her. She needs a sedative, something to give her a good spell of uninterrupted sleep so she can recover from her infection.

My conversation with Simpkins did not go well. He's freaked out by the counterfeit money. Already he's threatening lawsuits against me, threatening to turn the police on me. Why can't he just flush the money down the toilet? Toss it in an incinerator, light a match, and watch the black smoke rise from a chimney? It's impossible to tell good money from bad by the color of its ashes. Today. That's how long he's giving me. And then what? When I asked, he chuckled sardonically and slipped into a tough-guy voice. "Buddy, I've got ways of getting at you that are more immediate and more painful than anything the legal system can dish out, if you get my drift. You know what a knee-capping is?"

So I'm going to be kneecapped. Not by Simpkins, for I can't see him with a vicious streak deep enough to do the job himself, but a man in his profession knows unsavory types, paid thugs who'd gladly fuck up my ambulatory abilities for a fee. Simpkins talks a good ethical game, but as soon as serious money enters into play, everyone's ethics invariably take a hike.

"Are you still here?" Laurel murmurs.

"Sure, honey. But I need to leave in a few minutes," I say, getting out of bed. I need to get good money to replace the bad that Simpkins is holding. Do I know where to get the money? Yes, but it's not going to be easy. "I'll be back, though. You can trust me."

~

The call comes when I'm in my car, my cell phone showing an unrecognizable number that I mistake for being Simpkins's or some minion he's dispatched to whack or hack my knee to pieces. When I answer, I hear the voice of Jack Riggs over a wave of static so dense you'd think the voice was coming from the scratchiest of my old shellac 78s. An odd rhythmic, electronic pinging punctuates the call like the tick-tock of a metronome.

"Hey. Can I call you right back? We must have a bad line. I can hardly hear you."

"No!" Jack says. The echo of other conversations bleeds through the background static on this line. Jack's voice becomes clearer, but the posh quality I've long admired in his voice is absent. His words, his syllables, and even the *ah-umms* that punctuate his thoughtful pauses are slurred, mumbled, as if his lips were swollen or working off the effects of a dentist's Novocain injection. "Don't hang up on me. We need to talk."

"Jack, what's wrong?"

"Nothing's wrong. I . . . ah-umm . . . I heard the good news about you. About the baby. Tricia told me yesterday morning. She told me your good news. About your new baby. Congratulations!"

I feared Jack wouldn't welcome the news, that he'd reject me or tell Trish to keep me away from her money. However, he's happy. My heart stutters. He must realize I've been unfaithful to his daughter, but there's no anger or cynicism in his voice, and it boggles my mind that Jack Riggs—the most sardonic octogenarian alive—could be so bighearted as to welcome the birth of a child born to his son-in-law's mistress.

"You're okay with this?"

"Course I'm okay with that. I couldn't be happier for you. But that's not why I'm calling."

"Thank you, sir. This makes me glad. I can't tell you how grateful I am for your understanding of the situation."

"Roosters roost. That's why I'm calling. Level with me, James. Are you doing all right financially?"

No man desires to admit he's a deadbeat alcoholic loser, especially to his father-in-law, but prevarication is what makes the world go round. I tell Jack things couldn't be finer for us, which is what he wants to hear. "Work is going well, all my investments—both for myself and for my clients—are coming up roses. Absolute roses!"

"I mean, do you have money set aside that's separate and independent from Tricia's accounts?"

"Trust me, Jack. We're nobody's fool. We've got a diverse portfolio. Money in her name. Money in my name. Money in both our names. Hey, Jack, what's this all about?"

"Is it enough to tide you two over should something . . . ahumm . . . happen to eradicate Tricia's portfolio?"

"What's this all about, sir? Are you sure you're all right?"

"I already told you: roosters roost. That's why I'm calling. I'm making sure you've got yourself covered. You'll take care of Tricia, won't you?"

"Sure. You can count on me."

As the conversation becomes more stilted, the real purpose of Jack's call dawns on me. He needs money. Probably lots of money. Grizzled old goat that he is, he's finally racked up one floozy too many or at least encountered a woman who's demanding more money to hush up his misdeeds than he's able to pay. Sixteen years ago, he called me into his living room to tell me the then-current price of buying off a woman was $4 million. Times have changed. Just the other month, a former Fox News Channel honcho was forced to pay $32 million to settle a sexual harassment claim. Sometime soon, Jack's going to make a large withdrawal from Trish's account. He wouldn't be calling unless it was going to be a stupendously large amount. Maybe millions. Maybe more.

The distracting echoes of other conversations on this phone line become quieter. I can still hear the other voices, but not as loudly. Jack, too, is silent.

"You still there?" I ask.

"It's about women. Roosters have come to roost on my escapades. I finally bit off more than I can chew."

I think back to our conversation a year ago at the Coterie. Trish, enraged at the idea of surrogacy, had stormed out of the dining room, leaving me alone with Jack. I got up to run after her, but Jack urged me to stay. He was old, he said, and could deal with some companionship. I felt sorry for him, traveling up from the Caribbean only to have his daughter run out like she did. And besides, I knew I could charm my way back into Trish's good graces, so I reached for my Scotch and asked Jack how he'd been lately.

Jack leaned back, rolled up his sleeves, and cracked his knuckles. "Do you want to know?" he asked. His arms were scaly, reptilian, inflamed with xerosis and dried out by too much sun. He grinned, and when I assured him that I really wanted to know, he mentioned the wife of a famous movie star whom he befriended on the white-sand Cayman beaches. The movie star owned a compound not far from Jack's own beachside compound, and being that the movie star was stuck in Los Angeles filming a high-budget romcom, Jack and the wife had been laying out their beach blankets together every afternoon. He mentioned the chocolate heiress who lived on the other side of his compound and their yacht excursions to an uncharted atoll. He mentioned the ladies who flocked to the island in search of sugar daddies. He mentioned the scantily clad girlfriends of suspected drug lords who'd winter in nearby cabanas and were appreciative of his attentions.

Jack winked. His voice dropped down a level, requiring me to lean over the restaurant table to hear him. "These are by no means chaste endeavors. The urge gets worse the older I get. Maybe I'm lowering my standards too much, but gimp leg and all, I can't walk five feet without spotting another woman I want to stick my prick into."

In retrospect, I wondered if he engineered the whole restaurant conversation—including planting the seed of surrogacy in my mind and egging Trish to walk out on us—for the purpose of seeing the shock in my eyes. Now, listening to Jack on the phone, I feel no shock. Profligacy, even for wealthy septuagenarians, has a cost. No drug lord relishes being cuckolded by an aging banker, or so I guessed.

"I'll end up okay," Jack Riggs says over the phone with a voice that suddenly sounds tired and haggard. I could picture him slumped down on a chair in a darkened room, ruing his bad choices. "I'll have to transfer funds into my account here soon, though, so it's good to hear you and Tricia will be fine without my money. That's . . . that's all I can ask for at this step."

"I told you: we're fine."

"Good to hear, James. Good to hear. I've got to—"

The electronic ping . . . ping . . . ping reestablishes itself over the background static.

"Speak up, Jack. I can't hear you."

The call cuts off suddenly. My attempts to ring him back don't go through. He might have fallen down, had a heart attack, suffered a stroke, but there's no way to reach him. He's been good to me, a brother-in-arms who accepts my alcoholic foibles. He has people in his employ to watch over him—caretakers, valets, servants who will summon medical assistance should it be needed. But me? At this moment, I'm all alone without a nickel to my name.

Driving, I turn onto Georgetown's cobblestone streets. My mind races to the immediate questions I need to pose to Trish. Jack's not the only person who has designs on Trish's money. I park in Savory Mew's circular drive, where fresh tire tracks of a recently departed vehicle are visible in the dusting of snow beside Trish's Mercedes. Inside the house, I go through the rooms calling Trish's name. She's been popping Valiums by the handful, so many that it's easy to imagine her taking too many. A half-eaten rack of lamb, the leftovers from the meal Trish prepared the other night, sits cold on a ceramic platter on the kitchen counter. "Trish? Trish? Where are you?" I say, circling through the living room, the sitting room abundant in tapestries and gilded Louis XV settees, and the oak-paneled library shelved with first editions and leather-bound books that haven't been opened since Jack Riggs first acquired them decades earlier.

A high-tech electric baby bottle sterilizer lies in the center of the mahogany dining room table where normally a flowered centerpiece would sit. Through its clear plastic top, I peer at a batch of recently steam-sterilized bottles. I bought a sterilizer just like this for Anne Elise, and my first thought is that she must've somehow broken into Laurel's apartment and stolen it. But then I see the cases of baby formula and diapers sitting on chairs around the table. Some of the cases are ripped opened, the contents of those cases spilling to the floor. Plastic Babies"R"Us shopping bags sit on top of new rosewood cradle in the corner of the room. I'd wanted to buy a cradle just like this for Anne Elise, but I couldn't find one. I lift a pink baby dress from one of the shopping bags, finger its silk fabric. "I didn't hear you come in," Trish says, entering the room through the swinging doors leading from the kitchen. She's wrapped in an aqua-green silk robe I've only seen her wear when she's under the weather. Her hair is in a towel, but it's been hours since she stepped out of the shower. Upon seeing me, she smiles. "I was upstairs. In the study. Thank you for coming home."

I lay down the baby dress I'd been holding. No woman buys hundreds if not thousands of dollars' worth of baby goodies unless she has a baby. Anne Elise. Laurel said she suspected Trish had stolen her baby, but I didn't think Trish would stoop to such a criminal act. "Why do you have all these baby things?"

Trish sweeps her eyes over everything, expressing surprise, but she can't deny possessing them. Her smile becomes shakier. She pulls out a chair for herself, stretches her arms, and looks at me with tired eyes. "I'm glad you've come home. I've got some big news to share with you."

"What's that?"

"I threw up again this morning. The second morning in a row. Yesterday, I asked a pharmacist about it, but she said it was impossible to know this early. Today though, two days in a row, there's no denying it."

Trish doesn't seem sick, at least not now, but I ask if she needs me to take her to a doctor. Or an emergency room.

"I'm pregnant," Trish says. Something tightens within me. She holds her gaze to judge my reaction. "We're going to have a baby of our own. Isn't that grand?" She grabs my hand, places it against her cheek, her happy tears sliding from her eyes onto my fingertips.

"How can this be? How long have you known?"

"The other night. After we made love. I knew immediately. Something was happening inside me. Even while we were making love, it felt different. Down there. I called my friend Allie this morning. I asked her if she felt different immediately after conceiving. And you know what? She giggled! She said that at least for little Ellie, she had some kind of strange intuition she'd become pregnant again just after she and Clive finished making love one night. We're going to have a child!"

Trish's staring up at me, beatific, her cheeks aglow from the tears that slide over them. The fuzzy feeling of having stepped into a dream comes upon me. I'm not sure how this can be, the timing of it. Laurel was two months pregnant by the time she told me she missed her period. Trish asks if I love her. I don't know the answer. If this happened nine months earlier, I never would've gotten entangled with Laurel, but now that Laurel had her baby, I don't know what to do. The screws are tightening faster, harder. There's a dull ache in the back of my head, a tremble to my hands. I'm not man enough to be a father to two different babies, a partner to two different women. My mind races to the baby books I've read. I made love to Trish thirty-six hours ago. Actual fertilization would've occurred anywhere from a few hours to a full day after that. Trish's fertilized egg would still be traveling down the fallopian tube toward her uterus. How could Trish be aware of an embryo that has yet to implant itself in her uterus?

I'm not going to turn my back on Laurel, and there's no way I can turn my back on Trish if she's carrying my child. I'm a man smooshed between two alternate realities, one with Trish and one with Laurel, two opposed ideas of my future that are irreconcilable.

"Now that I'm pregnant, you don't need Laurel anymore. You can get rid of her. Call it a deacquisition," Trish says, with a giggle. "We're going to have a baby of our own. Who knows? Maybe we'll even have two babies! Aren't you happy?"

Chapter Thirty-One

TRISH

I take James's hand in mine and watch his startled eyes as I undo the silk sash to my bathrobe. There's a fire raging in my brain, ants in my fingertips. I'm so excited I can barely stand still. Surely, he sees it too: the burgeoning baby bump. In a few weeks, my breasts will become fuller, and my face will develop the healthy glow of pregnancy. This morning, I got sick again. Morning sickness. I took a Valium and then another and then another, the warmth of pregnancy radiating throughout me. A pregnant woman is attuned to her body. No one can tell me I'm not pregnant. The other night, I feasted upon James's touch, but today I need his touch in another way. I guide his hand to my body, feeling his warm fingers on my belly.

"Give it a moment," I say. James's breath becomes stilted. He looks at me questioningly. I press his hand to a spot inches below my belly button, where the top of my panties would sit if I were wearing panties. "Do you feel it?"

"What?"

"The baby, silly." For years, I yearned to be one of those glowing expectant mothers who'd lovingly guide friends' hands over their bellies, sharing with them the movements of their child. Something pulses inside me, startling me, a little trigger of excitement making me feel pink and rosy. "I think it just kicked. Isn't it amazing?"

James's hand jerks away.

"Honey. Please. It's our baby."

"Trish. Seriously. You're not pregnant. You can't be pregnant. Even if you were, you can't know it yet this early."

Just then, the baby—Laurel's baby—cries from upstairs. The sound is clear, distinct, a caterwaul of hunger and need. James's expression changes. The elation I expected from him upon feeling my baby kicks now comes over him—but it's Laurel's baby, not mine, who excites him. He pushes open the dining room door, but I charge past him, causing him to stumble and fall to the floor.

Last night, at Rock Creek Park, I found the perfect spot to abandon Anne Elise. The creek was just beyond her, the sound of its rushing waters loud enough to drown out the wind that shook the branches of the trees around us. I stripped off her receiving blanket, snatched away her knit cap. Given the weather—snow and slush and frigidity—Anne Elise wouldn't have survived more than a couple of hours. She was sleeping when I laid her down. I stood, debating whether to cover her with leaves and sticks to further conceal her should anyone happen by. A heaviness I had not expected came over me. I'm not immune to the tug of sympathy. I started to walk away, following back the path of distinctive hexagonal tread marks my new boots had made in the snow.

I turned back toward Anne Elise. She opened her eyes and sneezed. Already the cold was getting to her. Her face was alabaster white, her great blue eyes wide and vacant. It was more than just the fear of culpability and imprisonment should Anne Elise die that made me stomp back through the snow toward her. I could not turn away. Looking at her, I was looking at a baby-sized version of myself, the girl I might have been if I'd been born to lowlife reprobates with a drug-addled past. I hadn't even sat her down for a full minute. She knew she was being abandoned. I reached down and picked her up. I brought her to my chest, zippered up my bubble jacket. She was cold, and it took minutes to warm her. I'm a good person. James has told me so, several times, in the past. I rubbed Anne Elise's hands in mine, warming the color back in them, and pledged to raise her as my own.

"You've taken her!" James says, still on the floor where I pushed him.

I race up the stairs, running, panting, my heart pounding. I had hoped Anne Elise would stay quiet long enough for me to sweet-talk James into leaving Laurel. I reach for the bookshelf. A button is hidden beneath a loose plank on the bookcase's second shelf. I push it. The bookcase retracts into the wall, revealing the narrow passage that leads to the wood-paneled hideaway nook where my father retreated almost every night while I was growing up. It's something out of a spy movie or a cheap horror film, this hidden room. Musty and dusty, it's a veritable fire hazard cluttered with banking ledgers and secret papers far too valuable and compromising to store elsewhere. Only after I entered college and sounded out my classmates did I comprehend how unusual it was to grow up in a house with secret rooms.

I flick on a light switch. The room hasn't been renovated since the late 1940s. Splits and cracks run down the wall's wood paneling and the warped floorboards, the overhead light fixture discharging a burst of burned-electric ozone every time I turn it on. Anne Elise is in a cardboard box atop my father's old desk, about the only suitable place I could think to hide her. She'd been here all along, staring at the cobwebs drooping down from the ceiling. Amazingly, she slept without a sound while Adderly and his detectives searched the house last night. I lift Anne Elise out of the cardboard box. Holding her, I'm filled with a sense of calm and a sense of purpose that all my years of being Jack Riggs's daughter had never been able to provide.

James, having galloped upstairs, stands at the entrance to this secret nook. I point a baby bottle filled with formula toward Anne Elise's sweet mouth. Her pink cheeks redden with exasperation.

"What are you doing?" James says, dumbfounded, unable to believe it was me who took Laurel's baby. "How can you keep her in a . . . a box? In this musty room? Is this how you intend to keep her?"

Anne Elise, ignoring the bottle, butts her head against my silk robe. She's become more headstrong over the past day. What she wants is warm mother's milk, and she's learned from Laurel where warm mother's milk comes from, and yet she can't understand why I'm not offering her my breast. I shake a few drops of formula out of the bottle's nipple onto her pink lips, a trick I learned from an internet video. I'm not ashamed to admit my parenting knowledge comes from the YouTube videos I've streamed over the past day. The drops of formula I've shaken onto Anne Elise's lips whet her appetite. She licks the drops, and then, when I lower the bottle back to her mouth, her lips pucker around the bottle's silicone nipple, working it like a pump.

"You'll never get away with this. This is kidnapping."

"Honey, you're mistaken. This isn't kidnapping."

"What is it then?"

"Surrogacy," I say, invoking the word that's haunted my nightmares and preyed on James's mind ever since my father introduced us to it. Surrogacy has hovered over our marriage like a noose, strangling the love we have for each other. Surrogacy has let James's mind wander to other wombs to impregnate. Surrogacy has humiliated me. "Laurel's obligation to Anne Elise ended the moment of her delivery. We contracted Laurel to bear us a child. And now we've got Anne Elise. Don't you see? Laurel's nothing more than a surrogate mother."

James is stunned. Flabbergasted. He crosses his arm. "Are you crazy? Laurel's no surrogate."

"My father will advise us on lawyers who are comfortable backdating papers." Cradling Anne Elise in my arms, I tickle her. James turns to her as she giggles. This plan is all coming together in my mind. Together, James and I will raise Anne Elise as our own, in wealth and comfort, offering her greater opportunities than Laurel could ever provide. "We'll craft a story of how, months ago, we contracted with Laurel to bear our child. We'll make it look as if everything was signed last April or May."

"You're crazy. That's . . . that's . . . that's unethical. Laurel's not going to go along with this."

"Sure she is. I'll offer to pay her legal fees."

"Legal expenses? What are you talking about?"

I explain for James's benefit the circumstances of Laurel's episiotomy. Doctors had erroneously calculated Anne Elise would be so large that Laurel's health would be jeopardized by a natural vaginal delivery. They performed an episiotomy to lessen the risk of serious tearing. Although once practiced with great frequency, the medical community now realizes, in general, that episiotomies cause more complications than they alleviate; hence, there's been a widespread and well-documented effort to minimize the use of episiotomies in the delivery room. To complicate matters, the doctors angled their incisions incorrectly, increasing the likelihood her postdelivery wounds wouldn't heal correctly. On top of that, the hospital let an infection set in. They did not treat her with the right antibiotics. Or enough of them. They did not inform her of alternate treatment options or otherwise advise how to minimize the risk of complications. Added to all this, a hospital staffer endangered her child by providing a near-total stranger with a security bracelet that allowed that near-total stranger the opportunity to steal her baby.

James listens with exaggerated patience, but lacking my cunning, he merely blinks when I finish, unsure if there's a point to my explanation.

"Don't you get it?" It seems so obvious to me. A slam dunk. "Medical malpractice. I'll pay her legal fees to file a lawsuit. As incompetently as the hospital acted, Laurel will walk away from this with a multimillion-dollar cash settlement."

"She's not going to agree to this."

Having thought out all possible obstacles to my plan, I shrug. "Should Laurel contest this, we'll testify against her in court. It'll be two credible witnesses against her. We'll tell the court her refusal to acknowledge the facts as we present them owes to her desire to shake us down for more money. We're respectable people. She isn't! We'll prolong the case for years with delaying tactics and watch as she bankrupts herself to pay for her legal costs. She can't afford a protracted lawsuit. We'll simply dispossess her of her child."

"You forgot one thing."

James squints at me, his beady eyes giving me a small fright. Is it possible I forgot something? The incandescent light bulb above us in this ancient room fizzles out with an ominous crackle, discharging a burst of ozone into the air. I flip the light switch on and off until some connection reestablishes itself to let light again flow from the light bulb, but when I look at James, he sneers at me. He hasn't shaved today, and his cheeks are lined with a coarse stubble, giving him a more intimidating appearance. Again I wonder if, by some small chance, he has detected a chink in my surrogacy plan.

James lifts Anne Elise up. Hard to believe, but she's already hungry for more formula. About an ounce remains in the bottle I set down beside her box. He picks it up and begins to feed Anne Elise, filling the room with the sound of her sucking on the bottle. It amazes me how he knows how to do this all by himself without a woman henpecking him to do it. Has he watched the same YouTube videos as me? Looking into her eyes, he makes a funny face, sticks out his tongue, arches his eyebrows, the two of them transfixed in each other's expressions. "So what did I forget?" I ask.

"I love Laurel. That's what you forgot."

The admission pierces me like a knife. My throat tightens. I imagine them in bed together, James fondling Laurel's breasts, drawing her into an embrace, their hearts pounding with lust. I see him as he must have been when sticking the Debauve et Gallais box in her suitcase, the expectation in his face, the soft, encouraging words syrupping out of him as he drove her to the hospital.

"What if I don't go along with your plan, Trish? What if, instead, I pick up the phone and call the police?"

"You wouldn't do that, James. That wouldn't be wise."

"Why not?"

"Simpkins."

James's eyes narrow upon mine. It's like I passed gas, so immediate is his reaction. "What about Simpkins?"

"I know you've stooped to passing off counterfeit money to pay off your debts. That's how low you've sunk. People don't enjoy having counterfeit money sprung on them. Simpkins is angling to kill you—that's how angry he is. He told me so himself."

"He did?"

"Simpkins came here this morning. In fact, he was here when he called you."

I tell James only half of what happened, leaving out the choicest details. Simpkins had arrived, unannounced, at the doorstep demanding to see me. "What brings you here this morning?" I asked, first thinking Simpkins had come to collect the money I pledged to give him when I rescheduled our appointment and then fearing he had stumbled upon the fact I had stolen Anne Elise. "We need to talk," Simpkins said, brushing past me and walking into the living room. He hadn't slept all night, he said. Not a wink. He didn't comment upon how lovely the room's furnishings were or how impressed he was at my father's oil portrait. "Do you think anyone knows I'm here?" Simpkins asked, and when I inquired as to the reason for his fright, he told me someone outbid me for the Laurel Bloom information. For this, he apologized. And then he told me it was James who outbid me. I fell into the Hepplewhite, not believing James had it in him to be treacherous. But then Simpkins explained that James paid him with counterfeit money. "But there's good news," Simpkins said. "I'm giving you the opportunity to get your husband out of trouble. Otherwise, I'll fix it so that he goes to jail." To avoid this unpleasantness, Simpkins wanted me to make good on the counterfeit money, but the notion that I fork over $10,000 for James's misdeeds was crazy. I gave James's cell phone number to Simpkins and instructed him to tell James how upset he was at being tricked. I did all this because I knew James didn't have the money to satisfy Simpkins's demands for immediate repayment. I knew he'd be forced to come groveling back to me. "Tell him you're going to kneecap him," I said to Simpkins. "That'll light a fire under him to give you real money."

"He's going to kneecap you, James. That's what Simpkins said, right? And believe me—he means it."

James flops down on my father's old desk chair, which creaks under his weight, and buries his face in his hands, stricken. "Ten thousand dollars. He wants ten thousand dollars from me. Today. Where am I going to get ten thousand dollars? Trish, I need your help. I'm begging you for ten thousand dollars."

I pat James's hair. He looks so soft, so vulnerable, a shivering gray mouse caught in a warren of tomcats. He hadn't returned to rescue Anne Elise. He came back to throw himself on his hands and knees and grovel for money.

"You can have the ten thousand dollars. I can give it to you," I say, reaching into a desk drawer for the Montblanc fountain pen I've used for occasions like this. James has always been so easy to control, so responsive to the predictable male-motivating factors of money and sex. As my father said, most men will sell their souls for significantly less than you'd think possible. James doesn't know it yet, but $10,000 is the lowball price of his soul. "Let me have your signature on the promissory note so I can give you the money and make your problems disappear like I always do. You'd like that, wouldn't you? I'll get you the money. Won't you like that? You can have your knees. You can have Anne Elise. And you can have me."

Chapter Thirty-Two

JIM

Trish shoves the fountain pen in my hand. A sheaf of preprinted promissory notes, complete save for the blank spaces where she fills in the date and the dollar amounts, lies in an open drawer. Humiliation scorches my cheeks. I can't believe it's come to this. Normal people would help their spouse without bringing embarrassment upon them—wouldn't they?—but as Hemingway wrote of Zelda Fitzgerald, Trish's a hawk who doesn't share. Every quid brings a quo. Trish has never loved me. I know that now without a doubt. She might've loved the idea of me—a handsome, presentable flatterer gliding her into society dinners and onto the ballroom floors at charity fundraisers—and she might've liked the idea of me being the gentle, nurturing father of her children, but she never loved me. She's used me at every possibility, mocked me for my failed investments. She knows I despise signing these promissory notes, but it's the only way she'll give me the money.

"James. The money. Don't you want the money? You don't need to tell anyone I've got Anne Elise. Think of it: ten thousand dollars. Enough money to pay off Simpkins. Enough for you to avoid getting kneecapped."

Something hardens inside me. "I'm not going to sell out Laurel for ten thousand dollars."

Trish closes her eyes, sighs. "How about twenty thousand?"

I'm speechless. Twenty thousand dollars would be enough to pay off both Simpkins and Tully, who—counterfeit or not—sooner or later will demand his money back. Trish's never shown a willingness to negotiate when it comes to bailing me out, and from this willingness, I sense that I've got her over a barrel. Should I call the police, they'll arrest her. She can't buy me off as easily as her father has bought off all his floozies. She's been turning the screws on me, but now's my opportunity to reverse our positions. My livestock futures investment opportunity comes to mind. If I can pony up a quarter million dollars, I'll be set for life. I can pay off Laurel's student loans, giving her more reason to trust me. Never again will I need to grovel for more of Trish's money.

"Three hundred thousand dollars," I say, naming a figure that'll satisfy all my immediate needs. "That's what this is going to cost you."

Trish draws a breath, bites her lip. She reaches for the fountain pen in my hand. Without makeup, her skin's dry, in need of nourishment. Her open robe rakes across me as she takes the pen from me. She pulls out one of her preprinted promissory notes and fills in the date and the amount of $300,000 on the two blank lines in the form's opening paragraph. She's trembling, angry, and nervous. For once in her life she knows she can't dictate the terms of this negotiation, and I feel strangely elated. For once in my life I've outsmarted her, but then sadness falls over me: in getting the better of Trish, I'm pledging to sell out Laurel. It's a Pyrrhic victory, a lose-lose situation. Trish pushes the promissory note across the desk. Though the ink hasn't dried where she filled in the blanks, it's ready for my signature.

"I'm not going to sign another of your promissory notes," I say.

"Sure you are. We can't do this without a promissory note. I'm putting my foot down on that. My father told me long ago that whenever I give money to you—"

"Your *father's* the one who told you to make me sign these promissory notes?"

"If he hadn't suggested it, I never would have thought of it myself."

I thought Jack Riggs liked me; I thought he was a good guy. Though cognizant of my foibles, he got me my job, confided in me his lurid conquests. He must have known how humiliating these promissory notes are, but he's been forcing me to undergo this humiliation for years. I can't believe it. But then I do—men like him only respect money, their mercantile maneuverings pervading even into family relationships.

"What's wrong?" Trish asks. "Don't you want the money? I'll give you the money if you get rid of Laurel. We can have her baby! And we can have the baby I'm carrying too. Two babies for the price of one!"

My gut clenches up. Not an ounce of my soul wants to do as she tells me, but if Simpkins doesn't get his money, my kneecaps are history. I put Anne Elise down in the cardboard box. An amber plastic prescription bottle sits beside the cardboard box. I give it a shake. Dozens of pills rattle inside. "These the Valiums you've been popping?"

Trish glares at me. "It's no crime to be under a doctor's care."

"How many have you had today?"

"I don't know. Maybe a couple. I forget."

"You should keep track of these things. You don't want to overdose." I shove the bottle in my trouser pockets.

"Hey! What are you doing?"

"Maybe I need some for myself." I lay a soft hand on Trish's shoulder, gliding it over her silk robe. She looks up to me with her dazzling blue eyes. On any other day, she'd be in a designer dress, her face made up with cosmetics to conceal the wrinkles I now see. She's gorgeous, but all I can see is the humiliation she's caused me. We stand, embracing, while Anne Elise stares at us. Baby manuals say the eyesight of newborns is limited—they're only able to see eight to twelve inches in front of them—but Anne Elise is enthralled by what she's seeing. Perhaps Simpkins is right. Perhaps she's someone else's child, but it warms me, knowing she's transfixed by the sight of me. But I feel like such a heel. The screws can't possibly be turned any tighter on me. My mind is a stew of rage. I can hardly think. I'm selling out Anne Elise's mother, and I don't think I can live with myself. But what choice do I have?

"Can I have a few minutes to think this over?" I ask.

"Take all the time you need," Trish says, already confident she's done enough to persuade me to sign her note.

I turn around, head back downstairs. What I need is a long walk to clear my head, but there's no time for that. Inside, I'm about to explode. One way or another, I'm being forced into a choice I don't want to make. Trish and Laurel represent two irreconcilable paths I'll no longer be able to hold together in my life.

Shoving my hands into my pockets, I grab Trish's prescription bottle. The Valiums are like little pieces of candy, their color pale blue like the SweeTARTS I consumed by the handful as a child. A small *v* is cut into each pill, a fanciful touch I wouldn't have expected in a pharmaceutical, the *v*'s resembling little hearts when tilted sideways. If I march upstairs and sign Trish's agreement, forsaking Laurel, I won't be able to live with myself. So why should I live any longer? I spill the pills onto a bamboo cutting board, wonder how many I'll need to either lose the rage that's engulfing me or just plain kill myself.

I crush a few pills under the heel of a silver spoon, crumbling them into a blue dust. I open my wallet, take out the lone dollar remaining in it, and roll it up. I've never snorted cocaine or done drugs, but I've seen enough movies to know how it's done. Snorting the drugs allows them to enter into the bloodstream quicker than if ingested orally. The Valium will overwhelm me, or so I imagine, inducing a pleasant serenity in me, comforting me, and maybe numbing me, and if it doesn't knock me unconscious or kill me, I'll crush a few more pills and shove the rolled-up dollar bill up my nose again.

When I was a boy working with my father on the family Chevy, he'd look over my shoulder and caution me not to overtighten the

screws and bolts. Trish and Laurel, Simpkins, and Jack Riggs have tight-
ened the screws tighter than I can bear. I can't think anymore. Nor do
I want to think anymore. All my life, I've wondered what my father
meant. What would happen if I overtightened a screw? Would it strip
away the screw's threads? Would the screwhead twist off? Fracture? Burst
into a thousand fragments? I'm about to find out.

I lower my head to the cutting board, slip one end of the rolled-up
dollar bill into my nose, and close my eyes. Just as I'm about to inhale
the powder, though, another option flashes into my thoughts: it doesn't
need to be me who dies. I've got a baby daughter who needs me. I let go
of the dollar bill, go to the stove, and heat up a kettle of water. I can still
be the father I've always wanted to be, but for that to happen, I need to
brew up a special batch of chamomile tea for Trish. The blue dust will
dissolve easily when stirred into a hot liquid, but to make sure I have
enough, I grab the spoon again. Despite my anger, I become amazingly
calm as if under some spell, the spoon in my hand crushing more pills
as if under its own volition. The teapot whistles.

I select a fresh canister of loose-leaf chamomile tea from the pantry, still amazed at what I'm doing. I watch my hands shake tea from
the canister into a silver tea ball. I'm so calm it's as if I've swallowed a
Valium or two myself, but as I pour the hot water into a thermal-lined
carafe and as I deposit the tea ball into the carafe, the full import of
what I'm doing almost floors me: I'm killing my wife, the woman I've
loved from the moment we met. As the tea steeps, its color changes,
darkening, becoming a brownish yellow.

I worry what will happen to both of us when Trish tastes the tea,
but I've made my choice. I lift the cutting board to the carafe and watch
as the blue dust sprinkles into the tea. Soon I can take Anne Elise and
Laurel into my life with total undivided love. I lug the rosewood cradle
that had been in the dining room upstairs under one arm, blankets and
all, while balancing the carafe, a spoon, and a Wedgewood teacup in
the other hand.

"I figured Anne Elise would like this," I say, laying down the cradle on the square of free floor space at the side of the old desk.

Trish, spotting the carafe, bursts into a smile. "You've brought me tea!"

Usually, Trish offers me a sip of the tea I brew for her. Luckily, I've declined so often that, today, it won't provoke suspicions when I tell her I'm not thirsty. I lift Anne Elise into the cradle. The blankets are soft, maybe cashmere, and Anne Elise delights at the feel of them against her skin. She stretches out her arms. Trish prefers tea made from loose-leaf chamomile and an embarrassing amount of sugar. To mask whatever bitter flavor the pills might have, I stirred in even more sugar than usual. I'm not sure if she'll notice the difference. She's liable to have one sip and, declaring it not to her liking, dump the whole pot into the toilet. Or, not thinking, she may swallow a full cup in one swoop.

I pick the Montblanc pen off the desk and sign the promissory note, blowing air onto my signature to dry the ink. I know what I'm doing, and it still hits me when I drop the pen back on the desk: I'm selling out Laurel should Trish survive the tea. Trish perks up, her face filling with greedy-eyed happiness. She reaches out to me, kisses me, tells me she knew she could count on me.

"How soon do you need the money?" Trish asks.

I freeze, shocked. *The money.* In order for Trish to get me the money, she needs to be alive. I can't believe how badly I just botched the sequencing of events. How could I be so stupid? The carafe's already on the desk. I'd thought she'd drink the tea right away and then fall down, dead, allowing me a few minutes to destroy this promissory note before going through the motions and calling for an ambulance. If I tell her not to drink the tea, she'll figure out what I've done. If she drinks the tea, she'll not live long enough to get me my cash. I'm also running up against Jack Riggs. Pretty soon—maybe even later today—he's going to make his own sizeable withdrawal from Trish's account.

"I need the money soon, Trish. Real soon."

"Okay," Trish says, linking her arm around mine. We used to stroll through Rock Creek Park like this, arm in arm. I'm nervous. Incredibly nervous, so nervous I'm amazed she can't pick up on it, but she just stands and gazes contentedly at Anne Elise. "Just think! We're going to have two wonderful babies soon." She giggles. "After all these years of being childless, it'll be just like having Irish twins."

"Honey? I think I need to get going soon," I say, decoupling my arms from hers.

"James?"

"Yes?"

"James, you didn't even tell me I'm pretty today. Am I still pretty?"

I laugh, kiss her on the lips. Trish bats her eyes fetchingly. I touch her face, lifting her chin so she can look straight into my eyes. "Your lips. I've never said this before, but you've got beautiful lips." I kiss her, gently, but with more passion, more zest, than before. Her lips are soft, plump pillows. "Yes, you're still pretty. You're such a good kisser. I will never tire of kissing you."

Chapter Thirty-Three

LAUREL

I can barely keep my eyes open, awakening cotton headed for mere moments, shivering, and calling Jimmy's name before lulling myself back to sleep every few minutes. Hours seem to pass by. I find myself weaving in and out of consciousness. The room feels cold and then hot, perceptions having more to do with me and my infection-weakened body than any problems with the apartment's heating and cooling units. Though I'm dry as tumbleweed, it feels as if the mattress has sprung a leak, for my whole middle section is squishy, wet, and warm, and I wonder if I've involuntarily relieved myself, but there's no smell of pee, no smell of anything, and then I close my eyes again. I want to wake up; I want to drift out of this pampered bed into a normal, happy life.

Opening my eyes, I see Jimmy, still dressed in his gray flannel suit. He's holding the ibuprofen bottle in one hand and a glass of water in the other. I don't know where we are. This is not my gloomy basement studio apartment or the hospital room that smelled of iodine and lavender room fresheners. And then I remember that this is my new spacious sun-drenched apartment. And then I remember that it's only temporary. In six months, when the lease expires, I'll be homeless.

"How long have you been standing there?"

Jimmy looks at his gold wristwatch. "Twenty minutes. Give or take."

"And you didn't wake me?"

Jimmy puts his hand on my forehead to gauge my temperature. He seems different, more somber, as if he's had nothing but conflicted thoughts and worry for however long I've been asleep. He winces, shakes his head. "Your fever's back with a vengeance. You need something stronger than ibuprofen or aspirin."

"I woke up earlier and called your name, but you weren't here," I say, coughing. My throat's so dry that it hurts to talk. "Where were you?"

"Trish's house."

I suck down a breath and feel the air wheeze through my dry lungs. For a moment, I think Jimmy says he went back to Tricia's house. But he's here. Or am I delirious? Can he be in two places at once? I don't understand. "You're at Tricia's house?"

"No," he says, laughing. "I *was* at Trish's house. Now I'm here with you."

I can't believe he went back to see Tricia. He promised he'd stay with me. Doesn't he want to be with me any longer? Why can't I trust him to do what he says he'll do when it comes to being with me?

Tricia was right. Jimmy will never change. For all I know, because I've been sick and unable to sleep with him, he went back to her to get his rocks off. Here I am, sick in bed. I asked him to stay here in the apartment with me, asked him to look after me while I slept. Why can't he do something like that for me? Isn't that the minimum everyone's entitled to ask of their romantic partners—that they be there when you need them?

"I needed to sort out some things," Jimmy says. "That's why I had to go for a bit."

"I don't care about 'things.' I don't care about anything except you and me and Zerena," I say, but as soon as I say Zerena's name, I start crying. She's been missing for over twelve hours. If I were healthier, I'd prowl the streets looking for her. Now, my thoughts wobbly with fever, I don't know who to call or where to check to see if maybe she's already dead. "Aren't you scared? Aren't you worried about her?"

"Of course I'm worried." James takes another sip of water, wipes his lips, but otherwise appears unconcerned. "But I've got a good feeling. Karma's real. Think positive thoughts. That's what we need to do. Hopefully, she'll be back with us before the end of the day."

"Damn you and your good feelings. Damn you and your inability to keep your word with me."

"Honey, wheels are in motion. Honest, they are. Things are happening. Soon we'll have Anne Elise back."

I step out of bed to better give Jimmy a piece of my mind, but my legs are a pair of squishy licorice sticks, and I stumble and fall and hit my head against the floor. Jimmy reaches down and lifts me up, but then he gasps, and I feel woozy, and it seems like minutes pass before I'm seated on the bed. All the lights are on in the room. Or, actually, I see he's pulled back the window curtains to let the sunshine flood in. My eyes ache from the brightness. I can hardly keep them open without feeling the pain of a headache.

"Look at all the blood," Jimmy says. He stutters. I brush my hand over my ears and forehead, but my hand is dry. There's not a drop of blood where my head hit the floor, but when I tell him this—"Hey! I'm fine!"—he points to the bed. The formerly white sheets look as if they've been doused in ketchup. Something catches in my throat. The blood's thick and, in places, clotted. Am I the damsel in a slasher film? Did Jimmy somehow do this to me? Make me bleed? Wound me?

My throat is gravel, my voice hoarse. I'm a groggy, slow-witted sometime thing full of scattered reflections that scarcely qualify as thoughts. I run my fingers over the bloody sheet and then over my bloody pajamas and feel faint again. I don't know what to think—but then I do. Jimmy didn't do this to me. The hospital did. "See! I told you the hospital can't sew up an episiotomy right. They're incompetent! That's why I walked out when nobody was looking."

"They didn't discharge you? You just took it upon yourself to walk away? In the middle of the night?"

"If I'd stayed any longer, I'd be dead. That's how negligent they are."

Jimmy dips a finger in a mucuslike splotch of blood that stains the sheets, brings his finger to his nose, and sniffs, wrinkling his nose at the scent. "Honey. You can die. You know that, don't you? You're going to die unless we do something."

"You're not taking me back to that hospital."

"I told you how Tricia's been after me to get rid of you, right?"

Tricia? Why's he always bringing up Tricia? Is she lurking somewhere in the apartment too? I expect Jimmy to laugh, but his face is deadly serious. And still, it's like a light bulb just went on inside of him.

"I'd be getting rid of you—killing you—if I sat here and did nothing to get you back to the hospital. Don't you see? You'd be letting Trish get what she wants. Whatever's making you sick—your infection or whatever it is—is going to get worse before it gets better. Sooner or later, it will kill you. Do you understand? You'll die."

I'm shivering from exhaustion and worry, cold and infection. I touch my forehead and am surprised to find that I'm perspiring too, which makes no sense. How could I be both cold and perspiring at the same time? Someone shakes my wrist. It's Jimmy.

"Hey. Are you listening to me? If you stay here, you might die."

Jimmy's logic chills me. He's the man who I thought loved me, but he keeps bringing up how much Tricia wants to kill me. Is he her minion? Concern isn't exactly etched on his face. He furrows his brows, looks out the window into the distance as if charting out the different possibilities of what would happen to him if I died from this episiotomy infection. In the shafts of sunlight coming through the windows, I see dust motes. His eyes shift toward me with a glimmer of malice.

"If you were to die, I could sit here and do nothing, and you'd be dead, and Trish would be glad and happy. Do you understand? No one would be able to pin a thing on me. I'd say you refused to go back to the hospital. That's what I would say."

I'm a death waiting to happen, a body waiting to wither away. I don't know why Jimmy just stands there if I'm as sick as he says. I can't even step out of bed without falling down. Jimmy is standing there. Has he never truly loved me? More blood trickles down my thigh. There's only so much blood this special snowflake—me—has in her, but he's doing nothing to help me. Tully—and everyone else, for that matter—is right: I have no business messing around with a married man. Especially a married man I can't trust.

Chapter Thirty-Four

TRISH

After James leaves, I stare at the promissory note, scarcely believing he signed it. And then I sit down and bury my face in my hands.

I didn't tell James everything about my meeting with Simpkins. James might fear he's going to get kneecapped, but I've got my own fears. After Simpkins finished threatening James over the phone, he slapped his hands together, elated. I had pegged him as too meek to take satisfaction in the theatrics of tough-guy intimidation. But I was wrong. His call with James had gone well, and he was ecstatic. He smiled the same vicious grin I remembered seeing on my father whenever he demolished adversaries in business dealings or legal proceedings.

Because Anne Elise would likely wake up at any moment and start crying, I was eager to get Simpkins out of the house. Even from her cardboard box in my father's secret office, she'd be loud enough for him to hear. Simpkins glanced around the living room, his inquisitive eyes alighting on the ancient Victrola, the ebony-and-ivory-inlaid curio cabinet, and the Ming vase abloom with peacock feathers.

"That's your father, isn't it?" Simpkins said, gesturing to the oil portrait above the mantle.

"Do you know him? How'd you know it was him?"

Mornings had been my father's favorite time of day, and a rush of gratitude overtook me, for I was happy my father was not already a forgotten figure in this town. Unlike the DC detective who sat in the same room not more than twelve hours earlier, Simpkins recognized my father and, presumably, knew of his accomplishments.

"I've been reading up on your father over the last twenty-four hours. You two look a lot alike. You know that, don't you? Only a fool could fail to recognize the similarities," Simpkins said, turning his gaze from the portrait onto me. He was sitting close enough on the Hepplewhite that I saw my reflection in his wire-rimmed glasses. My father and I really do look alike. Simpkins clicked his tongue against the roof of his mouth, and his face hardened. Color rose to his cheeks. His ears reddened with disdain. "Your father," Simpkins said, shaking his head. "Your father's led an *interesting* life."

Instinctively, I leaned away from Simpkins. "Interesting" meant many things, but I knew from Simpkins's tone that I wouldn't cherish hearing what the word meant to him in the context of my father. Simpkins wasn't the only person who viewed my father in an unsavory light. Usually, I could tell who'd be polite and hide his or her reservations about my father's ethics, and Simpkins possessed no such hesitancy.

"Between you and me and what I read in my grandfather's old files, I'd say your father fled the country just in time."

I rose from the sofa. "Mr. Simpkins. I think it's time for you to leave this house."

My abrupt change in manner startled Simpkins. Perhaps he was fool enough to think I'd sit idly as he denigrated my father's reputation. What Simpkins said about my father and me looking alike came back to me, and suddenly, I felt like a fool. Simpkins must have known exactly who I was the very first time we met. Or perhaps he had an inkling when I sent him that first email. Whatever name I chose, Wainsborough or Riggs, wouldn't have thrown him off for long if he really wanted to learn my identity.

"Your father screwed my grandfather out of a whole lot of money," Simpkins said.

"That's impossible. My father was a man of impeccable honor and solid financial footing."

"No offense, ma'am, but no one gets to be 'on solid financial footing' unless they've screwed over a few people along the way. My grandfather also had a law degree. He did a lot of your father's personal legal work. Wills and deeds, things like that, and those NDAs almost every woman he ever touched signed as part of their financial settlements. For almost a decade, your father put off paying the bills for the work my grandfather did for him. Getting older himself, my grandfather couldn't put in as many billable hours as he'd been doing. Unlike your father, he wasn't on solid financial footing. He had a heart attack. And then another. Doctor bills stemming out of his triple-bypass surgery were coming due. He was too proud to beg, too proud to ask for help. He fell behind on his mortgage. When he finally confronted your father about the money he was owed, do you know what your father said?"

I shook my head.

"Your father said, 'Fuck off.' Pretty eloquent coming from a gentleman who, as you say, was of 'impeccable honor.'"

I stared at Simpkins, aghast. I wasn't sure if he was telling the truth, but I could see he'd been angling to screw me over from the time I first asked him to run a background check on Laurel. Simpkins crossed his arms and sank back into the Hepplewhite. Here and there, the Hepplewhite showed its age. In one corner, a small tear in the cream-colored silk upholstery had started to widen. Usually I covered it with a throw pillow, but now Simpkins stuck his finger in the hole and plucked out a wad of cotton stuffing. He inspected it for a moment and then flicked it at me.

"Go," I said.

Simpkins grabbed the sheepskin coat he'd earlier set down on the sofa and stood. "Mrs. Wainsborough, I have the feeling we're going to see each other again."

"Why's that?"

"Laurel Bloom's baby disappeared last night. That's why." If Simpkins's intent was to unnerve me, the way he stared at me accomplished the goal. I froze. He told me he had suspicions about who took the baby. He told me that once he was certain, he'd likely be amenable to accepting a large monetary donation to ensure that he kept whatever evidence he gathered to himself rather than run it over to the police. "A million dollars might be enough of an incentive for me to halt my investigation outright. Wouldn't that be nice?"

I couldn't control my anger. I closed my eyes, leaned against the wall, and steadied my composure. Although he struggled to pay rent, he viewed me as an easy mark, a golden ticket he'd cash in to make his life easier. I stuttered, amazed someone as young as Simpkins could manipulate me. A self-satisfied smile spread across his lips. I never met his grandfather, but from what my father told me about him, Simpkins was every bit as cunning.

Simpkins buttoned his sheepskin coat, took out a pair of brown leather gloves from his pockets. "There's something else I should tell you about your husband."

I crossed my arms. "He's an adulterer. Duh. I already knew that."

Simpkins let out a little laugh. "That, plus he's also about to become a very rich man."

My eyes widened. As much as I wanted to shoo Simpkins out of the house, I was eager to learn about James's new wealth. "How's that?"

"You know that prenup you made him sign?"

That prenup had been on my mind an awful lot since I learned of Laurel's pregnancy. If it wasn't for that prenup, James would be able to claim half my money and divorce me. It had been my father's idea that

I get lawyers to draw up a punishingly brutal prenup to preclude the possibility of James ever divorcing me.

"It's not the ironclad agreement you think it is," Simpkins said, smirking. "It was one of the last pieces of work my grandfather drafted at your father's request. By that time, he knew your father was going to stiff him. Have you ever actually read through the whole document?"

A horrible feeling came over me. My father had handed the document to me. I assumed he'd already read it over and given it a clean bill of health. I had no reason to question it. James, too careless to bother to read it once my father explained its supposed contents to him, signed it almost laughing, telling me, "Money or no money, I'm the luckiest groom in the world to be marrying a bride so beautiful and fair as you."

"It's a pity, isn't it? If you read it, you'd realize it actually obligates you to pay three-quarters of your estate to James should he find any reason whatsoever to divorce you." Simpkins's smirk widened. I must have looked absolutely horrified, for there was real joy on his face. He winked at me. He was such an unctuous little bastard.

∿

Picking up the phone as soon as James signs the promissory note and leaves, I dial Atavista Air, the private-jet charter company we've hired at a moment's notice whenever the capricious urge to fly out of the country strikes us. Simpkins had rattled me badly. I'm in no mood for the tea that James prepared for me, so I push aside the carafe. An hour or more has passed since I took my last Valium, and my thoughts flicker like little jagged flames. James thought he left my hideaway office with a grand bargain, but $300,000 is chump change compared to what he could take me for in divorce court. Or what I might have to pay Simpkins.

And Simpkins? Though I'm not constitutionally opposed to paying for Simpkins's silence, his grudge against my father and the steely manner in which he handled himself suggest that even if I pay him the $1 million he suggested, he'd demand further payments down the road, shaking me down periodically until, eventually, he'd claim my entire fortune—which is why, at least temporarily, I need to flee the country.

"I need to schedule a flight. To Grand Cayman Island," I say to the chipper young woman who answers my call to Atavista.

"Splendid!" the young woman professes. I picture her looking like Laurel, blonde and a tad pudgy, the kind of acne-blemished girl who'd wear a knockoff designer scarf around her neck even though such accoutrements are no longer in fashion. I tell her my name, and she punches it into her computer.

"For two," I add.

Our names must appear in Atavista's computer database, for the woman asks, "For you and James, Mrs. Wainsborough?"

"I'm not sure James will be accompanying me. I recently had a baby daughter. She and I will be traveling alone to visit my father so we can introduce him to his new granddaughter."

"And how long will you be staying? When should we schedule your return flight?"

Given the legal clouds, staying here with Anne Elise at Savory Mew is unwise. Even if Simpkins wasn't on to me, sooner or later, I'd open the door and find a police detective who's not as easy to mislead as the easily impressed Detective Adderly. Years ago, my father secured for me through his World Bank contacts a prized red United Nations laissez-passer, a kind of supernational passport to get me in and out of any country in the world, hassle-free. The Caymans are a British protectorate; American legal authorities and law enforcement personnel have no jurisdiction there.

"It'll be an indeterminate stay," I tell the attendant. How long we'll stay is dependent upon the speed with which my father's lawyers hatch up the necessary legal documents to paper over the issues of Anne Elise's surrogacy, which will then make Simpkins's claims that I "stole" Anne

Elise less compelling. My father might also have ideas about the prenup and how to best deal with Simpkins. "I'll need the flexibility to fly home or maybe elsewhere on twenty-four hours' notice."

"And when do you wish to depart?"

"This afternoon. Could you arrange a flight for two o'clock?"

"This afternoon?" The woman hesitates. Up until this point, she's enthused that everything I said or requested was "splendid." She puts my call on hold, and in the tick-tock moments that I wait for her to jump back on the line, I tuck the ends of a pink fleece baby blanket around Anne Elise.

"Mrs. Wainsborough? Two o'clock this afternoon might not be feasible for us."

My heart sinks. Atavista's ability to meet my travel needs is the one part of my plan that I failed to consider. I had hoped to be gone by the time James returns. He'd come home, see the pile of cash and the brief note I'd write him, saying goodbye.

"But we can commit to a four o'clock departure. Will that suffice?"

"Yes. That will do quite nicely."

"Splendid." The woman wishes us bon voyage, telling me it's been a pleasure serving me, and then asks if she can do anything else for me.

I feel like thanking the woman for her fawning obsequiousness. In this land where everyone is a potential customer and everyone wants a continuing share of the money in your purse, it's become an ingrained habit, this unquestioned respect afforded to the well-to-do.

After I finish the call, I make another call. I still bank at PNC, the bank that bought out Riggs, and after being patched through to the branch manager, I inform him of my wish to make a large cash withdrawal. Though humiliating on a personal level for my father, PNC's takeover of Riggs was free of animus. The level of customer service they've extended toward me has been impressive. To them, I'm just another high-asset customer whom they're eager to please.

"How much, Mrs. Wainsborough?" the branch manager asks.

"Three hundred thousand. Preferably in cash. And preferably in large denominations," I say, realizing I need to move quickly, for Anne Elise might wake at any moment. "I'd prefer to pick the money up shortly. In person. Will that be a problem?"

Over the phone, I hear the branch manager punch my records up on his computer and scroll through my account balances. A $10,000 banded packet of fresh-pressed $100 bills is about a half inch thick, meaning that $300,000 would fit comfortably in a leather tote bag. When the bank manager jumps back on the line, he bears good news. "That'll be no problem at all, Mrs. Wainsborough. When you come into the branch, ask for me. I'll take care of everything."

~

A gold-leaf dome tops the neoclassical bank building at the corner of Wisconsin Avenue and M Street, a ten-minute walk from Savory Mew. Because she'd fallen asleep again, I left Anne Elise in her cradle, but someday soon I will show her this dome. Suggesting permanence and integrity, the gold dome appeared in every television commercial produced for Riggs Bank, becoming synonymous with our family name. Seen from a distance, it still sends a shiver up my spine. We were as prominent in town as that dome, respected far and wide for our financial clout.

When I enter the building, the branch manager promptly identifies himself. Mr. Walters, courteous without being friendly, officious without being automatonic, is a throwback to the age of square jaws, 1950s-style crew cuts, pasty complexions, and coffee- and nicotine-stained teeth. Security officers—white shirts, blue blazers, and sidearms holstered at their waists—flank Walters at either side, a standard precaution whenever bank officials expect to handle exceptionally large cash transactions.

"I've been expecting you," Walters says, leading me toward his desk. The branch's open floor plan requires us to walk past the desks of Walters's colleagues. Everyone pays me undue attention, eyeing me. Someone raises her phone and snaps my picture. Walters and the security officers were waiting for me at the door. He must have told people that the daughter of the former bank's CEO would be withdrawing a ridiculous amount of cash, which strikes me as unprofessional—which I will mention after he hands me my money.

Walters invites me to sit down. Although other chairs are arranged around his desk, the security officers choose to stand directly behind my chair. Walters looks at the computer screen at the corner of his desk, and from that screen he reads my name, address, social security number, and the account number from which I'm withdrawing the money. "Is this information correct, ma'am?"

"Yes." I withdraw a Montblanc pen from my handbag in anticipation of the forms and withdrawal slips I'll have to fill out. "Do you have the paperwork ready for me to sign?"

"Mrs. Wainsborough? I'm afraid we have a problem."

"A problem?"

"I'm sorry, but I don't know how to tell you this in a nice way. There are insufficient funds in this account to cover the amount you wish to withdraw."

"How can that be? Tens of millions of dollars are parked in the account."

"Do you understand why we might find it *suspicious* that you'd ask to make a large withdrawal at the same time someone else is cleaning out the account of all its funds?"

"What are you saying?"

Walters glances at one of the security officers. "I don't believe this is a coincidence. When someone attempts to withdraw money from an empty account, something is amiss. Can I be honest with you? Attempted fraud popped into my mind when I realized what was happening. You called me right at the moment the funds were being transferred out of your account. Your timing was impeccable."

My thoughts spin to Simpkins. He must have hacked into my accounts, bled the funds into an untraceable destination, and compromised the bank's computers so thoroughly that he'll never be found. "You're not going to give me my money?"

"Mrs. Wainsborough? Does anyone else have legal access to the funds in your accounts?"

"No. Only my father. His name is still attached to my account. Why?"

"Your father," Walters says, peering at his computer monitor. "Does he happen to be in the Cayman Islands? The funds from your accounts were transferred into an account at a Cayman Island institution."

This can't be happening. There must be some explanation. It's not Simpkins but my father who's drained my account. I grab my cell phone, call his number. Walters and the security officers look at me with patience. The phone rings and rings. One of the security officers looks at his watch. An automated message comes over the line telling me that the number I dialed has been disconnected.

"Wait . . . wait . . . I must have misdialed," I say, but there's no way I could've misdialed. I can't believe my father took my money. Everything I have—my money, Savory Mew, the Mercedes, my clothes and fur coats, my carefree existence, the respect I'm still accorded at embassy parties and society events, and the belief that I'm more special, more dazzling and wonderful than other people—I owe to the fact that I'm Jack Riggs's daughter.

"Mrs. Wainsborough, unlike this building's previous occupants, PNC treats irregularities with great seriousness. I'll be reporting this incident through my bank's chain of command and to legal and regulatory authorities." Though Walters explains himself, I still have difficulty understanding his insinuations. He admits that, at this moment, the evidence is circumstantial, but he thinks I've colluded with my father to double dip into my bank account. Or at least try to double dip, which he insists is still a crime. Attempted fraud. Walters rises from his desk, signaling our meeting is finished. "Mrs. Wainsborough? Can I give you a piece of advice?"

Weakly, I nod.

"Don't make plans to leave the country anytime soon."

There's no end to my problems. Standing up, I freeze at the sensation of warm fluid dampening the inside of my thigh. I breathe, pretend it isn't happening, but when I take a step, I feel it again. I cry out, grab the back of a chair for support. Walters rises from his desk, and a security officer rushes to my side, both no doubt under the impression I must be having a nervous attack brought on by my financial mess, but what I feel is something far worse than the stress of impending bankruptcy.

I'm not pregnant.

All my life, I've been 100 percent regular. But now, for the first time ever, my period is early. I feel it soaking into my yoga pants, smell it when I shift my legs. In a few hours, I'll start cramping before the onset of my heavier menstrual flow over the coming days. Every woman is different, but this is how it's always been for me.

"Mrs. Wainsborough, are you all right? Do you need a doctor?"

The disappointment rocks me like a tidal wave. I sniffle, cry, wail. An hour ago, I guided James's hand to my belly, sure that I was pregnant. Was it all a delusion? Was every single hope, every single dream I shared with my husband a delusion?

Chapter Thirty-Five

LAUREL

One moment I'm beneath a half dozen blankets in my apartment bed, and the next I'm in the passenger seat of Jimmy's Volvo with no clue how I got here. I'm a fireball, a supernova, a comet blazing with fever, hot and woozy and near delirious, and though the car's heater blasts hot air at me at full strength, I'm shivering, my teeth chattering.

"We're almost there," Jimmy says.

Jimmy runs a stoplight. He makes a turn and then another turn, and we're barreling down the boulevard way too fast, hugging the curves with a momentum best measured in g-forces, but I'm too scared—and too sick—to say anything. I've got no idea why he's driving like a madman. Nor can I figure out where we're going. There's nothing but determination on his face—no compassion, no love, no sign of any consideration for me. Is he on some death wish? He's going to get pulled over by the police for speeding. Or the car's going to crash, mangling us in its wreckage. Sunlight glares off the surrounding snow. We fishtail onto a side street sheeted with ice. Cars honk at us. Jimmy presses his foot on the gas pedal, jolting the car faster—and then I hear a police siren.

"Oh, shit." Jimmy glances at the rearview mirror, bites his lip, and contemplates whether to pull over and let the cop write him up for speeding or whether he should lead foot it and try to rabbit out a getaway. The memory of every awful unlawful moment I spent in the company of my father floods through me. The Volvo's no go-fast car, but Jimmy guns the engine, speeding off on the kind of wild car chase that usually ends up on the evening news with someone either in handcuffs or in an ambulance. I glance over my shoulder and think I'm going to pass out. Why won't he slow down? Why does he never listen to me? The police car is right behind us, giving chase, its siren wailing.

"Pull over, Jimmy," I say, screaming.

Jimmy looks at me with astonished eyes. I've never raised my voice at him. He slams the brakes, but the forward momentum bounces me into the dashboard. Pulling the Volvo over to the curb, he runs his hand over his eyes, sighs mightily. I may have saved both our lives, but Jimmy just rolls down his window, letting in a blast of cold air. In the seconds that we wait for the police officer to step out of her patrol car and walk over to us, Jimmy tells me to let him do all the talking. Which is just as well, because I'm in no shape to talk. My heart pounds, but I'm so groggy I can't stay awake. Five minutes seem to pass before the police officer, a tall woman with short blonde hair, strolls up to the car.

"You know why I'm stopping you, don't you?" the police officer asks.

"I gotta get her to Sibley," Jimmy says. "I know I was speeding, but I think she's dying."

The officer peers into the car. Seeing me, her eyes widen, making me afraid Jimmy's right—I might really be dying. "Wait until I get back into my car, and then follow me, sir. You got that? I'll escort you to Sibley."

We follow the police officer onto the Whitehurst Freeway and then onto Canal Road and MacArthur Boulevard. She's got her lights flashing and her siren wailing, the sea of traffic on these congested streets parting to let us through. There's something exploding inside my head, a nervous pulse thrumming my heart. I feel like a trapped bird, a feathered thing too hot and feverish to flap her wings. Nor can I figure out why we're going back to Sibley. It's the one place I don't want to be. Is he taking me back there so they can finish off what they've already started—trying to kill me? The police officer must have radioed ahead, for two EMTs, a nurse, and an orderly stand outside waiting for me at Sibley's emergency admittance door. Everything is happening so quickly. Someone—maybe Jimmy, maybe a doctor—squeezes my hand, kisses me, tells me everything will be all right. I'm trembling, sweating. The orderly notices my hospital ID wristband and the plastic medallion dangling from my wrist, and someone else scans the barcode on the wristband with an iPad. The EMTs look at each other. "So you're the one," one of them says. Someone guides me into a wheelchair. I look around and panic.

"Where'd Jimmy go?" I ask.

"Never mind that—we need to get you upstairs immediately," the nurse says.

The elevator door opens. The orderly wheels me inside. The nurse takes my pulse. "You've lost a lot of blood," she says, as if I need her to state the obvious.

Chapter Thirty-Six

LAUREL

Somewhere near me, a baby cries when I awake, and it's impossible for me to hear a baby and not think of Zerena. In my mind I imagine Zerena crawling down the hallway, searching for me. She's a blur of a girl dressed only in a disposable diaper and white knit baby booties, her hands and knees supercharged and moving so fast she's leaving skid marks on the gleamingly clean hospital floors. I picture her peering into elevators, stairwells, broom-filled closets, and other patients' rooms trying to find me, her mommy, the one person capable of bringing her comfort and joy. She'll climb up my bed, navigate her way over the stainless steel bed railings so she can nestle in my lap, but then I grab one of the stainless steel bed railings and see it for what it would be: an impediment to Zerena's climb. The bed's elevated several feet off the ground, and I wish I was lying on the floor with no more than a blanket or a couple of sheets beneath me, a low-lying setting that my gummy-mouthed Zerena could mount without difficulty, but then this vision, too, comes crashing down with the crushing realization that she's too young to crawl, too young to do much of anything to get herself back to me.

Karma has its limits. No matter how much I wish, there's no Zerena nestled in my lap, no baby at my breast. Instead, the tubing from two different IVs—one for an antibiotic-laced saline solution and the other for a blood transfusion—is taped to my arm. Clamped to my index finger is an electronic sensor connected by wires to a computer near the nightstand, and on the computer's screen, a running graph displays my temperature and heart rate.

"You're doing well," Lois Belcher says. She reaches over and pats the back of my hand.

"How long have I been here?"

"Maybe an hour. The antibiotic you're on is really strong. Stronger than the vancomycin they gave you yesterday. A nurse already washed out your episiotomy wound and stitched it up better. We work quick around here when we have to."

I'm in the exact same room on the maternity ward as I had been in, which doesn't quite make sense. I hear babies cry outside my door, and my heart pangs. "Do you know where Zerena is?"

"I'm afraid we don't have good news on that front."

My heart sinks.

"The detectives can't issue Amber Alerts unless they're certain an abduction occurred. In your case, they thought it suspicious that both you and your baby vanished within hours of each other. That's what they said: 'suspicious.'" Disappointment lines Lois Belcher's voice. She shakes her head. "Or maybe the word they used was 'convenient.' Maybe that's the word they used."

"But I don't have anything to do with Zerena's disappearance. I was asleep when it happened."

"I know, but the detectives are going to need some convincing. I'm supposed to call them as soon as you're well enough for them to interview."

I glance around the room. Everything seems as it had been. Tricia's flowers stand in a vase on the nightstand right next to the box of chocolates Jimmy gave me. But though the room is the same, it feels emptier, sadder. Zerena's stainless steel bassinet is up against the wall, unoccupied.

"Is, um, Jimmy . . . Jimmy Wainsborough, my, uh . . ." After all that's happened, it's awkward asking about Jimmy. Lois Belcher, sensing my embarrassment, blushes. I don't know how to refer to him anymore. "Is my, uh, acquaintance Jimmy waiting for me in the waiting room?"

Lois Belcher shakes her head slowly. "He said he had something important to do."

Important, I want to yell out. Important? Like, why doesn't Jimmy think I'm an important enough reason for him to stay put and be with me?

"By the way, we found this on the floor by the closet," Lois Belcher says, handing me my cell phone. I haven't seen it since the previous night. "I've been holding on to it, hoping you'd come back."

After thanking Ms. Belcher, I tell her to let the police know I'm ready to talk. Before she leaves, she apologizes for what she's done. Later this afternoon, she'll attend an administrative hearing in the personnel department. She's going to lose her job, she says. Under the circumstances, it's hard for me to feel sorry for her, but I wish her good luck. She leaves to fetch the police.

While I wait for the police to arrive, I give my cell phone a little hug. My whole life is tied up in its computer chips and wiring. Never have I been separated from it for so long. I press a button, and its screen opens to a picture of Jimmy and me standing hand in hand in the Jefferson Memorial. Dozens if not hundreds of photos of Jimmy reside in my phone. Now, though, I don't want to look at a single one of them.

Instead, I notice a voice mail message has been waiting for me since last night—and then I remember how my phone started ringing when one of the doctors jabbed me with a hypodermic needle. The voice mail is from Tricia . . . making me wonder how she got my number. Had Jimmy given it to her? Against my better judgment, I play it.

"Laurel . . . Jimmy's going to kill me if he finds out I'm calling you," Trish says, her voice urgent and serious. I press my phone to my ear. She sounds seriously afraid. Might James have actually been near her when she called? "I just found out about your adorable baby being missing, and I'm heartbroken. I feel so sorry for you. What I've got to tell you is shocking, but yesterday Jimmy told me he was going to find a way to make sure you never had any contact with your baby. He was going to steal it, he said. He'd been drinking, and I thought it was just the alcohol in him that made him say crazy things. No woman deserves to have her baby stolen. I'm worried he's responsible for Anne Elise's disappearance. I've told the police everything I know, but I'm afraid, frankly, that DC cops are so incompetent they might never find out what he's done with Anne Elise. Laurel, I'm sure you know this by now, but you really can't trust him. Please don't say I didn't try to warn you."

I'm angry and seething, barely able to believe Jimmy's double-crossed me by taking Zerena. Tricia might be lying for some crazy psycho reason, but I think back to Jimmy's unflappable calm this morning when talking about Zerena. He never once mentioned going to the police himself to try to help the investigation, and yet he was dead certain we'd have Zerena back by the end of the day. How could he have been so certain Zerena would be back unless he knew exactly where she was and had the power to release her when he chose?

Tricia's message cuts off just as a commotion arises in the hallway. People argue, saying rude things to each other right outside my room.

"She's our daughter! Who wouldn't want to see their parents? It wouldn't be visiting hours if people aren't supposed to visit."

"But . . . but . . . but—"

"Woman, don't you 'but' me!"

Two kinds of drunks exist in this world—the gregarious but genial kind like Jimmy and the bitter, combative type like Tully. I thought he stopped drinking, but he's slurring his words and, from the heavy sound of his footfalls, stumbling. Hearing him bicker brings back bad memories of growing up in the trailer with them. No matter how well my mother tried to divert his anger, he'd always erupt something nasty, breaking plates and glasses and the fragile hopes of the little girl who once was me. I close my eyes with a sense of dread and pretend to be asleep, but my parents come into the room anyways.

"Aw, look at that, Tully," Belinda says, her voice hushed like it would be when I was a little girl and she'd find me curled asleep on the couch. "She's sleeping. I told you we shouldn't come here bothering her. Let's go and come back some other day."

"Nonsense," Tully says. He tugs my hand. Try as I might to still my breathing, it's impossible not to squirm at his touch. "Honey? Honey? You 'wake?"

"Aww . . . you gone and woke her," Belinda says.

"Wake up. Wake up."

I open my eyes. Tully hunches right above me, his graying ponytail slung over one shoulder, the odors of gasoline and motor oil clinging to his gray mechanic's coveralls. Seeing me awake, he steps back, scrunches his eyes, and says, "Man, you look horrible. What the hell happened to you?"

Before I can answer, he asks, "Has that man of yours shown up? I need to talk to him about my money."

I'm no troublemaker, no snarl girl who looks forward to giving pricks their comeuppance, but Tully's got to be told. "The money you gave Jimmy was bad money."

Tully narrows his eyes. Contrary to what I expect, he remains calm. He taps his fingers against my bed rail, pinging it in a metronomic rhythm. Belinda, who's holding my hand, tenses up as if she knows about the money. Tully asks her to leave the room.

"You're not going to hurt her, are you?" Belinda asks, letting go of my hand.

"Course not. Only a fool kills the messenger."

Belinda doesn't want to leave, but probably not wanting to provoke a confrontation with Tully, she slogs out of the room. Tully opens a pouch of Red Man loose-leaf chewing tobacco that he pulls from the back pocket of his coveralls and stuffs a lump between his cheek and gum. "So about this money. What you know about it?"

"It's counterfeit. Jimmy brought it to someone yesterday, and even before he could set up an investment account or whatever for the money, the money was flagged as counterfeit."

Tully takes this information in slowly, shifting his brows, nodding. Never has anything I've said so captured his attention. Bourbon vapors spill out of his every breath, comingling with the chewing tobacco. "So he'll give the money back to me. That's not so bad, is it?"

"Did you know it was counterfeit?"

"Do you got a cup I can use for my spit?"

"Paper cups are in the bathroom. Did you know the money wasn't real?"

"You don't need to know that." Tully walks into the bathroom of my maternity suite, and I hear him spit into a paper cup, and when he comes back into the room, he's carrying that paper cup. Sitting beside me on the bed, he balances it on his knee. "I'm your daddy, girl. I'm supposed to look out for you, so trust me. Don't go around asking about that money, okay?" He shoots me a glance, letting me know he's serious. "You don't want to learn anything that's going to put you in the middle of someone's crosshairs. The best thing in the world for you right now is to be a beautiful little fool. Stay stupid. Stupid's good. What you don't know can't hurt you."

In his own way, he's saying that he loves me. He doesn't want to see me dead, doesn't want to see me maimed or wounded or fallen victim to whoever fronted him the counterfeit money, which is more consideration than Jimmy's shown me lately. I asked that he divorce Tricia, but instead, he seems determined to leap into her arms every time he thinks I'm asleep or too sick to notice.

"So your Jimmy's going to give me back that money, right?"

"The money's still with whoever flagged it as counterfeit. They're threatening to kneecap Jimmy because of it." At the sound of that word—kneecap—Tully spits tobacco juice into his cup. "Jimmy gave them the money having no reason to think it wasn't real."

Tully looks off in the distance and whistles as if he can't believe Jimmy would do such a thing. "That was stupid. Your Jimmy should have known better. I'm going to have to talk some sense into him, tell him to get the money back. If whoever your Jimmy's dealing with turns the money over to the feds, it's going to be trouble for everyone. Understand? So how do I meet up with your Jimmy?"

A chill goes through me. Has Tully ever killed someone? I can't say for certain, but there's no question he'll turn violent if he can't get his counterfeit money. I warned Jimmy that Tully's a pit viper, but he chose not to listen. Now, one way or another, he's going to face the consequences. Is that what I want? Should I sic my father on him? What kind of asshole steals a baby? From his mistress? As eloquent as Jimmy sometimes is, my father will know that Jimmy lied to him—there's no way Jimmy can explain why he gave the money to a private investigator rather than investing it like my father expected.

"Come on, girl. I don't have all day. Tell me where I can find him."

I suck in a breath. What I'm doing is wrong, but what Jimmy's been doing to me is equally wrong. I tell my father the address Jimmy gave me yesterday.

Tully scratches his head. "Where's that?"

I grab my cell phone, punch in the address, which automatically loads it into the Google Maps app, and soon we're both staring at a map of upper Georgetown. I click a thumbnail picture of the house itself—which is absolutely humongous. The thumbnail picture expands, filling my phone's screen. Tully sucks in a breath. He, too, is shocked by the size of Jimmy's house. I could get lost in a house that big. He's totally played me. The house might really be in Tricia's name, but you can't tell me that a man who lives in a house that huge doesn't have ample resources of his own. He didn't even want to pay off my student loans.

"He lives there?" Tully asks.

"Go get him, Dad. Do what you have to do with him, okay?"

⁓

Five minutes later, Lois Belcher comes into the room again. "I don't know what's keeping the police so long." She's a nervous hen, that woman is. She goes up to the window, stares outside. "I called them up, just like you asked, but they still haven't come."

I glance at the chocolates next to the flowers and am filled with the desire to eat a couple of them. Because of the IV lines and electronic medical monitoring equipment hooked into me, I can't reach over far enough to grab the box. Not really being a chocolate person, it's the first time I've hungered for them, and I hope this hunger's a sign of a returning appetite, a sign that I'm getting better. "Mrs. Belcher, could you hand me my chocolates?"

Lois Belcher brings them to me. I open the box and bite into a little cube of dark chocolate that's rich and creamy and filled with some kind of coffee-flavored nougat. It's delicious. None of the cheap drugstore chocolates or Hershey bars I've ever had tasted so good.

"You know, you're real lucky to have Jimmy in your life."

"Yeah. Right." I nibble a milk chocolate swirl that tastes of cinnamon and citrus.

"Seriously. Bringing you here when he did, he saved your life. That's what the doctors are saying."

My head jolts up. "He did?"

"Uh-huh. If he hadn't stumbled on you just when he did, or if he found you maybe even a half hour later, you might not be alive right now."

I let this sink in. Any minute, Tully's apt to confront Jimmy about his counterfeit money, but I feel a rush of gratitude. And then a bolt of regret for siccing Tully on him. I never should have done that. I remember Jimmy driving me to the hospital—me being scared not because my life was in danger but because of his silly fast speed and reckless driving. He could have taken me anywhere, or he could have let me stay in my Watergate bedroom. Instead, he took me back here to ensure I'd be safe and healthy. Right about now, Tully's probably bullying him. Or worse.

But it's all theoretical, I tell myself, working out the possibilities in my mind. Maybe Tully's just finding out more about where his money is or plotting with Jimmy how to get it back. But it's Tully we're talking about, someone who'd never resort to reason when violence was a viable alternative. And then I just know it: Jimmy's going to be brutalized.

"What's wrong?" Lois Belcher asks.

I grab my phone. There's probably still time to let Jimmy know Tully's about to come after him. I cross my fingers and dial him up. But then I hear Jimmy's phone ring. It's on the nightstand next to the flowers, where it's probably been since yesterday. I start to cry. He may have saved my life, but I can't do anything to save his.

Chapter Thirty-Seven

TRISH

Stepping into Savory Mew after coming back from the bank, I'm woken out of my shattered spirits by the sound of Anne Elise crying upstairs in the hideaway office. She's hungry, thirsty, and in need of a calm shoulder on which to rest her tired body. I've lived most of my life in Georgetown, a tony enclave of privilege and power, but a sense of estrangement already settles over me. Without money, I won't be able to afford to live here much longer. My mind is numb, empty, a cotton field that has been picked clean. I can't even cover Laurel's legal expenses should we convince her to bring suit against the hospital.

I grab a baby bottle from the refrigerator, stick it in the electric bottle warmer. James's carafe of chamomile tea remains on the counter, untouched but still warm enough to drink thanks to its special thermal lining. In desperate need of a pick-me-up, I pour a cup and give it a taste. James has done something different to it. It's cloudier than it ought to be, as if he's dribbled a teaspoon of cream into the carafe. I take small sips to judge whether it's to my liking, the sips just large enough to wet my tongue. It's more bitter but with a sweet aftertaste that tingles and numbs the back of my throat. Anne Elise hasn't stopped crying since I entered the house, and I suspect she, too, would enjoy a little chamomile calm in her life. Chamomile's natural and totally safe, so I unscrew the top of the baby bottle, pour half its contents into the sink, and top the bottle off with tea.

Upstairs, I lift Anne Elise out of her cradle. She looks at me with anger in her eyes, her face red with anguish, her hands balled into fists no bigger than silver dollars, but she's smart: I show her the bottle, and she opens her mouth and reaches for it. Almost immediately, she's suckling the bottle, murmuring, seemingly contented, but then her eyes pop open. She pushes the bottle's nipple out of her mouth with the pink tip of her tongue and fusses, and when she stops fussing, she stares at the bottle as if trying to make sense of it. The taste must set her on edge. I dabble a few drops onto her lips, which she licks, but she's still hesitant to accept the bottle, so I jam it into her mouth, determined not to lose a battle of wills to a newborn.

"It's only a little bitty little tea. That's what you're tasting."

Rather than drinking the bottle, Anne Elise wails. I can't get her to drink from the bottle. I force it into her mouth a third time, and this time she actually presses her lips against the silicone nipple, chugging at it. Somewhere, I remember reading a magazine article saying that people can retrain their taste buds to become accustomed to and accepting of new foods or strange tastes just by eating them three times, which is exactly what seems to happen with Anne Elise and the tea. It's as if she's forgotten her initial aversion to the concoction. Satisfaction comes over me. She takes a few more sips. But then a look of sudden consternation falls over her. She pushes the nipple out of her mouth.

Frustrated, I carry her downstairs, grab a formula-only bottle from the refrigerator, stick it in the bottle warmer, and pour another cup of tea for myself. There'll be time tomorrow or some other day to teach Anne Elise to like the tea, but though she hasn't drunk that much, the chamomile's already done its trick on her: she's calmer, quieter, drowsier. When the formula bottle's warm, I feed Anne Elise, and such is her hunger that she drinks the entire bottle before I remember to burp her.

When Anne Elise falls asleep again, I take her back upstairs and lower her into the cradle. Her shallow breathing makes her seem like a lifeless doll, so calm does she appear. I stand, staring at her for ten minutes. Her chest barely rises with each breath. Is this normal? Is this how babies are meant to breathe?

The whole house is quiet. Walking downstairs, I feel like I'm a goose feather gliding in the air, ever downward. My father's portrait catches my attention. He was a dashing man in his top hat, but I never actually remembered seeing him with the silver-knobbed walking stick he holds in the portrait. When I was a little girl, he'd bend down in the hallway before leaving for his banking offices and let me lay his top hat on his head. I remember it like it was a privilege, a grand honor. The hat itself was something magnificent, with a fine satiny finish. Constructed of stiff brushed fur felt, I've never since felt anything like it. But the walking stick? I don't ever remember him with that one. In the painting, the stick's silver knob is the size of a grapefruit, too huge to be practical or manageable. For years, I've searched closets and attics without success for it. Might it have been the portrait artist's studio prop? Or did it exist solely in the painter's imagination, a fanciful touch to convey in the sitter, my father, a nobility he didn't actually possess?

The house abounds in objets d'art and heirlooms that can be quickly and quietly sold now that I'm in need of money. The rich always have their parachutes, their hidden assets, and I am no exception. The portrait of my father would be the first thing I'd let go, for how could I look at it after the betrayal and humiliation he's caused? Abandonment is my father's lasting legacy. I shiver with this understanding. He betrayed everyone who ever trusted him. My mother and the many lovers he took throughout his life. Shareholders lost vast sums when PNC absorbed his bank in the wake of his mismanagement. His best friend, Simpkins's grandfather, was not immune to his treachery. Why did I think I'd be different?

~

Back in the kitchen, I polish off the rest of the tea. My Valium bottle's on the counter, where I don't remember placing it. Though I'm calm and mellow, I spill out a couple of pills onto my palm and swallow them. My hands are slow and shaky. I can't remember taking many pills this morning, and yet I must have: the bottle is nearly empty. How many have I taken? Sights and sounds become foggy, dissolving into warmth and nothingness as I drift into a drowsiness that catches up fast on me. James had warned me to keep track of the pills I ingested. Should I be worried? Should I call for an ambulance? One moment, I'm staring at the porcelain teacup, wondering if I should wash it out, and the next moment I look up and see James patting my hand, asking me if I'm all right.

"I couldn't get the money," I say, worried how James's going to react. "My father. He took all my money."

James is so tall, so handsome. He's going to be disappointed when I tell him I'm not pregnant. The best moments in my life revolved around the months we fell in love. He hadn't yet learned how wealthy I was. Osama bin Laden had brought us together. That is what we told our friends: 9/11 was our blessing. I should have trusted him forever. I should have bought him that fancy Tesla he wanted; he would've been so happy. Instead, his eyes drift toward the carafe, which I've emptied. He rushes to the sink, fills a glass with water, and implores me to drink it.

"I'm sorry. I'm sorry," James says. "I was too late. I'm sorry."

Why is he apologizing? He must be telling me he's sorry about cheating on me. I'm feeling dopey, dumb, but it's cute, having him apologize for running around with Laurel. To make him happy, I drink the water and hand him back the glass. He would've been so happy if I bought him that Tesla. Why had I been so stingy when I had so much I could give him?

"Where's Anne Elise?"

"I gave her some tea. She fell asleep."

"You gave her tea?" James looks horrified. I try to tell him that babies are people too, that they can drink all sorts of things, but I'm mumbling my words, and nothing I say calms him. The glass falls from James's hand and shatters on the floor, the slivers and shards glistening in the sunbeams shining through the windows. James pulls out his cell phone.

Everything feels so cold and foggy.

"What are you doing?" I ask.

"I'm calling 911."

An ambulance. I should have called for one myself when I realized I'd taken so many Valiums. I'm grateful James is taking care of me. I grab the Valium bottle again. Yesterday, and even this morning, there were dozens of pills in the bottle. Now, only a few remain. Is this why I'm groggy?

James must see it too, the alarm in my expression. His face clamps up with concern. He puts his hand over the phone. "Don't worry, Trish. I'm getting someone to help you."

Chapter Thirty-Eight

Jim

The 911 dispatcher asks if Trish and Anne Elise are breathing. I'm a fool. I never should have crushed those Valium tablets, never should have placed them in the teapot or given the carafe to Trish. Despite Washington, DC, being, as locals like to say, "the most powerful city in the world," not a month goes by without some horror story hitting the news about the city's underfunded and unreliable 911 response services. Trish, seated at the breakfast nook in her lush sable coat, slumps forward, her forehead smacking the lip of the breakfast table. I had crushed the Valium tablets, stirred them into the tea, but it was as if I were in an altered state, possessed by the humiliation of Trish's promissory notes and the demands that I separate myself from Laurel. I'd been disoriented, knowing Anne Elise was upstairs. I couldn't fathom why I hadn't suspected Trish of abducting her. I hadn't truly anticipated something like this would happen. How was I to know Trish would give the tea to Anne Elise?

As soon as Laurel was in safe hands at the hospital, I ran back to my car, determined to do something about that carafe. My hope had been to get to Trish before she drank the tea. If need be, I was going to feign clumsiness and knock down the carafe, spilling the chamomile tea to the floor. Apologizing profusely, I'd offer to brew Trish a new pot and then sit down with her and chart out our separation. I'd spin this giant roulette wheel and see where the chips fell. Money is one thing Trish understands. To induce her to give up Anne Elise, I was going to sign away all claims on her fortune should we divorce. And about Trish's legal problems? Prosecutors would need Laurel's assistance to bring charges against Trish for the kidnapping, so I'd tell Laurel I'd marry her only on the condition she withhold such cooperation. It was as close to a win-win-win proposition as I could imagine. Now, I pray an ambulance will come quickly to save both Anne Elise and Trish.

"Sir? Sir?" the dispatcher asks.

Anne Elise starts crying upstairs. I put down the phone and run to her, overjoyed she's alive, but upstairs, Anne Elise is locked behind the bookcase in the hideaway office again. I never figured out how to spring open the bookcase to get inside that room. Out of frustration, I hurl books off the shelves and toss crystal bookends, decorative figurines, and a bowl of spare change down the stairs. One of the varnished shelves becomes loose. Kicking doesn't budge the bookcase. I heave myself at it, ramming my shoulder into it, but rather than moving the bookcase, I hear something pop in my shoulder. A flash of pain sears through me. For once in my life I wish I were a brute, a hulking goon capable of destroying anything and anyone in my path. I ram myself back at the bookcase using my other shoulder. The loose shelf falls off its support pegs. Just beneath one of the support pegs sits a small button such as you'd normally depress to activate a doorbell. I don't understand how I never noticed it before. I push the button. Something mechanical cranks to life behind the wall. The bookcase screeches backward, revealing the narrow passageway that leads to the secret office.

Downstairs, Savory Mew's front door bursts open. Someone rushes into the house. It's been mere minutes since I phoned 911 dispatch, and the speed of the ambulance's arrival fills me with hope for Anne Elise and Trish.

"I'm up here," I say, yelling downstairs as I dart into the hideaway office. Seeing me, Anne Elise stops crying. I lift her from the cradle, hug her to my chest. Her face is red with tears, but she's healthy. There'll be no more locked doors in her future, no more inaccessible secret offices. When I make a funny face, she smiles.

Footsteps stomp upstairs.

"We're going to be all right," I say to Anne Elise. Even if she might not be biologically mine, the bond we already share will keep us united throughout life. I'll hug her and cherish her, build a life with her and Laurel. Suddenly I can see it: the single-family detached home in the suburbs we'd own, the swing set in the backyard, the sandbox, the trips to the playground. The Christmas trees layered with tinsel and strands of twinkling lights, the Easter baskets overflowing with chocolate bunnies. I see us having more than one child—a little brother for Anne Elise and maybe, God willing, another child down the road. I see the happiness we'll share: it's all in our future.

The footsteps approach, and as they do, so too does the smell of gasoline and motor oil. The twin scents bring to mind my father, who I never saw again after he walked out on my mother when I was thirteen. Decades later, that moment of abandonment still reaches out to me, rubbing its salt in my wounds. Back then, I internalized my father's abandonment, resigned that some inferiority or latent defect within me caused him to leave my mother and me; ever since, I've fantasized about the regret that might one day befall him should he find out how well I'm doing in life. I wanted him to open the newspaper in whatever squalid surroundings he found himself in and discover the son he abandoned was now obscenely wealthy.

A man in gray mechanic's coveralls and a graying ponytail steps into the hideaway office. In my emotional state, I mistake his coveralls for the jumpsuit emergency medical personnel might wear. Seconds later, though, I recognize his true identity.

"Tull! What are you doing here?"

"Don't 'Tull' me."

"Huh?"

"For you, it's 'Tully.' Tully. Only my close friends can call me 'Tull' and get away with it. What did you do with my money?"

My heart clenches in fear. "Your money? You're here about your money?" I take a deep breath, grit my teeth. The overwhelming stench of bourbon oozes out of Tully. He's aggravated and frantic. I can't afford to lie to him. "It's counterfeit, Tully. All of it. It's not real."

"I know damn well it's counterfeit. That's not what I'm asking. I'm asking what you did with the money."

"There's a man in Chinatown who's got the money. A private investigator." I tell Tully about Simpkins, spinning a tale of how he refused to give back the money. Though I'm holding Anne Elise, he doesn't mention her, perhaps doesn't even notice her, so single-minded is he on learning what happened to his money. He drums his fingers on a dust-covered leather-bound ledger and tells me to tell him everything I know about the guy who's got his counterfeit money. Upon first meeting him, I thought Tully an unsophisticated grease monkey incapable of understanding anything more complicated than a hydraulic torque wrench or the workings of an internal combustion engine, but he takes in what I'm saying unflinchingly, assessing it. "Simpkins is a sharpie. I've tried to break him, tried to convince him it's not in *his* interest to hold on to counterfeit money. He's trying to blackmail me."

"Wait. I tell you to invest the money in stocks and bonds and whatever shit works best, and you're telling me you gave the money to some private investigator? Why the hell did you do that?"

I understand how bad this looks, me eschewing my fiduciary responsibility and, rather than plowing the money into actual investment-grade financial instruments—"stocks and bonds and shit"— giving the money to a private investigator. Tully squares me a look. "Anyways, why'd you spill the beans to Laurel that her old man's a crook? She was coming around to liking me again, and then you had to tell her about the money. Now she'll never respect me."

Tully's right: I shouldn't have told Laurel—not that I think it would have made a difference in how she views him. But I should've let Laurel believe Tully was working long hours at the garage, accruing overtime pay and maybe picking up a second job and saving his pennies. Myth has it that hard work and thrift—two qualities I've never embodied—are the pillars to financial well-being. I should have told Laurel her father had these qualities down in spades. Why couldn't I have lied?

"I'm sorry, Tully. I'll do what I can to get Laurel to respect you again. Honest, I will. Laurel's a good girl. She'll give you a second chance. She will. I know it."

Tully's eyes become glassy. I wouldn't have thought him the sentimental type, but maybe it's the bourbon turning him melancholy. He wipes his eyes with the sleeves of his mechanic's coveralls. And then he glances at me, clearly uncomfortable that I've witnessed him during an emotional moment. He weaves his hands together and cracks his knuckles. "You say you know where we can find this Simpkins guy who's got my money?"

"Sure do! Want me to write down the address for you?"

"You're going to do better than that. You and me. We're family, right? If we're going to rough this guy up, we gotta do it together."

"Who said anything about roughing Simpkins up?"

"I did. That's who. Haven't you been listening to a word I've been saying? You already tried to talk sense into him, right? That didn't work too well, did it? So we need to be ferocious and whack him some."

I'm scared, but cowardice isn't an argument likely to sway Tully. "Tully, I wouldn't bring the same skills into the situation as you would. That's not who I am. I'd be a liability in a down-and-dirty brawl. You'd be better off without me. Besides, I've seen Simpkins. He's a wimp! A tough guy like you can handle him no problem. Trust me."

Tully crosses his arms. "You're chicken. Admit it!"

"You're right: I'm a chicken. I'm ashamed to admit it, but I'm not half the man you are."

My implicit praise takes Tully aback. He eyes me over, taps his fingers against one of Jack Riggs's ancient oak filing cabinets. "You shitting me? You think that?"

"It's true: I'm not half the man you are."

"You got that right." Tully's laugh is deep, rich, a har-de-har laugh emanating from deep within his belly. "You're all right! I'm not going to make you do anything you're not A-okay, one hundred percent on board with."

"You're okay with this?" I ask with a wave of relief. I'm not going to have to rough up Simpkins. Or run the risk of Simpkins roughing me up. "You're really okay with this?"

"Sure am, buddy. You being a wimp's no skin off my nose." Tully holds out his hand for a handshake. "Let's shake on it."

I shift Anne Elise to my left shoulder, freeing up my right hand. As I reach for Tully's handshake, I hear the spring-action sound of the switchblade that Tully whips out from his coveralls. His eyes are big and green. He looks at the knife in his hand and then grins at me, fierce, near maniacal.

I back up against the oak-paneled wall, more scared than I've ever been. The knife is huge, and this cramped hideaway office is small and devoid of places to hide. There's not even space beneath the desk to crawl under. Tully blocks my path to the hallway, closing in on me so slowly that it makes me think his intent is to exert maximum fear. He could leap on me with that knife, pummel and stab me with it, killing me off quickly, but he inches up to me with exceedingly slow deliberation.

"Don't hurt Anne Elise," I say.

"It's not her I'm fixing to kill."

A braver man might fight off his assailant, but with Anne Elise nestled against my shoulder, a struggle seems futile. One way or another, she's bound to be hurt. I could set her down somewhere safe, but that would involve taking my eyes off Tully, allowing him the opportunity to lunge at me. Light glints off the polished steel blade of Tully's knife. It's six inches long, maybe longer, but staring at it, I become braver. This is my lucky day, I remind myself. I think happy thoughts. Survival thoughts. Tully reeks of booze. His eyes are wild and bloodshot. Sooner or later, he's bound to do something stupid—take his eyes off me or stumble over the cradle—allowing me to rush past him to safety. Time is his enemy. The longer he delays lunging at me, the greater the chance he'll screw up.

"Tully, why are you doing this? Let's talk this over. Like you said, we're family."

Tully snorts. "We're not family. I don't want any man in my family who's not willing to fight for his money."

"Let's talk about it. We can—"

Tully lunges at me. I dodge to my right, sidestepping his parry. I wish I could call a time-out to put Anne Elise down and guarantee her safety, but Tully lunges at me again. This time, the switchblade slices into my neck. For a half second, I think I've imagined it, but there's a terrible stinging pain in my neck. An ethereal calmness overtakes me. With my free hand, I press down on the slice in the skin around my Adam's apple. It's not deep, giving me hope. Although bloody, the wound's not the cinematic gusher depicted in movies and television dramas.

Another person, a woman judging by the light footsteps, steps upstairs. I allow myself to think that Trish has pulled herself up from the kitchen table to come to my rescue. I call out to her, but my throat is sore, and my voice is weak—"Trish? Trish, honey? I'm in here!"—but, rather than stepping inside this hideaway office or saying something, she remains in the hallway, listening in on us.

"Your own wife's not going to save you, is she?" Tully says. He points his knife at my neck. "What's the matter? You got yourself a little boo-boo?"

Tully's right. As Jack Riggs would say, "Roosters roost." After all I've put her through, I couldn't blame Trish for just standing in the hallway, safe and secure, while I'm being terrorized by this switchblade-wielding madman. Blood dribbles down my neck. I'm shocked by how thick, how viscous, this blood is. I'm pressing down on the wound to stanch the flow, conscious of the blood that slicks onto my hand, my white shirt, and the ancient warped floorboards.

In the distance, a siren wails. Hearing it, Tully cocks his head to one side. Simpkins told me about the warrants out for Tully's arrest, and on the lam, Tully must be hyperedgy and irrationally aware of sirens and police patrol cars.

"You call the police?" Tully asks.

I nod. There's no need to tell him about the Valium-laced tea or that Trish was supposed to lavish me with enough money to pay off both Simpkins and himself, no need to tell him how I was supposed to have enough money to make a killing on my investment tip and enough money to pay off Laurel's student loans. The ambulances and EMTs will arrive and save me from dying. I will live to see Laurel again. I will live to see Trish again so I can tell her how sorry I am. I hope she can forgive me. The siren becomes louder. More blood trickles from the gash in my neck, making me woozy and cold. What I need is a jumbo-sized Band-Aid and a doctor to stitch up the cut. That and a few fingers of twenty-one-year-old Scotch to ease my nerves.

"Why'd you do that? You trying to screw me? Is that what you're trying to do?"

"Anne Elise. I feared she'd been hurt, so I called 911. That was moments before you came."

Feeling dizzy, I worry about dropping Anne Elise. My toes and feet and hands are numb, and I'm cold. My shoulder still aches from bashing myself into the bookcase, but that pain pales when compared to the knife wound's sting. The trickle of blood from my throat becomes a small stream. There's a tingling sensation in my temples. Slowly, cautiously, I bend down and lay Anne Elise in her rosewood cradle, and as I'm doing so, my blood drips upon her forehead. Feeling the blood, Anne Elise frowns, something I haven't seen her do before. My movement or maybe my talking must have stretched the cut wider, deeper, causing this profusion of blood. Pressing my hand against it no longer keeps it from bleeding so much. I shiver. Weird memories—a youth soccer penalty kick I buried in the upper ninety to win an important tournament for my team, a lemon-raspberry birthday cake Trish made from scratch for me for my birthday just after we became engaged, the stench of Jack Riggs's cigars.

The woman who'd been waiting in the hallway limps into this hideaway office. It's Laurel. Pale and dressed in her flimsy hospital gown, she looks just as sick as when I drove her to the hospital hours earlier. She ought to return to the hospital immediately so she can finally recuperate, but I'm too tired and worn out to form the words in my mouth necessary to tell her this. I don't know why she thinks the hospital is so unsafe. Even someone as young as her should realize that the temptations and desires in the unquarantined world outside the hospital walls are far more dangerous.

Laurel, seeing the blood puddling over the floor from my neck, stutters. She turns to Tully. Her eyes grow large at the sight of his switchblade. "Wha-wha-wha—"

"Girl, leave us alone."

"You killed him."

"I did not. You didn't see anything. Anyways, what did you think was going to happen when you gave me his address and sent me on my way? You think I was coming here for a picnic? Maybe a tea party?" Tully says, flicking back the knife's blade to retract it into its hilt. The siren seems loud, the light around me getting dimmer. "Laurel, we better run. Quick."

I tumble to the floor. Anne Elise wails. She's so loud. The siren is so loud. Everything is so loud.

"What about the baby?"

"Leave it. We got to run."

"But—"

Tully runs out of the hideaway office, his feet rumbling on the floor. I hear him scramble downstairs. He calls for Laurel to join him but then leaves without her, slamming shut Savory Mew's front door, and I know he's gone from my life forever. Laurel's gripped in horror, her mouth hanging open. She stutters, cries, sobs, tells me she's sorry. Everything becomes still. I close my eyes. I want to comfort Laurel, tell her everything will be all right. *Be bold*, I want to tell her. *Embrace the child we have created.* The moments that follow stretch out forever. A soft hand presses against my cheek. Laurel, having lifted Anne Elise out of the cradle, kneels beside me. The hand on my cheek is Anne Elise's, and it feels so warm, so wonderful. I inhale her milky breath, feel her smooth hand on my face and the wisps of blonde hair around her ears. She's all I ever wanted: a baby of my own.

PART FOUR

Chapter Thirty-Nine

LAUREL

Seven Months Later

Out here in Oyster's Edge, you can hear the surf at any hour, the squawk of seagulls swooping down on the beach, pecking meat from the crab shells that wash ashore. You smell the salt water and the rotting algae and feel the grit of sand in your clothes whenever you step outside. Weathered skipjacks and oyster dredgers set sail from the piers before dawn, and if they're lucky, the watermen return by nightfall. After my lease ran out on the apartment Jimmy rented for me, Belinda packed my belongings and brought Anne Elise and me to live with her. The baby stuff Jimmy bought—the crib, the changing table, the stroller, the rocking chair, and the playpen—takes up most of the living room in her trailer. If she hadn't taken us in, I would've had to go into homeless shelters.

Situated about a two-hour drive from DC, Oyster's Edge is a declining fishing village on Maryland's Eastern Shore, one of many that have fallen on hard times. Though the town's name sounds like the kind of place where richy Washingtonians build summer homes, there's nothing fashionable about the place. Last month, the local McDonald's franchise shut down. Still, rumors persist that developers are about to buy this trailer park and tear everything down to make room for beachside McMansions or a yacht club, accoutrements that'll make summering Washingtonians happy but leave residents like Belinda and me with no place for our trailers.

In the early morning or in the early evening, or whenever the sun isn't too bright, I slather Anne Elise with SPF 50 and take her to the beach. Sand fascinates her. She loves the water, loves the driftwood, and will put smooth frosted sea glass into her mouth if I'm not watching. She's a happy baby, which, under the circumstances, makes me feel I'm doing something right. The locals claim to remember me, but what they really mean is they've read about my father in the newspapers or remember drinking Natty Boh and rolling dice with him after hours on someone's stoop. Sometimes they offer condolences—whether for Jimmy's death or for Tully's incarceration, I've never asked. After they spiel salty stories about the things Tully's said or done, they lean into me and say, "Your mother must be a saint, staying with him after all these years."

"Thank you," I say, for how else should one respond when someone accuses one's mother of sainthood?

But people continue to stare at me long after I thank them. They've heard the stories, gossiped among themselves, swapped speculations and insinuations, and as they stare into my face, assessing me, I know they're really trying to figure out if I, too, am a saint. Or am I a monster, someone coldhearted enough to be complicit in her lover's murder?

~

The hour leading up to Jimmy's death is a mad jumble in my mind. Distraught and unable to reach Jimmy from my hospital bed, I told Lois Belcher I feared for his life. I pointed to his red flip phone on the nightstand. Her eyes widened in horror as I recounted how Tully was on his way to bash in Jimmy's skull. She grabbed my hand and pulled me up from the hospital bed, disconnected my IV line, and yanked me through the back corridors and stairwells and out the employee entrance and into her little bitty mint-green Chevrolet Spark, about the smallest car imaginable. At one point, she said that if she wasn't already going to lose her job for giving a KISS bracelet to Tricia, she surely was going to lose it for this. And then she shook her head and said she'd been meaning to find another job anyways.

Lois Belcher drove fast, zipping in and out of lanes. Cars honked at her, their drivers enraged at her recklessness, but we caught all the green lights and were at Tricia's house within minutes. She waited in the car while I ran inside. I headed upstairs, where I heard voices. When I reached the landing, my heart skipped a beat at the hallway's disarray. Books, knickknacks, and crystal figurines lay on the floor, broken, all of them presumably thrown off a bookcase that had been turned aslant somehow to open up a narrow cobweb-filled passageway, beyond which Tully and Jimmy skirmished. My palms turned cold and clammy. I hugged the hallway walls, afraid of being seen and afraid of what I might see if I stepped into that narrow passageway and into whatever chambers lay beyond it.

From somewhere in the distance, I heard a siren. Tully must have heard it too, for his voice turned panicky, and he accused Jimmy of calling 911 on him. Thinking the police would soon arrive, I worked up the courage to walk through the narrow passageway and into a disconcertingly snug office filled with shoddy old wooden furniture and shelves of decaying leather-bound accounting ledgers.

Tully's eyes opened wide upon seeing me. I thought he was going to lecture me again to remain willfully stupid about the things that could land me in the middle of someone's crosshairs, but then I glanced at Jimmy and the blood that bubbled and oozed from a cut in his neck. Anne Elise lay in a crib. Blood dotted her forehead. Was she wounded too? My whole life got fuzzy and dizzy. I remember Tully urging me to make a getaway with him. He wanted me to abandon Anne Elise and Jimmy, but I couldn't do that, so he stomped out of the office and made his getaway on his own.

I looked at Jimmy. He smiled. I thought everything was going to be all right. The flow of blood down his neck had slowed. He reached out as if to hug me, but I was a step farther than he could reach, and he fell to the floor. I knelt beside him, saw the pallor that had already replaced the color in his face. No longer did I think everything was going to be all right. Jimmy closed his eyes. A serene smile came over his face. He was alive but just barely. As I convulsed in tears and agony, somehow I managed to summon a moment's courage. I lifted Anne Elise from her cradle and brought her to Jimmy so she could say goodbye to him.

An ambulance arrived soon after I knew Jimmy was dead. EMTs scrambled into the house, followed by policemen, who detained me for hours with their questions. My presence at the scene of the crime provoked their suspicion. They viewed me as a suspect or an accomplice. A plainclothes officer read me my Miranda rights. EMTs took Anne Elise from my hands. Standing there in the musty nook where Jimmy lost his life, I broke down. Nothing made sense. I looked at my hands, expecting to find Anne Elise, and not finding her, screamed at the police to find my baby. "She's been stolen!"

I was in shock. Two men from the coroner's office zippered Jimmy into a thick brown plastic body bag. Police asked me to retrace the events that brought me into this house where I'd never been before. I stuttered. Confusion took hold of me. I said Jimmy had driven me here himself, rushing me out of the bed in my Watergate apartment. And then I told them that, no, I'd been outside, shivering in the hospital parking lot when a cabbie invited me into his cab and brought me here.

The plainclothes officer who'd been interviewing me closed his notepad. "We're not getting anywhere."

Luckily for me, Lois Belcher filled the police in about the particulars and the man she saw run out of the house as the ambulance arrived.

Police apprehended Tully within an hour after he fled Tricia's house. Jimmy's blood was all over the switchblade found in his pocket. After some hours, I was released. A distance of less than four miles separates Tricia's house and Sibley Hospital, but it seemed like a lifetime was lost in the time it took Lois Belcher to drive me back to the hospital. I sank back onto my hospital bed and cried for two straight hours. My heart was pierced and empty, all hope drained from my soul. Belinda came back and held my hand. My eyes were so sore from crying that I couldn't keep them open.

A nurse brought Anne Elise to me after the doctors examined her, giving her a clean bill of health. I ran my fingers over her soft shoulders, her smooth neck, her dimpled chin, imagining them slashed and gashed, bleeding. In the back of my head, I heard Jimmy's voice encouraging me to think happy thoughts, good thoughts. He warned me that a baby instinctually picks up on a parent's psychic energy, but I couldn't control the recriminations jamming my thoughts. Although I didn't kill Jimmy, I was instrumental in bringing about his death. I'd given Tully the address where I thought he'd likely be found. Anne Elise, too, seemed confused. This should've been a happy reunion between us. She wanted to be nursed, but as she stared at me, it was as if she was trying to work out whether she knew me. Was I the woman who nursed her a day or two ago, or was I someone she need fear? Someone who was more than a little responsible for killing the man who might've been her father? She scrunched her lips, squeezed shut her eyes, making me feel useless, dispirited.

"Give it time," Belinda said. I hadn't told her what I did—nor had she asked. We both had our reasons to be quiet—she, too, had known something bad was going to happen when Tully stormed out of the hospital to go to Jimmy's house. Why else would she choose to watch repeats of *The Oprah Winfrey Show* on cable TV in the hospital's waiting room while Tully did whatever he was going to do? "She's been through a lot. You've been through a lot. We've all been through a lot."

I sucked in a breath and tried to beat back the sense of futility that came over me. Jimmy had managed to save two lives—mine and Anne Elise's—but I wished he was here with me, coaching me how to deal with my betrayal of him. Dark thoughts raced through me. I contemplated throwing up my arms and giving up. Because of me, Anne Elise would not have a father in her life. I could put her up for adoption and concede my failures, just like my father suggested. I could never be the responsible person I wanted to be. All the things Tully suggested about me being ill-equipped to be a single mom came back to me. *Honey, don't you know love's expensive? How are you going to afford a rug rat?*

Anne Elise smiled at me, shocking me with her cuteness.

I swear, if she hadn't smiled at me at that moment, I probably would've killed myself. This is not easy to admit. Her gummy smile reminded me of everything I had to live for: namely, her love, her joy, us together as mother and daughter. In her gummy smile, I found the strength to persevere. I drew her toward me, unsnapped the upper portion of my hospital gown, and felt her open mouth on my breast. And then I smelled something *off*. I scrunched my nose. Belinda, sitting beside me, smelled it too. Anne Elise hadn't flashed me a smile; she'd farted.

Although I didn't realize it, Tricia, too, was hospitalized at Sibley while I recuperated from my infection. She'd overdosed on Valium and, upon learning her husband died, was thought to be at risk of suicide. She was the woman I would have become if not for Anne Elise's gummy smile: someone who'd spend the rest of her life alone and unloved. Her bed, so I am told, was exactly a floor beneath mine. Had a hole been drilled into my floor, I could've looked down and waved at her or induced Anne Elise to smile down upon her, but Tricia would've been in no condition to acknowledge me. Doctors sedated her. Nurses sat with her twenty-four hours a day for two weeks. Lois Belcher, had she not been fired, would've made an excellent sitting partner for Tricia.

Despite my suspicions, Detective Adderly didn't believe Tricia kidnapped Anne Elise. Since he'd taken on the case, Adderly grew a mustache, which he kept neatly trimmed. Along with the mustache, he developed a habit of running his index finger over his mustache while he talked. Although paramedics found Anne Elise in Tricia's house, no definitive evidence existed as to how she got there. Adderly interviewed Tricia several times and concluded she was incapable of doing something like kidnapping. "A woman like that's not mentally tough enough to pull off a crime." Who did he think kidnapped Anne Elise? "James. I think James kidnapped the baby in order to give her to his wife. That's what she says happened, anyways. She had no idea what he was going to do before he showed up at her door with the baby. You really didn't know him well, did you?"

Jimmy was not Tricia's only sorrow.

A couple of weeks later, while Belinda strolled the hallways with Anne Elise, a young man with a sheepskin coat and wire-rimmed glasses knocked on my hospital door. I stiffened, for only policemen and security officers felt compelled to knock on my door before entering; everyone else came and went as they pleased. I'd answered enough questions about Jimmy and enough questions about Tully. The last batch of policemen assured me that, having assembled sufficient evidence to secure a conviction against Tully, they wouldn't bother me with further interrogations. This guy at my door seemed about my age, early twenties, but in the aftermath of what happened to Jimmy, I felt as if I'd aged twenty years. I wasn't a girl anymore but a woman who had to figure out how she'd feed and clothe and shelter a baby. I was twenty-four years old, going on forty.

"Can I come in?" the young man asked.

"Do I have a choice?"

"Yes, ma'am. This is America. You have every choice in the world to tell me you don't want to see me."

I laughed, which the man took as an invitation to step inside. He unbuttoned his sheepskin coat, tossed it over the back of a chair. He wore blue chinos and a cable-knit night-gray cashmere sweater with a blue insignia stitched right over where I presumed his heart would be. He stepped closer. The insignia was of a man on horseback swinging a polo mallet. It was the kind of sweater Jimmy would wear on his leisure hours. The floor to my room was wet from having been mopped, and as the man walked across the room, I saw the impression of his penny loafers in the drying floor.

"I'm sorry," he said.

"What are you sorry about?"

He sat down on the recliner and told me what Tricia was going through. Without her knowing it, her father stole all her money, sold her house and car, and saddled her with hundreds of thousands of dollars in unpaid taxes. I already learned Jimmy died in debt, but to have one's father steal from you struck me as just deserts for Tricia. She was able to keep some of her possessions, but she'd never again afford the lifestyle to which she'd become accustomed.

"There's more," the man said, raising his glance to meet my eyes.

The previous morning, Tricia's father's body had washed ashore on a Caribbean island. He'd gotten mixed up with drug lords. Or rather, drug lords got involved with him after he started messing around with their women. I couldn't imagine it. They shot him thirteen times in the chest, a dozen more times than necessary to kill him, and hurled his body off a yacht anchored in an exclusive sun-drenched cove where wealthy scuba diving tourists explored coral reefs and sunken fishing trawlers.

"How do you know this?" I was shocked, not only by the circumstances of Jack Riggs's death but also how this man had apparently already learned everything there was to know about it. "Why are you telling me all this?"

Without blinking, he said, "Everyone has the right to know the truth."

I stared at him, incredulous. Only someone brought up in privileged surroundings and pampered on a diet of anodyne bromides could spout off such weasel shit. He was hiding something but lacked the responsibility or the moral courage to man up to it. I wasn't a little girl anymore who'd rush into whatever lies and illusions spread out before her. I asked that he leave my room. He was courteous. He got up from the recliner, walked out the door, and retreated into whatever moneyed world would welcome a young man with a polo player insignia stitched to his cashmere sweater.

He never even told me his name.

∼

Jimmy's memorial service, when it finally happened weeks later, was held in an underused chapel not far from where he lived with Tricia. Though rosy light shone through the enormous stained glass windows behind the pulpit, the interior of the granite chapel was cold. Few people showed up to pay their respects, and those who did kept their winter coats and hats on. An aging minister, assisted with a black rubber-tipped cane, hobbled to the pulpit and asked that we bow our heads. Owing to my fear of how Tricia would react, I left Anne Elise with Belinda. The minister read a psalm about the Lord being our shepherd.

I loved Jimmy. I kept imagining him as he must have been, bravely seeing to Anne Elise's safety in his dying moments. I craved to see his smile, craved to hear him sing another of those Sinatra-era songs he loved so much. Outside of Lois Belcher, who sat alone in another pew, her hands bundled in wool mittens, I guessed none of the other eight people in this chapel knew of Jimmy's relationship with me, and it pained me to realize I couldn't express my grief to everyone as freely as Tricia. But Tricia wasn't in attendance.

The minister admitted not having known Jimmy very well. Like many in his particular aging Episcopal congregation, Jimmy wasn't a religious man. He didn't attend Sunday services, but the minister knew Jimmy enough to say with confidence that optimism was his defining trait. Jimmy was insanely optimistic about his personal prospects and the prospects of those he loved. "Did that not indicate a fundamental—perhaps even subconscious—trust in Providence's guiding hand?

"I'm told that Jimmy's favorite song was 'Ac-cent-tchu-ate the Positive.' It's an old Johnny Mercer/Harold Arlen composition. Does anyone here know it?"

My hand shot into the air. The minister squinted at me. Mine was the only hand raised.

The minister, standing behind the pulpit, started singing the song. He was probably old enough to be a boy when the song was first recorded. His black cassock swayed as he sang. Here and there, people sniggered, a miserly thing to do given the circumstances, but they couldn't help themselves. The minister's weak voice warbled, echoing throughout the cavernous chapel. It was strangely pathetic hearing the song this way when I'd only known it before through Jimmy's rich, warm baritone.

"Jimmy Wainsborough had the consoling grace to realize that however bad he or any of us might have screwed up in the past, we need not give up our faith in what the future holds for us."

At that moment, Tricia burst through the chapel's aged oak doors, letting in a frigid gust. I turned around. She was a haggard, wraithlike woman with sunken cheeks and glazed eyes wearing a sable coat, veiled black pillbox hat, and a tasteful black mourning dress. Seeing me, she rushed down the aisle. A man rose up from a nearby pew to assist her, but Tricia shoved him aside. Despite her expensive clothes, she looked like someone you might meet in a halfway house. Or, if she was younger, someone messed up enough to be your cellmate in a juvenile detention facility—which is to say she looked like the woman I might've remained had Jimmy never entered my life.

Tricia wrapped her arms around me. I feared she was going to wrestle me to the ground and smash my face into the stone floor, but she convulsed in tears on my shoulder. Her hands were freezing cold. She must have stood outside the chapel for a half hour, debating whether to come in. She was a little girl crying maniacally. I ran my hand though her hair, trying to console her. Her hair was greasy, and my hand got caught in its tangles. The minister, cane in hand, hobbled down from the pulpit and put his hand on Tricia's shoulder, trying to calm her. I worried Tricia would shove him aside, just as she did to that other man. Others gathered around us, trying to tell Tricia that everything was going to be all right.

"It's not going to be all right," Tricia said. Her voice had a dream-like, medicated quality. She leaned into me, whispering into my ear. I struggled to hear what she said. She seemed thinner than I remembered, bordering on malnourished. She was nothing more than a snowflake at risk of being blown away in a stiff breeze. She whispered again in my ear. "I should've bought him a Tesla. I should've consented to surrogacy."

The commotion around us made me uneasy. Tricia was near delirious. I wrapped my arms around her, persuading her to sit beside me. After some minutes, others returned to their pews. The man who tried to assist Tricia when she burst into the chapel assisted the minister back to the pulpit. He was the same man, I realized with a start, who had come into my hospital room and told me about Jack Riggs's death. Walking back to his seat, he tried to catch our attention, but we both looked away from him.

For Tricia's benefit, the minister repeated what he said about Jimmy's abundant optimism. Tricia trembled beside me. I couldn't tell if the minister's kind words assuaged Tricia's grief, but hearing it a second time filled me with the same optimism that imbued Jimmy's life. I felt at that moment I could do anything. I even had the strength to sit beside the woman I most detested and pretend we were best friends. I hated her for having left that message on my phone implying it was him who stole my baby. If I hadn't heard that message, I never would have told Tully to go after Jimmy. But I can never admit this to her—or anyone else. It's the secret I'll have to keep with me for the rest of my life, and I suppose she has her secrets too.

I squeezed Tricia's hand.

Tricia started crying again. I reached into my purse and produced a Kleenex. She took it from my hand and dabbed her eyes with it, seemingly at peace. Although I hadn't noticed it before, a gossamer-thin black veil was pinned up to the edge of her pillbox hat. With great deliberation, she unpinned the veil, lowering it over her face and becoming the very vision of a proper wife in mourning. She lowered her eyes, gave my hand a last squeeze, and then got up from the pew and walked out of the chapel. I haven't seen her since.

Chapter Forty

LAUREL

Another Month Later

I'm a helicopter parent, a one-woman safety patrol scooching after Anne Elise as she crawls on the narrow kitchen's linoleum floor in Belinda's trailer park home. A week ago, Anne Elise was immobile. Now, on her belly, pulling herself along, she wriggles and slithers, zipping back and forth over the length of the trailer, giggling, sticking her hands into the nooks and crannies along the baseboards, under the refrigerator and stove. Someday soon, she'll look at me and say "mama," but it breaks my heart that she'll never have the opportunity to say "dada." There are no guarantees in life. No amount of optimism, no amount of ac-cent-tchu-ating the positive can raise the dead, guarantee happiness, or prevent us from becoming poor and destitute, but I'll always have my Anne Elise. She's my daughter, and when I look at her, I recognize myself in the curve of her cheekbones. She's a kinder, better version of me, the warrior princess I always wanted to be.

Money's tight. I work evenings at the same grocery store where Belinda works six afternoons a week. I signed up for a few courses I need to get under my belt in order to get an internship with the county's

Child Services division. Classes start on Monday. Already I'm nervous. Not of the coursework but of the time I'll be away from Anne Elise. But I couldn't afford *not* to go back to school—as soon as I start attending classes again, I can defer payments on my Ethan Allen College student loans.

Anne Elise still doesn't sleep through the night. Like clockwork, she awakens tonight at three a.m., just when I return home from my grocery store shift. I take her outside and walk down the trailer park's crushed-oystershell driveway, the white shells shining luminescent under the moonlight's glow. We sit on a weathered beachside bench. The cool night air soothes us both. While she nurses, I throw my head back and gaze at the starlit sky. Even at night, gulls squawk. The noise from the surf can be so loud, and it's easy to imagine myself clinging to nothing but driftwood and being torn asunder by the waves.

"Don't you ever trust anyone but yourself," I say, patting Anne Elise's back.

Anne Elise turns her head to me, and it's as if a fleeting moment of comprehension comes over her. She squiggles her eyebrows, nods. She can't possibly know the meaning of what I say, but hopefully, she'll learn the message by watching my actions as she grows up.

～

Washing the dishes the next morning before Belinda goes to work, I hear an unfamiliar car rumble up the trailer park's oystershell driveway. I must be seeing things. It's a midnight-blue Volvo station wagon with DC plates. Jimmy's old car. It drives past the single-wides at the entrance and continues toward us. My heart starts beating faster. I know it can't be him, but there's no doubt it's the same car.

My mother, sensing something catch my attention, comes up behind me and asks, "What is it?"

"Wait inside," I say, dropping the dish towel I'd been using onto the counter. "And keep Anne Elise inside too."

The car halts right outside the trailer. Tinted windows make it impossible to identify the driver. I'm at the trailer's screen door, the hairs at the back of my neck standing at attention. The car's front door swings open, and suddenly I know I'm not going to like what's about to happen. Tricia steps out of the car. Though it's summer, she's wrapped in her elegant sable coat. She's skinnier than I remember, dressed in tight designer jeans, a pink camisole, and a lustrous pearl necklace that gleams on her tanned skin. Upon seeing me, she brings her hands together, looking contrite. Despite her attire, the vibe she gives off is needy. If not desperate.

"What are you doing here?" I shout at her from inside the screen door.

"I was in the neighborhood."

I cross my arms. If my mother wasn't locked in her bedroom guarding Anne Elise, I'd tell her to call 911.

"Okay. Fine. So I drove out special to be here. I wanted to see, uh, Zerena. Can I see her? Just for a minute?"

Though I know it won't do much good should she try to break in, I set the latch lock on the screen door and go outside. Only a madwoman would drive a hundred miles on the off chance some near stranger might let her hold her baby.

"Please let me hold Zerena."

"No. And her name's not Zerena. It's Anne Elise."

The sun, already scorching at nine o'clock, must get to her, for she takes off her sable coat and folds it over her arm. Without the coat, she looks thinner and weaker. Just like animals puff out their fur to look fiercer and scare off rivals and predators, she must have worn that coat to make herself look bigger, wealthier, more physically intimidating. "I thought you were going to change it to Zerena. As soon as I heard

James was dead, that's what I thought: you were going to rush out and change the name of his baby."

What she says just shows how different we are: when I saw Jimmy die, I realized I could never change Anne Elise's name.

"I'll make it worth your while to let me hold her for a few minutes." Tricia starts to cry. She turns away from me, embarrassed by her tears. She covers her eyes with her hand and sniffles. "Please?"

Watching her fall apart like this devastates me. So many times over the last many months I've cried just as hard over Jimmy's death. Just watching her, I tremble.

"Tricia. Don't you think you ought to head home now?" my mother says. I hadn't realized she'd come outside. When I turn around, I see she's right behind me, holding Anne Elise.

Tricia starts heading toward her car. She looks sad, pathetic, and I can't imagine the thoughts that will pour through her mind during her long drive home. Everyone needs a little mercy in life, but from the doomed look that shadows over her face, I'm guessing she's condemned never to find mercy again.

"Wait," I say. Scooping Anne Elise out of my mother's hands, I run after Tricia. "Hey. You can hold her. But only for a minute, okay?"

Tricia's jaw drops open. In her awestruck expression, I realize she never thought I had it in me to be this generous. I place Anne Elise in her arms. My mother comes up from behind me. She lays her hand on my shoulder. Something smells around us, fragrant and vaguely floral, that owes nothing to the sea. Tricia's wearing Shalimar, a perfume so expensive I've rarely smelled it. Tricia wraps both arms around Anne Elise and hugs her. She hasn't stopped crying, and Anne Elise is unsure what to make of this crying woman holding her. Two minutes pass, enough time that I start to question if it was wise to let Tricia hold Anne Elise.

"Hey? Are you okay?" I ask.

Tricia raises her head. The expression in her face is that of someone who's just been woken from a dream. She opens her mouth, sighs, and hands Anne Elise back to me. "I woke up this morning and knew I had to hold her one last time. Just one last time. Thank you."

One last time? The finality in her tone scares me. During her hospitalization, she became so depressed doctors placed her on suicide watch. I've heard that once suicidal ideation enters a person's thoughts, it can never be totally pushed aside, and suddenly I wonder if she might still be at risk. "Tricia. Are you all right? You aren't intending anything drastic, are you?"

Tricia opens the door to the Volvo and slides into the driver's seat. She puts the key in the ignition, starts the car up. "Laurel, do you remember what I said when we first met? About how a woman with a vendetta and lots of money in her purse will inflict great harm?"

I suck in a breath. Vaguely, I remember something like that, but I was heavily medicated and shaking with anger because Jimmy had brought Tricia into my maternity suite. I was feeling stressed out enough about Anne Elise and questioning if I could be a good mother. I didn't need Tricia to come barging into my life, causing friction between me and Jimmy.

"Laurel, you've got a beautiful daughter, but let me tell you, you're lucky you let me see her today. Thank you. It spared me the trouble of killing you. If you hadn't let me see her, I was going to shoot you."

And then I see it. A handgun rests on her dashboard. Tricia's got a wry smile on her face and steel in her eyes. I've gotten into some fights over the years, especially while in juvie. One girl tried to poke my eyes out with a pencil when she thought I ratted her out to the guards for an illicit candy bar she'd stolen from another inmate. Another time, a girl elbowed me from behind, knocking me down while we were outside. I forget what made her do it, but I sprang up from the ground and smacked her down something bad. So bad that the guards tossed me into solitary confinement for a week. But in all those fights, I never felt as if my life was in jeopardy. Now, though, I tremble.

"I will never leave you," Tricia says, buttoning back on her sable coat. A chill zips through me. She's looking straight at me, but I'm not sure if she's talking to me or Anne Elise, but then Tricia winks at me. We'll always be sisters of a kind, sinister sisters, drawn together by tragedy and a baby who's changed our lives forever.

Tricia puts the car into gear. I can tell she likes scaring me, but when she looks again at Anne Elise, sadness returns to her face. She waves goodbye, blows Anne Elise a kiss. Though I don't doubt for a minute Tricia will reappear again and again throughout my life, dogging me, right now, listening to the oystershells crunching beneath her tires as she leaves, I mainly feel relief.

I stand shoulder to shoulder with Belinda watching Tricia drive back down the same way she came. Reaching the end of the trailer park's driveway, she takes a right at the main road. In the distance, I hear the shriek of seagulls, the ocean's slow roar. I give Anne Elise another squeeze. She's always so warm in my hands. When the Volvo totally disappears from our view, we remain standing, listening to the thunderous waves of the ocean behind us.

"Wow. The rich are very different from you and me, aren't they?" Belinda asks, turning toward me.

It sounds like something Jimmy would have said, some quote he'd pluck from one of his favorite writers. Or maybe it's a song lyric, something from that Great American Songbook of his. But it's not true. I think about the handgun on Tricia's dashboard and how I trembled at the sight of it. The rich are no different from you and me, but had the shoe been on the other foot, I would have shot her.

ACKNOWLEDGMENTS

This novel could not have been written without the love, support, and encouragement of my wife, Alison, and our children—Stephen, Sebastian, and Ellie. Thank you for putting up with my stress-frazzled mind and all my insecurities throughout this whole process. Thank you, also, to my mother, Mary; my brother, Mike; and my mother-in-law, Elaine—I can't even begin to express my gratitude for all that you've done for me.

I'm extremely grateful to Rick Pascocello of Glass Literary Management, who took on my novel when it was still in its infancy. My first drafts were cartoonishly bad. His comments and suggestions helped each successive draft become better, more realistic, and tighter. Looking back, I can't believe the time he devoted to my novel, the patience and encouragement he offered during the novel's gestation. Thank you also to Alex Glass for his many insights and early critiques. And thank you to the many earlier readers whom Rick reached out to for comments—I don't know your names, but you've helped me tremendously.

I'll forever be in Megha Parekh's debt. Not only did she acquire my novel for Thomas & Mercer, but she also proposed a killer title for it—*I Will Never Leave You*—which I love for its urgency, its insistence. Beyond that, she suggested bringing Charlotte Herscher on board as developmental editor. Working with Charlotte has been a dream—she identified literally hundreds of problems within my manuscript and had the patience to read through three completely different drafts within a relatively few weeks. I've relied on her expertise, sensibilities, and problem-solving skills throughout my revision process—thank you! I'm also deeply in debt to Stephanie Chou, my wonderful copyeditor who single-handedly rid my manuscript of hundreds of spelling, grammar, and continuity errors. Thank you!

Many other people at Thomas & Mercer have also provided invaluable assistance, including Sarah Shaw, Laura Barrett, Oisin O'Malley, Jessica Tribble, Laura Sarasqueta, and Laura Costantino.

Over the years, a number of fantastic writers have helped me develop my craft: Frank Conroy, Keith Banner, John McNally, Claire Messud, Thomas Mallon, Joyce Hackett, Ed Falco, Jeff Mann, Lucinda Roy, and Fred D'Aguiar. Scarcely can I write a paragraph or structure a chapter without thinking of one lesson or another these writers have taught me. Thank you.

I'm also lucky to count so many writers among my friends, including Julie Lawson Timmer, Jenniey Tallman, Jeremy Griffin, Heather Ryan, Robert Kostuck, R. L. Maizes, Tracee de Hahn, and Thea Swanson. I've learned from your examples, benefited from your suggestions, and cried on your shoulders. Thank you for being there for me when I needed you.

Lastly, I began writing this novel after a period of profound disappointment. I was seriously thinking of packing it in and giving up on the writing thing. Two things happened—I started reading psychological thrillers for the first time. Paula Hawkins's *The Girl on the Train*. And then Mary Kubica's *The Good Girl*, Asa Harrison's *The Silent Wife*, and many others. Until then, I'd devoted myself to literary fiction with an aggressively outré, experimental, or absurdist orientation, but I was overwhelmed by the propulsive narrative momentum these psychological thrillers presented and by the real but terribly flawed characters.

Also around this time, I started attending the Wednesday evening "Refresh" services at Blacksburg Baptist Church during Lent 2016.

Before one of those services, I prayed an "Our Father" to myself. When I got to the "and lead us not into temptation" line, I experienced an epiphany of sorts: the biggest temptation that I consistently yielded to was allowing myself to fall prey to a stubborn sense of hopelessness. I vowed to give up that sense of hopelessness. During that same service, Rev. Todd Millsaps urged congregants to look into their lives and discern what wasn't working. He urged us not to cling to notions that were getting us nowhere. Instead, he urged us to be brave and step in different directions that might yield fruit. The aggressively outré, experimental, or absurdist thing wasn't working for me, and yet I had clung to that aesthetic out of pride. Rev. Millsaps's message touched me deeply. I let go of that aesthetic and became determined to try my hand at something different. Thank you, Todd!

Should anyone find themselves in Blacksburg, Virginia, on a Sunday morning (or a Wednesday evening during Lent), I encourage them to drop by our church. Blacksburg Baptist Church is truly the most open, giving, and invigorating church community I've ever had the pleasure to encounter.

ABOUT THE AUTHOR

S. M. Thayer is a pseudonym for an award-winning fiction writer and McDowell Fellow whose work has appeared in numerous publications and received several Pushcart Prize nominations. A native of New York, Thayer lived for decades in the Washington, DC, metropolitan region before moving to rural Virginia and earning an MFA from Virginia Tech. *I Will Never Leave You* is Thayer's debut novel.